The Raven and the Nightingale

The Corvid Chronicles
Book One

By K. Lawrence

Inkubus Publishing

Cover Art by TatteredWolf Studios

Inkubus Publishing LLC
1530 E. 58th St.
Tulsa, OK 74105
www.inkubuspublishingllc.com

ISBN-10: 0692955097
ISBN-13: 978-0692955093

Dedicated to Candy for her constant support and friendship, not just during the writing and editing of this book but also life in general.

Contents

1

Boston Fall

You ever have those mornings where you just can't face getting out of bed? Today is one of those for me. Ten years ago, on a damp October morning just like this one, I began a journey that lost me everything. My fiancé; my job; the man I once was. The case was closed, the perpetrator left to rot behind bars, but the unanswered questions have plagued me ever since. Something about it feels unfinished.

That feeling follows me as I make my way into my office. Leaves swirl with the wind and gather in the gutters in deep, russet toned, piles. The weather is damp, though there is no rain to speak of. It's just typical Boston fall weather, gloomy and cold.

The office however, is bright and warm. I visit the break room first, pour a good measure of coffee into my used mug and make my way past the other offices in the hallway until I reach the one with *J. Higgins, P.I.* etched into the window. I don't see any of my colleagues. Maybe they have finally learned not to talk to me when

October rolls around.

Door to my own office closed, I take off my coat and hang it up carefully before I sift through the documents on my desk. I sort them into things I can ignore and stuff I need to deal with straight away, then boot up my computer and go through my emails. Amongst the correspondence from clients and my fellow private investigators there are at least three different invites to Halloween parties. What is it about the death of the year that makes people want to dress up in greasepaint and Lycra and run wild? The rest is junk that I can pretty much discard on sight. That done I turn my attention to the first assignment in my urgent pile.

The rain comes around midday. Heavy drops hammer onto the pane and drum into my brain. I rub at my forehead to try and stave off a headache, then wander off to find more coffee. My colleagues make tentative attempts at conversation. I give nothing more than monosyllabic answers.

My limp sandwich is hardly a satisfying lunch, but it fills a hole and allows me to refocus.

Information whirls past my eyes. I glaze over and rub at my forehead again. It's getting dark outside. Surely, it’s too early for that? I click on the desk lamp. Its small pool of sickly yellow light does nothing to alleviate the pain behind my eyes.

Thunder joins the rain.

I glance at the clock out of habit. Six pm. I guess I should call it a day. My eyes stray to a framed photograph just below it. In a few weeks, it'll be ten years from that cold, fall morning when I found him dead. I shudder and quickly push the thought away.

My colleagues make their way out of the building, their cheerful chatter slowly fades as they leave the hallway. A flash of lightning illuminates my dreary office space, and highlights shelves full of relics of my former life. The thunder is soft, almost like a cat's purr as it rolls across the torn sky. The night is alive with the power of the storm. This is the type of night cops are wary of, a night when the feral side of human nature comes to the fore. People say it's just a superstition, but ask any cop, even ex cops, at any level, and they will tell you the same thing. We all know what storms and full moons bring. It's not superstition. It's just understanding human nature.

I haul the window open, and let in the sounds of the streets and the fecund smell of rotting, dying plant life. I take a deep drag on my cigarette and blow smoke out into the night, flaunting the smoking ban without a single care. People hurry by on the streets below me, their colorful umbrellas jarring against the bruised tones of the world around them.

There is a soft knock at my door. I'm not expecting anyone, but I shout "Enter!" anyway.

The heavy clump of boots on the rough wooden floor fills the room. I turn to face the man who has entered my office. His hair, which is streaked black and gold, curls softly around his heart-shaped face. The sickly light of the desk lamp illuminates pretty green eyes, a thin nose and full cupids-bow lips. I motion for him to sit and he does, crossing one leather clad leg over the other at the knee. The dark purple faux fur coat looks expensive. There is no way my visitor has been out wandering the streets in this weather, not with a jacket like that.

"Detective Higgins?"

A musical accent catches me off guard. Eyes painted up like the Egyptians of old fix me with a level gaze, waiting for my response. I sit down, lean back in my chair and prop my feet up on the edge of my desk, crossing them at the ankles. I take another drag on my cigarette and take my time exhaling. "That's me. How can I help you?" I ask. I try to speak slowly so he doesn't have to fight with my accent.

"My name is Lachlan Calhoun and I think someone is trying to threaten me."

"Either they are or they're not," I say.

He sighs. "Okay, someone is trying to threaten me."

"What makes you think that?"

He reaches into his coat and pulls out an envelope. Rather than handing it to me he clutches it in his hands, crinkling it slightly.

"I have been receiving letters for about two months, I think. They don't say who they are; they just write nasty words. It started off as graphic descriptions of what they wanted to do to me then, this morning, I received this." He leans over and hands me the envelope.

I turn it over, examining it. It's a standard plain postal envelope. The address has been printed, and there's a tiny smudge from the printer rollers in the left corner. There is no stamp, no post mark. I look up at my guest. "Where did you find this?"

"It was on my doormat this morning," he says flatly.

"Did it come with any other mail, or was it on its own?"

"It was on its own. I'm not sure what time it was dropped off, but it wasn't there when I went to bed at one am. I left for work at eight; that's when I saw it."

I study the address. "You're from New York?"

"Yes."

"I'm sorry, kid. I don't work in New York. What I am gonna do is put you in touch with a friend of mine in the NYPD. He works for one of the precincts in Manhattan. He can help—"

"No!" Calhoun shouts. "It has to be you."

I narrow my eyes. "Like I said, I don't work in New York. It's nothing personal. I have enough things to run through here in Boston, that's all."

"Please, just read the letter," he pleads. "You'll see why I need your help then."

"Kid, please listen," I say. "There's no point in my reading it because I won't be able to help you. If you really feel like someone is after you, then you have to take this to the cops. They'll help you out. I'll call my friend in Manhattan. We'll make sure you have protection from the minute you set foot back in the city." I smile in the hope that will soften my refusal to help. "Trust me, they aren't going to dismiss you. Someone has been hand delivering threatening notes to your home. At the very least, that's some kind of stalker." I grab a slip of paper and a pen. "What's your name again?"

He glares at me. "Do you really think I'd have come all this way if I could just go to the police?"

"Why can't you?" I ask. "And don't even think about lying. If I agree to work with you, I will be checking up on you first."

"I've never been arrested, if that's what you mean," he says and crosses his arms defensively over his chest. "Please just read the letter. You'll know why I came to you once you do."

I roll my eyes. What harm can it do to read the thing? I open the envelope carefully and pull out a single folded page. The text is typed just like the address on the envelope.

Would that I could clip the wings of my angel to keep him earthbound.
Would that I could envelope feathered black wings in my embrace but, alas.
My angel forsakes me, my angel no longer cares and so my angel will bleed human blood.
So, my angel will shed human skin, human flesh, piece by piece until I have consumed my angel whole.

I look at him over the thin paper. "And you said the rest weren't like this?"

"They were crude. This is the only one that's poetic."

"Do you think all the letters are from the same person?"

"In them all, I am referred to as an angel." He seems to have a sense of pride about that. A ghost of a smile plays on his lips.

What is this kid's game? I glance at the letter again and steel my resolve. Threat or no threat I am not being dragged all the way to New York. "Like I said, I don't work outside of Boston. I'm not even sure if I can. There's private agencies in New York if you don't want to work with the NYPD."

He uncrosses his legs, and places his hands on my desk. The weak lamplight illuminates more of his face as he leans forward. "Mr. Higgins, I come from a rich family, a very rich family. I heard you were one of the best, and I want to hire you. Not some guy from a New York agency, not an NYPD detective. You. Name your price."

His directness catches me off guard. For a moment, all I can do is stare. "I already explained—"

A flicker of anger passes over his face, and his lip curls back in a little snarl. This kitten does have claws after all. "I said name your price!"

"This isn't about money."

"If not money then tell me what it will take." He walks slowly around my desk, fingers gliding over the surface. I watch his shapely legs move with feline grace and scoot my chair back as he comes towards me.

"Kid, you have nothing I want."

He sits down on the corner of my desk, crosses one ankle over the other, and taps a heel of the vicious boots against the leg of it.

"Look, I don't mean to be rude, but you're gonna have to leave. I can't help, I'm sorry"

I turn back to the papers on my desk, and dismiss him from my attention and, hopefully, my office too. Out of the corner of my eye I see his body sag, his hands coming up to cover his face. Concerned, I look back over. His calm, steely exterior slides back in place as he reaches into the back pocket of his leather pants.

"Here's my number. Call me when you change your mind."

The kid is tenacious, got to give him that. I take the proffered card without reading it. "You've come a long way to get a 'no' for an answer."

"Why do you think I am not taking it?" he asks. He leans in close enough that I can smell the scent of fine cologne on him. He smiles. "Just promise me you will think about it," he whispers seductively.

I swallow hard. "Don't get your hopes up, kid."

He winks and swaggers from the office. The door clicks shut behind him. I stare at the card for a little while before flicking it into my trash can. Out of sight, out of mind.

§

Next morning, I awake to the sound of my cell phone ringing. Within the hour, I'm at a greasy table in a diner waiting for an old friend, Detective Greg Harris. I spot him through the glass and signal to the waitress to bring two coffees. We nod to each other in greeting, and he sits across from me. We're not ones for small talk, so he immediately hands me his phone. I read through the email on the screen.

"When did this happen?" I ask.

"Last night."

I read the details again. White male. Probably early twenties, and found wearing what the author of the report has referred to as Gothic clothing-plenty of leather and lace. Found brutally murdered in an alley off of 53rd street in Manhattan. My mind wanders back to my visitor last night. I wonder if I can get back to the office before the trash cans are emptied.

"McCray says it was a mess," Harris says over his coffee cup. "The kid was found with the flesh peeled from his upper arms and shoulders." He takes a deep swallow of the bitter liquid and makes a face. I wait impatiently as he shakes out a packet of sugar and pours it in. "There were all sorts of symbols on the ground, blood everywhere and black feathers." He taps the little spoon against the cup. "Whole heaps of them." I stare at him and he looks back at me. "Just like—"

"No, Harris, it's not!" I say sharply. "Why is McCray sending you info about New York crimes anyway?"

Harris glances at me, and I see the sadness in his eyes. "He's one of us, remember? Even if he did leave us for the Big Apple. He sees the similarities too. So does Novik."

I laugh derisively. Not this again. Every couple of years they bring up the same shit. There are so many unanswered questions from the murders a decade ago. Any little clue sets their minds whirring. More often than not those clues send them to look at the occult—demons, monsters. Things that can't be real.

We sit in silence for a bit, and I take the time to look through more of the email. McCray has provided just enough to give us a good picture of the grisly scene. The more I read the more I worry about the guy who showed up in my office. He almost fits the description of the victim exactly.

"Why are you showing me this?" I ask. "I'm not a cop anymore."

"I thought you'd want to know."

"Why? One murder is the same as any other in that cesspool," I say. "Leave the New York mess to the New York cops."

"The New York cops haven't dealt with a killer like this before."

I rest my elbows on the table so I am a little closer to Harris. "They haven't? What about the Bone Crusher? Toe Peeler Tom? The Cat Call killer?"

"They're all different!"

"In what way?"

"They were all human."

I force a laugh. "Our guy was human too."

"The one you caught, thinking it was our guy, was human. Something never really added up though."

I sit back and shrug angrily. "So, what? You, Novik and McCray starting a secret union of supernatural cops? Gonna start solving cases involving vampires and zombies now, are you?"

"We think it might be more of a demon."

I slap the table top in anger. The sullen faces of the other customers turn to us, each one wearing a slightly different look of disgust. I lean forward. "Is this shit funny to you?" I growl.

"I'm serious, Higgins."

"I know there was all sorts of talk about occult stuff at the time. I know the symbols found around…" I stop, my head filling with the images I don't want to see. No, why mention that particular murder out loud? "I know that there were a lot of symbols and ritualistic stuff in those deaths, but I still believe he was human."

"Why?"

"Because there is no such thing as demons or vampires. It's all just crazy-ass Halloween fan boys who get a kick out of fake Pagan rituals."

Now it is Harris' turn to roll his eyes. He rubs his temples briefly, like my refusal to accept his demon story has somehow given him a headache. "Jerry, come on. Stop pretending we didn't see the things we did!"

I stare at him. I know it's serious when he uses my first name. "What I saw was an evil guy, a human, who enjoyed cutting up young men who looked a little different. It was metal-heads last time, now it seems to be Goth kids. At the worst, we have a copy-cat killer. What's more likely is it's a coincidence. Not demons.

There are a lot of sick people out there."

"A human can't fall twenty floors and still run. A human can't take a point-blank shot to the chest. A human can't rip out—"

"Don't," I growl. I let my eyes drift to the dirty table top. "Just don't." Harris rests a gentle hand on my arm, but I pull back out of his grip. "No one saw how he died," I mutter half to myself. "Anything could have been used."

"He looked like a wild animal had been at him!"

I shake my head. "He was killed by an evil human being, not a werewolf or vampire or whatever you're thinking it is today."

"Jerry—"

"No!" I shout. "I saw his killer put behind bars. It was the last thing I ever did before they suspended me and all that anxiety shit drove me out of the force. I may have taken a dirty route to do it, but I did it!"

I get up from the table and hear Harris' chair squeak against the cheap linoleum. He attempts to grab my shoulder, but I twist away from him.

He falls into step behind me. "And what if it is the wrong guy? Are you willing to let more innocent people die just so you can rest easy?"

My mind reels back to a cold, tiled room. Splashes of red hitting the white walls as my fist slams into the face of the suspect again and again. He's lucky I didn't kill him. The possibility of that not being the right guy has occurred to me from time to time, but, if he didn't do it, then what does that make me? No, my mind is made up. Nothing is dragging me out to investigate murders again. I don't belong there.

"If you want to put yourself in New York, in Burbank's way might I add, then be my guest," I say.

"We don't have to go to New York. We can help them from here," Harris says. "And I am not scared of Burbank."

We step out into the damp streets almost in unison. A brisk breeze whips at our coats. Harris squeezes my shoulder, and this time I don't move away.

"Jerry, it's time to face your demons head on."

I lean in close to his face and grit my teeth. "I already have."

I stalk down the dreary streets, light a much-needed cigarette and let myself sink into the mire of sickly thoughts and worries. Two calls to go and help in New York in less than twenty-four hours? The universe is trying to tell me something.

The universe can kiss my ass!

Why do people feel the need to make a horror out of things? Isn't real life scary enough? I have seen some things on the job. Kids left so long in their own waste that their skin is rotting away. Women beaten to death by partners who felt like they owed them something. Isn't that horrifying enough? No one is safe from evil, but evil is inherently human. *That's* the truly horrific thing.

Harris and Novik weren't the ones that stumbled across the body that day. I was. I was the one who saw the damage for what it was. Wounds inflicted by the sick, twisted mind of another human, not some supernatural creature. An especially gruesome death for Myles, my partner. A cop who got too close. I chase the images away with cold hard facts.

A grisly death of a young man. A clearly ritualized murder that seems to have been described perfectly in a poetic note sent to a rich foreign kid in New York. Both the victim and my visitor are what can be described as Goth. Is there a link, or is there something else at play here? And, mores the point, why am I puzzling it over? I should hand over what I know to McCray and be done with it.

My wandering feet bring me to my favorite bar. It may be a little early on a Saturday, but Eddie's is always open. I push the swing door and enter the dim bar. There aren't many people in at this time of day, but the owner, Eddie, a short, curvy woman with a head full of thick, wavy brown hair, turns in my direction and smiles.

"Hey, man, the usual?" She asks.

I nod to Eddie, who fills a glass with two ice cubes and a good measure of Scotch. I down it in one go and shake it at her.

"That bad?"

"Looks like it's going to go that way."

Eddie refills my glass, and her brown curls bounce around her shoulders with her movements. "It's early, plenty of time to turn things around."

I offer her a wan smile then look around the bar. "Business okay?" I ask, changing the subject.

"Oh, yeah. We have a few of the younger bands on the books now. Not as jumping as it was in our day though." She gives me a sideways glance. "You ever think about picking up the guitar again?"

"No," I whisper. *The music in me died with Myles,* I add silently.

Eddie says nothing more.

As the bar fills, I remove myself to a far corner where I can watch the clientele. The skills you have as a cop never turn off, even after you quit. You can tell so much more from little gestures—the way they stand, how they greet people—than people think.

The new crop of college kids seems to be the same as any other year. They all wanna try the dive bar—soak up a little genuine Bostonian atmosphere—-but very few come back, unless they like listening to weekender bands like my old one.

Despite my best efforts, my thoughts wander off in the direction of my visitor last night. The kid didn't seem scared, didn't even appear a little shaken. He exuded a calm that was almost frightening, though it did slip every so often. Maybe he is simply an expert at projecting what he wants people to see.

I settle back against the worn leather of the cushions and lift my glass to my lips. Were there notes the first time round? Threats? Any other similarities at all? My instinct is trying to tell me something, and I don't like it. The more I think it over, the easier it is to contemplate going to New York.

I approach the bar again and grab a chance to pick Eddie's brains as she is pouring the golden liquor into my waiting glass. It's a long shot, but bartenders seem to know everything, and Eddie has a particular knack for picking up gossip.

"Hey, did you have any new faces in last night?" I ask.

"There's been a few," she says. "College kids. Most will fade out by Christmas."

"Any Goths?"

Eddie glances at me then laughs. "Goths?"

"Yeah. Were there any in the bar last night?"

Her eyebrow twitches up. "Out of all the places in Boston, what makes you think goths would hang out here? There're clubs downtown that're more their scene. Maybe you can check there?"

I raise my glass to my lips. "It's not that important."

"Are you sure?" Eddie asks. "I wasn't here all last night. I can check with Daryl when he comes in for his shift, see if he saw anyone."

"It's cool." I sigh. "I'm just thinking something over."

Eddie fixes me with the same smile she has been throwing my way since I first came to this bar. I was just a bright-eyed rookie then, and she was barely old enough to help her dad, the original Eddie, behind the bar. Eventually I return her grin.

"It's really nothing," I say.

"Well, you know where I am if you decide it is something," Eddie says with a wink. She crosses to the other side of the bar to deal with some customers.

I swirl the Scotch in the glass and think over my conversation with Harris. I have to listen to my gut on this one, but that means leaving Boston. My instincts have never let me down before though. Perhaps I should listen.

2

Help Wanted

Thank the Lord and his many angels for lazy cleaning staff; the business card is still lying in the trash can. I fish it out and dust a stray piece of discarded lettuce off of it. The bird design on the card shimmers in the light as I turn it over and dial the number.

"Lachlan Calhoun, tattoo artist," I read aloud. I allow myself a little chuckle at the kid's expense. Oh, to be rich and have hobbies as a job.

"Hello?"

"Mr. Calhoun, this is Detective Higgins."

I can almost hear the smile spreading across his face. "I was wondering when you'd call," he says warmly.

"Listen, kid, I been thinking about your offer." I lean back in my chair and prop my feet up on my desk. "Can we meet somewhere and talk?"

"How about my hotel?"

"Uh, no." Something about being alone with the kid makes me

feel uncomfortable. "How about a bar instead. You do drink, don't you?"

There is a musical little laugh from the other end. "Yeah, I drink. Where should I meet you and when?"

I give him the address for Eddies and wonder what I am getting myself into.

§

My watch flashes to ten pm, and I look towards the door. It opens almost instantly. Calhoun is dressed a little more low-key than when we first met— dark jeans and a black shirt—and his eyes are still painted, just not as heavily. His stance is strong, his back straight, and he easily meets people's gazes, but the chewing on his lower lip gives away his nerves. I raise my hand, and he spots me.

"Hi!" he says happily as he flops down onto the seat.

"Hey, kid, what you drinking?"

"Um. . ." He pushes his blond-and-black streaked hair out of his eyes. "Red wine. That okay?"

At the bar, Eddie takes my order.

"Wine?" I shrug, and she looks over my shoulder towards my table. She raises an eyebrow. "Who's the kid?"

"A friend from out of town."

Eddie gives me a slow nod as she pours the wine and hands me the glass. "A friend, huh?"

I don't respond.

Calhoun's eyes are on my back, and it makes my skin tingle. I return with a drink in either hand. He reaches up and takes his in both hands as if it is the most delicate thing in the world. I watch him as he takes a sip. His movements are quick and deliberate.

"Thanks," he says. His gaze never leaves mine.

"No problem," I reply and look away momentarily while I think of how to proceed. "You enjoying Boston?"

He nods, black fingernails tapping on the stem of the wine glass in a gesture that would seem like agitation in anyone else. "It's a braw city. Little damp though."

"Braw?" I ask, completely butchering the way he said it.

"Oh." He blushes. "It's a cool city."

"So where are you from?" I ask as I take a sip of my Scotch. I'm usually good at placing accents, but his musical lilt is throwing me off. "You don't sound like a New Yorker."

"Scotland. It's a little place in—"

"I know where Scotland is, kid." I smile to soften my words.

"Sorry. Anyway, I'm from the Shetland islands, actually."

"Oh yeah? Cool. Nice place?"

"Tiny place, hardly anyone around."

I take another sip. "You don't sound Scottish."

"You mean I don't sound Glaswegian," he says with a smirk.

"Well, yeah, I guess so."

"Scotland has loads of different accents, you know."

"So does the USA," is my terse reply.

Unaffected by my tone of voice, he carries on talking. "I grew up in this tiny town, and then I moved to the mainland at thirteen. My dad took up a job with. . ."

And he's off on a roll, giving me his life story. Where is the cool, collected kid from last night? The one with the quiet confidence and sultry voice. I fade back in as he is finishing up his monologue.

"Five years later, here I am."

I nod and try to look like I've been listening all along. That's not like me at all. It's my job to focus on what people are saying. In an attempt to fill in what I missed, I ask, "Why, did you come to America? Your home town not got tattoo studios or something?"

Calhoun's cheek indents like he is biting the inside of it. "I already told you I wanted to train with the best artists."

I ignore the annoyance in his voice. Sure, I wasn't listening before but he has my full attention now. "Scotland doesn't have a tattoo art scene?"

"Not like there is here. Plus, who wants to live in the same place forever?" He says with a little half-hearted shrug.

"And you've settled well here? Plenty of friends?" I ask.

He sips his wine before replying. "I wouldn't say plenty, but I go for quality not quantity."

I can understand that, I do the same myself. Plus, it makes my job easier if the suspect pool is small. "Never had any problems with anyone? Even a little fight with a neighbor?"

"Nope." He taps his fingers on the glass again as he stares into the burgundy depths.

"There's not anyone who bears a grudge? No one you have maybe rubbed the wrong way?"

He furrows his brow. "Not that I can think of."

"There's *no one* who maybe wants to get something from you, or your parents? You said you were rich. That's enough motive."

"Well everyone has someone who doesn't like them," he says almost dismissively.

Come on, kid, give me something to work with. "But enough to send you those letters?"

A warm grin spreads over his face. "Does this mean you're going to help me?"

"Looks that way," I mutter before downing the last of my Scotch.

"Want another?" he asks. His own glass has barely been touched. I hope he's not planning to get me drunk in the hopes I'm more easily swayed.

I hand my glass to him and watch him walk the bar. Once he's back I decide to iron out the details.

"So, what exactly is it you want me to do?" I ask.

Calhoun leans on crossed arms on the table. "I want you to come to New York and find out who is sending me these letters. I want them stopped. It's gone on long enough, and I'm sick looking over my shoulder," he says. His voice and face are surprisingly calm given what we're talking about.

"And you need me to do that? You'd be better off with someone local to New York and there's a whole police force full of them. P. I's too, if you don't want to deal with the cops." But I'd really like to know why that is.

His nose wrinkles as he takes a hissing breath. "Like I said last night," he says, and his voice drips with frustration. "It has to be you."

"But you haven't told me *why* that is."

He rolls his eyes and takes a sip of wine. A little bit of the hard edge he showed me last night seems to be slipping back into place. "You wouldn't believe me if I told you."

"Try me, kid."

"The cards told me."

I wait for him to laugh or give some other indication he is joking. He just gazes at me.

"Cards?"

"Tarot cards," he says. "I read them."

Of course he does. "And they told you to find me?"

"They told me to find the correct solution to my problem, and that's you."

How can he talk about this in the same tone someone would use to discuss the weather? "You sound pretty sure about that for someone who's known me for less than a day. Why?"

"Because, if the cards are right, you need this just as much as I do."

I narrow my eyes. "What makes you think I need a case like this?"

He sighs as if he's losing patience with me "Detective, I came here to find you because someone's threatening me. When I looked to my cards for help, like I do with everything else, they pointed me to you. Someone who has all the skills but no other cases to work on because of some self-imposed exile. You need me just as much as I need you."

"I do have other cases to work on," I snap. "Lots of them. And I'm not in exile, I'm working the job that best suits me."

"But you weren't always this way," Calhoun says like he's known me for more than five minutes. "You were one of the best detectives in Boston."

With a deep sigh I ask, "Who put you up to this, kid?"

His eyes widen. "No one!"

"Was it McCray?"

"Who?"

I rub my forehead. This is getting old. "Come on, you can come clean now. I won't be angry with you."

"No one put me up to this." Now there's iron in his voice, tinging his words with believable strength. "I was pointed in your direction by the cards, and, when I looked you up online, I found out the rest."

Tired of the conversation, I stand up. "Thanks for wasting my time, kid. See ya."

"Don't go," he pleads. His thin fingers close around my wrist.

Something in his gaze compels me to sink back into the booth. "I am not who you think I am," I mumble. It doesn't seem right to talk louder about something so personal.

His fingers remain around my wrist, and neither of us attempt to change that.

"The only one who believes that is you." Calhoun's voice is

low, his tone soothing. “I read all about your previous cases. This will be a piece of cake for you.”

I bark a laugh. “You really have some explaining to do, you know that? You can start by telling me what you really think is going on.”

His grip tightens as he leans closer. I can't look away—something in his expression commands my attention.

“I told you what I know. I have been getting letters for ages, and I think they may be planning to do something else. Something worse.”

“Do you think it might be linked in to the murder last night?” I ask. My mouth feels like it's moving sluggishly. My head is fuzzy.

“Could be,” Calhoun says. His voice is soothing, almost hypnotic. “I don't like to think about it if I'm honest.”

That makes sense. No one likes to believe they're in danger.

Calhoun's hand slips from his wrist and he squeezes my hand. My skin tingles at his touch, like static is passing over it. “You want to help me, don't you?”

“I want to, yeah,” I say.

“Good. Now, name your terms.”

Calhoun lets go of my hand. My senses are suddenly assaulted by the smells and sounds of the bar as the fuzz clears from my brain. I push my glass to the side. Too much of that tonight, I think. “I will come to New York for a week,” I say as I fish a cigarette out of the packet. “That'll give me time to assess the situation and form a report for my boss here.” I light up, take a drag, and blow a plume of smoke into the air.

“A week?”

“If I need to stay longer, I will.” I explain. “I only ask for payment for expenses incurred through the job. Hotel fees, travel costs, that kind of thing. I record everything and retain receipts. I'm not gonna rip you off.”

"Done. When can you come to New York?"

"Gimme a few days to tie up some loose ends and clear things with my boss." I flick ash into my glass. "I'll bring the contracts with me."

He smiles warmly. "You won't regret this."

I hope not. I hand him my card. "I'll call you when I get there. If you have any information about this case between now and then, then call me. Don't be afraid to call the cops either if you feel you need to. I can arrange a watch on your apartment if you want?"

"That's okay. It's a secure building, and there's cameras," Calhoun says.

My eyebrow raises. "Someone got in to mail those letters."

"Really, it's fine," Calhoun reassures me. "It's been going on for months, and no one has tried to do anything."

"But—"

Calhoun's hand closes over mine again. "Trust me. You don't have to do that."

"If you're sure," I say slowly. At least it feels like I'm speaking slowly.

His hand slips from mine, and leaves a ticklish feeling in its wake. I shake myself to try and shift the sluggishness I feel. This is just great. I'm staring down a long drive into another state, and I'm coming down with the flu or something.

"I guess I'll see you in a week unless anything changes." I take another drag.

"Yeah. See you then." He squirrels my card into his jeans pocket.

§

I get back home around midnight and start drawing up the contracts. When I finally get to bed, it's a little after two am, yet sleep alludes me. The rain makes a soft pitter-patter against the window, reminding me of black lacquered nails clicking against glass. I push the thoughts away, but they return. It's just a simple stalking case. Someone will have taken a dislike to Calhoun, possibly because he's pushy and will fight to get his way, no matter what other people want. I'll find out who the stalker is, stop them, and be home long before Halloween.

But what if it becomes more? There are already tiny similarities between the letter and the murder case Harris showed me, plus the fact Calhoun has a lot of physical similarities with the victim. It's not completely out of the realms of possibility that he could be next.

My hand closes around the ring that hangs on a thin chain around my neck. Myles' engagement ring. Its cold metal brings me no comfort though.

I have to think rationally. My job is to make sure these letters don't turn into anything more serious. The chances of me having to deal with anything that sent me into my breakdown are slim to none. And, who knows, maybe getting out of my little bubble for a bit will do me good.

§

The beeping of my alarm clock rouses me. I claw dark snarls of hair from my face and force myself through my morning routine. The rain is heavy this morning—it drips from the brim of my fedora and soaks my shoulders. Work, on a Sunday. This shit should be illegal.

Same routine at the office as always. Fill coffee cup, walk to office, head down, don't speak to anyone, open door, safe.

Except this time someone has beaten me to my sanctuary.

Detective sergeant Martin Novik stands up as I enter. He looks in a similar state to me, shoulders damp, cheeks flushed from the cold. Novik was my mentor when I first became a cop, and we have remained friends ever since. Even now he calls me up every so often to help with cases he is assigned to.

"To what do I owe this pleasure?"

"Can't I visit you for no reason?" he asks, his lip curling up in a little smirk.

"After the weekend I have had? No." I turn from him as I hang my coat up. After retrieving my cigarettes and lighter, I sit behind my desk. "If you're here to give me the same line Harris did, I don't want to hear it."

"But—"

"No," I bark. "Goodbye, Novik."

Novik is too much like me, a quiet man with a dangerous slow-burning temper. I see it flare up in him now. "Why won't you even consider it?"

"Because the right guy has been rotting behind bars for years."

Novik shrugs. "Whatever helps you sleep better, man."

I take a deep gulp of my coffee, wishing it was Scotch, and boot up my computer. Novik stares at me. His tall, muscular frame takes up more space in my office than the average human, and it's hard to ignore him. I know he is waiting for me to speak, but I refuse to give in. I lose myself in looking for the best route into New York and somewhere to hole myself up for the week.

I jump as Novik's voice rattles from next to my right ear. "Nah, you ain't thinking about this case at all."

I minimize the windows. "It's not related."

"Bullshit, Higgins!" he says. He drops to a squatting position and looks me in the eyes. "You're heading to New York, a place you can't stand, for what? A vacation?"

"Yes," I say and turn from him.

"Come on, man, aren't we better friends than that?" He stands up and walks slowly towards my shelves. I click my internet browser back open. "We all slept better when you got that guy, but we can't ignore this. This is almost the exact same shit."

He slips a folder from the shelf. I know instinctively what case it is. He plops it down in front of me and opens it up over my keyboard. "Symbols on the ground, flaying, dissection, and decapitation."

"What I'm working on has nothing to do with that," I say.

Novik glances at me and then back at the page. "All victims had the same look—long, wavy blond hair, brown eyes, Caucasian. All male. No one older than twenty-eight."

There was one older, I think and quickly chase the thought away.

"What is it this time? New York City. Goth kids." His green eyes narrow in anger. "Do we need to wait until we find the beheaded one before we act?"

"We tried to act before that, but we had no leads. No clues. A whole heap of nothing!" I snap.

"Yeah, but we have a head start this time," Novik insists. "We have to help them out. We know stuff McCray and his team don't."

I pinch the bridge of my nose. "Stop."

"Are you going to let it all happen again? Could you live with yourself if you did?"

"Why is it my problem?" I ask. I don't know what got into him, but he better drop it and fast. Why is he suddenly the authority on these kinds of murders?

"It's *our* problem," Novik says firmly. "We have a duty to help."

I stand up, anything to get away from the pictures in the folder. Each one is a searing-hot scar on my mind. "I don't want it to happen again," I whisper half to myself. My thoughts fill with images of Myles' body lying on the ground—throat ripped out, ribs splayed open, *not a worthy offering* scrawled in blood on the wall behind him.

Novik's voice crashes into my waking nightmare. "Then stop it! Join up with us and McCray. We are all thinking of heading to New York anyway, so why don't you come with us?"

"Because I'm not a cop anymore!" I shout "Plus, I already have something to work on out there."

"We could hire you like I've done before. You can work with us, give us your insights since you were lead investigator last time around. Come on. You know it makes sense."

Am I putting Calhoun in danger by insisting on working on the letters in isolation? Will the course of action I'm taking be too little too late just like last time?

I wearily scrub my hands over my face. "I'll entertain the idea, for now, but no more demon talk, okay? All I'm doing is going to New York to investigate some poison pen letters."

Novik sigh. "Fine. But you can't deny something weird was going on. We saw some strange shit."

"Amazing what you can do with a bit of makeup and wax nowadays." I say dismissively. "You saw those guys and gals at the comic convention we had to attend."

"Even a rotting skull with moving parts?" he asks. I can tell he's not buying it.

"Yeah, even that," I say, even though I am becoming less sure with every word.

And just like that we are getting the old gang back together. Well, what's left of us.

§

"Your friend not with you tonight?" Eddie smirks at me. I roll my eyes and shake my glass at her. "That's why you were asking if I'd seen any Goths in here, right?"

"He wants to hire my services." Before she can deliver one of her trademark filthy jokes, I say, "Not those kinds of services, ya gutter rat! Though they would probably make me more money." I savor the smell of the Scotch before drinking it down.

Eddie leans on the bar, her chin resting on her upturned hands. "So, you've been enticed back, have you?"

"Looks that way."

"And all it took was a pretty little thing with big goo-goo eyes."

I scowl. "It's not like that. He's just a kid."

"He can't be that young."

"Young enough. Plus, I wouldn't be interested even if he were my age."

Eddie's shining dark curls shiver over her shoulders as a small chuckle shakes her body "You need to get back on the horse, dude, even if it is a young stallion like that."

"You're a crude bitch, you know that?"

"I try my best."

I can't help but smile at her goofy grin. She's right, it has been ages since I had, well, anything in that department. I haven't even thought about it for years.

"Who's playing tonight?" I ask, hoping to divert attention away from my non-existent love life.

"Anyone who wants to," Eddie replies. "Why don't you play something? You and your band were always a hit here."

"I'm seriously out of practice. Plus, I should be going. I just wanted to stop in and ask if you would mind keeping an eye on my place while I'm away."

"Sure, man. Any time."

"Thanks." I hand her my glass and pay up. "I better go. I need to get some shut eye."

"You know what always helps me sleep?"

I laugh. "You offering your services now?"

"You couldn't afford me even if I was."

I roll my eyes. "Night, Eddie," I say and head out into the dark streets.

3

New York, New York

New York—a shining, glittering facade spread thinly over a quagmire of wasted lives and shattered dreams. The bright lights may draw many kids to its crowded streets, but it is the dark shadows that claim most of them. Presiding over this cesspool of human corruption is one Stanley Burbank, a hot tempered, nasty little man who is possibly the most corrupted of all the cops I have ever had the misfortune to meet.

Shit always rises to the top.

My number one objective while I am here is to stay under his radar. He can't stop me working here as long as I'm not interfering in police work, but drawing attention to myself is more trouble than it's worth.

I gaze out of the large window of my room at the Park 79 Hotel, trying to get my bearings in this maze. I'm too hot and uncomfortable from my drive. Six hours point to point isn't bad I suppose, but my back is sounding its protests. I don't do well with downtime though, so rather than chilling in my room, I call Calhoun.

This time I do agree to go to his house to meet up. It's better than hanging out in any bar in this jerk-water burg. I grab my laptop bag and head out.

§

I decide to brave the walk to his apartment. The Gothic facade of the building rises in front of me and, suddenly I recognize it. Well, I'll be damned. I step past the very spot where John Lennon lost his life and enter the large archway. It's a fancy place if a little gloomy. The nickname Gotham really suits New York when you see buildings like this.

After a quick discussion with the doorman and an even quicker phone call by him to Calhoun's apartment, I am making my way up. Top floor? Very fancy. As I reach the right door, I fix my face into a neutral expression and knock. A few seconds pass, the door opens, and Calhoun smiles at me. His face and long baggy painters smock are splattered with so many colors of paint it's like a unicorn threw up on him.

"Oh, hey. Sorry. I lost track of time. Just let me clean up." He gestures for me to come in, and I do, following him through the hallway and into a large living room. The walls are a pale green. Little birds and plant life painted with a delicate hand break up the solid color. It doesn't look wet though. I wonder what he has been working on?

"I thought the doorman called you before I came up?" I ask.

"Oh, he did, but I didn't have enough time to clean up, and I kind of got sucked into my work again," he explains as he wipes at his nose. A smear of purple appears on his pale skin. "So, uh, this is my home," he announces and raises his arms as if to indicate the room.

I obediently cast my eyes over everything. The couches and armchairs are covered in swathes of dark green fabric. Shelves, bookcases, and a TV stand, are all made from bleached driftwood. There is little in the way of photographs, but there are loads of DVD's, CD's and books, which I plan on looking over as soon as I get the chance.

"Nice place," I say. Nice place? My entire apartment could probably fit in one room here.

"Thanks, my, uh, my parents insisted. They didn't want me living just anywhere in New York."

I nod a little and make a mental note of the information. "So, what do your parents do?"

He scratches his forehead, gaining another purple streak. "My dad is high up in one of the big oil companies, that's why we moved to Aberdeen. He used to work offshore on the oil rigs, but he climbed the ranks."

"Must've gotten pretty high up to afford this place."

He smiles a little tightly. "Yeah I guess. But I do okay for myself. I own a tattoo store that's going pretty strong, and if I do decide to sell any artwork, I can get a few hundred per painting."

"That's great." He isn't telling me anything yet that I haven't found out for myself. I glance around again. Two big windows grace the wall to my left, overlooking the street. The room is light, airy, with a subtle floral fragrance mingling with the chalky smell of paint.

"Well, uh, make yourself at home," he says. "I'm going to go grab a shower. Won't be long." He pads barefoot down the hallway before I can answer.

I remain where he left me. I sit down on one of the couches, finding it a lot more comfortable than it looked, and pull my notebook out of my pants pocket. I write down what he has told me so far and my own observations since I got here. Nothing is piquing my interest just yet.

While I'm alone I have a look at his book and DVD collection, but all I learn from it is that he has an eclectic taste. His musical taste, too, spans decades and genres with no apparent preference.

I give up on finding any hints to his personality in the living room and wander into the hallway. The ceiling is higher out here and is covered in plaster molding common in old buildings. The floors are a shining dark wood. The walls, where they are not punctuated by the large doors, are a stark white. There's no artwork of any kind.

A few doors are open. Through one I spy a modern kitchen done up in scarlet and black. Another room, painted in soft purples, contains a large bed and a mishmash of furniture.

From this end of the hallway, I can hear the shower running and decide to return to the living room. As I turn, something catches my eye. The door at the end of the hall is halfway open, and through it I can see colors, lots of colors. I slowly push the door open and gasp.

The room is completely white down to the dust sheets on the floor, but on the wall facing the door is something spectacular. I move towards it, carefully stepping over the paints and the airbrushing equipment. The sun streaming in through the windows catches every hue. It's a mural made out of little vignettes. I can make out the shape of a man wandering a forest and another of a palace under a shining blue sky. In the next little image, one that still glistens wetly, the man has a little brown bird sitting on his finger.

"Do you like it?"

I turn sharply and find Calhoun standing beside me in sweats and a black tank top. He rubs at his hair with a dark towel.

"Sorry, I uh…" I laugh under my breath to hide my

embarrassment at being caught unawares.

"It's okay, you can wander around." His voice is cheerful. The permission to snoop around seems genuine. I catch myself staring. Something is different about him, but I can't quite figure out what. I turn back to the mural. "This is what you were working on?"

"Aye."

"It's really good."

"Thanks. It was my favorite story as a kid." A wistful look crosses his face. His voice becomes softer, intimate. "My mum used to tell it to my brother and me all the time."

He points to the first vignette of the man in the forest. "It's about the Emperor of China hearing this beautiful song in the woods, and, when he finds the bird responsible, he takes it home so it can sing for him always. He ends up building a mechanical version since the real one has to sleep and stuff and can't sing whenever the Emperor wants. The little bird goes back to the forest, the mechanical bird breaks, and the ruler of China gets so ill his subjects think he is dying. They search out the original songbird and ask it to come back to sing for the emperor one last time."

A dreamy smile spreads over Calhoun's face. "The bird agrees and its song is so beautiful that Death decides he isn't going to take the dying ruler. When he fully recovers, the Emperor and the bird reach an arrangement that works for them both. The bird can go wherever he wants, but he returns to the palace every year to sing about all the things he has seen throughout the empire."

Calhoun steps back and looks over the wall. "Ever since hearing that story I have been obsessed with those birds. They're called nightingales. They even sing at night. Imagine that, a beautiful song to soothe you through the darkness. I always wanted to hear one for real, but there's not really any of them in the Shetlands."

"Nightingale?" I laugh, "I thought a little Goth kid like you would be more interested in crows or ravens."

"A fairy story about death, slavery, and captivity isn't Goth to you?" Calhoun asks.

"Well when you put it like that."

"Some Goths have Poe. I have Hans Christian Anderson, and he, to me anyway, is a lot darker. You should read his stuff. Children's stories? He must've been mad." He gives a little shake of his head, whether that's to his assumption about the author or my comment I'm not sure.

I make another mental note in my head. Must check out this author. If nothing else it will give me a little more insight into Calhoun.

Calhoun's eyes are still on the painting. He chews his lip as he studies each vignette in turn.

"So, you like all this morbid shit then? Death?"

"Is death morbid?"

I stand there, shocked. What kind of question is that? "There speaks a man who has never lost someone," I mutter bitterly.

"And there speaks a man who has lost too much," he retorts as he raises a cloth to the newly painted vignette and blots at a stray drip. "Death comes to us all, Detective. What matters is how we live and how we remember those gone from us."

"And what would you know about it?" The words come out harsher than I intended, but his romanticism of death and morbidity is starting to grate on me.

He meets my gaze, eyes flashing. "I am the only survivor out of a car of four that crashed into the side of a lorry. The only one! My older brother is included in that death toll. You tell me what I know?"

Without another word, he returns to the painting and continues fixing little bits and pieces. I fight for words to try and explain, but I have none. Not even sorry seems to do, so I stay silent. I must have made some sort of noise because Calhoun narrows his eyes at me. It's then I realize what is so different. It's the first time I have seen him without eye-liner on. His irises are an almost impossible shade of green and flecked with gold. I rouse myself from my thoughts with a shake as he begins to speak again.

"Anyway," his voice is back to its sunny tone. "Don't you think that's the most romantic story? Music bringing you so much joy that it cures your ills."

"I think it's a commentary on how analogue recordings will always be better than digital," I say dryly.

He laughs, clutching his sides. I glad that our little bitter moment seems to have been forgotten.

"So," he says, "what's this change of plans?"

I scratch at the back of my neck. How am I going to tell him this without scaring him? "I, uh, I don't mean to worry you, kid." Wrong track. I can see concern crossing his face already. "Some of my colleagues think the murder here is linked to ones we dealt with in Boston. There are two of them thinking of coming through here to liaise with a New York officer to investigate them."

"What's that got to do with why you are here?" His whole posture stiffens. He's not a dumb kid; he already knows what I am getting at.

"We've already discussed this briefly." I keep my voice calm and gentle. "There's a possibility, a small one, that the letters you're getting are linked, too. This means I am duty bound to work with the officers investigating the murder if I find anything that I think could help them. That's standard procedure."

He chews his lower lip. "Do *you* think they're related?"

"There are elements in your letter that seem to describe things at the murder scene. I think it makes sense to, at least, consider the possibility of a connection."

Calhoun folds his arms across his chest. "Are you working with the police now?"

"No, you hired me, so I am working for you. I won't pass on any information about you unless it is for your own safety, and I will discuss everything I find with you." I keep my voice level and calm to prove there is very little to worry about. "Chances are this person heard about the murder and decided to use its details in the letters they were already sending. You've been getting them for months, right?"

Calhoun nods and rubs his face with his hands before looking at me again. "Aye, but in your professional opinion do you think I'm in danger?"

I smile, hoping it's enough to reassure him "Not any more than you were before. Like I said, it's a slim chance."

The calm, steely exterior that he displayed in my office slides effortlessly back into place, completely concealing the happy young man I was speaking to moments ago. "Thank you for doing this."

"No problem, kid. You got anyone that can stay with you? A girlfriend, friends, relatives maybe?" I ask. It might push his worry into overdrive but it has to be asked. He shouldn't be left alone.

"No, I'm on my own." A half-hearted shrug barely conceals his agitation, especially when he starts to look around as if expecting something to jump out at him. "My best friend, Morrigan, is back in Scotland at the moment, and I don't want any other friends knowing about this."

I suppress a grimace and feel my mouth open before my brain fully engages. "Why don't I stay with you? We have lots to talk about to start this case anyway, contracts to sign. Might as well kill two birds with one stone."

"Are you sure?" he says then quickly dismisses the idea with a wave of his hand. "I'll be fine, and I have your number if anything happens."

"Yeah, it's cool. We can use the time to make a good head

start."

Calhoun grins. The slump in his shoulders that appeared when we started talking about the murders disappears. "Sure, okay. It's not like I don't have plenty of space."

So much for not wanting to be alone with him. Still, a little bit of uneasiness on my part is far better than the alternative.

§

Once the contracts have been talked through and signed, I take a notebook and pen from my bag and glean as much information from him as possible. "You have many friends in New York?"

"Some," he replies. "Only one I am that close to."

"What about the artists you work with? The people you trained with?" He shakes his head sadly, and my senses tell me to push in. "Why not?"

"We had a falling out, a pretty bad one. A whole series of falling outs actually."

"Could you tell me about them, please?" I ask.

He looks at me, eyes darkening as he picks at the upholstery. "It's not any of them."

I raise an eyebrow and scratch the side of my mouth with the end of the pen. "All the more reason to tell me then, isn't it? Rules them out completely."

He takes a deep breath as if I am wasting his time. "The guy who trained me didn't like the fact that I started hanging around with bikers."

I raise an eyebrow. "Bikers?"

He nods and fiddles with the green throw that covers the couch.

"And I take it we're not talking about some guys who like to take a leisurely drive on the weekend?"

"Yeah, but… but I wasn't involved in… I mean I tried to change… They've gone straight now."

"Ain't no such thing, kid." Calhoun concentrates on trying to pull a stray thread out of the throw, so I decide to assuage his fears. "Look, you're not in trouble. I just need to know about people you know here. Talk to me."

"I did a tattoo for a biker named Alex Newlin not long after I first arrived here," Calhoun begins. "He was so pleased with it he asked me if I would be interested in doing work on some friends of his. I was still an apprentice then and really wanted to branch out on my own so I took the chance."

"And what was it like working with them?"

"It was …" Calhoun looks away for a moment, lost in thought. "It was good. The guys were friendly. I hung out with them a lot. I didn't take payment from them because I didn't need the money. I saw it as a chance to expand my portfolio and experience, and I think that smoothed the way for me a lot when it came to making friends."

I write as he speaks, taking short hand notes that I can expand on later. "Okay, let's get back to Newlin for a moment. What can you tell me about him?"

Calhoun shifts a little and clears his throat. "He's the leader of this biker gang called the Wolves. We were close from the beginning. I was flattered that he wanted to hang around with me so much. He's this big strong guy, gorgeous too, and loads of people obey his word like it's the law. It was fun being pulled into that kind of world. People respected me by proxy."

"Did anyone within the gang act differently towards you when you and Newlin became close?"

"No. I didn't get involved in anything they were doing, although I did speak to Newlin a few times about trying more legitimate business ventures. He listened to me more and more; I guess that could make people upset."

"Do you want to take a break?" I ask when I notice how much he is fidgeting.

"No. I'm fine," he replies. "I'm finding this harder to talk about than I thought."

"You're not going to say anything that's gonna shock me," I say reassuringly. "The most important thing here is that we get as much detail as you remember. Anything that you think could help me, no matter how small it seems to you, just talk it out."

Calhoun takes another deep breath. "No one seemed bothered by how close we were. Chris Duclos—that was his second in command—he was always a little off with me but it was more indifference than anything else."

"How do you mean?"

"He didn't really talk to me. He would stop talking when I got near him, especially if he was speaking to Newlin. He never threatened me, though, or said anything nasty, and we had been alone more than once when I did tattoos for him."

I write down Duclos' name along with what little I know about him so far. "Okay, so you were hanging out with the biker gang and doing tattoos?"

"Aye. When I finished my apprenticeship, I was taken on full time at the shop I had trained with, but I was spending more and more time with Newlin and his gang. The owner gave me an ultimatum. The bikers or his shop, and I chose the bikers." He starts to pick at the throw again. "I had a crush on Newlin from the day I met him. I didn't do anything about it because I had seen him chatting up girls, and he never did anything that made me think he was attracted to me. One night, I think about three months in to our friendship, we got drunk together, and, since no one else was around, I kissed him." He pulls his knees up to his chest and rests his chin on them. "I thought he was going to hit me at first, he looked so shocked, but he kissed me back, and then we went back to his place."

"Was it just a one-time thing?"

Calhoun shakes his head. "We started a relationship of a sort after that. It was a secret though. He kept telling me we had to do that. If anyone found out, we could have been in serious trouble."

"And how did you feel about that arrangement?"

"I was a little annoyed at first, but things with Alex were really great. He was never cold or distant with me in front of people. We just didn't act like we were any more than friends." Calhoun drags a hand through his streaked hair. "The longer we went without being found out the more risks we took. I'm sure some of the others knew. We had a few near misses—people almost catching us kissing or holding hands, but they never said a word."

I look back through the notes from earlier in the conversation. "And Chris Duclos. Newlin's right hand man. Do you think he knew?"

Calhoun's eyes flash as his lip curls up in a snarl. "He's the one that ruined everything."

So much for Duclos never being a problem for him. When the pause stretches out, I wave my hand to indicate he should continue.

"We were careless," Calhoun says. "We thought no one else was around, and then Duclos barges into the office and just stares at us. I have never moved so fast in my life. I mean, we weren't fucking, but what we were doing was bad enough."

I give him a moment to compose himself. "What happened? Did he threaten you or Newlin? Was there a fight?"

"There was a lot of shouting." His gaze is unfocused as he speaks. He's lost in his recollection. "Newlin tried to deny everything but Duclos had caught us red handed. Duclos left, and he said he was going to tell everyone."

"But he didn't?"

Calhoun shakes his head. "Didn't get a chance to. I'm not sure how he did it, but, by the next day, Newlin had managed to come up with a link between Duclos and another one of the guys that had been shot a month before. He held a meeting with the rest of the gang, and they kicked Duclos out."

I frown. "They just kicked him out? What exactly was the connection?"

Calhoun shrugs. "Newlin never told me. No one seemed willing to talk about it either. All I know is that Duclos got kicked out, and he took the members he was closest to with him."

"Be honest with me, Calhoun," I say. "Did you tell Newlin not to harm Duclos? Because, if he decided to let him go, when Duclos had that kind of dirt on him, then that's the first time I've heard of someone getting off so easily."

Calhoun starts to pick at his nails. "I told him not to, yes, but that was straight after the fight. I didn't want Newlin running after him and either of them getting killed."

I write all of this down but add my own notes to it. It doesn't add up. If Newlin was worried enough to get rid of Duclos from the gang, then why not finish the job and have him killed? Even if they were stepping away from the criminal side of things, it would still take a massive change of character for someone like Newlin to let a threat remain alive.

"Was the information Newlin had true?"

"I don't know." Calhoun sighs wearily. "Newlin never spoke to me directly about it. I was as much in the dark as anyone else."

Smart move there, Newlin. Calhoun couldn't have been accused of having anything to do with the plan if he knew nothing about it.

"Okay, so what happened after Duclos left?"

Calhoun looks down at his hands for a moment. "It was all quiet for a few weeks. Newlin listened to me and began to move the gang out of criminal dealings. Duclos got a new gang together, and they started a feud with us. A few people were killed on both sides, and then Newlin went to meet Duclos, to try and sort things out. I don't know what happened, but I do know Duclos isn't a biker anymore, and that gang is no more."

"You don't know, or you don't want to think about it?" I ask.

"I don't know," Calhoun snaps.

"You don't seem to know a lot when it comes to their more dangerous side." The words sound as harsh as I intend them to. Maybe if I piss him off in just the right way, he'll tell me something he might not otherwise want to say.

"What do you want me to say?" Calhoun asks. "I kept away from that side of stuff. I know they were dangerous people, I'm not an idiot, but Newlin never showed that side to me. Whatever happened to that gang, I know nothing about it."

I look at my notes and give Calhoun a few moments of calm before continuing. "Did you and Newlin continue your relationship after Duclos left?

"We started to drift apart after all the crap." Calhoun says. He's fidgeting once more. "Newlin was constantly worried that someone else was going to find out about us again, so our sex life dwindled away to pretty much nothing. He seemed to be afraid to be around me in public; he barely spoke to me."

"Did you leave him?"

"No. I wanted to make things work." He sighs and brushes his hair back from his face. "I sound like a lovesick puppy, don't I?"

"Not at all," I reassure him.

"That's good. Because I feel like an idiot about it all now." He crosses his arms over his chest. "I didn't leave him, but he forced me away. There was an incident."

"Go on."

He takes a deep breath. "I was walking home from work. We

had a late opening on a Thursday, and it was near Christmas. Dark, pretty damn cold too. I was walking along, headphones on, not paying attention, and some guys jumped me. Left me for dead."

"Can you elaborate?"

"They pushed me to the ground and started punching and kicking me. I managed to get up and fought back but they—" He toys with the hem of his shirt as he talks then lifts it a little revealing a five-inch scar running along his abdomen. "—they stabbed me."

"Jeez. That looks painful."

"Yeah, it was pretty bad. I probably would have died if Duclos hadn't found me."

I can't keep the disbelief off my face or out of my voice. "Duclos found you? Are you sure?"

Calhoun nods. "He got me to the hospital. It was definitely him, I remember speaking to him."

"Do you remember what hospital you were taken to?"

He chews his lip as he thinks. "I think it was the ER down on Madison. That would be the closest one."

I jot down the details I need to follow up that part. "And this is why you and Newlin are no longer together?"

"He abandoned me. He never came to see me once, not even when I was out of the hospital. Took me ages to feel safe enough to go out again, and when I did…." His face falls. Poor kid, I can almost feel his pain myself.

"And when you did?"

His face twists up like there's a bad taste in his mouth. "He was with some girl."

"I'm sorry," I say. "That must've been rough."

"Wasn't the best few months, that's for sure," Calhoun says. His whole body sags. "We were together for nearly a year, and he drops me without a thought in the world, right when I needed him most." He rubs his hands over his face then stands. "I'm sorry, can we take a break?"

"Sure thing, kid," I reply. "Take as long as you need."

I read over my notes while Calhoun is away. An exiled biker who may have already made an attempt on Calhoun's life, and an ex-lover who might want to chase him out of the city if it means he can keep their relationship a secret. It's a tiny suspect list but I've started bigger cases with less.

4

Dancing Steps

I wake with a start and stretch out. My stiff back pops loudly. It takes a while for me to realize where I am. I vaguely remember allowing myself a few minutes' rest in the armchair and hoping sitting upright would be enough to keep me in a light doze. I guess not. I throw off the comforter Calhoun laid over me, and head to the bathroom. On my way, I can't help sneaking a little look into Calhoun's room to make sure he's there. He's curled up amongst a mess of blankets and pillows like a little cat. Satisfied that he is safe, I continue to the bathroom.

Once I'm back in the living room, I grab the comforter and lie down on the couch. I need some proper sleep. After much deliberation, I strip to my underwear—the apartment may be old but it's warm, and sleeping in a shirt and pants isn't exactly comfortable. The rain drums against the window, and a warm scent—cinnamon with maybe a hint of vanilla through it, drifts off if the comforter. I take a deep breath and slowly relax into a proper sleep.

"You don't have to sleep on the couch," says a soft voice.

"Where else am I gonna sleep?"

Myles smirks and lazily rakes one hand through short blond curls. "Well, there's a perfectly good bed upstairs."

"With you in it."

My heart is hammering in my chest as I watch him come closer. My best friend since the academy, my partner from the day we became cops. I stand up.

His expression grows serious. "Jerry, I think we need to stop pretending."

"Who's pretending?"

He laughs. "Why are you on my couch tonight?"

I take a deep breath. "Because Kate kicked me out, for good this time!"

"Why?"

I take a step towards him; there is almost no gap between us now. "Because I told her I had fallen for someone else."

"Yet you won't share my bed."

"You cocky shit!" I laugh. "What makes you think I mean you?"

"I know it was more than some drunken fumble. For me anyway." He drapes his arms around my neck while mine slide around his waist. "I fell for you too, Jerry."

He kisses me. It's soft, tentative, but quickly deepens. I hold him to me, savoring his warmth when suddenly his body stiffens. I hear a whimper, and my mouth fills with blood.

I step back. Myles stares at me, eyes wide with fright, blood dribbling from his mouth. I look down as a blade bursts through his chest, splattering me with hot gobs of gore. He reaches out for me, and I clamp his hands in mine, powerless to do anything else. I watch dumbstruck as the skin melts from his face, and the rotting carcass of a laughing skull appears in its place. I want to scream, but my body is cold. Frozen. I can't move.

"Now here is a worthy offering," the skull says, its deep timbre shaking me. The skull snaps forward.

I hit the ground before the jaws clamp shut around me, and the force wakes me immediately. I stare up at the high ceiling, barely visible in the first light of dawn, and fight for control of my heart. It hammers in my ears.

The apartment is silent. Good. I don't want to be seen like this. I pull myself up, wince as my shoulder twinges, then wander over on bare feet to where my coat is hanging up.

I'm not sure if this is a non-smoking house, but it's for medicinal reasons. Calhoun will understand. I light up and take a drag. It does nothing to settle my nerves.

§

I must have drifted back to sleep because the next thing I know sunlight is burning my eyes. I rouse myself from the little nest I've made on the couch and head into the kitchen.

"You look really different with your hair down."

I jump. "You need a bell, kid."

"I was already here. I didn't sneak up on you," he says and holds out a mug to me. "Here, I made coffee."

I take the cup from him and sip the black nectar. Not bad, little weak compared to my usual. I mutter a thanks to him and lean back against the counter top. "What time is it?"

He glances at his phone. "Um, nine-thirty."

I relax a little; it's not as late I as thought.

"Would you like some breakfast?" Calhoun asked quietly.

"No, thank you."

Why are we both treating this like an awkward morning after? Or is it just me that's feeling the tension.

"You sure?" He jabs his thumb towards the stove. "I can make you something?"

"No, thanks, kid, I'm really not a breakfast person. You go ahead."

"I've already eaten," he says flatly.

I look over at him. He is chewing on his thumbnail, eyes trained on the world outside. There's definitely something wrong. His jaw is clenched tight.

"What's up, kid?"

He turns sharply to me, as if he is seeing me for the first time. "Nothing."

"You sure?"

Calhoun nods.

"I know you're not okay." Why am I pushing him? It's none of my business if the kid is in a mood. Still, something feels wrong, and the longer he stays silent, the more I ask about it. Finally, he thrusts an envelope at me. I open it up.

Such delicate footsteps my angel takes,
Flitting from one life to the next, uncaring.
My angel does not see how dancing feet trample dreams,
And so, my angel will dance no more.

It's typed, just like the first one. There is nothing on the letter to identify anyone or any place, just the same cheap, plain paper. Before I can ask anything about it, Calhoun pushes past me into the hall. I follow him, but he locks himself in the bathroom.

"Hey, kid, you okay?"

No answer.

"Calhoun, answer me!"

Finally, the door clicks open, and he steps back out. His face is pale, and he looks terrified. I fight the urge to pat his shoulder. "Are you okay?" I ask again.

He nods and brushes past me.

"It's just a letter, nothing to worry about," I say trying to assuage his concerns even though I am worrying right along with him. He looks like he is about to say something, but the words don't come. His eyes meet mine, wide and unblinking.

"Kid, what is it? You look more spooked than you have before."

"There's no stamp on the envelope," he says softly.

"Like the first one?"

"Aye," he confirms. "But that means they've gotten up to my apartment twice to drop these off."

"These are the only two that were hand delivered?" I ask.

"The rest were all posted. I'll get them all for you so you can take them with you when you leave."

"Thanks. We may be able to get some forensics from the stamps if we're lucky. I'm also going to have a word with your doorman. Everyone coming in here gets checked out, don't they?"

"They should be," Calhoun says. "Look, you don't have to stay here again." His sudden change of heart surprises me. "I can call Morrigan. I should have done that last night. Maybe she can fly back from Scotland early."

"I can stay here until she does," I say.

"No, it's cool, really," he insists. "One of the guys at my shop can stay with me until she gets back."

"Have I done something to make you uncomfortable?"

"No. Not at all."

"Then I can stay until your friend arrives."

"I can protect myself," he says and softens his words with a smile "I'm not incapable of it, you know."

I take a moment to look him over. Oh yeah, I have every confidence that a five foot eleven, one-hundred-forty-pound guy can fight off a sadistic killer all on his own. "I never said you were," I say after managing to stop my eyes from rolling. "But everyone needs help now and again."

He chews his lip as he ponders this. "Okay, sure. It would be nice having your company longer. I'm about to head into work, but you can stay here. I'll give you my keys so you can get your stuff from the hotel and whatever else you need to do."

"Sounds like a plan."

After Calhoun leaves for work, I boot up my laptop, and type up my notes from our conversation the night before. I run quick checks on any names he has given me, but only two really stand out. By the time I receive Calhoun's text to tell me he has arrived safely at work, I have a basic profile written for my prime suspects.

Number one on my list is Christian Duclos. A thirty-year-old of French extraction. Around five foot eleven, thin, with light brown hair and blue eyes. A native of Poughkeepsie. Second in command of the Wolves. Just like Calhoun said he is no longer a biker but is working as a record producer.

Suspect number two, Alexander Newlin. The leader of the Wolves. Thirty-three, six foot four. Black hair and hazel eyes. Light brown skin. Built like the proverbial brick outhouse. He's still with the Wolves and owns a body shop near the East River. This also seems to be the Wolves' headquarters.

I scour newspaper reports online, looking for any mentions of their names. They have both had dealings with firearm smuggling and drug running. Both have served time too. There is no connection to a crime for either name in the last six years.

With the basic checks done, I read through the pile of letters Calhoun gave me. All of them are typed, their envelopes bearing postmarks from all over New York state and New Jersey. I map them out on my laptop to see if there is a central location, but there isn't. No post office comes up more than once.

The contents themselves reveal very little. They're full of violent sexual descriptions and crude language but nothing that reveals much about the sender. I read over my suspects' profiles again. Could either of them be this cruel? They are violent men, that's for certain, and Newlin was Calhoun's lover. He could know enough to make these letters really personal to Calhoun.

Around midday I call Novik. I need someone to air my thoughts to, and there's no one I trust more than him.

"Did you find anything out on your own check?" I ask him as soon as he answers.

"Nothing more than what you did, Jer. The kid's clean, nothing to suggest he's delusional or in any way unstable. He's got quite a low profile for someone with such a rich family. No real mentions in the news, good or bad."

"What about the family, anything in their past?"

"Nope, his ma got arrested for possession in her teens. Dad's record is as clean as a whistle. The brother died about thirteen years ago. A car accident. He had no criminal record either, not that he had much chance to get one. He was only eighteen."

I juggle my phone into my right hand, then type up what he told me. "Thanks, man. That was pretty much all I found out too, but I thought I better double check."

"So, how's it going?"

I click open another window of my internet browser and Google the local news sites. "It's going okay. I've got a few people I want to speak to, one more promising than the other. They're members of the Wolves."

Novik sucks in air sharply. "That's unlucky."

"Yeah, but these guys don't sound as bad as the chapter out our way. I can find nothing on them for the past couple of years, which is impressive. I haven't run their names through every database yet, so something could still pop up."

"Yeah. Still, it might be worth your while asking someone for some insider info. McCray, he worked as a cop for a few years out there before becoming a detective, and he could know something. Jameson grew up in Manhattan, didn't he? He's bound to know stuff."

I ponder this as I scroll through one of the news pages. "I guess. I don't wanna get either of them into trouble though."

"It's not like you're asking for classified information, is it?"

A breaking news banner flashes up on the site. I click on it and read the headline. "Shit," I whisper.

"What's up?"

I read the first few lines of the article then manage to get my brain in gear to voice my concerns. "Did you know there had been another murder?"

There is a pause before Novik asks, "When?"

I scroll further. Details are sketchy at best. "Says any time between midnight and three am." A little tingle of worry tickles the base of my skull. What time had the letter arrived?

"Does it say what happened?"

"No. Same MO though. Symbols on the ground, quiet location, Manhattan again. They removed the legs of the victim. That's all it says. You've had no word from McCray?"

"Nope, nothing."

"Weird."

I hear Novik make a gentle *hmmm* sound, a sure sign the cogs of his brain are hard at work, possibly following the same path mine are. "What was our second murder like?"

Yup, we are walking the same path on this one.

"I can't remember off the top of my head, but I have a bad feeling it was similar to this one. Can you guys bring the old case folders when you come here?"

"Already planning on it," Novik says, "How's Calhoun holding up?"

"He seems to be okay for the most part," I reply as I continue to read the article. "He's scared, but he doesn't want to show it. I'm staying with him at the moment."

"At least he's had a warning of some sort and can protect himself."

Novik is right. It's not just Calhoun that's in danger here, any Goth kid in New York is. And, as far as I know, no previous victim received notes.

"We've gotta move fast on this, Jerry," Novik states.

"I know. We only have a few days until the next one."

"You think they'll last all the way to Halloween again?"

"I hope not. That's almost a month of this shit," I say with a bit of annoyance." I don't think I can stomach New York for a month."

"It ain't that bad a place," Novik says with a little laugh.

I scoff. "Yeah, right. Of course, a Brooklyn native is gonna say that. Anyway, who says these murders are the same?"

He doesn't need to say anything. I already know everyone thinks this a foregone conclusion.

"Are you going to call McCray or Jameson?" Novik asks, tactfully steering himself away from talk of the murders.

I sigh deeply. "Yeah, I guess I should. I don't want to go in there blind. Any info Calhoun can give me is a few years old at least."

"Maybe Jameson will want to help you out with the rest of it too."

"I can manage on my own, thank you." His concern is edging into mothering.

"I know you can, but it might do you good to have local knowledge."

"Yeah," I concede. "I guess that couldn't hurt."

"Awesome. You call him, and we'll see you in a few days. Take care of yourself, Jer."

"Yeah, you too, man," I say and hang up.

I look through my contact list and sure enough Jameson's number is still there. What are the chances he hasn't changed his number in almost ten years? I press the call button, hold the phone to my ear and wait for an answer.

§

"So, this is the base of operations?" Jameson says. He follows me through to the living room and lets out a low whistle. "This place is gorgeous."

"I know. This place dwarfs my entire apartment."

"Mine too. So, you said you wanted my help with something?"

I sit down on the couch and flick my ponytail back over my shoulder. "I'm working on a possible stalking case. My client used to be friends with members of the Wolves, and that means I have to go talk to them too. I was wondering if you had any information on them?"

He takes a seat next to me. "They operate out of a body shop near the East River. They have been trying to paint themselves as model citizens for the last few years, and, to be fair to them, we haven't had any reason to suspect them of anything in ages."

"Do you think it'll be safe enough for me to go there alone?"

"I think so." Jameson says after a moment's thought. "I've not had to interview any of them personally, but the cops that do have never had any real problems. They would refuse to talk from time to time. Get kinda angry. Swear at the cops if they didn't like the questions. That sort of thing. Never any threats though."

"Hmm. Do you think it'll be safe to tell them I'm a P.I. from the get go, or should I do this undercover?"

"It's just interviews, right?" Jameson asks. "There's no point in being undercover for what could be a few conversations." He looks me up and down. "Might not be the best idea to go in there dressed like Sam Spade though."

"I don't look like Sam Spade," I mutter.

"You look like a cop is all I'm saying."

Jameson has a point. I'm not going to hide what I am there for from Newlin, but the rest of the gang don't need to know who I am. "I'll change before I go." I angle my laptop so Jameson can see what I'm working on. "Do you know anything about these guys in particular?"

Jameson studies the screen. "Their names are well known. Newlin has been in and out of trouble since his teens. Duclos is the more dangerous of the two. He was usually at the heart of any kind of fighting. I'll come with you when you speak to him if you like."

"Is that gonna be okay with your boss?"

"It's just a bit of support, Higgins. I'm not jumping ship."

"I appreciate it, really," I say. "Are you sure you won't get in shit over it?"

"I'm just gonna accompany you," Jameson say. "I'm not going to take notes or work any further on this with you. It's just back up."

"Thanks, man." I lean back on the couch and, relax a little. "I've also done a quick check on a friend Calhoun keeps mentioning. Her name is Morrigan Pendragon. I doubt that's her real name, but I can't find any other for her."

"It's not unheard of as a last name," Jameson says.

"No. Anyway, she's not a suspect, but she is close to Calhoun. She could have some useful information."

Jameson thinks for a bit. "Is this the same Pendragon that has the nightclubs?"

"That's the one." I pull up her picture and show him. "She's fifty-two. A tiny woman, barely over five foot tall. Everything I've found about her seems to be positive."

"Yeah, that's what I've heard to. She's a nice lady."

"Who owns a fetish club," I say. That particular fact is still amusing to me.

"What's so weird with that?"

"Nothing. She just doesn't seem the type."

"She could be exactly the type," Jameson smirks. "Who knows what people are hiding about themselves?"

"I guess I'll find out, won't I?" I grin. "She's out of the country right now, but Calhoun says he's going to ask her to come back early and stay with him for a bit. I'll talk to her as soon as I can." I brush my hand through my hair. "So, how's it going with the murder case?"

Jameson takes a deep breath and settles back on the couch. "We have information on the victims, and that's it. The first guy was an art school student, close to graduating. The second guy is still a John Doe right now."

I start typing. "What about ages, place of birth, family?"

Jameson let's a slow breath out through his nose. "You know I'm not supposed to tell you details."

"I won't tell anyone," I reassure him. "But, I understand if you don't want to tell me. I won't be offended."

Jameson chews on the inside of his cheek as he thinks. "Still looking into it for number two like I said," he says in an almost conspiratorial whisper. "But the first guy was twenty-three. Magnus Erikson. From a little town in Norway. Can't remember the name of it for the life of me."

There's a few similarities to Calhoun. Artist. European. Granted not the same country, but northern Europe just the same.

"Three sisters, no brothers," Jameson continues. "Single parent household. Won some sort of scholarship to study here. Quiet kid. Kept to himself, though he had a few friends in his year. Preliminary reports are pointing at the death happening pretty far into the attack. There was no killing blow from what they have found so far."

I suck air in through my teeth. Poor kid, what must it have been like for him?

"Toxicology is clean. No drink or drugs in his system. Autopsy shows he had been raped, and the skin around the shoulder blades, chest and upper arms was flayed off and some muscle removed. All while he was still alive. Looks like the killer had tried to make wings out of flesh he pulled off. The shape was kind of there, but whether he was interrupted or just sucks at that kinda thing is up for debate."

I shudder. What kind of sick person could do that to another human being. "What about victim number two?"

"Pretty similar from what we can see so far. Violent assault, rape, mutilation. Legs severed at the hips and wrapped around the neck. Looks like it was the trauma that killed him."

"These happened on residential streets. Did no one hear anything?"

"One happened in an alley just off 53rd. The other in a disused subway station No one heard or saw anything," Jameson confirms.

"And 53rd is a busy street, right?"

"What street here isn't? This place never sleeps."

After a few moments' deliberation, I silently hand Jameson the latest letters. He reads them, and his eyebrow raises

"Where did you get these?" he asks.

"One was sent to my client at some point last week. He brought it to me in Boston. The other arrived this morning. Both were hand delivered. What do you think of them?"

"They have some pretty dark imagery in them," he muses as he reads.

I keep silent. I don't want to push him towards the answer I want.

"They kinda describe the crime scenes, don't they?"

"I think they may, yeah," I say with a sigh. "Whether that's because someone is hearing about these crimes and using them to scare Calhoun or it's the killer sending them is another matter entirely."

"Yeah, it could be either," Jameson says. "But if they are coming through on the same day as the murders, then that really narrows down the pool. The person sending them could be a reporter. Maybe a cop."

"Could be. Or someone who is watching the news sites like a hawk. Or it could all be a weird coincidence."

"We get very few of those in this job, Higgins," Jameson sighs.

"I know. My client even fits the basic descriptions of the victims so far. There are some differences, but they're pretty small." I scrub my hands over my face. "But there's every chance he could be on the killer's radar."

Jameson pats my knee consolingly; his sudden affection makes me flinch. "Try not to worry too much," he says, his voice soothing. "We'll stop this guy. We're already a few steps ahead cos we have the Boston case to look back on."

"And all my mistakes to miss," I laugh bitterly.

"You didn't make mistakes. You did what you could with the information and evidence you guys had."

"It was still a complete train wreck."

"You guys did your best." His tone lets me know this is the end if he argument, as far as he's concerned.

I fall quiet, mulling over the case that almost ruined my entire life. Jameson is right; we were completely blind last time. There was no forensic evidence at the murder scenes to link us to a killer. The weapon couldn't be fully traced. We had no witnesses. This time the detectives have our case notes, and I have something entirely new. The letters. These murders will not end the same way.

Jameson's voice cuts through my thoughts. "Who do you want to go interview first?"

"Newlin." I say without missing a beat. "He was closest to Calhoun. He'll hopefully be able to shed light on a few details."

"Sounds good. I know where the shop is so I'll drive you there," he says.

"Don't you have a better way to spend your day off?" I grin.

Jameson laughs. "Hey, you wanted my help so I'm helping."

I glance at my phone. Calhoun's hourly check in text is late so I send off a quick message. He replies quickly, stating he's fine and was so busy tattooing he forgot to text me. It's almost like he doesn't understand how dangerous this situation could be.

"Okay, I think we're good to go." I slip my phone back into my pocket. "Do you mind if we stop by my hotel on the way out? My bags are still there."

"Not at all," Jameson says. He stands and fishes his car keys out of his pocket. "Lead the way."

I double check that the apartment is locked up tight, leave a note with the doorman that no one is to be allowed up apart from Calhoun and me, then head to the hotel.

5

Interview with a Biker

I approach the garage and surreptitiously scan my surroundings. It's in a quiet area. There are a few businesses around it—a little store, a tattoo parlor, and what looks like a hair salon long closed down. I sweep my hair back from my face and slow my stride, trying to look like I fit in here.

I've taken the advice of Jameson and Calhoun, who I called to double check the address. Calhoun stressed Jameson's point about not looking like a cop, which only strengthened my suspicion that he was holding back on what he knows about Newlin and Duclos.

And so here I am, standing in the damp New York fall in clothes I borrowed from Jameson. Dark blue jeans that are maybe a touch too long, Motorhead t-shirt and Jameson's leather jacket. My dark hair is loose around my shoulders and catching every breath of wind. I never wear it loose. I feel odd—uncomfortable, exposed—yet I press on.

The sign above the garage reads Newlin and Sons. Something

tells me that doesn't mean biological sons. I take one last look around. I know Jameson is there, watching from the car, but I don't look straight at him. He is in enough danger just hanging around. Biker gangs don’t like people who aren't like them, and an African American cop is about as far removed from their kinda people as we are likely to get. I square my shoulders and step into the garage.

Loud bangs and the squeal of impact wrenches greet me as I step inside. The scent of oil is strong, but the reception area itself is clean and painted a soft blue. It looks just like any other body shop you might happen to wander into.

I walk up to the small window and press the bell. A tall man with a face like a bulldog chewing a wasp appears almost immediately. “Yeah?” he grunts.

“I'm looking for Alexander Newlin,” I say and dig around in my brain for the words Calhoun told me to use. “I need to book a custom paint job.”

“Uh huh?” the hulk grumbles, large arms folded over his chest. “What kinda custom job?”

I try not to pause too long. “I need a wolf's head on my body.”

Is that right? Calhoun seemed to stress the “my body” part. It's a coded way of asking to be considered for membership. I'm not sure those words have worked. Maybe they have changed since Calhoun was with the gang. I use every ounce of training I have to look calm while he stares at me for several long seconds.

“He's in the back office,” he grunts over the noise of the mechanics at work. He steps away and a door opens, leading me into the shop itself. It's a busy place. There’s at least twenty mechanics at work on a range of vehicles.

At first, I think I'm going to be left alone and consider taking the time to glance over the workshop with an ex-cop’s eye, but the mountain of a man leads me through and delivers me straight to the boss.

Newlin is sitting at a worn wooden desk hunched over a pile of paperwork. The little radio on the shelf is blasting out some sort of generic rock, and he's bobbing his head along with it. Raven hair obscures his face a little. His head is shaved on one side, and through the gray fuzz of new growth I can see the wolf's head emblem. He turns to us when the guy catches his attention and looks me up and down. His gaze is intense.

"Guy looking to join, boss," the giant says and leaves us to it.

Newlin leans back in his chair and crosses his arms across his wide chest. He's a lot more muscular than the pictures I found led me to believe. I fight the urge to look away from his glare.

"You're not looking to be a prospect. You're a cop, ain't ya?"

"Not exactly, no," I say. "And if you'd let me introduce myself, I would have told you who I am."

"You stand like a cop. You don't dress like one, but you look like you got a poker up your ass." He smiles at his own joke, a half sneer that pulls at the messy mustache along his top lip.

"And all cops look like that, do they?"

"Most of them do. Comes with being shafted by the man all day, every day."

I allow myself a little smile at that. "I'm a private detective, there's a difference."

"I got no beef with any kind of detective, especially outta state ones."

My strong accent strikes again!

"And I ain't got no beef with you." I say firmly. "This has to do with an old friend of yours, Lachlan Calhoun. I'd like to ask you a few questions, if that's okay?"

A flicker passes over his face, but it is too quick for me to catch what it is. He scratches the side of his face with the nail of his little finger.

"What does he want?" His chair makes a loud *squeak* as he

leans forward and rests his chin on one upturned hand.

"You used to date, didn't you?" I ask and make a valiant effort at pretending I'm not intimidated by his ever-present glare.

Newlin's lip curls up in a snarl. "Who told you that?"

"He did."

He makes the little scratching movement again and gives a dismissive shrug. "It wasn't dating."

"But you were involved?" I'm overly conscious of my tone of voice and posture. I don't want to do anything to set this guy off.

"What's it got to do with you?"

"Everything when I'm trying to keep him safe."

"Safe?" Gone is the death stare as Newlin's mask of bravado slips. "Why, what's happened?"

"How about you answer my question first?" I try to prove to him through tone alone that I won't back down.

It's a wrong move. Newlin furrows his dark eyebrows. His defenses are up again. "What's going on here? What's happened to him? Are you trying to say one of my guys has done something? And why are *you* here, not NYPD?"

I slip a copy of the newest letter from my jeans pocket and hand it to him. "Calhoun has been receiving threatening letters for the best part of a month. He hired me to find out who is sending them."

"And he thinks it's me or one of my boys?" Newlin barks. He ignores the letter completely. "That little—"

"No, he doesn't," I cut in. "But you were close to him, and I thought you may be able to help me with my inquiries." I soften my voice. "Look, I just want to talk. You're not under suspicion. I just want a better picture of what type of relationship you two had and what he was like with other members."

"What makes you think I will tell you anything?" Newlin asks.

I keep my arms loose by my sides. Nothing is tensed up.

Nothing is a threat. "Because I know you still care about him. You don't want to see him get hurt."

It's a little bit of a gamble—Newlin abandoned Calhoun when the kid needed him the most, but it works. A small grimace crosses Newlin's face before he rubs it with both hands. "Okay, what do you want to know?"

"Let's start with how you two met."

Newlin's eyes roll upwards as he thinks. "He did this tattoo for me." He pulls his shirt up and shows me the coiling dragon that covers his side. I nod appreciatively. Calhoun's work is really good.

"I went to this studio on the upper east side to get this done," Newlin continues. "The artists told me they had this guy who was apprenticing, said that he was really good at the type of shit I wanted done, and I could get it cheaper if I let an apprentice do it. I said no, but then I saw Lachlan's portfolio. It was amazing and just what I was looking for. So, I let him do it. We got to talking, and he was pretty cool. Quick worker too. I asked him if he wanted to do some work for the boys here. He said yes."

"Were you guys close?"

"Yeah, we were," he says.

I keep my gaze on him, eager to spot any change in his demeanor. "Close enough to date?"

He sighs. "Yeah. But it was just fucking, you know?"

I shift my weight to my other leg. "And not just the once, right?"

"No. He's, uh, he's something special. One taste ain't enough."

I raise an eyebrow at the blush that colors Newlin's cheeks. I give him a second as he pushes his hair back, scratches his ear, pops his knuckles—all those little nervous tics people have when they are trying to think. When he doesn't pick up the thread again, I prompt him. "You guys had a sexual relationship for how long?"

He answers without missing a beat. "About a year."

"And that's all it was? Just sex?"

I am treated to the killer stare again before he looks down at his desk. "No. We were already close, and that stuck around after we started fucking."

"I guess this closeness was not something you could hide from the gang?" I soften my voice. I know this isn't going to be comfortable for him to discuss.

"No. I started to hear whispers. That kinda closeness could be tolerated for an old lady but not for some foreign punk kid."

"Did you ignore those whispers?"

"I didn't think anyone was planning to hurt him," Newlin says. "I had no reason to. He wasn't a danger to us. If anything, he was more of a help."

I shift my weight again. My back is a little stiff from sleeping on the couch, and it's making it hard to stay still. "He put you guys on the straight and narrow, is that correct?"

Newlin nods. "Yeah, but I don't discuss club business with outsiders."

I manage to refrain from pointing out that he shared a lot of it with Calhoun and turn my questioning elsewhere. "So why did you guys break up?"

Newlin gets up and begins pacing the small office. "I couldn't deal with him being upset and hurt, so I ignored him." He sits down on the edge of his desk apparently done with moving around for the time being. "I've grown up now," he says. "I can see how fucking stupid I was to do that. I didn't mean to hurt him, but I had to protect the both of us."

"From what?"

"We attracted a little trouble from… others," he says, obviously uncomfortable with revealing the real details. "If they knew we were close, they could've used him against me."

"Did that trouble have anything to do with Chris Duclos?"

His hazel eyes narrow. "What did you know about him?"

"I know he found out about you two, and he threatened to tell everyone."

"I rule here!" His sudden burst of anger raises my hackles. "I can be with who I want. Anyone who dares to challenge me over that gets a sharp lesson into why I'm in charge."

I have no doubt Newlin can handle himself, but it's still funny hearing the way he puts it. "So, I guess that means Duclos finding out was no big deal?"

His lip lifts in a ghost of a snarl. "Course it's a big deal. Don't tell me they got some rookie out here who knows nothing asking me questions?"

"What I am asking," I say firmly, "is if you rule here and no one gets a say in what you do, then why didn't you tell people you were with Calhoun?" Of course, I know the answer to that, but I want to hear it from his own mouth. Newlin doesn't respond so I ask, "Why, if you're in charge here, did you find it necessary to get rid of your second-in-command when he found out? And why did you turn your back on Calhoun after he was attacked?"

There is a deep rumble in Newlin's chest before he fixes me with a gaze that turns my insides cold. "You sure know a lot of New York business for someone from Boston," he snarls.

"Just answer my question please. If you are so sure of your place here, why did Duclos have to go?"

"Cos there ain't no place for queers here. Queers are weak, that's what many of my own brothers think, and if Duclos told everybody, then they would try to get rid of me. Don't matter how well they respected me before." His shoulders sag and he looks down at his hands. "You don't understand what it's like to have to hide who you are every damn day of your life and then someone finds out. He could've got me killed, or worse!"

He doesn't need to know I may know a little bit about how that feels. “If he was so dangerous then why is he still alive?”

Newlin smirks. “Lachlan really ran his mouth to you, didn't he?”

“I need to know as much as I can if I'm going to solve this case for him,” I say.

“I didn't do anything to him.”

“Then answer my questions and help me prove that.”

“I promised Lachlan I wouldn't hurt him,” Newlin mutters under his breath. “I couldn't do anything that was noticeable, or he'd know I lied.”

My eyebrow quirks reflexively. “Calhoun's opinion meant that much to you?”

“Are you dumb or something?” he snaps. “We'd been together for nearly a year. I wasn't about to throw that away.”

“But you did,” I say. I keep my voice soft. “You said yourself you couldn't handle him being upset or hurt. You did it for his own protection.”

Newlin’s hands ball up into tight fists, and I clench my own, ready to defend myself. With a heavy sigh, he sits down in the desk chair and covers his face with his hands.

“All right,” he says. He slaps his large hands down on the desk and takes a minute to compose himself. “The truth is the rumors about us were getting worse. No one had challenged me outright, but I was noticing the looks. People would stop talking when I walked in. I had to start watching my back, for both our sakes.”

“But you let Duclos live.” I punctuate each word by slapping my fist into my palm. “He was the only one who knew for sure what was going on between you two.”

“Yeah, and killing him would've made people wonder why I was shutting him up,” Newlin explains. “I needed to discredit him. I needed to make everything that came out of his mouth appear to be a lie.” All trace of aggression bleeds from him. “It was the wrong move, but it seemed the best way at the time. Duclos was always going to meet other chapters, so I told everyone that he had let something slip unintentionally, and that information got someone killed."

"Did everyone believe you?"

"Not everyone, but enough people did to sway the others." Newlin scratches at the side of his mouth then clears his throat. "During that meeting, I told them about enough little coincidences and stories to make it look like Duclos was running his mouth too much. I made sure nothing came out that made him a danger to us, just careless. I talked people down from a tougher punishment for him, and we roughed him up a bit before sending him on his way."

I blow a stray lock of hair out of my face. "But getting rid of him didn't make things any easier, did it?"

Newlin shakes his head. "Duclos had told everyone in that meeting that he had caught me and Lachlan together, and that was enough for some people to begin to suspect. I had to be more careful, so I stopped hanging around with Lachlan so much in public. I didn't want to do anything to add fuel to the rumors."

I can't say I understand. It seems pretty heartless to me, but then what do I know? I've never been in a biker gang. "Did anyone challenge you outright over your friendship with Calhoun?"

"I got told a few times that I was too close to him, that he might be a cop, and I was putting everyone in danger. But most people liked him too much to do anything about what they had heard. Lachlan didn't get involved in club business unless I asked him shit. He did amazing tattoos for half the price of any studio, if he wasn't doing them for free, and he was sharp as a tack. He didn't take shit from no one, and that gained him a lot of respect."

My hair is beginning to annoy me, and I blow strands out of my face again. "So, you decided it was better to cut all ties with him, without explanation, when he was at his lowest? Self-preservation at its finest."

"I did it for him! It was safer for us both." Newlin says sharply. "I never hated him. I wouldn't hurt him, and I wouldn't send him shit like this!" He shakes the letter at me.

"No one's saying you did. I just wanna know what happened." I take a deep breath and soften my voice again. "What happened after Duclos left?"

"He took anyone that believed him," Newlin says, "and he attempted to start a war. They interfered with everything. We were losing our friends, business deals, everything."

"Did you fight back?"

"Course we did."

I wait for him to elaborate, but he doesn't.

"Were any threats made against Lachlan during this time?" I ask.

Newlin seems to think it over. He drums his fingers on the desk. "No," he finally says. "No one was targeted individually."

I pull my notebook out of my pocket to make sure I've covered all the questions I wanted to ask. "Thank you for your time so far," I say. "I have one more question, if I may?"

Newlin sighs and scrubs his hands over his face. "Sure. Why not?"

"What do you know about the attack on Calhoun?"

"Nothing. That's the truth."

"You had no idea he was attacked?" I put just enough disbelief into my voice to goad him.

Newlin snorts. "Course I knew that. But that's all I know."

I move closer to the desk and look down on him. "Tell me what you know."

"I didn't do anything to hurt him," Newlin growls. "I don't know anyone who would."

"Even Duclos?"

"Even him," Newlin says without missing a beat. "Duclos hated me cos I pushed him from the Wolves, but I dealt with his little offshoot gang. There wasn't anyone left afterwards that would dare to attack Lachlan."

"Apart from Duclos."

"Why would he beat him up then take him to the hospital?"

"Ah, so you do know something?" I say with a smirk.

Newlin grinds his teeth when he realizes I've caught him out. "I was informed that Lachlan had been hospitalized, yeah."

"But you didn't try to find out why?"

"Why should I have?"

"Because he was someone that you had been seeing. He was someone you were close to," I rest my hands on the desk and get up in his face "He was someone that you cared about so much that you let Duclos live on his word."

Newlin stands and forces me back. "You have no idea what I had to do to try and keep him, us, safe. I had to balance everything just right to make sure no one got hurt. When he got beat up, I had to make a tough choice again, so I decided it was safer to cut all ties. Like I keep telling you. There were too many whispers, too many rumors."

"There was no talk about an attack beforehand?"

"Not a thing, and that's the truth," he grumbles. "And I heard nothing after the fact that made me think any of my guys were responsible." Newlin picks up the letter, folds it, and hands it back to me. "I'm sorry, I have no idea who could be sending these things. If I did, I'd tell you."

I push my hair away from my face and read over what Calhoun told me. Even if I did have anything more to ask, Newlin doesn't seem in the mood to continue. Best to call it a day and return later.

"Thank you for your time," I say. I fish a business card from my pocket. "If you think of anything else, then call me. Please."

"Yeah, right!" Newlin snorts. "Working with the cops ain't worth my life." As I turn to leave, Newlin asks, "Hey, uh, he's okay, isn't he?"

I think about using his worry as leverage for future interviews, but he's told me so much I decide to throw him a bone. "Like you said, he's a smart kid. He knows how to take care of himself."

Newlin nods and opens the door for me.

Back out onto the street, Jameson's car is not in the place it was when I left. I look around, trying to make it seem like this is exactly not what I am doing, and suppress the tiny lick of panic I feel incubating in my stomach. Just as I start to suspect that Newlin talking to me for so long was some sort of a diversion, Jameson rolls up into his original spot. I keep myself in character and jam my hands into the pockets of my jeans as I stroll to the car.

"How was it?" Jameson asks.

I slide into the passenger seat. "Illuminating in a way. Seems to be a lot of guilt floating around that guy. That and lot of repressed feelings."

"You still think he could be a suspect?"

I write down the bullet points from the interview. "I think he is safe to leave for now, but we'll keep an eye on him though. He was a little too evasive at times for my liking."

Jameson taps his fingers against the steering wheel, "Okay, where to now?"

"Calhoun hasn't mentioned anything about Pendragon being back in the city," I say after I've checked my phone. "I guess it's off to see Duclos."

Jameson nods and pulls the car out into the road.

§

Duclos' home is a big house in a good neighborhood out on

Long Island. Not overly flashy, but the guy is obviously doing well for himself. This time, with Duclos' reputation fresh in our heads, Jameson accompanies me for the interview.

We knock on the door, and after a few minutes, we are greeted by a happy looking guy with a wild mop of brown curls. "Hey, guys, what can I do for you?"

Christian Duclos?" I ask.

"Who's asking?"

"My name is Jerry Higgins. I'm a private investigator. This is Detective Jameson from the NYPD. We'd like to ask you some questions."

His expression never changes. "Sure, guys, come in."

We follow him into the house. It's a normal enough home. No stupidly expensive gadgets or furniture, though there is a large flat screen TV on the wall of the living room. Duclos motions for us to sit and offers us a drink. We both ask for coffee.

"First impressions?" I ask Jameson when we are left alone.

"Seems a nice guy. Doing okay for himself."

I nod. "No sign of any hostility either."

"Not yet," Jameson whispers.

Once we are all sitting with our coffees—good, strong coffee, too—I begin the questioning. "We are here about some correspondence that is being sent to an old friend of yours. Lachlan Calhoun."

Duclos lets out a short bark of laughter. "He's no friend of mine."

I don't react. Jameson scratches the side of his face. I know what he is thinking—this is the answer we expected based on everything we know so far.

"But you do know him?"

"I did, once." Duclos rakes a hand through his unruly hair and fixes me with a slightly confrontational stare.

"Care to elaborate?"

"Depends. Am I under arrest?"

"Not at all," I say and keep my voice as level as possible. "We are only here to talk."

"Did that little shit blame me for whatever you guys are here about?"

"No, he was actually shocked that I had even considered talking to you in relation to it."

Duclos snorts. "Wow, he's changed his tune."

"Mr. Duclos," Jameson says in a commanding tone. "Would you please answer our questions rather than asking your own?"

He shrugs. "Okay, ask away."

"What was the nature of your relationship with Lachlan Calhoun?" I ask as I take over questioning again.

"We had none."

My eyebrow raises. "He was with the leader of the biker gang you used to be a part of, yet you say you had no relationship with him? Not even on a professional level?"

Duclos rests one ankle on the knee of the opposite leg. His knuckles are white where his hands clasp his leg. "We were never really friends. I found him a little weird. He talked funny and seemed to be in his own little world most of the time. Alex put him under my protection, just like all of his stuff."

I wince at his choice of words but say nothing. Jameson picks up the thread. "Would you say you disliked him?"

"I wouldn't say that. Not at first. He had a good business head, helped us iron out a few things. All legit business stuff, I might add. But then he used his influence on Alex to pull us out of everything we were used to. He destroyed that gang from the inside. Now they are just a bunch of guys who play at being bikers. There's no bite to them anymore."

"Tell me about the incident that resulted in you being kicked from the gang?" I say calmly.

He smiles at me, blue eyes glittering dangerously. "He told you about that, huh?"

We look at him until he gives a huffing breath and shrugs. "It was late, and most of the guys had gone home. There was only me and a handful of others left in the club house, but I knew Alex and Lachlan were around. He had said that Lachlan was doing another tattoo on him. Lachlan had gotten Alex into all kinds of Pagan shit, and it was some sorta protection symbol he was getting." He pauses to rake a pale hand through his hair again. "I got this phone call, important business. Someone wanted to talk to Alex, and they weren't waiting around so I went to go find him. I opened the door to his office, and there was Alex sucking off Lachlan."

"Musta been a hell of a shock. What did you do?" I ask.

"I kicked up hell. What kinda sick fuck do you gotta be to willingly suck another man's dick?"

I fight to keep my expression neutral. Letting him know he's pissing me off isn't a good idea. "I'm pretty sure there is worse shit to walk in on than that."

"Well, yeah, least he wasn't fucking him!"

This isn't the place to slap the ignorance from him, much as I would like to. "You kicked up hell? In what form?"

"We all shouted a lot. I couldn't get near Lachlan. Alex held me back. Even in a situation like that hitting the boss man ain't the best of ideas, so I told it to him straight. He either got rid of Lachlan or I would, permanently."

Neither Newlin nor Calhoun mentioned that. Interesting. "Just because he was in a relationship with Newlin you think he deserved to die?" A little bit of a growl slips into my voice.

"So, what happened next?" Jameson asks, quickly diffusing the tense atmosphere between Duclos and me.

Duclos throws me one last glare before answering. "A couple

of days later I was called into this big meeting. Alex said he knew I had been running my mouth and that got someone killed. It was all bullshit." He sweeps his hand through his hair. I can't tell if it's because he's nervous, mad, or just out of habit. "But almost everyone in that room was on his side. Next thing I know I'm out on my ass. I guess I should be grateful they didn't kill me."

"And that was the last you saw of either of them?"

"Yeah."

His story doesn't match Newlin's or Calhoun's, but I decide to see where his own narrative is going. "Have you tried to contact either of them since the incident?"

He shrugs angrily. "Why should I? They kicked me out, and I made my peace with it. I moved on. I hooked up with an old buddy of mine and started working in his recording studio. Sure, it's a different life to what I wanted, but it pays well. Very well. I don't need them and their faggy bullshit."

"You didn't try contact Calhoun at all? Not even after he ended up in the hospital?" I ask.

"He was in the hospital? Why?" His shock appears to be genuine, but I decide to push him further.

"Some guys jumped him, left him for dead."

No recognition passes over his face. Just how good a poker player is this guy? He does the old hand raking the curls bit again and looks right at me, dark blue eyes meeting mine without flinching. "Well, damn. No, I didn't try to contact him. I didn't even know about that."

A little shock of apprehension shivers up my back. I signal to Jameson that we should leave.

"Okay, that about wraps things up. We'll be in touch if there is anything else."

"Oh, I doubt there will be," he replies sweetly. The grin is back in place, just like that.

I give him my card, and tell him to call if he can think of anything else. I have a feeling it will find itself at the bottom of the trash can before we have left his yard.

"Why did you wanna leave so quick?" Jameson asks once we are on the road again. The sky is beginning to grow dark, and there is a promise of a storm in the clouds over the skyline. I rake my dark hair back from my forehead then mentally curse myself for copying Duclos' well-worn gesture.

"He's lying." There's no doubt in my mind that that's the case. "I've had two people who have had no contact whatsoever in years telling one story, and then his is completely different."

"Well, there is another possibility." Jameson says. "Maybe Duclos was genuinely doing his job as some sort of enforcer. Protecting the interests of the club. They wouldn't have survived with an openly gay leader. Maybe he really has put it all behind him?"

I consider this for a second. "He could have, but that's a hell of a lot of made up shit from Calhoun and Newlin if that's the case."

"Maybe Calhoun got it wrong."

"Nah, he's pretty switched on."

"Yeah, but think about it," Jameson presses on. "You're new to the country. You don't really have anyone apart from this guy who suddenly takes an interest in you, so you try to fit in to his world. I'm guessing Calhoun hadn't been in a biker gang before. He probably had no idea of the dynamics involved. Maybe what he saw in that office scared him enough that he pinned the other events on Duclos?"

"You could be right. However, Newlin pinned it all on him too," I say. "The only one who hasn't wanted to talk is Duclos. What does that tell you?"

"Depends where you are looking from, doesn't it?" Jameson says. He looks at me quickly before turning his eyes to the road.

"Either Duclos doesn't want to talk because he doesn't like cops and he's a hateful, dangerous, man or he can't talk cos he has nothing else to say. Maybe Calhoun and Newlin are pinning it all on him for some reason."

"Why?" I ask, my tone a little harsher than I intended.

"I don't know, but every angle be explored. Right?"

I nod thoughtfully. Jameson has a good point. I have to look at everything, no matter how unlikely the story seems. Maybe a second opinion would be a wise decision.

"Hey, why don't you meet Calhoun for yourself?"

"What for?" Jameson asks skeptically.

"So, you can see what he's like."

Jameson laughs. "I don't care what he's like. I'm not working with you on this."

"Then do it to help a friend. A second opinion on him won't hurt."

Jameson thinks for a second. "Sure. Why not?"

§

Calhoun walks up to the apartment building just as we arrive. The girl he's with gives him a quick hug then crosses the street. At least he seems to be following some of my advice and not walking alone.

"Wow, look at you," Calhoun says, a cheeky smile playing on his lips. He is in his full Goth get-up again, dressed in a short-sleeved black shirt with a silver and electric blue dragon design on it, leather pants, hair falling around his face in soft waves, eyes lined thickly. "You look like a rock star," he laughs.

"Don't get used to it, kid," I say, but I can't help but smile at the compliment. I introduce him to Jameson, and they shake hands. I give Calhoun his keys back, and he leads the way up to his apartment.

"We went to see your friends today," I inform him once we are seated in the living room, coffee in hand.

"Oh, yeah?" He curls up in the big chair, legs folded under him. "What did they have to say for themselves?"

I glance at Jameson, trying to see what he is making of Calhoun, but I get no response. Not even a flicker.

"Newlin basically tells the same story you do. Duclos wasn't so forthcoming." Calhoun does that kind of deep nod people do to show they are following you and motions for me to go on. "He says he never had any contact with you after he was kicked out."

"Well, that's a pile of shit for starters," he hisses, his face screwing up in sudden anger. "He was there! He carried me into that damn hospital. You can go check with them."

I hold my empty hand up. "Wait just a second there, kid. I never said I believed anyone over the other, but you give me the details for the hospital, and I'll check it out."

He seems to settle at that and is quiet for a bit. In one swift movement, he downs what is left of his coffee. "Another coffee or something stronger?" he asks, and unwinds himself from his position.

We both refrain as our cups have barely been touched. Once he leaves the room, I look at Jameson, eager for his opinion.

"Well, one of them is clearly lying about that little incident," he whispers "and maybe a few others, but I'm not entirely sure who."

I narrow my eyes. I think it's perfectly clear who is lying and it's not Calhoun.

6

The Fog

Frustration, that is what has driven me out in the thick fog that has blanketed New York since the early evening. I can barely see two feet in front of my face. Boston can be a foggy city, but this is different. It is isolating, shutting off not only my visibility but my hearing too. It's exactly the type of seclusion I need in this bustling metropolis.

My steps are muffled in the shrouded streets. My clothes cling to me, and my hair feels weighed down. The very air is oppressive, squeezing down on my thin shoulders and the top of my head. I add to the veil by blowing smoke into it, a little blue-gray swirl in a sea of white. I have no idea where I am, but that doesn't bother me. All I want to do is get out of my hotel room and step away from the case for a bit.

It has been three days since I spoke with Duclos and Newlin. I moved back to the hotel that same night. Calhoun had someone staying with him, one of the other artists from his shop. Maybe the girl we saw him with. I'd rather be staying myself, but we have a system in place with hourly check-ins throughout the day, and the doormen are under strict instructions about letting people up. His supposed best friend, Morrigan Pendragon, still hasn't shown up. I can't speak for her circumstances, but I know where I would be if my best friend was being threatened.

There've been no new notes, but no more murders either. No DNA has been found on the letters. The stamps were self-adhesive. The stationary used was generic. It could have been bought at any store in the country. Not even my visit to the hospital to check out Calhoun's story helped me. His medical records don't list who brought him in, and none of the staff remember.

I've kept myself busy outside of my own work by helping my friends. Novik, Harris, and I spent a chunk of time discussing everything we remembered from the Boston murders. The last series had gone like so. The first involved skin and muscle being removed from the arms and back but there were no wings in our crime scene, just a pile of flesh. The second one was pretty much identical to the New York murder. Our third had the lower jaw removed. Fourth was bled dry through small holes in the wrist. Fifth and sixth were killed together, half the body taken from each and the resulting halves lain together to make a new body. It carried on like that, each body missing a different part—teeth, eyes, hands, feet, hair. Sometimes the trophies were removed from the scene only to be found somewhere else. The only missing parts we never found were the blood and the severed head. To this day there has been no sign. Blood is pretty easy to get rid of but a head? Why take that and nothing else?

The only death that didn't fit the ritualistic pattern was my partner's. His had looked like a frenzied attack. He fit the same description of the other victims with wavy blond hair—even if it was pretty short in comparison—and brown eyes, but he was thirty-one when he died. He told me he had found something out about the case, but, like an idiot, I didn't want to listen. He left our home in a rage and never came back. Whatever he knew, he took it with him to the grave.

A loud bang makes me jump. A high-pitched meow echoes out, and I can just about make out the shape of a few cats running into street. Stupid strays! How can a tiny animal make so much noise?

I pull my sleeve back and check my watch. It's one am. I should really think about finding my way back to my hotel. My head is clear enough to start working again, and the foggy, quiet streets don't seem quite so welcoming any more.

Wandering back the way I came, I focus on the other gripes I have with both cases. I don't like the fact that Calhoun is being dragged into this as anything other than a victim of a cruel campaign to scare him. Jameson thinks the kid is lonely and may have constructed some sort of fantasy world around himself to combat it. Why else did he insist on me, someone who is single and has no kids? Someone else who is lonely, to use Jameson's own words. Part of me can see his reasons for thinking it, but it still annoys me. The kid is a lot of things but…

My spine prickles, like someone is watching me. I turn around but can't see anything at all through the damn fog. The street seems to be completely empty. That's a little weird. Yeah, it's the middle of the night, but I would have thought there would have been some people out. A few cars, at least. I start walking again. My pulse pounds in my neck.

As sudden as the feeling came, it's gone again. I constantly look around. The streets are still empty, the air still thick and quiet. I carry on towards the end of the block. My hands are sweating. I ball them into tight fists just in case I run into whoever is watching me.

A figure materializes out of the fog. It looks like a man who's a little too tall, a little out of proportion. It takes a step towards me. "Halt. I have a gun," I warn him. He doesn't stop.

I close my trembling hand around my gun and attempt to pull it from its holster. It jams. I try again, but I can't pull it free. The man is getting closer so I warn him again. "Stop or I will shoot!"

Please don't let this be happening. I fight for breath, my stomach churns. No, not another damn panic attack. I did this job for years before these damn attacks forced me from working in homicide. But all the others were kicked off by seeing murder victims. I shouldn't be scared of some guy in the street.

Before I can give him another warning, he charges. I turn and run as fast as I can. Suddenly I am ten years old again. The night I got lost in the woods while on vacation in Alberta. Hoof beats fill my ears as the rider charges down the forest path towards me. The waking dream clears, but the noise remains. It's the same thing all over again!

The little boy that fought for survival that night takes over. I tear around the corner, and the hollow clop of the creature's feet echo just behind me.

I throw myself at the door of a convenience store. It's locked. I hammer on the glass and shout for help until the creature's pursuit drives me on. Another doorway, this time a bar. It's locked up tight, and all the lights are out. Why?! It's hours away from closing time. Despite my shouts, no one answers. Not a single person in all the apartments on the block looks out.

All those brutal murders and no one heard a thing, I remind myself. Even the people who had windows backing onto the locations the bodies were found. You're on your own!

I stumble and fall onto the slabs. The thing is so close I can feel the warmth from its breath. In a desperate attempt to lose it, I dive under its nose and start running in the opposite direction. My chest burns, my legs are shaking with exertion. Another desperate grab at my gun pulls it free. The monster yelps when I fire, but I keep running without waiting to see how badly I've wounded it. I turn blindly into an alley and, in my attempt to turn back, lose my footing, landing heavily on my left side. Pain radiates from my ribs and over my chest as I roll onto my back and angrily push garbage bags out of my way.

A soft, singsong voice breaks through the silence. "I know where you are"

My hands shake as I aim my gun at the entrance to the alleyway. "Don't come any closer. I will shoot you dead!" I shout.

The creatures laugh is harsh—there's no joy in it. It bounces off the walls of the alley, echoing over and over again. It steps into view, a vague shadow in the fog. I fire at it. It folds in on itself with a grunt. When it straightens up again, I am ready for it. This time it's head snaps back as the bullet slams into its skull. The noise it unleashes is like the death howls of a thousand tortured souls. It sets my teeth on edge and reverberates through my bones. The monster claws at its head and roars again. Before I can take another shot, it disappears like it was never there.

I lie still and struggle to get my breath back. My ribs are on fire. My knuckles are scraped up, but nothing seems to be broken. I roll onto my hands and knees and try to get up. The left side of my torso feels like a mass of jagged, rusty, nails. The mere act of breathing is torture. Just as I ease one foot forward, I slip and land hard on the ground. In a rage, I throw my hands out, looking for anything I can use to pull myself up, and recoil when they come into contact with something unexpected.

There's something that feels a lot like a human leg in that pile of garbage.

A thin, naked, body lies discarded amongst the bags. Blood runs over the pale flesh in thick rivers. Even without a lower jaw to complete the silent scream I can still see the terror frozen on the youthful face.

It's still warm, the body and the blood.

I scrabble away from it. No! I will not give in to panic, not this time. Yes, it's a body, but it's one of hundreds I've had to see. It's not the same as Myles. It's not the same!

I hug myself and try to remember the breathing exercises I was taught long ago. No matter what I try all I can see is my partner's body lying there and the awful, soul crushing despair returns with the image. One minute he was there, the next gone. Every hope I had of my life with him, every ounce of love we shared, destroyed.

I wrench my gaze away from the body and lean my head against the cool brickwork. It's okay, just breathe. Get your phone out and do what you must. It takes a few attempts with blood-slicked fingers, but I finally find the right contact and make the call.

"Jameson?" I say, fighting and failing to keep the tremor out of my voice. "You better come see this."

§

"You know we have to call this in, don't you?" Jameson asks.

"Fine," I say as I pace around. "Just give me a chance to leave first." I hold a cigarette to my lips, and the smell of blood fills my nostrils. I flick the unlit cigarette away in disgust.

"Are you kidding!" he hisses. "You fell right into the middle of a crime scene. You left a fucking body print and who knows how much DNA. You can't go."

"I have to! I have to make sure Calhoun is okay!"

"You know he is. You have your cell, and we both know it's working because you just called me." He looks at the corpse and mutters. "Why you didn't call nine-one-one instead I don't know."

"Because you are my friend, and I thought you'd help me!" I

snap.

"With what, Jerry?" Jameson asks angrily. "I can't do anything, okay. This is a crime scene! I can't process this on my own. I'm gonna call it in, and you are going to stay here and explain what happened."

"I have to go," I insist. "I need to wash all this fucking blood off and get my ribs checked. I need to call Calhoun."

Jameson stands in front of me and blocks me from pacing. "You need to calm down. Stop tracking blood all around the damn place. Go and sit there, by the wall, and fucking breathe."

"I don't need to breathe. I am calm!" I insist.

Jameson raises an eyebrow. There's no point in arguing. If I leave, it's going to make my being here a whole lot more suspicious. I lean back against the wall and watch Jameson make the call.

The alleyway is soon bustling with cops. I give my story over and over again and spare no detail, even the stranger ones. With each reiteration, my confidence in my recollection slips. They don't believe the whole story, and who can blame them? Monsters aren't real.

Finally left alone, I take a seat between the open doors at the back of the ambulance. One of the EMTs, a young guy, with short, bouncy, red hair and big blue eyes, sidles up to me. "We need to take some blood."

He looks terrified by whatever look I have given him. "Why?"

"Well, um, you fell in a huge puddle of it. It got on your mouth and scraped hand," he shrugs. "It's a precaution."

With a sigh, I remove my coat and roll up my shirtsleeve. I can't stand to watch this toddler as he prepares the needle or my arm so I avert my gaze.

A pair of shiny black boots appear in my field of vision. I look up and smile when I see a familiar face.

"This fucking guy, huh?" McCray says with a grin.

I take his insult with the humor it's intended. "McCray." I hold out my hand, see the crimson stains on it and retract it with an apologetic shrug. "How the fuck are you, man? How's life treating you?"

"I think you just collided with how life is treating me right now," he replies and waves towards the crime scene.

Ben McCray is short and kinda round, always has been. He shifts his weight from one leg to the other, and his face changes, all pretense of happiness gone "Burbank wants to see you."

"Fucking fantastic!" I groan.

The EMT sticks the needle in my arm, and I don't even flinch. There's worse pain to come.

Once I have been checked over, McCray drives me to the station.

"I thought you'd wanna stay away from a case like this," I say.

"A lot's changed since I left Boston," he explains. "I decided I could either let seeing that body scare the shit out of me for good, or I could put myself in a position to directly fight the scum who commit these crimes. I've been working in homicide for five years."

"I know. Harris has been keeping us all updated since you two keep in touch so much." I soften my words with a smile. "I meant this specific case."

"The same reason you didn't stay away, I guess," he says.

"I'm not working on this. I'm investigating a stalking and harassment case."

He gives me a confused frown. "But Novik said you were helping us."

"I was and I am. I've given them everything I know about the Boston murders, but that's as far as I can get involved." Maybe if I keep saying that to myself, it'll eventually come true.

"Seems to me like you might be getting dragged into this case whether you like it or not, Higgins." McCray taps his fingers on the steering wheel as he drives. "This guy chased you down. He didn't try to shoot you or hurt you in any other way. He just scared the crap outta you. This wasn't some random attack."

Silence fills the car as I chew on that statement. The thing I met in the street was definitely playing with me, like a cat with a mouse, but it's a bit of a stretch to say it wasn't trying to hurt me. Who knows what would have happened if I hadn't shot it?

We park outside the station and head inside. They take samples of the blood on my skin, do a DNA swab, take fingerprints, then let me shower and change. I hand over everything I have on me—clothes, boots, phone—and dress in the blue scrubs the forensic team hand over.

McCray looks me up and down as I step into the hallway. "Are you sure you don't want to call anyone?"

"I'll probably be done by the time they get here," I grumble. "I can change into my own clothes again when I get back."

"Okay, if you're sure."

The borrowed sneakers are probably half a size too small, and they rub unpleasantly on the back of my bare heels as we walk to Burbank's office. With a deep, calming breath, I knock on the door and go inside when he bids me to.

Burbank plasters on a fake grin as he greets me.

"Well, well, well, if it isn't Jerry Higgins."

I say nothing, just glare at him. Burbank's once dark brown hair now has a liberal dusting of gray. His brown eyes sparkle with calculating intelligence.

"So, what brings you to New York? Oh, no, wait, I bet I can guess. You want to play the hero again, don't you?"

"I'm just doing my job," I mutter. All I want to do is get out of here and call Calhoun. I know Jameson is going to call him and fill him in on what happened, but I'd rather speak to him myself.

"You are too fucking far west to be doing any job, just like with

Toe Peeler Tom." His voice drops into a soft, low pitch, but I'm not fooled. This is when he is at his most dangerous. "We don't need you here."

"That's where you're wrong," I say, my voice equally low and dangerous. "I was hired to work here. *Someone* needs me."

Burbank smirks. "Bet your boss doesn't see it that way."

"I cleared it with her. I'm not a cop any more. I take the cases I want, wherever they happen to be."

Burbank gets up from the desk, stalks around it like a big cat, and shoves his pale face into mine. "Understand this! You may be a big shot up in Boston, but here you are nothing!"

I stifle a laugh. Big shot! Someone clearly hasn't been paying attention to recent events.

Burbank jabs his finger at my face. "I don't want you here contaminating my crime scenes. I don't want you here poaching my officers and dragging them along on this little chase of yours. You had your chance ten years ago to finish this, and you failed. Now ship back on up to Boston."

"I didn't fail. I solved it!"

His smile is full of impish glee. "Oh, yeah? Then, why are you here now? Why is McCray shitting his pants over this particular case and muttering about what happened in Boston? Why do I have three Boston officers sniffing around my case?"

"Two," I correct him.

Burbank glares. "Three. You may have given up your badge, but it changes nothing."

A sudden pulse of pain radiates out from my left side, stealing my breath and robbing me of my retort. I grit my teeth and hug myself, hoping to ease it a little. Burbank carries on berating me.

"Higgins, let me make one thing clear. I may not be able to shift your little buddies since McCray actually went through the correct channels *for once* when looking for help, but you were not included. I want you gone! Hand over the Calhoun case to my team and leave."

"Calhoun didn't want to go to the NYPD." I say through gritted teeth. "He came to me for help."

I don't give a rat's ass. I'm not having this case go the same way as the Toe Peeler."

"You mean you don't want to actually solve the thing?" I gloat.

"Solve it? You destroyed one of the most influential families in New York?"

I shrug as much as my painful ribs with allow. "Not my fault the son was a serial killer."

Burbank looms over me. "There are ways of getting things done without blowing open and sinking a whole dynasty. You rush in and cause too much trouble. That's probably why you were fired. Why don't you just leave this to the real cops?"

"I wasn't fired. I left the police force. It was my decision!"

"Hardly your own decision when everyone is already pushing you out the door."

"You know nothing about what happened!" I snap.

Burbank rolls his eyes. "I am done talking to you. Get out of my damn city and keep your mitts off of this case!"

"I can't leave. I told you why."

"Then you'll just have to disappoint your client, won't you?" He straightens up and wanders back to his seat. "We can do this the easy way or the hard way. Believe me, you won't like the hard way. Now go." He dismisses me with a wave of his hand, and I bite back my scathing remark.

McCray is waiting for me as I exit the office, and he grabs my arm. I snatch it back but follow him into one of the other offices. There are four officers in there. I don't know them personally, but the names of three of them are known to me from times our work has brought us together before. Gail Rodowski, Paul Gordon, and

Anthony Micheli. The fourth guy is a new face. He looks younger than the rest of us, not the tallest of guys but broad in the chest. McCray takes up the introductions, and we shake each other's hands. The younger guy, who McCray introduces as Jason Robertson, seems nervous, a little shy maybe. His blue eyes fix on mine when we clasp hands then dart away as soon as they can. He sits back down, a little apart from the others.

"Look, I better go," I whisper to McCray. "If Burbank catches me in here, he'll fire me over the nearest state line."

"Fuck him!" Rodowski says, blond ponytail bouncing as she jabs her pointed fingernail at me. "We went through the proper channels securing you guys to help. We don't need his permission."

"Not with me, you didn't. I came here under my own volition," I say, echoing Burbank's words. The pain in my left side makes me irritable. I just want to go home, call Calhoun, and sleep. "And there's no denying the fact me being here has bent him out of shape."

"That's because he likes to be the big boss. His guys do it alone or not at all. No outside help allowed." Rodowski says.

"But we know better," Gordon adds.

I roll my eyes. "You already have Novik and Harris. Do you need me too?"

They all look at me as if the answer is obvious. "You stopped it before, didn't you?" Micheli asks.

"I thought I had," I say, and those words suddenly bring everything into focus for me. I nabbed the wrong guy. Sure, he was a nasty piece of work and a dangerous killer, but he wasn't *our* killer. And now my blinkered search for revenge has allowed the most prolific murderer we ever dealt with to strike again.

"I'm willing to do everything I can to help you guys, but I'm not a cop. I can't do anything more than hand over what we have from the Boston case, and I've done that."

McCray sits down heavily in his desk chair. "We could really use your help, and not just in some old files and hunches."

"What do you want me to do?" I do nothing to temper the hard edge to my voice. "I can't roll the clock back and stay a cop. I already have a case I'm working on, and I don't want another one taking up my time."

The uncomfortable silence stretches on and on.

"Can I go now?" I growl.

They all look at each other. "I'll call you a cab," McCray says flatly.

McCray walks me out of the building without a word and waits with me for my cab. In a way, I'm glad of the silence. It gives me time to think. When the cab arrives, I mumble my goodbyes and get in.

The drive seems to take forever. The street lamps give the sidewalks an eerie glow through the fog. There's a few people around going about whatever business they have tonight. Everything seems too normal after the few hours I've just had.

The hotel desk clerk jumps to her feet, but I wave away her concern. She buys my lie about leaving my key in my locker at the hospital—it was the only way to explain the scrubs—and issues me a new key. She watches me with the same look of concern until the elevator doors close.

The dry heaves hit me as soon as I get into my room. Nothing comes up but what little water I had to drink. I kick the sneakers off, stuff the scrubs into the trash can, and throw myself under the shower. No amount of scrubbing my skin and hair makes me feel any cleaner. I pull on fresh underwear, knock back a few Tylenol to take the edge off the pain, and slide into the cool sheets. Curling up on my side, I try to empty my mind, but all I can think about is that poor kid lying there in the alley. Three young men dead, and, as far as I know, not a single lead. Exactly like last time.

I can't just watch this unfold from the side lines. If the wrong guy is behind bars, then that means that the killer is still out there. He killed all those guys in Boston and got away with it. He mutilated the love of my life and left him to rot in the damn street! If there's any justice in this world, I shot him dead tonight. If not, I will not rest until I have brought his reign of terror to an end.

7

Lucky Charm

Incessant knocking on my door forces me awake. I pull myself from my sweaty cocoon and pad across the floor. As soon as the door opens, a whirlwind of dark clothing and wild streaked hair rushes at me, catching me in a tight hug. My ribs on my left side explode with pain.

"I was so worried when your friend told me what had happened," Calhoun shouts. His arms are clamped around my back, but I manage to prise him off.

"I'm okay, kid, now let go."

He pouts. "*Are* you okay? Really?" His hands still rest on my waist, but I hold him by the shoulders, putting distance between him and my injured body. "Jerry?" He protests as I push him away completely.

"I'm fine. Can I get dressed before we talk, please?"

He gives me a few moments of silence to pull my clothes on. When I emerge from the bathroom, he is sitting on the couch chewing on his black painted fingernail.

"That's poisonous if you swallow it," I say in a poor attempt at humor. He doesn't answer but looks up at me, his emerald eyes wider than usual. His makeup looks a little smudged.

"What about you?" I ask as I sit down on the bed. Now that I've recovered from the shock I'm actually glad he's here. "You okay?"

"Yeah," he says, but his voice is shaking. "I wanted to make sure you're safe, that's all."

"Come on, kid, you gotta be straight with me if you expect me to help you. You can't be that worried about me."

He looks at the floor before taking something from his pocket. Another note, this one is short and to the point.

Make the pigs fly or you die.

No description of the victim, no poetic words, just an open threat.

"What time did this arrive?"

"Around six am."

I turn the note over in my hands, and look for any distinctive marks. "Stamp this time?"

"Nope." He slumps back into the couch cushions, arms tight around his waist. I fold the letter carefully and set it aside.

"Have you told anyone else?"

"No. I came here to see you straight away."

I glance at the clock display in the corner of the television screen. "It's seven am!" I shout. "You came here just after getting a letter like that rather than staying in your apartment? Why didn't you call? Why didn't your friend come with you?"

"You said if I needed anything then to speak to you," he says.

"Yeah, kid, call me! Don't just show up. I don't want you

running around New York alone at night!"

"I tried to call!" he shouts back. "But your fucking mobile is disconnected!"

I forgot about that. I run my hand through my hair. "Look, kid, I—"

"You're hurt," he gasps, cutting me off. Calhoun pulls my left hand from my hair and examines it. His touch is soft against my damaged skin, and my hand tingles slightly. I gently pull it from his grasp.

"It's just a graze."

He looks down at me through his heavy bangs. "I saw the rest before you got dressed. You're all bruised up." He sits down beside me, his thigh rests against mine. I shift uncomfortably. Calhoun narrows his eyes. "Let me help you."

"It's nothing I haven't had before," I reassure him.

"Jerry…" He looks away as he trails off. "I think that it may be a good idea if you leave here."

"Why?"

"Because you were attacked last night, and all because you're trying to help me."

"No. That's not why it happened," I say. "I must have disturbed the killer or something. Maybe he just saw me and decided to have a little fun. Either way, it's got nothing to do with me helping you."

"It does!" Calhoun insists. "Look at the letter they sent. They were warning you."

"It's not the first time, and it won't be the last."

"That doesn't make it okay," Calhoun growls. "I don't want you getting hurt."

I squeeze his shoulder. "I'm not going anywhere. Not until whoever is sending you those letters is stopped."

"But—"

"No buts!" I grab his other shoulder and force him to look at me. "You just said yourself that the letter and that guy chasing me last night are a warning. That means we have our proof. They *are* connected. And if you think I'm gonna go anywhere while that bastard is still at large, then you can think again."

Calhoun opens his mouth but says nothing. He chews on his lip. "If that's what you want, then let me give you something to protect you, for next time."

"There won't be a next time," I say, even though I don't believe my own words.

He snorts at my confidence and reaches into his pocket. "I meant to give this to you before you left my apartment, but I hadn't finished it." He holds up a silver chain with a thin metal spiral on the end. Inside is a stone which looks black, but the light reveals a pale rainbow sheen. It reminds me of mercury or the color of spilled gasoline. A small piece of what looks like dark thread is wound around the top of the gemstone.

"It's a hematite," Calhoun says as he dangles it in front of my face. "Good for the mind. Helps people think and solve problems. Orders thoughts. All that shite. It's also a protection stone. One I've added an extra spell to."

"And the thread?"

He blushes slightly. "Um, well, that's your hair. I needed it or the spell wouldn't bind to you."

I raise an eyebrow. "How the hell did you get my hair?"

He lets out a little nervous laugh. "From my sofa after you stayed over. I know you don't believe in this stuff. I saw your face when I told you I read tarot cards, but humor me, please? It either works, in which case great, or it doesn't, and you can gloat about being right. Either way it isn't going to do you any harm to wear."

I shrug. "Sure, why not."

Before I can take it from him he unfastens it and drapes the cold chain around my neck. He reaches under my hair to fasten it.

The stone rests just below the hollow of my throat, a bit high for my liking, but at least it won't tangle with the other chain with the ring on it. Calhoun's breath is warm on my neck. The warm, spicy scent of his cologne surrounds me. Another lingers underneath it. A hint of something soft, floral, comforting. His fingertips brush my skin. The thin hairs rise under his touch. My scalp tingles as he lifts my hair clear of the necklaces and lets it fall again. I am equal parts relieved and saddened when he pulls away from me.

"Looks good on you," he says with a smile.

"Thanks. So, are you some sort of wizard or something?" I ask as I take the little spiral in my hand. It feels warm, probably from being in Calhoun's pocket.

"Well, no. Most of us call ourselves witches."

"Us? You mean there's a group of you?" An entertaining image of naked Goths dancing in the moonlight fills my mind.

"Sort of. It's mostly an on-line group. We meet up sometimes, but it's more like a party or hanging out with friends. Not a coven."

"You're not linked to any other witches here in New York?"

"Just one," he says.

"Is it Pendragon by any chance?" I ask, but I already know the answer.

"Aye," Calhoun says. "She's a lot better at this stuff than I am though.

I let the pendent go again, and it rests snugly against my throat. The whole chain feels warm on my skin now.

"Everything okay?" Calhoun asks.

"Yeah. The metal feels warm is all. Is it supposed to?"

A toothy grin spreads over his face. "That means it working."

"That makes sense, I guess." I make a mental note to see if any of the victims had any connection to Wicca. It's a long shot, but there's so little to go on that I'm clutching at anything.

I jump out of my thoughts as Calhoun's thin fingers touch my ribs. I scoot away from him.

"Sorry," he says.

I gently press my fingers to my side and wince. "You a healer now too?"

"No but I can tell by the way your leaning on this side here that you should probably get to the ER and have that broken rib seen to."

"It's not broken."

"I'm telling you it is, and I know which one," He gently taps his finger midway down my ribcage. I feel the pain bloom for a second before it settles back into a dull ache. "That one."

I stare at him. "How the fuck do you know that?"

"I'm just winding you up," he says, chuckling. "But you need to get it looked at. You're holding yourself all wrong."

I try to sit up straighter, but it's agony. "Okay, you win. I'll go to the emergency room."

"Good," he says. "I'll drive."

§

I hate hospitals. The smell of them always makes my skin crawl, but I can't think of any reason why. Calhoun sits by my side until my name is called. The doctor checks me over then decides that, yup, I need an x-ray on my ribs. Everything else is just bruising and minor cuts. I could have told him that from the quick check I got last night.

Back out in the waiting room, Calhoun is a pretty comforting presence. He doesn't keep asking me if I'm okay, which is exactly what I need when I'm worrying over how bad my injured ribs may be, but talks enough about other things to keep me distracted.

Finally, after x-rays and another chat with the doctor, I am free to go.

"You were right," I tell Calhoun as we make our way back to the car. "One broken rib in exactly the place you said it was."

His face is full of happy surprise. "Really? That's amazing. Not the broken rib, obviously, but the fact I knew. Wow. That was pretty good, huh?"

"It was a lucky guess," I tease him. "But thanks for forcing me to come here all the same."

"No problem," he replies. He unlocks the car but stops before getting in. "Are you sure you want to keep working here?"

"For the last time, yes." I soften my words with a smile. "I'm not going anywhere until this is all over."

Calhoun gazes at me and worries his bottom lip between his teeth. "Okay, Jerry. Just stay safe."

"Hey, that's my line," I joke.

We get into the car. I glance quickly at Calhoun. I'm not ready to lose his company just yet. "Hey, uh, do you know of a store nearby where I can get a new phone?"

"Sure. There's one we can swing by en route to the hotel."

"Sounds good."

I lean back as comfortably as I can with my tightly-bound ribs and settle in for the ride.

As soon as I get back to the hotel, I head to Novik's room. He's not there. Harris isn't in his room either. I go back to mine, set up my phone, and text Calhoun so he has my new number. I should float the idea by him about me staying there again, but it would be purely for my benefit since he isn't alone anymore. I was the one who was chased, not him. I don't want to draw attention his way if I can help it.

The throbbing in my side forces me to take the pain pills the doctor gave me. While I wait for them to take effect, I sit on the bed, boot up my laptop, and open up my list of phone numbers. I call Novik first and introduce myself as soon as he answers.

"Hey, Jerry. How'd it go at the ER?"

"Fine. They strapped my side but it's still fucking painful," I complain.

"Could've been worse, man."

"Don't remind me. Speaking of that, I take it they never found the guy I shot?"

Novik sighs heavily. "'Fraid not. We've widened the search to cover seven blocks in every direction, and we're looking at doing more. We've called all the hospitals and still nothing."

"Did anything show up on the security cameras?"

"Nothing. The businesses with outside cameras are either facing the wrong way, or not working at all."

"That sucks," I say, deflated that we are, once again, out of leads.

"The good news, if you can call it that, is that this crime scene is different." Novik rustles a few papers. "The whole scene looks like the body was abandoned. There's no symbols either."

"So, I *did* interrupt him."

"Looks that way. Not that it helps. You heard nothing, saw nothing?" Novik says.

"Sorry I couldn't be more help while I was running for my life," I grumble.

Novik huffs out an angry breath. "That's not what I meant. Don't pretend you're not as frustrated with this as I am."

"You know I am. Listen, I didn't tell the guys last night, they wouldn't understand, but I *recognized* that thing that chased me. I'm sure that we're dealing with the same killer as last time. If not, then there's got to be a group of them."

"I thought you didn't get a good look at him?"

"I didn't, but it was a feeling, you know?" I shake my head at how dumb that sounds.

Novik makes his thinking *hmm* sound. "We've been playing it that way all along, but it's nice to have it confirmed."

"Is there anything else about last night I should know?" I ask.

"Just that you need to be careful. You're on Burbank's radar."

"He doesn't scare me," I say. "I've got a job to do, and I'm not leaving until it's done."

"That's the spirit, Jer," Novik says in a happier tone. "We'll be heading back to the hotel in around three hours. Do you need anything brought back? You got all the pills you need?"

"Yeah, I do. There is one thing you can do for me though."

"Sure."

"Can you organize some sort of watch on the Dakota building? After the attack last night and the other lett—"

Novik cuts me off. "Consider it done, man."

"Thanks. That's a load off of my mind."

We hang up. I rub my eyes. Tiredness is hitting me hard. It won't hurt to grab a nap. I've done all I can right now to keep Calhoun safe.

My eyes drift closed. These pills are good; I can barely feel my ribs any more. Hopefully I can grab some much-needed sleep while I can.

Soft musical moans reach my ear, and I match them note for note. I reach out, desperately grasping my lover's back with one hand and the sheets with the other. Anything at all to anchor myself fully in what is happening. We kiss, but our need for air forces us apart. I can feel every inch of him moving inside me. My angel. My Myles. The only person I have ever truly loved. I grip his back tighter, pull him close and nuzzle my face against his cheek. His beard scratches my skin. He moans my name again, and I answer him with a whine of my own.

He thrusts deeper, faster. His back muscles flex under my hands. I hold onto him with everything I have. My legs tight around his waist; my nails scratch his back; my body surges to meet his as I melt into the exquisite feelings coursing through me. He looks down, but instead of brown eyes I see green. Where there should be blond hair I see onyx.

"Let me protect you," he whispers.

My fingers slide up through thick tresses of black and gold. "Yes," I say, my aroused mind and body barely cares about the change in my lover. He leans in to kiss me, and steals my breath away. My ears pick up a noise, like wing beats, and each thrust is punctuated by the new sound. When he pulls back from me, I see huge wings sprouting from his shoulders, the feathers are black and shining like the stone that hangs around my neck.

"Let me in. Let me love you!" he moans, "Let me heal you."

I can only nod in response. Yes. Love me, protect me. But, most of all, don't stop fucking me!

I wake up abruptly, utterly frustrated by the dream's sudden end and for myriad different reasons. My mind's eye can still see Calhoun above me. Green eyes glittering in the golden half-light that filled the dream. It shouldn't have been him. It will never be him or anyone else, never again. I roll over, ignore the bulge in my shorts, and try to sleep again.

When next I awake, it is after a restful dreamless sleep. I sit up and feel the new chain pull slightly as the stone moves around my neck. I glance down at it. An image of shining wings fills my mind. Why does my subconscious punish me? It lets me relive my first time with my love—someone I will never have the pleasure of holding again—then it taints that memory by slotting someone else into his place. It's not fair.

I try to chase the dreams away with actions and dress as quickly as my injuries will allow. Over breakfast I check my messages. Calhoun has sent me three overnight, and all of them say that he is safe. One from Novik informs me that the patrol outside Calhoun's building is in place. Another states that the patrol hasn't picked up anything unusual.

I make another call to Novik. "Any word from the others about the latest victim?"

"Yeah. Unlike victims one and two this kid was American. A local kid. Twenty-four years old. From the upper east side."

"They identified him quickly."

"His wallet was in his pocket. He also had a record—possession of narcotics, disturbing the peace."

The killer leaving behind evidence like that is further confirmation I disturbed him. "Anything else?"

"They're still finalizing the autopsy. You know these things take time."

I shift into a more comfortable sitting position. "Yeah. Listen I need to ask another favor."

"Just say the word."

"Can you or Harris run a check on these kids and see if any of them have a connection to anything like witchcraft, Wicca or Paganism? I'd do it myself, but I don't have all their details."

After a pause Novik says, "Sure. Can I ask, why?"

"Just another avenue I'm looking into." I say.

"Alrighty. I'll get back in touch with the results as soon as I have them."

"Thanks, Novik. I can always count on you.

I place the phone on the nightstand and reach for the little stone around my neck. It's still warm.

I devote the day to going over all the evidence I have at my disposal. I know the details of the Boston case like the back of my hand, but it's been years since I've been through the actual folders. Something new could pop up. I open a new file on my computer and begin the laborious task of transferring what I need from the physical case binders onto my computer.

The hours are punctuated by Calhoun's texts. Occasionally he sends a selfie, further proving he's alive and well. I reply quickly to each one then return to my work. My eyes water with the strain of reading for so long. The pain pills draw me into fuzzy periods where I can't think straight, but I keep working until I have looked through everything.

I am at a dead end.

I hurl one of the old folders against the wall and let out a roar of frustration. All those hours devoted to one task, and I am not a single step further forward.

My phone bleeps. It hasn't been an hour since Calhoun's last text so I grab it up in a panic. Rather than being bad news, it gives me my first reason to smile all day.

8

The Lady Pendragon

It's late in the evening when I arrive at Pendragon's strip club. I wait at the bar, drinking lemonade since I can't drink with the painkillers—unless I want to fall off the bar stool—and scan the room. No one is looking my way, but I've dressed to blend in. Dark shirt, dark jeans, hair loose around my face and annoying me no end. This look is becoming a bad habit.

There are two rooms to this club. One for the men to get their jollies and one for women to get theirs. The dancers I see on stage from where I am sitting are more punk rock than the average stripper. I suppose Pendragon is going for a theme.

Finally, she appears at my side. She is small, barely five feet tall and waif-like. Her thin frame is swathed in a floating, shimmery dress. Poker straight, pale blond hair spills over her shoulders.

"We meet at last," she says and offers me a dainty hand. Her voice is a little deeper than I was expecting, and it carries well through the noise of the room. There’s the slightest hint of an accent similar to Calhoun's.

“Good to meet you,” I say warmly as I shake her hand.

“We can talk here, or would you prefer somewhere more… secluded?” she purrs, drawing out the last word for all it is worth. The dimmed lights catch her tongue piercing as she speaks.

I ignore whatever she is implying and ask to speak in private. She leads the way through the building to a large, lavishly appointed, office. Along two walls are massive ebony book cases, and I get the impression the books aren't for show. Pendragon oozes intelligence the same way she oozes confidence. An ornate desk made of the same kind of wood dominates the room, facing a blood red couch on the opposite wall. The chairs either side of the desk have the same deep colored upholstery. A fire crackles in the grate and throws dancing shadows over the walls. Pendragon switches on an antique standing lamp, adding some much-needed illumination to the office. “Please sit,” she says and indicates the couch.

The leather creaks as I sit down and releases the scent of cleaning oils. The whole room carries the smell of tree sap, wood smoke, and furniture polish. It's strangely homely. More like some drawing room in a mansion than an office.

“Now,” she says as she sits next to me. She takes the time to rearrange her full skirts before going on. “Tell me what you want to know. I won't hold anything back. In fact, I'll start. Lachlan is a good friend of mine. He told me you would be coming to see me and not to worry about why. He wouldn't tell me anything else, but I know he's worried. I could hear it in his voice. Lachlan doesn't have an emotional filter. Everything spills out of him despite his best efforts.”

I nod though my experience of Calhoun's emotional barriers is a touch different. I take out my notebook and pen. "Ms. Pendragon—"

"Call me Morrigan, please."

I ignore the request politely. Familiarity isn't a good thing in this job. "Can you tell me how you met Mr. Calhoun?"

"Well let me see," she begins, and I get the feeling she is mocking me, even if it is nicely. "We met about five years ago. We were almost neighbors actually. I had been looking at an apartment in his building, but I decided against it. Isn't quite to my tastes."

I look around her darkly colored office. "I thought a building with that kind of architecture would be right up your alley."

Her large blue eyes sparkle as she replies. "It is a lovely building but not quite for me. I need a lot of light and open spaces, so I moved up to a penthouse on fifth avenue."

"How exactly did you guys meet?"

"We ran into each other in the corridor. He was moving in and I walked right into him. Silly goose that I am." Her laugh is like a little bell. "Naturally, I had to help him since he dropped a pile of sketch books when I bumped into him. We talked as we worked and realized we both came from the North of Scotland. I was amazed. I knew I had to hold onto him. Gaelic speakers are like gold dust outside of the highlands."

"Gaelic?"

"It's the language of Scotland, my dear. Not that many of my own country folk speak it."

I nod. "What were your first impressions of him?"

Pendragon looks toward the fire as she thinks. "I thought that he was very sweet, very loving. I still think that. He spoke of people with a lot of affection. I adore that about him. He is also very passionate about things. Once he gets started on a subject he likes he can talk for hours without pause. He is very focused. Has a good analytical and creative mind too. He does have a petty temper though."

I look up from my note writing. "How do you mean?"

"He can be childish sometimes. If things don't go the way he expected. It's almost arrogance, but other times it's just frustration. Putting all that effort in and having nothing to show for it. I think he fears failing."

"Don't we all?" I say.

Pendragon smiles brightly at me. "You're a sharp one, Mr. Higgins."

I press my hand gently to my ribs and straighten up a little to relieve the ache. "Would you say he's your friend?"

"Oh, more than that, I count him as the son I never had." Her warm smile echoes the affection she obviously feels. "After that first meeting we have spoken to each other almost every day in some form or other. We have taken holidays together. Gone to parties. He even helped me with artwork for this club. Yes, we are very close."

"And as his close friend what did you think when he started receiving letters?" I ask.

She smooths out her skirts. "I was all for ignoring them at first. You get famous enough and people get jealous. They send you letters, make nasty comments online and anything else they think they will get away with. At first it just seemed like the usual horrible stuff I myself have received. I asked him to get rid of them, burn them. I thought they would stop eventually."

"What did Calhoun want to do with them?" I say through gritted teeth as my ribs throb.

Pendragon looks me over. "He wanted to… I'm sorry, dear." She lightly touches my knee. "Are you okay?"

"I'm fine, thanks," I reply. "Carry on please."

"He wanted to do the same at first, ignore them," Pendragon continues. She takes her hand from my knee. "But they got worse. When it was clear they weren't going to stop, I told him to go the police"

"Did he take your advice?"

"He didn't want to, not at first. The next day, however, I called his mobile because I couldn't reach him at home, and he told me he was in Boston. He told me he was looking for someone that could help him. I guess that's you, dear." She pats my leg again.

"Yeah, I guess so." I shift my leg away. "What're your thoughts on these letters? Can you think of anyone who'd want to scare him like this?"

"I suppose anyone could hold a grudge for any number of reasons. Maybe they don't like the way he looks or his orientation. Maybe he was just a name someone pointed at in the phone book and thought, 'now here's someone we can have fun with.'"

"That's not entirely helpful," I say.

She shrugs her thin shoulders. "But it is the truth is it not? Lachlan has been here for five years, give or take a few months, and has made connections with very few people. I know, because of the nature of your investigative mind, you've already spoken to two of them before you came here. Tell me, Mr. Higgins, do you believe they have hurt my Lachlan?"

I manage to keep my face neutral. "I'm afraid I am not at liberty to discuss that information."

Pendragon grins. "I suppose, if you did think that, you wouldn't need to ask me about the letters." She twirls a lock of her hair around her finger.

"I'm gathering as much information as I can, that's all," I flatly reply.

She rises fluidly from the couch. "May I speak candidly with you for a moment, Mr. Higgins, off the record?"

I hesitate. Off the record is not usually a good plan. That's when a person will give you the best bit of information you could ever hope for, but you can do nothing with it.

Pendragon seems to sense my hesitation. "On the record if it makes you feel any better." She studies the titles on the shelves. "All I am really asking is that you listen to an old lady while she says some silly things and hopes to steer you onto the right track."

"With all due respect, I came here to speak to you about Calhoun and the letters. That's all."

She hauls a large hardback from the shelf and places it on the desk before turning back to the shelves. "That's all well and good, my dear boy, but I want to help. I am trying to arm you with the knowledge and tools you need to face this head on because, Mr.—"

"Detective," I correct her. It's not strictly true but, hopefully, it will remind her I am actually conducting an investigation.

Her blue eyes seem almost otherworldly big above her amused smirk. "—because *Detective* Higgins, I know what you really want to ask but are afraid to. You think you have stepped down that road enough, and any farther will begin your descent into madness. I am telling you now, *Detective*, that you are on the right track. Grab onto that little flash in the dark, murky, depths of this case, cling to it for dear life and ask me, ask away!"

I can't keep the smirk off my face. I fold my arms in front of my chest. "Let's play it your way. What should I ask about?"

"Why don't you ask me about magic?" she says as if it's the most normal suggestion in the world.

"Magic?"

Pendragon begins looking through her books again, trailing a silver-painted fingernail over the spines. "Yes, magic." She lifts another text reverently from the shelf. "You have seen enough things over the years that you are beginning to wonder if there is something else to this case. Am I right?"

"No," I say a little too quickly.

She picks up her little stack and heads back to the couch. "For someone not interested, you don't seem to mind wearing something with a powerful spell on it."

My hand instinctively rises to my chest, where the gem sits hidden under my shirt. How did she know it was there? Pendragon smiles at me, perfect, little teeth flashing.

"I have to wear it. It was a gift," I explain.

"The gift giver isn't here though, is he? And he won't know if you take it off."

In annoyance, I look away from her. She is enjoying this way too much for my liking.

"Not taking it off yet?"

I roll my eyes. Pendragon gazes at me expectantly.

"Look, I don't believe in this stuff." I say sharply. "I've got other people to talk to, so if you don't mind, I'll be on my way."

"If you don't believe, why haven't you taken the necklace off?"

"Because…" I can't answer her. My hands refuse to reach for the clasp. "I don't want to take it off," I say, sounding like a petulant child. "I like it. It's got nothing to do with magic."

Pendragon seems to consider my answer before replying. "That stone around your neck brings you comfort. Doesn't matter why, it just does." Her voice is soft, persuasive. "And the longer you wear it, the deeper it becomes tuned to you, and the harder it will be to remove it." She shrugs "Whether you believe that is by magic or a growing fondness for that bauble or the gift giver is by the by. Magic is believing that by saying the right words and lighting the right candles you can actually do something, make a difference. It's maybe an oversimplification, but it's accurate nonetheless."

"So, it's all just bullshit then. It doesn't actually work?"

She fixes me with a Cheshire cat grin. "If you pray hard to get that promotion and the next day you receive the phone call, does it matter whether it was divine intervention or not? Does it matter if a penny really is lucky, or that it's just a coincidence that you have it on you whenever good things happen?"

"So that's a yes? I say. "It is just bullshit."

A deep exasperated breath from her wipes the smirk right off my face. "What I am saying, *Detective—*" her heavy emphasis on the word makes it almost seem like an insult "—is that there is magic like that. The type of magic almost everyone is happy to entertain exists. And then there is magic like the stuff in this case. The darker stuff." She taps the cover of the book with her nail.

"Do you mean the letters or the murders?"

Pendragon recovers her composure quickly. "I didn't think they were separate."

"You think the killer is sending Calhoun these letters?"

She twiddles the rings on her fingers and chews at the inside of her cheek through the lengthy pause. "He told me that's why he had gone to find you in Boston. You had worked on a similar case. As far as I was concerned, they were never separate."

I let her stew for a minute with her nerves then put her out of her misery. "A lot of things have come to light that make it seem like they may be related."

"Lachlan was probably too worried to say it out loud at first." Her smile is tight. "Either way it is magic that is part of the answer for it all. I'm sure of it."

"Why are you telling me this?"

Pendragon's face loses all traces of her sunny disposition—her eyes even lose their sparkle. "Because you are like many people who meet a real witch for the first time. You can't separate us from the hocus pocus, toil and trouble type witches. The stuff that is, to use your own words, bullshit."

"I don't think you guys fly around on broomsticks," I say. I don't want any offense I cause to stop this conversation in its tracks.

Pendragon clasps her hands tidily in her lap and leans towards me. "No, but you think this is all some sort of faddy mumbo jumbo, don't you?" she says abruptly. "All you see right now is some crazy old lady wearing a fake name, and that automatically means you will be expecting something odd to come out of my mouth. You expect me to act the way Wiccans are portrayed on TV. There is so much more to what I can do than that," she says with a hint of pride. "So much more that Lachlan and so many other seemingly normal people can do. I think it's important that you start listening."

I drum my fingers against my leg. "I really don't understand what this has to do with this case."

She plops one of the books down on my lap. "Read these. I think you need to start looking beyond what you are comfortable with if you ever want to solve this thing. You are so close to considering it, but you need a little push."

"I already have considered it!" I state sharply.

"No, I mean *really* consider it," Pendragon demands as she places the rest of the pile onto the first book. "Don't dismiss something because it doesn't fit your world view. Who knows what kind of information you'd be missing out on." She gently touches my knee and gazes into my eyes. "Why don't you actually investigate a magical reason behind these killings? Look at the symbols and the way the victims were killed. Use the information in the letters, maybe there's a clue in them. Study the cards with Lachlan or learn to read them yourself. Use all the tools you would in a normal case but just expand on them."

I glare at her. "How much about this case do you actually know?"

She shrugs off the suspicion in my tone. "Just what's in the news and what Lachlan has told me, but it's enough for me to know that something isn't right. You can feel it in the air Mr. Higgins. Can't you? Just promise me you will look at all angles?"

"Detective! And I don't owe you anything," I growl, possibly a little harshly, but she is really starting to annoy me.

"No, but there is *someone* you owe."

There is no way she can know about Myles and our fight before he died. I drop my eyes from her intense gaze and study the covers of the books. The top one is a thick volume of urban and ancient legends.

"I don't have time for horror stories," I say. I try to give them back, but she closes her hands around mine.

"Just read them. Humor me," she implores. "You might even find the answer, or at least something to point you the right way."

I put the texts down on the coffee table and stand. "Alright look, this is a police investigation not an episode of *American Horror Story*. Now, if you don't mind, I've got a killer, a *human* killer, to catch." I make an attempt to soften my tone but my words come out harshly all the same. "Thanks for your time. If you have anything that is actually helpful that you would like to add, call me."

I drop my card on the desk on the way out. Pendragon doesn't make any move to stop me.

I leave the club then get into my car. When a calming breath does nothing, I punch the hell out of the steering wheel. How dare Pendragon, with her weird fairy dress sense and condescending smile, think she can tell me how to run an investigation? A wannabe cop drawing her own conclusions is definitely *not* what I need. Yet, I reached the same conclusion she did. We all have. Still, the fact Pendragon was so sure of the connection is a little suspicious. I send off a quick text to Novik, giving him

Pendragon's description and the suggestion that she may be another person to watch. She doesn't strike me as the killer type, but I wouldn't be surprised if she took an unhealthy interest in them. Maybe enough to send notes to Calhoun?

It's a long shot, but there's no harm in running with it for now.

I check the time on my phone. Eleven pm. It's not too late to call and check on Calhoun. Maybe I can pick his brains for further info about Pendragon too.

§

The faint, chalky, smell of paint fills the air and tickles my noise. A soft hissing punctuates the silence every so often. Calhoun works tirelessly on his mural, having only paused to let me into his apartment. He seems moody. He's barely spoken to me, and doesn't want to look my way. All my attempts at a normal conversation have been shot down in monosyllabic responses.

"So, what did Morrigan say?" he asks. If his clipped tone is anything to go by, it's almost as if he begrudges having to waste words on me.

"Not much of any use," I say. "She wanted to talk about magic and stuff."

"Magic has a lot to do with this case."

I pick at my nails. "It could have, if it were real."

"So what else would you call all those symbols then?" he snaps.

"Rituals." Whatever he thinks, I am not going to change my view just because he raised his voice.

Calhoun faces me. "Do you think it's all make believe? That no one that's doing this has any idea how to make real magic work?"

"My grandfather could make a quarter appear out of my ear but that doesn't make him Gandalf," I retort.

Calhoun tenses for a moment then gets back to painting. He clenches his jaw tightly. "Are you, at least, satisfied it's not anyone I know who's doing this?" he says without looking at me.

"I never said I thought it was." I shift to rest my back against the side of the window frame rather than on the cold glass. "But I have to talk to anyone that has a connection to you. That's how investigations work."

Another hiss from the airbrush. The vignette is slowly coming to life, one spray of paint at a time.

"I know," Calhoun says. His concentration is fully trained on the painting. "It's just…"

"Just what?"

He shakes his head. "Nothing," he mutters.

"You don't wanna think someone you know could do this to you?" I venture. He makes a show of changing the color canister on the airbrush and then nods. "No one does," I say in what I hope is a comforting tone. "That's why guys like me have to consider that angle. Unfortunately, it usually *is* someone who knows the victim."

"I am not a victim," he hisses.

"Well in police terms you are." I rest my head against the glass and peer into the darkness. The small turrets on the roof are visible, thanks to the lights around the building, but most of it is dark. I turn back to Calhoun. Maybe joking around with him will soften his mood. "So, you're a witch, huh? Is Pendragon your coven leader?" I say with a smile.

Calhoun whips around to face me, his shoulders tense. "What's that supposed to mean?"

"Nothing." I hold my hands up, silently asking for calm. "It was just a comment."

"You seem to have a lot of comments to make about what I believe in."

I frown. "What's got you so pissed?"

He stabs his finger in my direction "You!"

"I'm not taking the blame for this," I say. "You were in a mood long before I got here."

He steps towards me with the airbrush clutched tightly in his white knuckled hand. I keep my eyes on it, ready to duck out of the way if the nozzle is pointed my way. "You're flailing around talking to my friends and people I used to know rather than looking at what's right in fucking front of you." The hose from the airbrush writhes and jumps like an angry snake when he gestures. "That's why I'm pissed."

"You asked me to find out who was sending those letters, and that's what I'm doing. I'm sorry if it seems to be taking time, but these things do." In an attempt to diffuse the situation, I turn away from him and look out the window. "I'm moving as fast as I can with this."

"Hey! Look at me when you're talking to me." His authoritative tone shocks me enough that I look back almost immediately. Calhoun's whole body is tense. Shoulders strong, arms held stiffly by his side. How the hell has one little comment warranted this reaction? "You're wasting time, and you're too pig headed to even listen to reason about it."

"I have to look at real life shit, okay," I say sharply. "And magic isn't real."

"Just because you can't understand something doesn't mean it isn't real."

I roll my eyes. "Magic doesn't exist. It's all tricks and rituals. Any normal person knows that." I dismiss the argument with a wave of my hand.

"I am normal!"

"You're acting like a big baby." I cross my arms defensively over my chest. "I trained for years to do this job. Can't you just trust that I know what I'm doing?"

"Not when you're ignoring big clues." Calhoun dumps the airbrush and digs a pencil out the pocket of his painter's smock. "All the murders had this symbol, right?" he quickly sketches the elaborate circular pattern that was found under almost every body. "If the killer is using it then it means something to them. It's important! It's something magical, but you're refusing to look at it."

"Then you look it up," I say. "Work with me instead of against me."

He steps close to me, his face inches from mine. "I tried, but the answer I got won't mean anything to you since magic isn't real!"

"Get outta my face." I growl. He steps back. "Why are you on my case if you know? This is the kind of stuff you should tell me when I ask for any information that could help!"

"That symbol isn't the only thing that needs looked at! There's a whole ton of stuff you're just—"

The sudden darkness is blinding and disorientating—every light in the apartment seems to have gone out at once, without any warning.

I order Calhoun to the ground and drop down with him. The apartment is silent apart from our breathing. The sky is overcast—no light spills through the windows—but I can see the glow of the street lamps on the clouds above the rooftops. It's not a cut that's affecting the block.

"Where's your fuse box?" I whisper.

"In my bedroom."

I switch on my cell's flashlight and draw my gun. "We're gonna run for the door, okay? Be as quiet as you can. Stay low. Follow me."

We make quick progress across the floor. The door is open and the hallway beyond is an inky black broken by a few slivers of orange light from the street-facing rooms. Aiming my gun over my phone, I sweep the beam around. There's nothing lurking in the dark.

"This is stupid," Calhoun complains. "It's an old building. The electrics trip a lot."

"Keep your voice down," I scold. "Have you forgotten that you have some sick fuck mailing letters right to your front door? This is the same guy you and Pendragon have decided is our killer, apparently."

Mumbling angrily to himself, Calhoun follows me the short distance down the hallway. I reach for the handle of his bedroom door.

A heavy clatter against the front door stops us in our tracks. Gun aimed, light illuminating the entrance way, I creep towards it, and motion for Calhoun to follow. The hairs rise on the back of my neck. I don't blink. Barely breathe. I point towards the wall, and Calhoun presses his back to it. The silence is deafening as I slide into position beside him. My fingers close around the lock and slowly click it open. There's no noise from outside. Breath held, I grasp the handle, and yank the door open.

9

Fight or Flight

A whoosh of air hits me from behind. I stumble forward and trip over a bag left on the doormat. Before I can see what's inside, footsteps in the dark stairwell call my attention.

"Stay…" My words die on my lips as I turn around. Calhoun isn't behind me. I dive back inside, calling his name as I search each room in turn, but the apartment is empty. Fearing the worst, I take the stairs two at a time, shouting his name as I go.

"Did you see anyone run past here?" I shout at the doorman as I pass him. "Not Calhoun; someone else?"

He raises his hands reflexively when he sees my gun and stammers something about the lights being out. There's no help coming from him so I carry on running out onto the street, hoping I'll be fast enough to catch sight of them.

"Calhoun!" I roar. Painful coughs wrack my body but I press my hand to my broken ribs and keep going.

The sidewalk is busy. I force my way through the bustling crowd and keep my eyes peeled. He can't have gone far with this many people out. He was barefoot for one thing. Lost on where to begin I start asking people if they saw anything, but most of them shrug me off.

A piercing scream shatters the night. Forcing myself into a run I take the corner onto 71st Street West. I dodge my way through people and search for the source of the wail.

"Calhoun. Where are you?" I yell.

A woman stumbles past clutching her arm. When I ask her what happened, she points down the street with her good arm and stammers something at me. I catch a glimpse of Calhoun and, after reassuring the woman that I'll call for help, I follow him. My side is in agony, but I refuse to slow down. A cab screeches to a halt, narrowly missing me when I sprint across the street. The driver flips me off. I return the gesture.

A coughing fit grips me. I double over, hugging myself tightly, until it passes. My breath catches and rattles in my throat. Spitting up the gunk barely relieves the pressure. I'm never going to catch them, not when I can barely get a breath. I need help.

"Jesus, Jer," Novik exclaims when he answers the call. "What's up with you? You sound like death."

"It's… this… fucking rib," I wheeze. "We need people down here. Central Park—" A rib shattering cough stops me mid-sentence. "Central Park West, Seventy-first, seventieth, maybe the next few streets over too. We need medical support too. There's at least one injured person out here so far."

"Why? What's going on?"

I relay the story to Novik as quickly as I can through my coughs and wheezes. I walk as I talk, and scan the alley for any sign of Calhoun and the intruder.

Finally, I spot them. After a quick goodbye to Novik, I force my unwilling body into a run.

Calhoun has a young man held up against the alley wall by the neck. The guy is dressed all in black, from knitted cap to scuffed leather boots. He glances at me, gray eyes pleading for help. I squeeze Calhoun's shoulder. "Let him go."

"He got into my building!" Calhoun growls.

"Yeah, and the cops are on their way. They'll deal with him."

Calhoun's grip tightens on the guy's neck. "It's my problem. I'm dealing with it!"

"You're the reason for all of this evil, you inhuman scum!" his captive hisses. He spits in Calhoun's face and attempts to kick him. "I am Rex—" Calhoun slams him against the wall, cutting off his words, then lifts him off his feet. Rex squeals like a stuck pig.

"Inhuman!" Calhoun growls. "I'll show you inhuman." His fingers tighten again. Rex gasps for breath, and claws at Calhoun's arm.

"Let him go!" I order. Calhoun ignores me. Rex gapes like a fish, and even in the sickly orange light of the streetlamp nearby, I see his face flush purple. In desperation, I press the muzzle of my gun at the back of Calhoun's head. "Drop him now!"

Calhoun casually releases his grip, and wanders over to lean against the far wall. Rex falls to the filthy ground. He gulps air and rubs his neck. I squat down beside him in the deep shadows of the alley.

"You have no idea what you're dealing with," he whispers to me. He glances up at Calhoun. His face contorts with rage. "Monster! I am the last defense! I will destroy you."

Calhoun takes a step towards us. Rex cowers and raises his hands above his head. I order Calhoun to wait against the opposite wall then turn my attention to Rex. "What were you doing in the Dakota?"

"I came to warn you," he says. His gaze drifts towards where Calhoun is sitting, at least it looks like it does—it's hard to see in the dim light. "You're on the wrong side."

"Wrong side?" I frown. "What the hell is that supposed to mean?"

He rubs his neck where a bruise has started to form. "He's not who he says he is. He's tricking you! They've tricked people before, and those people all have one thing in common. They're all dead!"

"You lying piece of shit!" Calhoun spits at him.

"Who?" I demand, and call Rex's attention to me. "You want me to believe you then give me something I can check."

Calhoun shoves me to the side and grabs the guy by the shoulders before he can utter a word. He shakes him violently. "You're lying! Tell him you're lying, you fucker!"

"I'm not lying!" he screams.

Calhoun shakes him again. Trying to pull him off doesn't work, he just shoves me back. "Tell him it's all lies," Calhoun commands. He goes for the guy's throat again. "Tell him all about your little conspiracy theory group."

Rex fights at first but then, all emotion drains from his face. He looks up at me, his movements like drunken exaggerations. The air feels thick, charged, like before a thunderstorm.

A siren and the squeal of tires makes us all jump. Calhoun backs away from Rex who takes up his raving from before, shouting accusations at Calhoun. Calhoun doesn't retaliate, not in front of Jameson and Novik.

"This the guy?" Novik asks with a quick nod of his head towards Rex. He gives Calhoun, who's wearing his painters smock and no shoes, a curious glance.

"That's him," I confirm. "I think his name is Rex. There's something in the hallway, just outside Calhoun's apartment. He threw it at the door then ran. I didn't get a chance to check what it was."

"It's proof!" Rex shouts. He runs at me and grabs my shirt. "You gotta read it. You have to believe us! He tried to change my mind just then, did you see?"

Novik pulls the guy away from me and slaps cuffs on him. "You'll have every chance to talk down at the station."

"You should be arresting him!" Rex protests and jerks his head towards Calhoun. Novik leads the guy back towards the car.

Jameson, who has been silent since he arrived, looks around the alley. "I'll come back to your apartment with you both. We need to check this package, and make sure there are no intruders."

"There won't be," Calhoun states defiantly.

Jameson's demeanor seems calm on the outside but I can easily see through it. His jaw is clenched. "All the same I would prefer to make sure of that for myself."

"Sounds good to me," I say.

Calhoun says nothing. He crosses his arms over his chest and glares at Jameson.

Jameson calmly stares back. "I'd like you both to come back to the station. We need to take statements, maybe fingerprints. This guy might decide to press charges."

"He can try," Calhoun growls. "But he won't get anywhere."

"We should get going," I say in an attempt to diffuse the tension. "The sooner we talk to this guy the better."

"Lead the way," Jameson says.

Calhoun walks off with Jameson following. Neither spare me a second glance.

We take my car to the station after the apartment has been checked out and locked up tight. The area around it is filled with squad cars and uniformed officers combing the streets in search of clues. Jameson and Calhoun don't speak at all. Their animosity towards one another is delivered in narrow-eyed glances and tightly pursed lips. I can sympathize with Jameson—Calhoun has been antagonistic since I showed up at his place.

At the station Calhoun is taken to an interview room by Rodowski and Gordon. Jameson interviews me on his own. The room is bare save for the table and chairs in the center. All the walls are a sickly, off-white. A florescent strip light hums overhead.

"We just need a written statement," Jameson says as he sits at one side of the table. "Calhoun is gonna be interviewed on tape just like the guy we brought in."

I take the seat across from him. "Why?"

"I saw the marks on the guys neck. It's going to come down to one word against the other. Tapes are the better way to go." Jameson pushes a yellow legal pad and pen towards me. "You know the drill, Higgins. Write down everything you can remember as clear as you can and sign it."

I pick up the pen. "Yeah, I know what I'm doing," I reply.

I diligently write down everything. From the lights going off in the apartment to the accusations the intruder made about Calhoun, not a thing is missed. Jameson glances up from his cell every so often but doesn't speak. A soft knock on the door finally breaks the silence.

Novik steps inside and closes the door behind him. "Hey, do you mind talking to this guy with me?" he asks me. "He won't talk to us, but he says he wants to tell you something."

"Sure. I want a chance to interview him anyway. If that's okay with you guys?"

They both answer with a "Yeah." I finish off my statement, sign it, then follow Novik.

The interview room we enter is about the same as the last one except one wall is dominated by a large mirror. I glance at the glass, wondering who, if anyone, is behind it.

Robertson, who is already present, addresses the recorder. “Detective Novik and Private Investigator Higgins have entered the room.”

Novik indicates I should sit next to Robertson so I do. Novik leaves again, probably to watch from the other side of the two-way mirror.

“Interview recommenced at zero-hundred hours and fifteen minutes,” Robertson says. He turns to the young man on the other side of the table. “Okay, Mr. Higgins is here. Will you talk to him?”

Rex meets my gaze without flinching. His hair, now free from the woolen hat he was wearing, is a reddish-brown, short and spiky. A light dusting of freckles covers his pale face. I try to imagine this guy typing up the kind of notes Calhoun was receiving or, worse still, butchering other men around his own age, but the image doesn't stick all that well. Still, killers come in all shapes and sizes.

“I believe you have something you want to tell me,” I prompt. “I'm listening.”

“I told you most of it already,” he answers. “You're on the wrong side. You're in danger.”

I wait a beat before replying, long enough to keep my voice and face neutral. “What makes you think that?”

He seems completely at ease as he lounges back in the chair. “They call me Rexus. I'm a member of a group whose sole purpose is to keep the world safe from all things inhuman.”

“That doesn't quite answer my question, Rexus,” I reply. “What does this have to do with you thinking I’m in danger?”

Rexus leans in a little. Robertson and I do the same. In a conspiratorial whisper he says, “That is not Lachlan Calhoun. It's an imposter.”

“Do you have proof?”

"I gave you proof in that bag. We've been tracing the inhuman since it turned up here, in Manhattan. There's no record of him before that."

I know that's a lie, I checked for myself, but I let him ramble on.

"It's been working with other inhumans to manipulate world events. They're everywhere."

I look at Robertson. His expression is blank, and he's focused on what Rexus is saying. "What have you seen that makes you believe Calhoun is not human?"

"It manipulates people." Rexus continues quietly. "Changes their minds about things. Takes away their free will."

"I asked for evidence," I say firmly. "Hearsay isn't that."

Rexus whacks his hand on the table, his face contorts with anger. "It is *not* hearsay. I'm talking about people coming onto our forums and sharing stories about their experiences. We have spoken to people who've dealt with that thing directly. It is dangerous, and it's pulled you into its little web of lies."

"I'm still not hearing any evidence," I say.

"Can we bring in the bags?" Robertson says into the little intercom. Novik appears a couple of seconds letter with the evidence and hands it to me.

I read the first sheet of paper through the plastic. It's a detailed account of Calhoun's involvement in the Wolves, all told through numerous posts to a forum. Names and the forum title have been removed.

"How did you get these stories?"

"We are everywhere," Rexus says with a smirk.

"Even within the Wolves?"

"We operate where the inhumans operate."

The other evidence bags contain more print outs—supposed evidence for their claims in the form of anecdotes and loosely formed conclusions. Another contains a rock. I guess I know what caused the bang on the door. The last bag holds a blood-soaked scrap of material and what looks like a chunk of black and gold hair.

"What's this?" I ask as I turn the bag to Rexus. Robertson narrates my movements for the benefit of the tape.

"It's samples. We've tried to get them tested, but all the labs refused our requests. We know why that is," Rexus replies smugly.

"There's no medical technicians or DNA analysts in your little army?" I mock.

Rexus' smile fades. "Not yet."

I turn the evidence bag over in my hand. It's impossible to see the color of the cloth due to the blood, but the hair is unmistakable. The blond is the same golden shade of Calhoun's hair, assuming it's always been the same color. I'm willing to bet I know where he got the samples too. Time to mine this guy for every last piece of information before we lock him up.

I fold my arms on the table. "What's the name of this group you work for?"

Rexus smirks. "Like I'm going to tell you."

"You expect me to trust you then give me something in return," I say firmly. "The name of your group. A list of inhumans. Something."

Rexus just smiles. "I've given you all I'm going to. There's enough there to prove everything if you test those samples. It's you who should be paying us back."

"You expect us just to test random samples on your say so?" I say.

"You're not a cop so you can't, but he will." Rexus jabs his finger towards Robertson.

Robertson frowns. "Me? What makes you so sure?"

Once again the smug look drops right off Rexus' face. "Cops are supposed to follow all the evidence. This is evidence!" he shouts and points at the bags that litter the table.

"Tell me where the samples are from," I demand. "You have to give us something back in return if you want us to trust you." I pick up the evidence again. "This could be from an animal. It could be doll hair. You obviously know a lot, Rexus. Share it with us. Prove you know what you're talking about."

Rexus' eyes dart quickly to Robertson and then back to me. "I want a lawyer. I'm not saying anything else."

Robertson sighs. "Interview terminated at zero-hundred hours and twenty-three minutes." He picks up the evidence bags, and glances at Rexus. "You can wait in here for your lawyer to arrive."

Sure enough, Novik is waiting in the dark room behind the two-way mirror. On the other side Rexus sits with his head on his folded arms. He probably knows the game is up just as much as we do.

Robertson dumps the evidence on the desk. I pick up the bag containing the hair and shake it at Novik. "This is from Calhoun; they got it by beating him up. I'll bet any money on it."

Novik takes the bag. He studies it for a long moment. "The blood is real old, but we took samples for testing. If it matches Calhoun then—"

"We can't wait that long," I cut in. "This guy has a serious screw loose."

"You're basing your hunch on that bag of junk?" Robertson scoffs.

"Were you in the same interview as me?" I snap. I point towards Rexus. "This guy has been calling Calhoun 'it' since he entered the room. He's dehumanized him. You know why people do that? Cos it makes it easier to justify hurting them."

"Higgins has a point," Novik says. "Plus, those printouts he left at Calhoun's place show they've been watching him for a very long time."

Robertson chews thoughtfully at his nail. "So, you think he did it then?"

The question catches Novik and me off guard. "Attacked Calhoun?" I ask.

"No, the murders," Robertson replies. "If not that then what do you think he's done?"

I look down at the bag in my hand. "I'm not sure. What I do know is he has kept surveillance on one person already. He's made threats. He somehow has Calhoun's blood and hair. I think we should keep the possibility in mind that he could be behind it all."

I grab my notebook out of my pocket and rip a bit of paper out. "Here's what we're gonna do." I talk and write all at once. "One, we find out who this guy is and who he's working with. Two, find out the identity of their contact within the Wolves. Three…" I trail off and glance up at Novik.

He meets my gaze. "Don't stop now," he says, amused. "You got a plan to sink this guy and his gang so let's hear it."

Smiling I return to my list. I jot down the last few things I can think of and hand it over to Novik. "We need to get the Cyber branch in on this. They can find that site, trace IP's. Any name we find must be run through the databases. Any issues flagged as priority. I don't care how small or seemingly unrelated. Focus on New York State, New Jersey and Massachusetts first then widen the net."

"Why Massachusetts?" Robertson asks.

"Because the murders are almost exactly the same, right? If that's the case then I'm willing to bet this group is active back home in Boston."

Robertson rolls his eyes. "Do you think this Rexus guy murdered these people or not?"

"That, *Detective*," I say, "is your job to find out."

As soon as no one is looking I grab the evidence bag with the print out inside and slip it into my pocket. It's a seriously dangerous move, but I really need something as proof when I start asking questions to Wolves members again. I pull Novik to one side. "Is he acting a little weird or is it just me?" I nod my head toward Robertson.

"This is his first major homicide case," Novik explains. "I get the impression he's double checking everything rather than just coming out with what he thinks."

"What did he work as before?"

"He did some sort of deep cover job." Novik says. "McCray says the rumor is he was moved down here cos his cover was blown."

"Shit." I sigh. "I guess that would make anyone jumpy."

"Yeah, I wouldn't worry about his attitude. So, what should we do next?" Novik asks, directing the conversation back to the case.

"That's not really my call," I reply.

Novik looks down at the list. "If it was your call, what would you do first?" When I hesitate he continues, "This is *our* case, Jer. Catching Rexus has pretty much confirmed the link, and you have as much say as any detective on this team." He squeezes my shoulder. "We got this."

"Yeah, we do," I agree. I swipe my hand through my hair and take a minute to order my thoughts. "We get this Rexus guy his lawyer, and I'll talk to him when I get back. Robertson can't interview him again. I don't know why, but him being there doesn't sit right."

"Agreed." Novik reads the list. "I'll get everyone gathered, and we'll start assigning people stuff. We'll run Rexus' prints and photo and get Cyber on finding this website."

"Awesome. Make sure Calhoun stays here," I demand. "Where he's safe."

"Why, where are you going?"

"I have a few people I need to speak to," I answer. "Call me if you need me. I'll be back as soon as I can to interview Rexus."

"Be careful, man. If Calhoun is on their radar, you could be too."

"Then we better move fast, before they have a chance to target anyone else," I say with a smile, then head back out into the night.

§

Despite the lateness of the hour there are lights on in the reception of Newlin and Sons. I ring the bell since the door is locked, and wait for an answer. The streets are deathly quiet except for the ever-present hum of distant traffic. A street light flickers then blinks out altogether. I ring the bell again.

"We're closed," Newlin barks from the other side of the door.

"It's Jerry Higgins," I shout back. "I know it's late, but I need to talk to you. Now."

There's a lengthy pause before the locks start to slide back.

"Don't you sleep?" Newlin grumbles as he opens the door.

"I could ask the same about you," I reply. I step into the warm reception area and rub the cold from my arms.

Newlin walks past me and into the body shop itself. The overalls he wears are spattered with oil. He unzips them halfway, and slips out of the top half before tying the sleeves around his waist.

"We can sit here." He points to a room containing a long table, a mismatched bunch of chairs, and a small kitchen. "Or the office. There's no one else here, though, so we might as well sit close to the coffee machine."

"Sounds good."

Newlin steps into the room and kicks a chair out. "Make yourself comfy. I take it you want coffee?"

"Yeah. Thanks." I sit down and lean my elbows on the worn table top. "I take it black."

The place reeks of motor oil and spray paint. Maybe it's Newlin that smells so strongly of it. That and sweat. The coffee from the machine just adds another layer to the nose wrinkling mixture. At least he scrubbed his hands clean before making it.

Newlin sits at the table and copies my posture—arms folded on the table top. His biceps bulge against the thin material of his shirt. "How'd it happen?" he asks. His voice is soft, a little shaky.

"What?"

"Lachlan. They got him, didn't they?" He slowly scrubs his knuckles against the shaved side of his head. "Why else would you be here in the middle of the night if he wasn't dead?"

"He's not dead." I stop myself reaching out to touch his arm. "He's fine, I promise."

With a deep sigh, he visibly relaxes. "Why the hell are you here then?"

"We caught someone tonight. He said he was trying to warn me about Calhoun." I pull the folded evidence bag out of my jeans pocket and flatten it out. I hope this interview is going to be worth the risk of taking it. "This is one of the things he showed me."

Newlin picks it up when I pass it to him. His brow furrows as he reads. "He was keeping tabs on us?"

"On Calhoun mostly, but your name cropped up a few times." I sip at my coffee, valiantly swallow the scalding, acrid liquid, then push the mug to one side. "Can you confirm if any of it is true?"

"Wait there," Newlin says. He strides out of the room. It's so quiet I can plainly hear him banging around in his office and cursing to himself. Finally, he returns with a large, leather-bound diary in his hands. He drops it down and starts to read through it.

"Here!" he triumphantly announces. "May 16th. Angel spent four hours in the afternoon with the Wolves' leader working on bikes." He turns the book to me and taps an entry. "Sixteenth of May. Bike check special offer. Keep extra mechanics on hand."

I nod to show I understand. "Do any of the others match up?"

Newlin goes back to reading. "Yeah! I remember this one asshole kicking off cos his car wasn't the exact right shade of red, even though he picked the color himself. That's noted on their list. This guy here." He taps the print out in the evidence bag. "Yeti? He had to go the ER. Lost his finger working on an engine. They knew about that too."

I read what he indicates. Sure enough, the exact same story is logged in Newlin's notebook.

"Do you have any idea who this is?" I ask.

Newlin frowns. "He's got to have been one of us. He knows all of our nicknames. But knowing that Lachlan's was Angel…" He shakes his head. "Only I called him that. It was…"

I can almost see the light bulb switching on above his head.

"What is it?" I prompt.

The chair *squeals* loudly as Newlin scoots it back then marches into the body shop. I have no choice but to follow.

"Why didn't you tell me you used to call him Angel?" I demand."

Newlin kicks the office door open. "Why would I incriminate myself?" he says sharply as I step inside beside him. "I didn't hurt him. Lachlan knows I didn't hurt him. It was useless information." he throws a bike helmet at me. "Put that on."

"Like hell am I getting on a bike!" I say forcibly, and throw the helmet back at him.

"Then stay here for all I care!" Newlin grabs his helmet and leather jacket and stalks out. He swings one leg over his bike and sits. "See you around."

"What's with people not telling me shit?" I say furiously. "I'm trying to do my fucking job here, which, by the way, involves keeping Calhoun alive, and all I'm getting is a pile of lies and omitted truths."

Newlin snarls. "I told you everything I could remember!"

"Apart from the fact his nickname was Angel."

"I told you why I didn't—"

I cut him off. "No! You don't get to decide what information is important to me. I do." I step close, looming over him where he sits on the bike. "Holding back information, protecting your own, stopping justice being done. Does that make you feel good? Huh?"

"I was protecting no one," Newlin growls.

"Just yourself," I continue. "And you can do that all you want, but just remember this. Those guys had someone in your gang tracking Calhoun. That means they probably know about you and your connection to him. Who's the only person taking time to try and protect you from them?"

Newlin slowly loses his snarl. "I was gonna take you with me, that's why I gave you the helmet."

"Do you really expect me, anyone for that matter, to get on a bike with someone they don't know in the middle of the night to go fuck knows where?"

"You expected me to get in your car," he retorts.

I rub my hands over my face. "Then tell me where we're going and I'll follow you. Best of both the worlds."

Newlin seems to consider my proposal for a few moments before responding. “We're going to pay Duclos a visit.”

10

A Strike Close to Home

Lightning splits the sky as we pull up near Duclos' house. A few lights flicker on in the houses, probably due to the noisy approach of Newlin's Harley, but they quickly shut off again. The rain, which falls in fat globs, quickly soaks me as I get out of my car. Thunder rumbles somewhere close by. I hug myself as we walk, trying to retain what little warmth I have.

Newlin stalks up the yard, hair flying out behind him in the wind, and pounds his fist against the door. It swings open on the first knock—it clearly wasn't shut all the way. I grab Newlin's shoulder.

"Let me go in first," I whisper.

I push past him and into the house. My hand rests on my hip over my gun. Newlin's heavy boots clump on the carpet, he's making no attempt to be quiet. I hold my finger to my lips, but Newlin just rolls his eyes.

The TV murmurs on, and floods the living room with a soft, pale glow. It flickers now and then as the scenes and colors change. I draw my gun and slowly walk forward. At first the room doesn't seem disturbed, but there's a broken beer bottle lying on the carpet and slashes in the couch cushions. The metallic smell in the air grows stronger the further we go.

"Fuck," Newlin whispers

Duclos is lying half on his stomach behind an armchair, his hair covers his face. Blood soaks the thick, cream carpet around him. His once blue bathrobe is now a deep purple in places. I drop to my knees beside him and press my fingers to his neck. Duclos coughs, and I jump.

"Call an ambulance!" I yell back at Newlin who is hovering nearby, staring.

I roll Duclos onto his back. Four deep cuts run diagonally across his body. Blood seeps from the wounds in thick rivulets and fills my nose with its coppery stench. With shaking hands, I rip my t-shirt off and press it to the worst of the injuries. The flesh gives way a little under my hands with a soft squelch. The fabric is quickly soaked in blood.

"Help… me." Duclos croaks.

"Help is on its way," I say in as soothing a voice as I can.

With what little strength he has, Duclos grasps at my wrist. He stares at nothing, blue eyes darting around as he struggles to focus. "… sword. They had… a sword."

"What did they look like?" I ask.

Duclos' eyes drift closed. His breath rattles. Just when I think he's gone he speaks again. "Lachlan," he wheezes.

Newlin and I share a look of disbelief. "Lachlan did this?"

"No." Duclos chokes on the word and coughs violently. Behind us Newlin relays information to dispatch, his voice trembling.

Duclos loses his grip on my wrist, so I take his hand in mine. "Help... him," he pleads.

"Who?"

"La—Lachlan."

"I am."

"No... listen." He takes a deep, shaking breath and coughs again. Blood sputters onto my chest. "I lied. I... I'm his friend..." Another deep shuddering breath. "Under... cover. We had to lie. But they know." he whispers. His eyes flutter shut again. His chest heaves.

"Who knows?" I ask.

The only answer is a rattle deep in Duclos' throat.

His grip on my hand relaxes but I tighten mine. "Stay with me. Help is coming."

"He... promised." Duclos' grip tightens suddenly. "Make him... keep it. Take... me... home."

Slowly mumbling the words over and over again, Duclos relaxes. All tension washes out of him. His fingers slip from my grasp, and his arm lands heavily on the soaked carpet.

I shake him. "Duclos? Christian?"

Newlin drops to his knees beside me and cups Duclos' face in his hands. "Talk to me, buddy. I'm here."

A weak smile spreads slowly over Duclos' bloodstained lips.

The rattle echoes out of his mouth again. Long, drawn out. The final breath. Newlin grabs his shoulders and pulls him into a desperate hug. The force ruptures the perilous hold Duclos' torn abdominal muscles had. I back away, and fall over the edge of the armchair as Duclos' insides peek through the tear. My stomach churns. A cold sweat breaks out on my forehead.

Newlin talks to him. He pets his hair and face. He even tries to put him back together as if it was stuffing falling out of an old cushion and not the guts of someone he knew. I understand him.

No matter what you see, they are still the person you knew, the person you loved.

I touched his heart. Those were the only words I could say to anyone right after Myles was killed. *I touched his heart, and it was cold. It's not supposed to be cold.*

I curl up in a little ball in the corner. Newlin needs me. He needs some sort of comfort in this moment, and all I can do is sit here like a scared kid and whimper. Telling myself that over and over again doesn't make me move. I can't. I can't even look at them.

The cops and the EMT's arrive simultaneously a few moments later. Once I pull myself back together I talk the uniformed officers through everything and lead them through the house, pointing out things that caught my notice. A kindly EMT wraps a blanket around my shoulders and offers to check me over. I wave her off. I know why I'm shaken, and the residual effects of the anxiety attack will pass. They always do.

Newlin is already outside when I leave. The rain pounds against his hunched shoulders. His inky black hair clings to his neck and cheek in sodden strands. Blood drips from his hands as the water washes it away.

The lights of the emergency vehicles have called the neighbors from their beds, and many stand in the doorways of their homes, watching. At least the heavy rain has stopped them gathering around the ambulance itself.

"Want me to drive you somewhere?" I ask in a soft voice. I hug the now wet blanket tightly around me.

Newlin slowly shakes his head. "I've got my bike."

"I don't think you're in any fit state to drive. Plus, the rain is coming down pretty heavy." I rest my hand on his back, between his shoulder blades. "Come on, I'll take you home or wherever you want to be right now."

Newlin sighs. "Home would be fine."

I keep my hand on his back as we trudge to the car. "There's going to be cops in and out of here all day. They'll keep an eye on your bike," I say.

Newlin nods towards the ambulance. "Where are they gonna take him?"

"To the Medical Examiner's office," I reply as I get into the car.

"After that?"

"I'm not sure," I admit. "We need to get in touch with his family. Do you have any contact for them?"

"Nope."

"We'll find them," I say as warmly as I can. It's best to keep to myself the fact that Duclos admitted to working undercover before he died.

The rest of the journey passes in silence. Newlin stares blankly out of the windshield. His hands grip his knees. I don't know what to say to help.

As we approach Manhattan, he says, "Actually, can you take me back to the body shop? I don't wanna just sit around doing nothing. I should get some more work done."

"Sure. What are you working on?" I ask, hoping to take his mind off what he just saw, even if it is for a few moments only.

"Got this real old Triumph Thunderbird I'm fixing up." He pushes his hair behind his ear. "She was rusted up pretty bad."

"Was that what you were working on tonight?"

"Yup." He rests his head against the window and lapses into silence again.

We pull up in front of Newlin's shop. The rain drums on the roof of the car, but at least the wind has died down. Newlin grasps the door handle, then lets go.

"Thanks," he says. He thrusts out his hand, and I shake it. His grip is strong as his large hand covers mine. "You did some good for him at the end."

"So did you."

Newlin shrugs. "At least he's not hurting no more." He gets out of the car without another word.

§

The homicide offices are a whirlwind of activity when I return. "Do we know any more about Rexus?" I ask as I burst in.

Everyone stares. Novik approaches me. "You've had a tough night," he soothes. "Why don't you get some sleep?"

"I'm fine," I insist. "We need to find out who Rexus is, who he is working for, and then we need to ask why Duclos was fucking killed when he was the one supplying them with information."

Murmuring breaks out in the room. Novik steps closer and whispers. "You're half naked and covered in someone else's blood. Go get cleaned up, grab a coffee, chill for a few minutes, and then tackle this."

"Don't patronize me," I hiss. "Everyone else has been up for hours."

"No one else has seen a murder tonight." He drops his voice further. "No one else suffers from anxiety attacks."

"I didn't panic!" My raised voice calls the attention of the others again. "I got kinda shaky but—"

"Jer," Novik sighs. "I'm telling you as your friend that you need to regroup and get yourself sorted out before you pass out. You can use the locker rooms here." He looks to McCray. "Jerry can use the locker rooms here to shower, right?"

McCray nods. "Sure."

"And I got a spare t-shirt in my bag," Novik continues, his attention back on me. "Please just do as I ask. You're coiled up like a damn spring."

I give into his demands and follow Novik to the locker rooms. He pulls a t-shirt from his bag and tosses it to me. I hold it up against myself. It's easily two sizes too big, but at least it's clean. I shiver violently, suddenly feeling cold all over. The adrenaline must be wearing off.

"We need to find out who they are and quick," I say.

"I know." Novik says. "McCray, Harris, and Rodowski are on it along with some of the guys from the Cyber division. We have Rexus' prints and his mugshot. We'll find out who he really is."

"It's not just him, is it. It can't be?" My voice shakes. My lip trembles. I back out of Novik's attempted hug. "Don't touch me, okay," I snap. "I'm fine."

Novik visibly flinches at my words. "Sure you are." He pulls a towel from his bag and tosses it to me. "You can use that. It's clean, I never got a chance to go to the gym today."

And with that he leaves.

Alone, and with no need to hold myself in check, the tears come fast. Novik is right. I need time to get myself back in order. I don't need to be blubbering in front of the others.

As I shower, I go over what Duclos said. The two tie in—Rexus' accusation that Calhoun isn't who he says he is and Duclos' death bed admittance at being undercover—but why is Rexus so convinced that means Calhoun isn't human. And why did Duclos help Rexus' gang out if he is working with Calhoun? Could he be a double agent?

Shit. Calhoun doesn't know Duclos is dead. I need to let him know. I have so many answers I have to get from him too.

I shut off the shower, dry off, and dress quickly. Novik's t-shirt comes halfway to my knees, but it'll do for now. By the time I arrive back in the office, the investigating team on Duclos' murder has handed the case over to McCray—there's no point in two teams working on the same case—and they are discussing the evidence gathered so far.

"A trip out to Long Island at five am," Robertson grumbles. "Just what I need." He sees me and his complaining stops. "Sorry."

"I know. We're all tired." I sketch a map quickly in my notebook and hand the page to him. "We found him lying behind the armchair in the living room. There was glass on the floor, and the couch was slashed. The front door wasn't closed to, either."

"Thanks," Robertson says with a smile. He folds the note up neatly and slips it into his jeans pocket. "Any idea what killed him?"

"He'd been pretty much ripped open," I say flatly.

Robertson shoves his hands into his pockets. "Yeah. They think it was a knife or a sword or something."

"Yeah. Duclos said it was a sword."

Robertson's eyes narrow for a second. "You spoke to him? What did he say?"

"Not a lot." I say. "It's all in the notes."

"Nothing was found at the scene? Weapon wise I mean?"

"I don't know. I was more interested in helping Duclos."

Robertson shrugs his shoulders. "We'll take a look around in that case. Maybe we'll get lucky."

"We can hope." I fight back a yawn. "Do you know where Calhoun is? I should tell him what happened."

"He went home."

"I thought I said to keep him here?!"

Robertson scowls. "Well no one told me that. He was done with the interviews, and he wanted to go, so I let him."

I run my hands through my hair, gripping it tightly as I force down my anger. "He's got people like Rexus on his tail, who know where he lives, and you let him go?"

"What was I supposed to do? Lock him up so he stayed put. He wanted to go, and we have no reason to keep him here."

"I just gave…" I take a deep breath." Never mind. I'll find him at home."

My car stinks of blood. There are smears of it on the dash and seats—anywhere Newlin and I touched. That's another thing I'll need to deal with later. The traffic is building, the roads filled with the city's early birds, but I manage to keep a good pace. When I reach the apartment, the door is locked, but Calhoun answers quickly to my knock.

"Oh, it's you," he says. His jaw is clenched tightly. "What do you want?"

"We go some stuff we need to talk about." I push back on the door when he moves to close it. "Just a minute, please. That's all I'm asking."

"I'm not letting you in so you might as well say it here.

I sigh and force the words out. "Duclos is dead."

Calhoun's eyes open wide. He barks a laugh. "Don't be stupid."

"I'm telling you the truth," I whisper, all too aware that behind every apartment door there could be eavesdropping neighbors. "He's gone. I'm sorry."

Calhoun steps back from the door and lets me in. His face is unreadable; he looks everywhere except at me. I follow him into the living room and watch as he sits down heavily on the couch. He looks up at me, eyebrows furrowed in a confused frown.

"Why?"

"I'm not sure," I say. I take a seat at the other end. "He was attacked—that much was obvious—but we don't know by whom or why."

He pulls a cushion into his lap, hugs it to his chest and stares into space. "Was it like the other ones?"

"No." I move a little closer to him. "You okay?"

"Yup," he answers a little too quickly.

I take a long look at him. He chews on his nail. His other arm is hugged around the cushion, the long sleeves of the black shirt stretched tight over his shoulders and upper arms. Everything about him is coiled tight like a spring. I pat his shoulder. "Is there anyone you want me to call? Maybe Morrigan?"

Confused, he asks. "Why? She didn't know him."

"No, I meant for you."

Calhoun hugs the cushion tighter. "I'm fine. It's not like he was a friend or anything."

"That's the other thing I want to talk to you about. He told me some stuff before he died. He said you two were undercover together."

Calhoun laughs bitterly. "So, he's still lying."

"Duclos said that you promised to take him home."

"What are you accusing me of?" he snaps.

"Nothing." I keep my tone soft. He's clearly upset and I don't want to push that further. "I want to talk over some stuff with you."

He throws the cushion at me. "Leave me the fuck alone!" He storms out and into another room.

I go after him. "Please talk to me. It sounds like this group has blown your cover. All this secrecy has gone far enough. I need you to tell me who you are, who you work for, and what exactly you have to do with all this. If you don't, I can't keep you safe."

"You have no idea!" Calhoun roars in my face. He shoves me backwards. "You don't understand what we've been through to get this far. All the lies. Watching my back every damn day!"

"Then tell me," I plead. "Help me to help you."

"You don't get it! You never can." He covers his face with his hands. "Never."

I gather him into my arms at the first sob. His fists grip at my shirt, scrunching the fabric up, and his nails catch my skin. I hold him tight, gently rocking us both as he sobs. He buries his face into the curve of my shoulder.

"It's going to be okay," I soothe. I rub his back slowly.

"I know." He slides his arms around my waist. "I know."

11

Ties That Bind

What kind of person can watch someone cry themselves into an exhausted slumber and feel jealous? I guess that would be me. I did my best to comfort Calhoun, but seeing that kind of emotion come pouring out of someone has always made me uncomfortable. Men, real men as my dad had once stressed, don't break down and cry, even when they are burying their lover. How can you deal with someone else being upset if you can't deal with your own emotions?

Being here seems to have been enough. A warm shoulder to cry on, a safe pair of arms to wrap around a shaking body, that was all Calhoun needed. Eventually, he cried himself out and fell asleep with his face buried into the side of my neck.

He's still asleep now. I can't bring myself to move him in case he wakes up and goes through the same tumult of emotions he did when I first told him. It's best he sleeps while he can get it. The conversation we need to have when he wakes up isn't going to be a comfortable one.

I only know one thing for sure. Duclos is a lot more than a mere side character in Calhoun's personal narrative. All I can glean so far is that there is some sort of undercover mission going on here, and they worked together for a time. Was the animosity between them real? Did Calhoun get in over his head by starting a relationship with Newlin? Or is the whole thing some sort of ruse?

Calhoun sniffs and snuggles in tighter. I bite my tongue against a yelp of pain and gently move his arm down from my ribs. H shows no sign of waking despite the little snuffles and occasional fidgeting.

Rexus' accusations slip into my mind. There is nothing inhuman about Calhoun. What could Rexus or any one of the people he works with, have seen to make them think that? Is it as simple as what I said to Robertson? They've extracted the humanity from their victims, turned them into a threat, and made it easier to kill them?

Too many questions, not enough answers, and the main person who could give me a really good insight into it all is currently snoring on my shoulder.

It's nice to have a moment of calm like this, I suppose. No rushing around, no searches, no blood and seeing body parts that should remain under skin at all times. Yeah, might as well take the gift of quiet. I've comforted Calhoun as best I could. Why not let my mind and body rest and be refreshed for later when, no doubt, the shit will really hit the fan?

I rest my cheek on top of his head. His hair is soft and cool against my skin, and a soft scent of coconut lingers in it. I close my eyes.

"Jer…" he mumbles.

"I'm still here," I say and gently stroke his back. "Sleep. It's okay. I'll keep an ear out."

He nuzzles against my neck. "Safest place…" he trails off.

"Yeah." I loosen my hold on him and try to put a little bit of space between us, but he clings just as tight as before. At least the nuzzling has stopped.

A loud snore breaks the silence, and I can't help but smile. This isn't so bad. It's been a long time since I had this much contact with someone. I didn't realize how much I missed it.

My phone buzzes in my pocket. I ignore it at first, but it keeps vibrating. Calhoun whines softly as he wakes up, then moves away from me and rubs his eyes. With a whispered apology, I answer the call.

McCray sounds weary. I can almost picture him sitting slumped at his desk as he talks. "Hey. Thought I should let you know that our killer has struck again. Do you wanna come check this out?"

"Burbank is going to have my guts if I keep running around with you guys," I say, hoping the excuse will fly and I won't have to see what the murderer has done.

"This is your case too," McCray says. "Everything is connected, and, whether Burbank likes it or not, that makes you part of the team. We'll share what we have. It doesn't matter if you come or not."

I look over at Calhoun, who glances back and forces a smile. I need to see what's going on first hand if I'm going to keep him safe. That's the only way I can be sure the information I am getting is correct.

"I'll come," I reply. "Text me the directions, and I'll meet you guys in a bit."

Calhoun worries his lip between his teeth then says, "It happened again, didn't it?" when I hang up.

"Yeah," I sigh. "I'm going to go down there and check it out, see if there're any clues."

"There won't be. There never is." He scrubs his hands over his face. "I should have been ready. I should know—"

"What exactly could you have done?" It's not an accusation. I genuinely want to know.

Calhoun remains silent. He wraps his arms protectively around himself and stares at the floor. With a bit of effort, I swallow down my frustration and place my hand on his knee.

"We're going to have to talk about this, all of this, eventually," I say. I try to look in his eyes, but he refuses to meet my gaze. "For now, though, I want you to go stay in a hotel room. Don't tell anyone where you are. Don't contact anyone either, except for me."

He frowns. I can't blame him for being unhappy with that. I know I would be. "Why? I'm perfectly safe here."

"No, you're not. We have no idea who is in this gang of Rexus', but we do know they had someone in the Wolves watching you, and there are probably people tailing you now. You need to get away. Right now, I think you'd be okay in New York itself, with us around to protect you, but you need to get out of this apartment."

He forces himself up from the couch. "Let me grab some stuff first and wash my face."

I watch him leave. The urge to wrap him up safe in my arms and tell him everything is going to be okay is a strong one. He looks defeated. Like every ounce of self-confidence and happiness he had has been sucked out of him, leaving behind a frail shell of what he was.

It'll pass. There's a lot going through his head right now that I don't have the first clue about, but I *will* find out. No matter whom he works for, no matter what they are up to, his silence is probably the biggest threat to his safety.

Calhoun has obviously been busy thinking while packing. In quick succession, we hit several different costume and make up stores, following Calhoun's plan to the letter. By the time we walk through the doors of The Michelangelo down in Midtown, we are disguised as Mr. and Mrs. Lovatt. Rich tourists from England. Calhoun handles booking the rooms in a flawless aristocratic English accent, and flashes enough cash to make our lack of ID no problem.

"You're good at this," I say once we are safely in the room.

Calhoun checks the room over. He runs his hands over the door frames and peers into the ornate light fittings. "I've had a lot of practice."

I watch him walk around effortlessly in five-inch heels. His eyes are blue now thanks to contacts, and his hair is hidden under a wavy blond wig. My own costume is simpler. Jeans, dark shirt, short brown wig and the same color contacts. It's the eye color that really makes the difference. I'd be surprised if my own mother recognized me like this.

"This is what you do then?" I ask. "You're a spy or something?"

Calhoun simply stares at me. "You have somewhere to be, don't you?"

"You are going to talk," I say firmly. "Please tell me you can see how serious this is."

"We'll talk later." He sits down heavily on the king-size bed and kicks off his shoes. "I need to sort some stuff out in my head."

With nothing left to be said, I head back out of the hotel, deftly avoiding conversation with any of the staff, and dive into the first fast food place I see on the way back to the car. When I am back to my old self—or as much as I can be trying to wash make up off my face in a McDonald's bathroom—I run back to where we hid the car.

I hope Calhoun is safe alone in the hotel. It may have been a major overreaction, but, until we know who Rexus is working with, anyone is a suspect. Like Jameson said days ago, it has to be someone who can find stuff out about the crime scenes. It could be a reporter. And, of course, there is the uncomfortable possibility that there are other cops actively working against us.

§

The subway tunnels echo with our footsteps as we trudge through the filth towards our destination. Novik has assured me again and again that the line is closed and the third rail is off. There's no danger of us electrocuting ourselves, but all I can see in my mind's eye is the headlights of squealing subway trains hurtling towards us.

It's just the kind of place I would expect to find mutilated bodies.

We walk single file down the rails. The air is the kind of icy cold only damp concrete and brickwork can bring. Stinking water drips around us, occasionally hitting my shoulders. I pull my shirt up over my nose to block out the putrid smell.

"You okay?" Novik whispers from behind me. Anything louder than a whisper echoes really bad.

"Yeah, fine," I say. I glance over my shoulder at him and catch my foot on the rail. Novik catches me before I can fall.

"Careful," he says. I pull my arm back out of his grasp and turn around, ignoring him.

A few more steps pass in eerie silence, and then voices start to filter through. We're getting close; there's a lot of light up ahead. We follow a curve in the tunnel, and it opens up into an ornate brick station. Leaded glass skylights punctuate the roof, letting pale daylight filter down into the space. It's impressive for a subway station, even more impressive considering it's been shut off for years.

McCray steps up onto the platform behind me and shoves his hands in his pockets. "They picked a pretty place," he says and glances upwards at the glass work.

I follow his gaze. "Do you think it's deliberate? It's almost like a church."

McCray shrugs. "I think it's been chosen on purpose, but not for the look of the place." He looks along the tunnel we just walked. "The six-train comes through here after the Brooklyn Bridge station on its way back up the line. It's not a stop, just a turning point, but the trains run twenty-four hours, meaning there's no way the victims would go undiscovered. The drivers can't help but see in here thanks to the amount of light." McCray grits his teeth. "The sick bastard wants all his victims to be found."

"Is there any other way out of here?" I ask as I look around.

"There's one street entrance, but it's locked up tight. Uniform says it hasn't been tampered with at all." He pulls a set of latex gloves out of his pocket and hands a pair to me. "Let's see what we can find out," he says wearily.

Under the harsh flood lights the CSI teams brought in, the bodies resting near the platform edge look otherworldly pale. Ugly black stitching holds the two naked halves together like some sort of Frankenstein's monster. Mottled skin surrounds the stitching, and bruising dots their inner thighs. Two eyes—one a darker blue than the other, stare are the vaulted ceiling. The mismatched lips are open enough to reveal shattered incisors. The rest of the teeth are intact—the severing blow must have been delivered with pinpoint accuracy. Underneath the victims, the familiar swirl pattern weaves its way along the otherwise unmarked concrete. Where's the blood? They must have been moved, but how? They could have used the same route we did, but the line would have been open then.

I give the bodies a wide berth as I skirt around them to the platform's edge. Just like in Boston the victims look posed—arms outstretched, legs spread, even the hair seems deliberately fanned out. The halves don't quite match. Victim one is about half an inch shorter than victim two.

I lower myself back onto the track, switch on the flashlight on my phone, and look around. There's nothing but the usual debris—rubble, trash, the remains of animals that weren't fast enough to avoid the trains. I jump as I spy something pale in the darkness. It's the hand of one of the victims dangling over the platform edge. His fingernails are painted blue, just like the tips of the young man's hair. At closer inspection, the edges of the nails are ragged, the paint chipped. Wrapped around the ring and middle finger is a tiny strip of beige fabric. I carefully prise it free.

There're paint spots on it.

The sight of it makes my stomach churn, but I quickly chastise myself for the thought. How many other artists are in New York besides him?

"What you got there?" Novik says, startling me.

"Oh it…" I look down at the scrap in my grasp. I can't exactly deny I have it. "One of the victims had a hold of it.

With my heart hammering in my ears, I place it into the bag Novik gives me. He holds out his hand to help pull me back up.

"We actually found something at one of these scenes? That's awesome!" Novik grins. How he can still be this perky when he's probably been up nearly twenty-four hours like the rest of us is lost on me.

"Yeah. A breakthrough at last." I give the bag over to Novik when he gestures for it. I have no choice. "Anything interesting up here?"

"It's all the same as usual except this." He points to the swirling symbols. They're the same designs we have seen at every murder except, this time, the stuff used to draw them is different."

I squat down and carefully touch the design It's drawn in a soft powder, gray, like fine ash.

"What the hell is it?"

Novik shrugs. "Who knows? We'll take a few samples and…"

"If you want my opinion," one of the CSI's, a petite, Hispanic woman, cuts in. "I'd say it's human ashes."

"You can tell just by looking at it?" The residue on my gloves could be from anything to my untrained eye.

"I could be wrong," she concedes. "But we've found a few larger fragments that look like they might be bone. It could be animal, but it's definitely from cremated remains."

"Is there any hope of getting DNA out of it, detective…?" Novik asks.

"Alvarez." She looks around the scene. "The more fragments we find the better chance we have. It's pretty slim though. Plus, with the amount of ash used, we are looking at more than one adult human for sure. More if it's smaller bodies."

Novik's nose wrinkles in disgust. "Lovely."

Detective Alverez kneels and scoops up a small amount of the ash. With a small brush, she cleans away more of the residue. "Look at this."

Novik and I examine the little patch of concrete. "It's burned," I say.

She rests her hand against the mark. "And a while ago too. The ground is just as cold here as anywhere."

Novik studies the powder a bit closer. "Maybe it's gunpowder?"

Alvarez takes a few photos of the scorched ground. "The consistency doesn't feel right. We'll get it tested, and then we'll know for sure.

We straighten up in unison. I step away carefully from the bodies to avoid damaging the patterns around them, and lean against the cool brick wall. Novik joins me.

"You're doing good, man," he whispers. He glances towards the others as if making sure they haven't overheard.

I pull my gloves off with a loud snap. "It's not so bad. This one," I gesture towards the bodies, "it's not as gory as the others. Everything's contained."

Novik leans beside me. "Yeah, I know what you mean."

"It's not like the last one where—" I stop mid-sentence as a light bulb flashes on in my head. "Novik, what's wrong with this scene?"

"Everything is wrong with it, Jer," he says. "This is some sick—"

"I know," I say over the top of him. "But what's *wrong* with it compared to the Boston ones?"

Novik furrows his brows as he looks around, "I don't know. Everything looks the same."

"They've skipped one," I say. "Where's number four? The one that was bled out through the wrists?"

I can almost see the pieces fall into place in his mind. "You're right."

"And the first murder was ever so slightly different."

"Yup. There were feathers here and none at the first Boston one," he says.

A small smile tugs at the side of my mouth. "You know what that means, right?"

Novik mimics my expression. "We most likely have a copy-cat killer."

A plan quickly forms in my head. "I'm gonna go back to Calhoun's place. Hopefully the guy who did this left him another little note."

"McCray and I will finish up here." Novik says. "We'll meet you back at the station and hit Rexus where it hurts."

§

The apartment is locked up just as tight as when we left. A letter is lying on the floor behind the door, like I hoped it would be. I open it up quickly and read it.

They're getting too close. They make you nervous.
Lean in, whisper. They say, "tell me all."
And with each secret the black chords bind you.
Are you even your own person anymore?

I guess that's proof. Whoever is sending the letters is aware of the murders as they happen in New York. They are not gleaning information from the Boston case. The real question now is how are they connected? Well there're eight detectives working on that answer as we speak, so I'm going to devote time to a little mystery of my own.

I lock the front door of the apartment behind me then head for Calhoun's room. By the time the scrap I found had been tested I want to have evidence to prove it's not Calhoun's.

I check the laundry hamper in the bathroom first. The smock isn't in there. The room itself has nothing interesting either, no clues at all to who Calhoun really is.

Calhoun's bedroom is huge. The bed is king-size and piled with blankets and pillows. The door to a walk-in closet is ajar. Next to it, a desk made of the same drift wood as the furniture in the living room. Across the other side of the room is a dresser, six drawers high by two wide. I start my search in there.

It's filled with what I expected. Underwear, clothes, junk like pens, hair ties, cologne bottles with just a few drops left inside. In the bottom drawers are piles of sketchbooks and art supplies. I look through them all. One features a lot of birds, people with wings, feathers. A small, hardback book with canvas pages contains beautiful fantasy portraits—men and women with pointy ears and strangely colored eyes. A third is full of landscapes, some recognizable, some clearly from his own imagination. There's no sign of the painter's smock, so I tidy everything away and cross the room.

In the desk, I find paperwork confirming what my preliminary searches on him did—he does own a tattoo studio, and he is licensed. The desk top is in tidy disarray. There's a hairbrush, some pendants lying in a tangle, a small box of make-up, and a set of three Japanese swords on an ornate rack. I open up the smallest one and gently press my finger to the blade. It's dull; they're just ornamental.

I jump when my phone vibrates. It's Calhoun. He's safe, and he hasn't left his room. The message is nothing more than that, but the timing makes me nervous. Does he know I'm here digging around?

He would know I'm doing it for him. We need a preemptive strike.

The bedroom is clean so I move on to other rooms and slowly eliminate them. One of the doors in the hallway is locked. I try the handle a few times then look around for a key, but, when I return with a few I've found, I realize there's no keyhole in the door. A swift kick earns me nothing but pain in my ankle. Before I can try again, I get another phone call. I let out a stream of curses before answering.

"What?!"

"Sorry," Rodowski answers. "Is this a bad time?"

I lean against the wall and sigh. "No, sorry about that. I was—" I look at the small crack in the door where I kicked it. "I've been digging around and not getting anywhere. It's frustrating."

"Ah, then I got just the thing to make your day a whole lot better."

§

Rodowski meets me at the front desk, and we exchange pleasantries as we make our way through the building.

"We have a cunning plan," she says and beckons me into the main office with a crook of her finger. "He's going to lead us right to his little friends."

I drag a chair over and sit down as Rodowski boots up her computer. She almost dances in her seat as she opens up her browser, flicks through her notebook, then types in the web address she finds in it.

"Welcome to *thelastdefense.com.*" Rodowski says with a grin.

The website is a busy message board filled with seemingly benign topics about aliens, conspiracy theories, and even Sci-Fi literature.

I point at the screen. "This is it? Rexus' site?"

"Yup. And it's a whole heap of crazy too." Rodowski logs into the site and opens up a thread enticingly titled *Just what exactly are they putting in the water?*

"There's everything on here," she continues. "Chem-trails, ancient aliens, the moon landings. Some of it is pretty harmless discussion, and then we have these guys."

She maneuvers her way easily through the forum and brings up a thread entitled *They Walk Amongst Us.* It's a long-running thread, too. The first post is about seven years old, but the newest is barely a few months.

"There're a lot of half-finished conversations on here," I say half to myself.

Rodowski taps her finger against the mouse as she reads. "Yeah, that's what we were thinking too. We think they're taking it off site, but we're not sure where."

"Do you have enough to get a warrant to seize Rexus' computer?"

"Working on that as we speak," she says, and a little smile tugs at the corner of her mouth. "We have accounts for this, as you can see. There's no vetting procedure on the site, and anyone can join. It's getting into this next level…" she trails off back into her own thoughts.

Rexus' user name is strangely absent from the thread but as Rodowski scrolls through it, I do see another that seems strangely familiar.

I tap my finger on the screen, over the name *Nightingale*. "Can you see the profile of this guy?"

Rodowski opens it up. It's pretty empty. Just the name, a blank profile picture, and a location listed as New York City. My stomach clenches. Things are not looking good.

"Nightingale's posts are mostly fighting back against the more extreme of the believers," Rodowski says when she returns to skimming the thread. "They really aren't happy about some of the stuff that the other guys are talking about."

All I can do is nod numbly. There'll be a simple explanation for this. It's not like the Nightingale profile is actively engaging with these people in anything other than online arguments.

"'Scuse me," I say as I stand up. "I need to use the restroom. I'll be right back."

Rodowski points towards the door. “Down the hallway then take a right.”

Once inside the restroom I quickly check the cubicles, making sure I'm alone, then lock the main door. I wait a beat before dialing, just long enough to get my story straight.

“Hey, listen, just a quick one,” I say before Calhoun can speak. “Were your clothes taken for testing last night?”

Please say yes. Give me something I can work with.

“Nope, why would they need that for testing?” He sounds confused, and I don't blame him.

“Just wondering is all,” I say in as nonchalant a manner as I can manage.

“Well I hope they haven't changed their minds now,” Calhoun grumbles. “I had to throw it away. There was a big tear out of it. I must have caught it on something.”

I swallow hard. “Yeah. That's probably it. I didn't think tearing it up would matter since it's covered in paint anyway?”

“I have more than one. What's the point in keeping ripped clothes?”

“You're right, there's no point,” I reply. I'm struggling to keep my voice normal, but if it does carry any suspicions, he doesn't seem to notice. After making sure that no one has spoken to him and that he is safe, I hang up.

Shit. Why can't I just ask him outright about stuff? What's the worst that's going to happen? I either get it right from his mouth that he's innocent and then I can work on proving it, or he turns out to be someone we should be keeping a closer eye on. If he is using the site, then he could help us, maybe point us in the direction of some of the more antagonistic members!

Suddenly it hits me. I could answer a lot of different questions all in one smooth move and without alerting anyone, including Calhoun.

The website opens on my phone. Perfect. I quickly create an account, making sure that there is as little information as possible that could link back to me on it, and then pick the most innocuous thread there is and leave a comment. I'll work my way in slowly, let them watch me, fathom me out, then I'll start digging deeper and access their inner circle.

12

A Strange Trip

It takes a few hours for Rexus' lawyer to show up, hours that I spend slowly building a rapport with the conspiracy theorists on *The Last Defense.* I called myself Raven after a comment from a bereaved and angry mother who once accused me—and the Boston homicide squad as a whole—of being like ravens picking at a carcass. No dignity given to the victims, no thought to who they were before the murder, just using them and taking what we could until we got our answers. I was just a kid back then in my first year as a homicide detective, but that comment stuck with me because she had a point. Yeah, we need to gather evidence and do autopsies, but we can't forget that the body on the slab used to be a real, live someone.

Well, this raven is picking at a whole different carcass this time. Somewhere underneath this flesh made of nonsense theories and scaremongering, there is something so sweet I can't wait to get my hands on it. The identities of whoever is hunting these men down.

I'm so engrossed in digging around in the forum that I don't realize someone has crept up behind me until their hand lands on my shoulder. I jump to my feet and grab their wrist.

Harris blinks up at me, bewildered. "It's only me." He pulls his hand out of my grasp. "I did say hi, but you must've not heard me."

"Sorry. I was—" I shut off the screen on my phone before Harris can see it. "I was daydreaming."

Harris glances at my now black phone screen and then back to me. "We're ready to interview Rexus again. Did you read the file I gave you on him?"

I pick it up off the desk. "Yup. And I got it all stored up here," I say and tap my temple.

We head to the interview room. Rodowski slips into the space at the other side of the two-way mirror to monitor things while we step inside and sit across from Rexus and his lawyer. Rexus looks a little rough. He has the start of bags under his eyes, and his shoulders are slumped. Sleeping in a cell with the thought of major charges hanging over you makes a sleepless night pretty much a guarantee.

His lawyer, a smug faced man with cold dark eyes, whispers something to Rexus as soon as we set foot in the room. This guy is going to be fun to deal with.

Harris does the introduction for the taped interview then leaves Rexus hanging while he looks through his file.

"The name Steven Lee Morrell mean anything to you?" he says. He doesn't look at Rexus until he has finished speaking.

Rexus stares back blankly.

"That's you, isn't it?" Harris pulls a couple of photos of Rexus from the file and lays them on the desk. "You're twenty-eight. You live in Queens. Any of this ringing a bell?"

The lawyer whispers something, and Rexus smiles. "I have no idea what you're talking about."

Harris smiles sweetly. “That's okay. We don't need to know who you are or what you do or why no one listened when you claimed to be abducted by aliens. We can find all that out for ourselves.”

“It wasn't a claim!”

Harris rests his folded arms on the table. “Then what was it, Steven?”

The lawyer cuts in before Morrell can reply. “My client doesn't have to answer any of your questions.”

Harris throws a stern look the lawyer’s way. “He does if he doesn't want to go down for breaking and entering, stalking, or…” He looks pointedly back to Morrell. “Assault.”

“And what about the assault charges my client wishes to raise?” the lawyer says, his haughty tone raising my hackles. “My client has suffered *terrible* injuries at the hands of Lachlan Calhoun, as well as a verbal assault.”

“Because *he* got into Calhoun's building and has been stalking him for years,” I say.

The lawyer smirks. “And what proof do you have?”

I dig the print out from my pocket, where it's been since I showed it to Newlin, and hand it to the lawyer. “It's all there. Morrell himself gave it to us.”

The lawyers face quickly falls as he reads through the information. He whispers to Morrell, but Morrell shrugs him off. “No! They need to know everything. It's important.”

“Go ahead,” Harris says. “What should we know?”

“My client,” the lawyer butts in, “is emotionally unstable after his ordeal last night. He will not be answering any more questions.”

“Aw, that's a shame,” Harris says. He leans in close, almost as if he is going to share a secret with Morrell. “Because we have found *Thelastdefense.com* and it’s only a matter of time before you and your friends are caught. If you tell us what you know now, we may be lenient when we sentence you. Otherwise, it's left up to fate, isn't it?"

"My client has done—"

Harris cuts him off by raising his hand. "But he has. We have reason to suspect that he attacked Lachlan Calhoun. We know, thanks to him handing us the evidence himself, that he has been stalking Calhoun for a number of years. Now, with so many young men who fit Calhoun's description being killed, I'm sure you can see why we may suspect he's been up to more than just stalking."

Morrell punches the table. "I haven't killed anyone!" he shouts. Spit splatters the table top.

"But you don't consider Calhoun to be anyone, do you?" I say. "What's it you called him, inhuman?"

Morrell laughs derisively. "You think you're so smart, don't you?" He jabs his finger at me. "That *thing* has got under your skin. It's been manipulating your brain every time you let it get its mitts on you. People are going to die because *you* let yourself be tricked by it."

Harris tuts loudly. I glance at him and give a tiny shake of my head. I've got Morrell where I want him.

"Why do you believe Calhoun isn't human?"

The lawyer tries to stop him talking, but Morrell is warming up to his subject. "It looks weird; it acts weird. It started causing a lot of trouble for people around it. I know guys who have had run-ins with it in the past. They say they get migraines a lot. Fits, too. Some have holes in their memory."

I wait a second, long enough to keep my voice neutral, before asking, "but what have you personally seen?"

The lawyer tries to push his way between us, but Morrell is having none of it. He slaps the lawyers arm away, then claps his hand over mine on the tabletop. I fight the urge to pull away and wave Harris off intervening.

"I'm trying to help you here, Jerry." Morrell tightens his grip. "That's all we want, to stop this thing getting its claws any deeper into you. We are not bad people. Even you must realize that we have to exterminate things that want to hurt us."

I hold his gaze. "Is that what you do? Exterminate threats?"

Morrell scoots closer. Most of his upper body is on the table now. My bones creak when he squeezes my hand. "We try," he whispers. "Monsters don't deserve to live!"

"So, you identified this inhuman, and you tracked him down. Got people to spy on him. Then what?"

"We tried to take it out before he did any more damage," Morrell says. His breath hits my face like a damp mist. "And we nearly managed it until it…" he trails off, his gray eyes unfocused as he drifts into memories.

I give his hand enough of a shake to bring him out of his daydream. "Until what?"

"He flew," Morrell says with a little smile on his face. "I stuck that knife right into his stomach, and he just took off, right into the sky."

"You stabbed him?"

"Yeah, I stabbed it," Morrell says. "He was beaten real bad, but he still got away. "

Morrell's lawyer elbows his way between us. "My client is not fit to be interviewed right now."

"Your client," Harris says with a little bit of a growl in his voice, "has said enough." He takes Morrell's hand and forcibly separates it from mine. "Steven Lee Morrell, you are under arrest for the attempted murder of Lachlan Calhoun."

Morrell doesn't flinch or try to fight. His calm gaze remains on me. "There're thousands of us all over the world. You'll never catch us all. You'll never stop us!" He glances at Harris then back to me. "We are on your side. We are trying to catch this killer too, but you can't just dive in there and confront it. It's too strong in that form. You've got to catch it when it is unawares, in its human form. Where it feels safe."

With those last words, Morrell allows himself to be led to the holding cells.

The lawyer glares at me. "You don't seem all that concerned about labeling a victim as a criminal despite overwhelming evidence to the contrary."

I smile sweetly. "For a lawyer, you're not all that observant. Morrell just confessed to a stabbing."

I leave without waiting for a reply.

Morrell's parting words stick with me. Was he bragging that they were going to go after Calhoun? If he tries, all they are going to find is an empty apartment, but is Calhoun the only one they have on their list? He can't be if these other men are dying. Maybe they will try to correct the murder pattern tonight.

"We need to put an alert out!" I shout to Harris as he comes back into the office.

He wearily rubs his face as he sits down at his desk. "Why?"

"Cos, to me, it sounded like Morrell was saying there's going to be another murder, tonight."

Harris starts digging through the mess on his desk. "He was just trying to sound important, Jerry." He flips through folders and digs through his drawers. "Trying to distract us."

"Lost something?" I scoot my chair closer, ready to help if I can.

"Yeah. Novik gave me the tape from Morrell's first interview, and I can't find it." He covers his face with his hands and groans. "This is just great! I knew I should've locked it away."

I pat his shoulder consolingly. "Don't worry. It'll be here."

Harris kicks the bottom drawer of his desk shut.

Rodowski looks up from where she is working. “Hey! Gordon isn't gonna be too happy if you break his drawer.”

“Sorry,” Harris says. He runs his hands through his hair and sighs. “I need to get some sleep. I swear I'm gonna start hallucinating soon.”

“Okay, but first, can you please issue that alert?”

Harris gives me a puzzled look. “What alert?”

“The one I just mentioned,” I say, exasperated. “I think we should advise that anyone who fits the description should stay inside tonight. I know there isn't much to go on, but there was something different at the murder scene today too. I’ve got a bad feeling.”

Harris looks at me like I've lost my mind “You're wanting to issue that kind of warning based on a throwaway comment? When we already have cops on the streets and at every Goth hangout in Manhattan?”

“It's just a precaution,” I insist. I move closer and drop my voice to a whisper. “Something really isn't sitting well with me. I think they might try to step up their game. They know we're onto them.”

“Morrell doesn't have a phone. He can’t let anyone know he’s been arrested.”

“We don't know how deep this goes. His lawyer could be involved. Cops in this very building!”

Harris sighs angrily. “What makes you think that?”

“They had people in the biker gang, why not cops?”

Harris shakes his head. “Give me a stronger indication that something is going to go down tonight, and we'll issue an alert. Until then, security is tight, and we're already getting bite back for being too heavy handed.” He stands up. “I'm going to go grab a few hours’ sleep while everything is quiet.” He turns to Rodowski. “Call me if it all kicks off.”

Rodowski gives him a thumbs-up, and Harris leaves. Frustrated by his lack of help, I jump back onto *The Last Defense* to see if I can dig up clues there. There's a message in my in-box. Curious, I open it up.

I know who you are! It reads. Frowning, I look around the office. Rodowski catches my eye and smiles. The message isn't from the account she's using. It's been active for years, but, maybe, she has another. Any cop in this precinct could have an account. Or maybe this user, *Nomad,* is making a good guess based on the fact we've arrested one of their own.

Okay, I'll bite. Who do you think I am? I type back.

There's a moment's pause before the message flashes through. *You're a cop and you're a traitor.*

Nomad must be online now. I slip my hand into my pocket and wander over to Rodowski. She looks up but doesn't close anything down or scramble to hide what's she's doing.

"Hey," she says pleasantly. "Don't you have a bed to go to?"

I surreptitiously glance at her screen. "Gonna be hard to sleep with all this going on."

"Tell me about it. Why do you think I'm spending all my hours on this damn site?"

"Yeah. Hard to sleep when your mind is on something," I say as I look at my phone again. There's another message from *Nomad.* "Hey, do you have someone you trust in Cyber?"

"I used to work up there before I decided I needed to get my teeth into something a bit juicier. I know a few of them pretty well." She looks up at me, eyebrow raised. "What's up?"

I squat down next to her chair. "Promise not to tell anyone?"

Rodowski frowns. "Depends what it is?"

That's pretty much the answer I expected. I decide to trust her. Plus, if word gets out, I know Rodowski is in on it too. I quickly fill her in on my little plan to burrow into the site undetected and *Nomad's* claim that they know who I am.

Rodowski nods thoughtfully. "I'll pass that name on to Cyber. They're dealing with this side of the case. I just like to dig around, keep the skills oiled."

"Can you hack in to the accounts then?" I ask.

Rodowski laughs. "It's not as easy as the movies make it look, and a lot of it is an ethical gray area." She turns back to the computer. "I could, maybe, get in, but then I'd have to explain why I broke into the accounts of innocent people with no warrant and no evidence that they are involved. That's *if* they could trace me."

I click to her insinuation pretty fast. "But if someone was to do this and got a bunch of evidence out of it, it couldn't be used in court anyway."

She winks "Maybe a friendly hacker will send us an email with just the information we're looking for. There's ways to make that kind of evidence admissible." She shrugs. "Cyber has got it covered though. They have the means and the clearance, but every little bit helps."

I smile. "I wonder if this friendly hacker might contact someone on this site, maybe one of the newest users, and—"

I shut up pretty quick as soon as we hear footsteps. We share a look. Rodowski winks again. "Maybe they will, Raven."

We both try to cover our grins when McCray steps into the office He looks at us both then around the office. "Where's everyone else?"

"Either sleeping, gathering evidence or slacking off somewhere," Rodowski says dryly.

McCray sits down heavily at his desk. "Any developments?"

I listen to them discuss the case so far and check on the messages from *Nomad.* There's one that was sent a few minutes earlier, then nothing.

You and the other traitors will die! Just like the monsters you are trying to protect. How many more innocents will you see killed just to keep that thing safe?!

Harris wanted some evidence that we needed to up the stakes tonight, and I think I just got it. I show the message to McCray and Rodowski and ask, once again, for the alert to be put out.

McCray heaves a deep sigh and picks up the phone. "This is just what we fucking need."

§

The day passes in a blur of activity. Rodowski and I spend our time neck deep in the discussions on *The Last Defense,* identifying accounts that require further investigation. We exchange a constant stream of emails and Skype calls with Cyber, trading information and hunches. By the time it's getting dark again, we have five more people identified for questioning. Unfortunately, they are just bit players, none of the core group.

Nomad seems to be on a mission to become the biggest thorn in my side they possibly can be. As well as their threat laden messages, they start dogging every post I've made, stirring up trouble and turning everyone else on the site against me. Interestingly, *Nightingale* jumps to my defense and demands proof from *Nomad* for every one of their accusations. None is ever given.

The others work on both of our newest murders. Evidence is thin on the ground in the subway station, like every other scene in this case, but a few things are found at Duclos' place. Nothing big, a few fibers and a partial thumb print, but at least it's something. Hopefully we'll find out who killed him before another person dies.

An agitated murmur starts in the hallway. We all glance over as one.

"Ah shit," Rodowski sighs. "Here comes trouble."

Burbank strides into the office and brushes aside anyone who tries to intercept him. "You!" He growls and jabs his finger at me. "Get out!"

Novik and a few of the other detectives try to jump to my defense, but Burbank roars at them all to be quiet. He looms over me where I sit.

"I thought I told you I didn't want you here messing up my case." He punctuates each word with a point to my face. "I thought I told you to go home!"

"And I told you I was working here," I growl.

Burbank leans in close. "You ain't a cop! Get out!"

I get to my feet. "I'm going nowhere. Our cases have overlapped!"

Burbank grabs a pile of paper from Robertson, who followed him in, and hurls it at me. "You have blown the cover of anyone we have working on that site. Are you some kind of fucking idiot?!"

"They don't even know why—"

"Not another fucking word," Burbank snaps. "Get out before I have you arrested for perverting the course of justice."

I snort a laugh. "Oh, yeah, I'd like to see you make that stick."

"Don't test me, Higgins. You've been at crime scenes, sat in on interviews, had information shared with you that never should have." He throws a nasty look at Jameson. "I have more than enough here to get you locked up, and your friends with you. So, what's it to be?"

Burbank doesn't back up when I step towards him. For a breath stealing moment we stare at each other, mere inches between us as we glare and snarl like angry cats. All eyes are on us, waiting. Is he really worth the assault charge?

I look him up and down, making sure my face shows every bit of disgust I feel just being in his presence, then walk away. There is a collective sigh of relief from the others in the room. On my way out, I step close to Robertson.

"No one likes a snitch," I hiss.

Robertson glares, but I'm already walking away. I'm not interested in whatever shit he has to say.

By the time I get out of the precinct, my mood has softened a little. Burbank had a point, no matter how much I begrudge saying it. It was me creating an account on that site and making so many posts that drew them to us. *Nomad* started causing trouble and shouting about cops because of me, but I don't regret my decision. Because of the attack against me online, we were able to single out a few more names to follow. We'll find others too. There's no stopping it now.

I suppose I'll have to thank Robertson at one point for his parting gift too. He ratted me out to Burbank with a whole stack of print-outs from *The Last Defense*. It seems I'm not the only cop digging where I shouldn't be.

I wander aimlessly in the rough direction of the hotel. It's going to be a long walk, but I need it. Maybe I'll hit a bar along the way. I could really use a stiff drink after all this crap. I light a cigarette, the first I've had time for in a while, and start to relax a little. Maybe sleep would be better than the drink, or I could do both? Grab a couple of beers or...

My thoughts trail off as I turn a corner. A few feet in front of me is a wall of mist. I look at the cigarette in my hand then back to the barrier. Has someone switched out my tobacco for something more potent?

Curious, I walk towards it. It doesn't get any less real up close. It covers the whole street and brushes up against the buildings, turning everything inside it into a hazy portrait. Gingerly I put my hand out. The wall holds then depresses. It's like sticking my fingers in cold honey.

There're a few people milling around the streets, but no one passes as close as I am to the barrier. No one walks through it, from either side. Can anyone else see it? Am I really so tired after about forty-eight hours with no sleep that I'm hallucinating?

Something moves on the other side. It's nothing more than a few shadows, but the way they are interacting doesn't look good. As soon as I see what looks like one of the distorted figures hitting the ground, I force my way through. For a few seconds, it's like pushing into Jell-O, cold and cloying, and then I burst into the mist beyond.

My ears ring in the sudden silence. The air presses down on me and irritates my sinuses, but it's not affecting my movements. The little pendent that Calhoun gave me warms against my skin. Strange, but it's just one thing in a whole pile of strange. I allow myself a little nervous laugh as I walk on. I've fallen asleep somewhere, and this is some fucked up dream. Or I'm creeping up the middle of some New York street, hallucinating, and everyone who can see me is laughing.

There's no sign of the shadows I saw, so I walk on, listening, watching, gun drawn just in case. Something feels familiar about the way the fog clings to my skin and hair, the silence, the weight of the air.

A scream splits the stillness.

I follow the noise at a dead run. It echoes strangely. My directions are thrown off. The constant shouts of protest and the terrifying noises-clothes ripping, flesh tearing, help me find my way. I skid around the corner and aim my gun.

The two of them lie tangled on the ground, one rutting savagely between the naked, splayed legs of the other. Dark red blood drips from the victim's wrists, which are pinned to the concrete. No matter how much he struggles and screams, he can't escape.

"Hey!" I roar to get the attackers attention. "Let him go, or I will shoot!"

The murderer sits back on his heels, and turns his head a full one hundred and eighty degrees. Red eyes bore into me from a gray, almost featureless face. My stomach knots up at the sight of him.

"We meet again, son of fire," the murderer says. He jabs a long nail into the victim's wrist, and makes another hole for blood to seep through. The young man whines in pain, his cry muffled in the mist.

"Let him go!" I demand, but my shaking hands dull the effect.

He stares me down. "Or what?"

The longer I stare back the more things come to my notice. His skin is gray and mottled. Eyes are dark red, his head bald. He holds his prey down with two hands on his wrist, but another two hold his hips. What the fuck is he?

The top half of the killer's body moves forward like some grotesque piece of taffy. I'm rooted to the spot, like a mouse facing a snake. I can barely breathe. My teeth knock together and my gun slides from my shuddering hands.

A gray, bulging eyed face looms over mine. His mouth opens wide, showing jagged, dripping teeth. Hot breath scalds my face. Spittle peppers my skin. A slimy tongue slowly licks my cheek. My stomach churns, and bile rises in my throat.

Run, you idiot!

"It's not your time," he hisses. "But we'll be back."

His body snaps back to normal proportions like a rubber band. At the first scream from the victim the hold on me is broken. I lunge and swing my leg, aiming for the murderer's head with all my might.

Quick as a flash he grabs my leg, and throws me clear across the alley. I hit the wall on the other side. My body explodes with pain. When I try to get up a wind rushes over me and knocks me back. Feathers, so many feathers, brush my skin. The murderer roars as he is engulfed in the swirling, down-filled, tornado. A bright flash of metal flickers amongst the swarm.

As soon as the killer is far enough away, I run to the young man. The wounds in his wrists are small. He's not losing a lot of blood through them, but the trauma of the attack has left him a quivering, barely conscious, mess. He's in no state to move under his own power. I lift him up, cradling him like a child, and carry him towards the barrier.

"Can you tell me your name?" I hurriedly say.

His lips move a few times before any noise comes out. "Ma…" He mutters the same sound over and over again.

Has he been drugged? His sluggish movements and impaired awareness make that seem likely.

An ear piercing, inhuman shriek like nails down a blackboard sets my teeth on edge. The man in my arms reaches behind me His pointed chin digs into my shoulder.

"Far…" he whispers.

"And we'll keep him far, don't worry," I hiss through the ache in my back and ribs. The man may be thin, but he's a grown adult, and his weight is growing heavier the longer I carry him.

A wet tearing sound echoes down the street, and a blood curdling wail that raises the hairs on the back of my neck follows it. I stop in my tracks. I should turn back. There's someone fighting that thing. I can't just leave them to it.

The young man clings to me with what little strength he has. His pale body shakes, and his black hair is a matted mess of sweat and blood. No, I have to get this guy out of here and call for help. I risk a glance back. Whoever is fighting that monster is still on their feet, still attacking with everything they have. If I move quickly, I can help them both!

The victim whines pitifully as I break into a run. I urge him to hold on to me and talk about whatever I can think of to keep him awake. He looks over my shoulder again and lets out a howl so raw, so pure in its illustration of the horror following us, that my knees quake in fear.

My ankle is yanked backwards. I fall heavily. The man rolls out of my arms and tries to scrabble away, but the killer is soon on him. I curse myself for leaving my gun behind and root around for something I can use as a weapon. I hurl a discarded traffic cone at him followed by whatever crap I can find.

I am nothing more than a mere irritant to him.

The killer's fingers elongate and wrap around the victim's neck. I move in to stop him, but he bats me aside like a bug. He lifts the young man high in the air and stretches his mouth open. Rows of upon rows of needle-like teeth spring out of his stretched gums.

I hammer my fists against him, but it's like punching memory foam—my hands just sink in and leave a temporary mark. He swats me again and lowers the screaming victim towards his mouth.

"*No!*" I scream, forcing every bit of rage into it that I can muster. I drive my hands as deep as I can into the killer's spongy body. A guttural roar thunders out of my throat, a noise I didn't even know I could make. I break out in a sweat, and my hands tingle. The killers flesh sizzles.

The murderer clutches at his stretched belly and whines like a beaten dog. Suddenly, it hurls the man into the air and rushes off into the night, it's skin still smoking. I make a dive for the victim but miss by inches. He hits the ground with a sickening crunch. Blood slowly pools from the back of his head.

I try to call nine-one-one, but my cellphone refuses to connect. With no more time to waste on fiddling with it, I lift the victim into my arms again. His head lolls over my arm, and his eyes roll until they are mostly whites. I maneuver him so he is leaning against my chest and gain a smear of blood and hair for my troubles. There's no response from him this time when I run. He's completely limp in my arms.

I hit the barrier. It clings to us, and slows us down as it stretches around us, but, eventually, we burst through it. My senses are flooded, overpowered, by the city and all its sounds and smells. My chest heaves violently. I can't breathe, why can't I breathe?!

I try to take another step, but fall to my knees. The young man slides to the ground in front of me when I can no longer muster the strength to hold onto him. I scratch at my throat. My fingers tangle in the thin chains around my neck, and they snap. The hematite and Myles' ring crash to the asphalt, but there's no relief from the constricting squeeze on my windpipe. I hear nothing but my heart's racing beat as darkness rushes up to claim me.

§

The hospital room is dimly lit and quiet. I woke up about a half hour ago with a splitting headache, and puked everywhere. The guy I brought in is still alive according to the nurse I spoke to, but barely. Which is more than can be said for any other victims in either of these murder cases.

I open my eyes at the soft knock on the door and wave to Novik through the glass. I still feel weary and strangely heavy, but I guess that will pass.

Novik looks around as he steps into the room. There's an IV attached to my left hand and an oxygen mask hanging off the rail on the bed in case I need it. I look a lot sicker than I feel, no doubt.

"There you are," Novik says with false cheeriness.

I force a smile to my lips. "Yay, you found me." I try to make it a joke, but my heart isn't in it, and it just sounds sarcastic.

Novik pulls up a chair and sits by my bed. "How are you feeling?"

"Better," I say. "I can breathe freely. I should be out of here soon."

Novik raises an eyebrow at that. "They brought you in here unconscious, and you think you're gonna be out tonight?"

"There's nothing wrong with me," I insist. "I think it was some sort of over exertion"

"Over exertion?" Novik rubs his forehead in exasperation. "Jer, when are you gonna start taking your health seriously?"

"Oh, stop worrying." I mutter. I move the IV line out from under my elbow. "I was running and trying to carry someone who probably weighs just a little less than me. 'Course I was struggling to breathe"

Novik points at my neck. "You got nasty marks where you clawed at yourself. That's more than struggling."

"Good job I'm in a hospital then and the docs can give me a clean bill of health before I leave."

Novik looks down at his feet for a long moment. "Jay, I think you should go back to Boston."

I laugh. "Why?"

"Do I really need to say why? Look at where you are?"

"Just overnight."

Novik claps his hand over mine and squeezes. "Twice this murderer has got real close to doing something to you. They're targeting you. You need to get out of here."

"I'm not running away," I say defiantly. "Plus, you were one of the people saying I should come here."

"I didn't think you'd end up running for your damn life twice in two weeks. Look, we need to face facts. You look like the victims."

"Save for the fact I'm almost twice the age of some of 'em and American. I don't even have Germanic blood in my ancestry."

Novik's reply is cut short by the doctor knocking on the door. I slip my hand out from Novik's and sit up a little.

"Mr. Higgins," she says. "I wanted to ask you a few questions if I may." She glances at Novik.

"He's a friend. He can stay while we talk," I reassure her.

The doctor nods and looks over her notes. "Mr. Higgins, had you taken anything last night?"

Confused I say, "No. Well, I smoked like half a cigarette, but that was it. Oh, and I've been taking Tylenol for a rib injury, but I haven't had since yesterday."

The doctor holds my gaze. "If you tell us what you took, it's going to be a lot easier to treat you."

I narrow my eyes. "I've told you everything."

"We found traces of hallucinogens in your system, Mr. Higgins," the doctor says, and it's obvious from her tone she thinks she's dealing with another low-life who can't admit they have a problem. "Perhaps you can enlighten me as to how they got there."

"Okay, first of all, you can stop with the condescending tone. Second, I've never taken hallucinogens in my life."

The doctor's eye roll is a clear sign she doesn't believe me. "We can't pinpoint exactly what it was, but I would advise that you stay away from it in the future. It's pretty strong."

"But I didn't take anything. I…" I trail off as an idea pops into my head. "The guy that was brought in with me, did he have any in his system?"

"I'm afraid I can't discuss the health of another patient."

"Can hallucinogens get into your system through the air?"

The doctor's body sags as she sighs. It's clearly been a long shift for her. "Mr. Higgins, an airborne drug wouldn't gain the concentration that—"

I dig out my cigarettes from the storage cabinet and toss them on the bed. "Test them. That's the last thing I did before all this happened, smoke. Like I told you when I was first asked what happened, we were trapped in a thick mist. There could've been something in that, especially if the other guy has them in his system too."

The doctor appears to mull this over. "I'll be back in a bit to see how you're getting on," she says and then leaves.

"Well she was a delight," Novik grumbles. "Course you didn't take anything. Did you?"

"No!" I snap. "You saw me less than an hour before I ended up in here. Did I look high to you?"

"No," Novik concedes. He leans in and whispers. "You think someone drugged you?"

I nod. "And I think I may have a hunch why we've never had any witnesses to these murders. When you interview the people who live around the area, ask them if they had any headaches or nausea in the last twelve hours. There's a possibility they've been drugged too."

13

Caging Songbirds

Run! Got to go faster!

The man I'm carrying grips tighter around my neck. He whispers constantly.

"Mad… mad… they're all mad."

I keep running. There's no end to the foggy streets. Suddenly, I lose my footing and we both crash painfully to the ground.

I pull myself to my feet, pick up the injured guy, and start sprinting again. Just when I think I can see the way out of our foggy prison something wraps around my neck. The murderer's vermilion eyes bore into my soul as he laughs triumphantly. He squeezes my neck.

I gasp for breath and sit up. The nurse checking my vitals yelps and drops the chart. I apologize over and over again while I try to catch my breath and slow my racing heart. The nurse gives me a concerned frown, then checks me over.

"Bad dream?" he says softly. At first, I feel a little put out by his tone, but he must be used to talking to people under all kinds of different levels of stress. I let the fact he talked to me like I'm a kid slide.

"Yeah, but, I'm okay now." I offer him my friendliest smile. "Sorry I scared you."

He waves away my apology. "Do you want something to help you sleep?"

I shake my head. "I'd rather keep my wits about me if it's all the same."

The nurse smiles. "Let me know if you change your mind."

He picks up his chart and leaves.

I check the time on my phone. It's nine am. I've slept for nearly four hours after Novik left, and despite the nightmare, I actually feel clear headed, refreshed. There's several missed texts on my phone. Most are Calhoun's check in texts. I fire a quick one back to let him know what happened to me and that I'm okay. The others are from Novik. I give him an update on my situation, not that there's much to tell. I still don't know when I'll get out of here.

The rest of the day is a parade of tests, police interviews, and probing medical questions. Because the victim survived the case isn't assigned to McCray's team, but my insistence that the attack fits the pattern gains me the assurance that they will pass information between the two departments. I am finally left alone around eleven-thirty. As soon as the silence surrounds me I feel the familiar tendrils of anxiety wrapping around my insides. What happened last night was bad enough, but now I don't have any idea what was real, and the only other person who could possibly know is comatose.

By early afternoon I am free to go. Since I still feel kind of dizzy I call Novik to ask if he'll pick me up. He arrives about ten minutes later.

“I've got some good news and some bad news,” he says.

I sigh. “Hit me with it.”

“The bad news,” Novik begins as he sits down next to my hospital bed. “Is that we tested the samples Rexus’ gave us. They're fake. It’s dolls hair and special effects blood.”

I frown. “Okay. How’s that bad news?”

“Because his weasel of a lawyer is using it build an insanity plea. He's happy enough for Rexus to go down as some crazy stalker but not one who went far enough to actually attack someone.”

“But we can prove that’s not the case, right?” I ask. “He admitted he stabbed Calhoun.”

Novik shrugs. “The lawyer will try to twist it up into a false memory. And the best part is,” he says, his voice dripping with sarcasm “when we interviewed Rexus again, and told him the samples were fake, he went nuts. He’s adamant they’re real.”

I rub my forehead wearily. Rexus can't get away on something as weak as that, not when he confessed. “The good news better be real good.”

“We identified the guy from last night,” Novik says with a grin. “His clothes were found in a dumpster at the scene and his wallet was in his jeans pocket.”

“That’s great.” It's a weight off my mind. His family can find out he's here and we won't be alone. “So, who is he?”

“His name is Mads Rasmussen. He's from Denmark. We found a guitar at the scene, too, with his name on the case.” Novik pulls up a picture on his phone. “It looks pretty much like this. It’s an expensive piece of kit.”

I let out an appreciative whistle. “Not too shabby. It looks well looked after too.”

“He’s a member of a band actually. *Storms of Jupiter*. They’re a Prog rock band, they do all that weird time signature, twenty-minute song stuff.”

I can't help but smile at his description. "Not your kinda thing, is it?"

Novik slumps back in the chair. "Nah. But the good thing is, since the band was on tour here, we had people close to him that we could contact straight away. They were due to move on to New Jersey tonight but obviously canceled." He taps his fingers off the knuckles on his other hand. "They've only been here about three days according to the rest of the band. I wonder why he was targeted?"

"He fits the description and he's Scandinavian," I say. "I'm guessing he was in the same age range too?"

"Thirty, so he's the oldest yet." Novik sighs and glances up at the ceiling. "Well, at least he's safe and he has people who care for him at his bedside. Here's hoping for a speedy recovery."

"Yeah," I say flatly. I'm not holding out much hope of that—I heard the crack when Mads' head hit the road.

Novik sits up as if rousing himself from a daydream. "Oh, and your drugging theory is holding up. There's a few of the residents in that area reporting that they woke up feeling sick. Some said they had crazy nightmares too. We're going back to speak to the residents around the other sites to check if they say the same."

"That's awesome," I say. For the first time since this case began I feel a genuine smile pull at my lips. "We're getting somewhere, finally."

"So..." Novik looks down at hands for a second. "Any clearer in what happened now that you've slept on it?'

"I know what I saw," I say tersely. "And I know it was some hallucination, but it was real to me. My whole memory of it is fucked up. The only reason I know something happened outside my own head is because that guy is in the intensive care unit with the back of his head cracked open."

Novik looks away. His shoulders sag. He starts to speak, but before he can say anything his phone rings. "Be right back," he says and places a bag on the bed. "I brought you clothes like you asked. Why don't you get ready while I take this?"

I dress quickly while he's out of the room, and immediately feel more grounded once I'm back in my own clothes. After a moment's hesitation, I decide to forgo my tie—the thought of anything around my neck right now is not a pleasant one. I fish the broken pendants out of the cabinet. Myles' ring is a little scratched, but I can polish it up. The hematite looks unscathed, but when I pick it up it crumbles into sparkling dust.

That can't be good.

With no other choice, I place the remains of the supposed protection charm—it didn't exactly do its job last night, into the trash, and slide the ring into the photo compartment in my wallet.

Novik's smile is tight when he returns a few moments later. "Come on, Jay. I thought you wanted to get home?"

I frown. "I just need to get my boots on. What's the rush?"

He scrubs his hand over his face and has another attempt at a smile. "Nothing. Just wanna get out of here is all."

I put my puzzlement at his change in demeanor to one side, pull my boots on, and follow him from the room.

§

The drive back to the hotel is quiet. I'm too deep in thought, and I don't want to voice what I'm thinking about. Is that really all this has been? Some sort of drug-induced waking nightmare? I look down at my hands. I touched that monster's flesh for real. I know I did, but that thing can't exist. So, who was I fighting? Mads is obviously real, and he didn't appear as some sort of grotesque in my hallucination. Maybe the killers are wearing some sort of costume or armor?

"I just don't get it. It was like a barrier," I say, finally giving a voice to what's on my mind. I mime pushing my hands through it. "Everything on one side was misty and the other was clear. It felt like honey or syrup or something."

"It's most likely part of the hallucination," Novik says offhandedly.

"I guess," I concede.

As we pull up in front of the hotel, Novik asks, "Do you want me to stay with you?"

"Nah, man, I'm going to sleep this off. I'll be right as rain in a few hours," I say in what I hope is a warm tone.

He smiles but it doesn't quite reach his eyes. "Glad to hear it, Jay."

I frown. "What's with calling me Jay all of a sudden."

"I always call you Jay."

"No, you've only called me Jay a handful of times and never since…" I trail off unable to finish.

Novik shrugs. "Well it was always what he called you, and it kinda stuck I suppose. I just prefer using it sometimes. Does it bother you?"

"No, not really." I say after a moment pondering. "I'm just not used to hearing it nowadays."

"Then I'll stop using it," he says with another forced smile. "Gimme your keys and I'll drive your car back from the station when I finish. We can grab a bite, and I'll fill you in on everything you're missing now that you're banned from the precinct."

"Sounds good, man." I toss him my keys. "Careful with her, the steering's been a little sensitive."

"You got it, Jer."

The dizziness has all but gone, and I walk confidently into the hotel lobby. I hide out of sight from Novik, and, once he is gone, I head back out to get the first subway into midtown.

§

No one stops me as I make my way through The Michelangelo's lobby and up to the room Calhoun is hiding in. I've forgot my disguise, it's still in my car at the station, but there's nothing I can do about that now that except pull my hat down low and hope no one recognizes me.

Calhoun pulls me into a warm hug as soon as he answers the door. "I was so worried about you. I sent the texts every hour, just like you said, but you didn't reply."

"I know," I say softly. "I'm sorry. I was out cold for a while."

He rests his forehead against mine. His warmth is comforting. "What happened to you? I know you explained some of it in your message, but tell me the rest."

"I ran into our murderer."

"You what?" Calhoun takes a step back and looks me over.

"Don't worry, I'm fine." I say in what I hope is a reassuring tone. "And we saved one of the victims."

"That's…" he trails off, his face is a mess of emotions. "How?"

"I just got in there and grabbed him." I start to tremble as I relive that night. "Someone else was fighting him too

Calhoun sits down heavily on the bed and hugs himself. "What did they look like?"

"I don't know. I didn't get a good look." I sit down next to him. "The doctor said I had some kind of hallucinogen in my system. Everything was all twisted up in my head. That's what I rushed over here for. I had to tell you! There's no magic or anything else. It's all this drug they put in the air."

Calhoun shakes his head and rubs his face wearily. “No. Don't let them trick you like this. Yes, they have a mist, but it's not for what you think. What you saw is real.”

“How would you know? You weren't—” I glance at his shirt. There’s a wet spot at his side. “What's wrong with you?”

He covers it with his hand. “Oh, that. It's nothing.”

“Don't lie.” I try to touch his side but he moves out of reach. “You're hurt, aren't you?”

He refuses to answer. I grab his hand before he can shift out of my grasp. His palm is stained with blood. “Shit! You're bleeding. What happened to you?”

Calhoun smiles nervously. “You remember when I mentioned working undercover?”

“Yeah?”

We are interrupted by a sharp knock at the door. I motion for Calhoun to be quiet and creep over to look through the spy hole. McCray and Jameson are on the other side.

“How the hell did they find you?” I wonder half to myself.

There's another knock, louder this time. “Police! Open up!”

Calhoun sighs. “Just answer, Jerry. I'm not hiding from them, am I?”

I open the door. Both McCray and Jameson give me a look then turn their attention to Calhoun.

“Lachlan Calhoun,” McCray says. “You're under arrest for the attempted murder of Alexander Newlin.”

“What? When was Newlin attacked?” I blurt out.

They both ignore me as McCray reads Calhoun his rights and Jameson cuffs him. Calhoun stares at me with wide, fear-filled eyes.

“I didn't do anything,” he protests. “I haven't seen Alex in years.”

“Tell it to the judge,” McCray says through gritted teeth. They spare me no more than a glance as they lead Calhoun out.

"Jerry, you have to believe me," Calhoun yells. "I didn't do anything! I'd never hurt Alex."

I follow them along the hallway. "Don't say anything, Lachlan. Not without a lawyer. I'm going to get to the bottom of this."

McCray pushes me back. "I would suggest you keep your nose well out of this unless you want to join him in the cells. You're on thin ice as it is."

"I've done nothing!" I say sharply.

"Let's keep it that way." He follows Jameson and Calhoun into the elevator. The doors close before I can jump in with them.

I take the stairs as fast as I can, jarring my busted rib and bruised knees. I hit the foyer just after the elevator opens and run straight in Novik. He wraps his arms around me like a straight-jacket and doesn't let go until Calhoun, Jameson, and McCray are gone.

I break out of Novik's hold and point my finger accusingly in his face. "You knew about this, didn't you? You let them follow me?"

"I did, yeah," he admits. At least he has the good grace to look guilty about it.

I shove him hard. "You're supposed to be my friend! Why didn't you tell me?"

"Because you would've protected him," Novik says.

"Of course I would have!" I give him another shove to keep him back from me. "I'm trying to keep him out of the hands of people who want to kill him, and you let them follow me right to him!"

"We got a positive ID," Novik hisses. He glances at the people in the foyer. "Can we go somewhere private and talk?"

"You can take me to the station, now." I demand. "I wanna see Lachlan."

Novik folds his arms over his wide chest. "That's not going to happen, man."

I start pacing around like a caged animal. "Why? He's *my* client. I should get to talk to him and get answers for myself!"

"Oh, I'm sorry," Novik sneers. "I didn't realize you were a lawyer now."

"Fuck you!" I growl. "Let me talk to him!"

"He's not talking to someone who's been taking evidence and fucking around on that website."

"What evidence?"

"That printout Rexus gave us." He steps closer to me. "Did you think no one noticed it was gone, or that Harris didn't see you take it out your pocket in that interview?" He gives me a disparaging shake of his head. "You don't think he's innocent either or he wouldn't be in hiding."

I recover from my shock from that revelation quickly. "There are all sorts of people in that group, and that includes cops. I had to do what I thought was right, and that meant keeping him away from those that could hurt him."

Novik rolls his eyes. "All I know is when they interviewed Newlin he told them it was Calhoun."

I stare down at the pale marble floor and scrape my hair back from my face while I compose myself. That can't be true. "Did you actually hear him say that?"

"No, I didn't interview him."

"Then someone is setting Calhoun up, like I said. Who interviewed him?" I ask.

"I wouldn't tell you even if I knew. You'll try to talk to them and get yourself in even more trouble."

"Why the fuck am I in trouble?"

Novik sighs angrily. "Take the fucking blindfold off, Jer, and look at what's going on. You've been working with Calhoun, and you've spoken to both guys who've been attacked. We have you at a murder scene and an attempted murder without explanation and, you're actively trying to turn our attention away from Calhoun. You're real lucky you haven't been arrested too."

A bitter laugh bursts from my throat. "When did you start to think so little of me?"

"You don't get to have the moral high ground here," Novik snaps. "I was there in Boston, trying to cover your ass when you beat a suspect half to death. Jameson is the only reason you didn't murder that guy. Now here we are again with me running around trying to cover your tracks while you hide evidence and do whatever you damn well please."

"I'm trying to solve this case!"

"So are we," Novik say. His face flushes red with rage. "We have a positive ID. We have a possible weapon. There's enough to pull Calhoun in, more than enough. Do yourself a favor and let justice run its course."

"And I suppose you'll call it justice when one of your fellow officers dismembers Calhoun in his cell."

Novik rolls his eyes. "Maybe you should go back to your shrink, Jay."

"Don't call me Jay!" I say through gritted teeth. "You saw all the stuff on that website. You've already identified a doctor and a cop from another precinct as being part of it. Why can't you see what's going on here?"

"Because it's bullshit." His voice drops into a dangerous growl. "I've worked with these people every day for weeks. Closely, too. I would know if one of them was up to something."

"This person is probably used to hiding themselves. Check out Robertson, please." I squeeze his shoulder. I know he doesn't believe a word I've said, but I have to try to make him understand and maybe physical contact is the way to do that. "He's been undercover for ages. He has a good poker face. Rodowski used to work in Cyber. She could be doing all sorts of stuff on that site, and we would know nothing. Even McCray could be part of it. He moved after our case in Boston. He could—"

"Just shut up!" Novik roars. Several people in the lobby turn our way. "You know, you're starting to sound like Myles did, and if you keep going down this route and getting yourself mixed up in dangerous stuff, you are gonna end up the same way he did."

"This is not the same!" I insist. "I'm not talking about demons or any other shit."

"You're still making up theories without any evidence."

"Someone on that site knew who I was! That's proof that—"

Novik grabs me by the shoulders and forces me to look in his eyes. "Jerry, I am warning you. Back the hell off!" I fall silent but glare at him until he rolls his eyes. "We are gonna interview Calhoun. Newlin was attacked last night, hopefully Calhoun has an alibi. We'll see if his fingerprints and DNA are a match to the scene too. If they aren't, then we'll let him go. We're not treating him any different from anyone else."

I say nothing, just stare. Novik groans angrily then leaves without another word.

I step out onto the busy sidewalk and look around. All the parked cars look empty, and there's no one I recognize on the sidewalk. Satisfied that there's a slim chance I'll be tailed I hail a cab.

The body shop is a hive of activity when I arrive. A bunch of bikes line the street out front with more visible through the gate into the back lot. Oh, this can't be good.

The man mountain I spoke to on my first visit appears at the door before I can ring the bell.

"Wha' d'ya want?" he grumbles.

I hold his gaze. "I'm looking for Alex."

"He's not here, and the shop's closed for a private meeting. Come back another day."

"Wait!" I yell when he moves to close the door. "I need to speak to him. It's important."

The man rolls his eyes. "Are your ears painted on? I said he's not here." He rests his huge hand in the frame as he talks. He's missing a finger. "See ya."

"Wait, Yeti!"

Yeti glares. "How d'ya know who I am?"

"I'm a friend of Newlin's, that's how I know. If he's not here then can I speak to you. It's important."

Yeti rolls his gray eyes and sighs. "Come around back."

I head around to the gate where he's waiting. "If you're another cop buddy of his, then I'd keep that to yourself."

"Another…" I shut up quickly as we enter the yard. It's wall-to-wall bikers in here.

Yeti waves to one of the others, an equally tall guy with long blond hair. "Keep them occupied, but don't let them drink too much. I'll be done in a sec."

The blond guy rolls his eyes. "Might as well ask me to stop the tide."

Yeti leads me to Newlin's office and locks the door behind us. My skin prickles. He takes up a hell of a lot of space in the tiny room.

"So, you're a friend of Alex's, huh?" he asks and rests his hands on his large hips. "Then how come you don't know he's in the hospital."

"Hospital? I didn't think it was that bad?"

"That's the kinda thing a friend would know."

'Look, I don't have time for these fucking games!" I snap and cross my arms defensively over my chest. "I need to know who Newlin spoke to from the NYPD today."

"What're you talking about?"

"He spoke to the cops after he was attacked last night."

Yeti's laugh is deep and rumbling. "Alex doesn't talk to the cops. What kinda friend are you if you don't know that?" He makes grab for me, but I dance out of the way. "Why the hell are you he—"

His words die away to a yelp as I wrench his hand away from me. "Keep your damn hands off me. What do you mean Newlin doesn't talk to cops?"

"Just what I said. Look, who the fuck are you?"

"My name's Jerry. You can call Newlin if you want. Ask him if he knows me, and while you're at it, you can ask him if he reported his assault to the cops."

Yeti grabs the receiver from the desk phone then hesitates. Obviously, my invite to call Newlin is enough to convince him of my credentials.

"He's in the hospital still," Yeti says, his voice softer than before. "He's not too bad, got a few cuts and bruises. He'll probably be out in a day or two."

That news relaxes me more than I thought it would. "Good. Now, did he, at any point, speak to the cops?"

"Not that I know. Unless the docs called it in. I picked him up last night and took him to the ER. Stayed with him until I knew what was what, and he sent me home."

"Okay, when did you come back?"

Yeti shrugs his huge shoulders. "I dunno. About four am, maybe five."

"And you've not seen him since then?"

"What's with all the questions? I already told you what you wanted."

I nod. "You're right, you did. Sorry. Thanks for your time, man."

Yeti moves quickly for his bulk and gets in between me and the door. "Where do you think you're going?"

I fight hard to stay in one place, stand my ground. "Out. Unless you have some reason for keeping me here?"

Yeti tries for a few more seconds to intimidate me, but I stare him down until he steps aside. My heart is in my throat on my way through the lot. One word from him and I'll never leave here, not under my own steam at least. The eyes of the other bikers follow me. Words are whispered, but I slip out of the gate without incident. I immediately call Novik.

"Newlin didn't call the cops."

"Huh?"

"The positive ID, the arrest?" I say exasperated. "It's all bullshit. Newlin never spoke to anyone. The neighbors didn't call."

"Jer…"

"No listen. It's a set up! They—"

I drop and roll as a loud gunshot rings out from the road. A parked car nearby is poor cover, but it's better than being in the open. I press my back to the wheel and cover my head with my arms as glass and shards of metal spill from the car.

The gate to Newlin and Son's rolls back, and a few bikes roar past in pursuit of the gunmen. The blond guy Yeti had spoken to runs over to me.

"You okay?"

I nod, stand up, and brush the splinters of metal from me like it's no big deal. "Yeah. I didn't hear any screams, so I guess no one else got caught up in that."

Blondie strides out into the road and looks in the direction the bikes went. "They don't look like any of our guys. I can't see any patches at all."

I join him on the asphalt. "Is something going on?"

"Fucked if I know. There's always some shit going on," he says dismissively. "You sure they didn't get you?"

I can't help but laugh at that. "Yeah, pretty sure I'd be able to feel it if they did."

It sounds like someone is calling my name, very faintly or from real far away. Suddenly, I remember my phone. I pick it up from the sidewalk, where I dropped it, and place it to my ear.

"Jerry!"

"I'm here, man, calm down."

"Calm down? That was gunfire! Where the hell are you?"

"I'm fine, don't panic. But I'm thinking I must be getting a little close to our little online vigilantes."

"I told you to leave it alone!"

"Would you?" I retort. The silence is the only answer I need. "Can you to do me a favor. Will you meet me at a place I'm going to text you? Don't tell anyone about it. If you can't get away, can you send Harris? I need whoever is coming to bring me photographs of everyone on your team."

"Ah, come on, Jer." Novik whines. "You're really flogging the shit outta this dead horse now."

"Just let me do this last thing, please. If it comes to nothing, I'll drop that angle. You owe me one for that shrink jibe earlier."

Novik sighs loudly. "Fine. Text me the directions, and one of us will meet you there."

"And you'll tell no one?"

"Yup."

"Good."

I hang up. The blond biker gives me a strange look, but, before he can ask anything, I cut in with a question of my own. "What's your name?"

He frowns, puzzled. "It's Trey."

"Jerry." I offer him my hand and he shakes it. "You wouldn't happen to know where Newlin is, would you?"

Confusion reigns supreme on his face. "New— Oh, Alex. Yeah, I do. Why?"

"Can you please take me to him, and bring a few of your trusted buddies along too? I think it's a good idea to give Alex a little protection in light of this."

He glares at me. "You think we haven't already? Someone attacked him! In his own home! That shit doesn't fly."

"Glad to see we're on the same page there." I say with a grin. "Now, can you take me to him? I'm trying to find out who did this."

There's a split second of hesitation from the Trey. He quickly looks me over—taking my measure, I suspect—then nods

14

In the Flesh

Trey stays with me as I wait for Novik to show up. After a harrowing ride through Manhattan on the back of Trey's bike, I am grateful for a few minutes of silence and use them to refine my hastily put together plan. It's a hell of a long shot, hinging on a ton of variables, but, short of waiting for anything to pop up from Cyber's investigation, it's my only option.

Novik shows up and quickly hands over a folder to me. Trey silently watches us both out of the corner of his eye. Novik glances over at him too.

"What are you up to?" he whispers.

"Newlin is a biker leader. Why are you surprised to see other bikers protecting him?"

"Be careful," he says. "You don't want to get mixed up in all that."

"I'm not. I'm just trying to get answers." I look through the folder then close it again. "Thanks. You can hang out here. I'll be out in just a bit."

"Don't you want me to come with you?" He almost looks hurt that I'm not taking him along.

"Newlin doesn't talk to cops," I say. I have to admit, I'm feeling pretty damn good about the fact Newlin has decided to trust and talk to me when I am basically a cop without a badge. I nod to Trey, and we make our way into the unit.

Trey wasn't kidding when he said they were guarding Newlin. Two well-muscled bikers stand either side of the room door, their bulging arms crossed over equally t-shirt straining chests. A few more loiter in the hallway between Newlin's room and the main door to the unit. They nod to Trey as we pass.

Newlin looks up from the book he is reading. His smile quickly turns sour as I step in beside Trey. "What the hell are you doing here?" he asks.

"I need to talk to you."

Newlin shakes his head. "Talking to you is what got me knee deep in this shit." He glances at Trey. "Get him outta here, man."

"Sure thing, boss," Trey says. He lays his hand on my shoulder.

I shrug him off and move closer to Newlin. "They're saying Lachlan did this." I point at the bandages swathing his chest. "Did he?"

"Who's saying that?" Newlin growls.

I look over my shoulder at Trey. Newlin must get what I'm thinking because he asks Trey to leave.

Trey frowns. "But boss, you ju—"

"Jerry's cool," Newlin says, cutting him off. "He ain't gonna do nothing."

Trey reluctantly leaves. I pull a chair over and sit close to the bed. "I don't know exactly who said it, but the cops I'm friends with just arrested him."

"Are you fucking serious?" Newlin says through gritted teeth.

I nod. "But we're gonna fix this." I show him the folder in my hand before opening it up. "I need your help." I spread the pictures out on the bed. "Do you recognize any of these guys from any other biker gangs?"

Newlin looks at the photos. "No, but I do know this guy." He picks up McCray's photo. "He's a cop. He's been around the shop a few times, when shits been going down and we get the blame, like usual."

My heart sinks. "You don't recognize anyone else?"

"You obviously came in here with your mind already made up, so who do you think I should recognize?"

I sigh. "Never mind, thanks." I put the photos back. "So, how are you doing?"

"Oh, I'm great. Never better," he says sarcastically. "That's why they're keeping me in here."

"Stupid question, huh?"

"Ya think?"

I smile a little at that. "Okay, so what's the damage?"

Newlin traces a line across his bandaged abdomen. "They tried to open me up like they did to Duclos, but I got outta the way. Cut's still pretty bad, but I'm all sewn up now. Everything else is pretty much cat scratches."

"Did you get a good look at them?"

"Nah, they had their face covered. They were shorter than me." He frowns as he thinks. "They had some sort of armor on."

"But you're sure it wasn't Lachlan?"

"Course I am! Lachlan knows how to fight. If he had wanted me dead, I would've been."

Well, that's a load off my mind. "Could it have been someone from a rival gang?"

"Sneaking into someone's home in the middle of the night and trying to stab them in their bed ain't exactly our style."

"What about a drive by shooting? That their style?"

Newlin narrows his eyes. "When did this happen?"

"Just before I came here. I went to your body-shop to talk to you, and some guys on bikes tried to shoot me on the way out."

Newlin sits up a little straighter and looks me over. "Shit. I take it they didn't get you."

"You think I'd be sitting here talking to you if they did?"

"Fair point." He says, and scratches at the side if his mouth. "Do you remember the make of the bike or see a patch?"

"Nope. I didn't get a good enough look at them."

Newlin sighs. "This is to do with those letters, right? That's the only connection all three of us have."

"And Lachlan. But you're right. Someone is trying to stop us from getting to the truth." I lean back in the chair and think for a minute. There's got to be some way of finding out who's doing this. It has to be a cop who knows just as much about the connections between Newlin, Duclos, and Calhoun, as I do. Maybe someone who was in the Wolves at one point and splintered off when Duclos did, or someone who at least met him or other members enough to know what was going on in the gang. A trusted friend. I already have someone in mind, but I need proof.

"Do you have photos of past members and stuff like that?" I ask.

Newlin gives me a puzzled frown. "Yeah. There's some up in the clubhouse and in a few photo albums in my office. Yeti has the keys. Tell him I said you could look around, and if he has any problem with that then he can call me."

"Thanks, man, I appreci—"

"Don't go thinking something into it that isn't there," he cuts in. "I want these guys caught, and you got a head start on that, so I gotta help."

A smirk pulls at the sides of my mouth. "No, I get it. You don't talk to cops."

"But you're not a cop," Newlin says. He gives me a wink and smiles.

I chuckle. "Well you seem to be feeling okay anyway."

"Take a lot more than a few scratches to finish me off."

"Glad to hear it." I stand. "I'll let you know what happens."

Newlin catches my hand as I turn to leave. "I'll give you my number. If you need me or my brothers help with any of this, then call. Don't let anything happen to him."

I give his fingers a quick squeeze. He rattles off his number and I type it into my phone. "Thanks. I'm doing everything I can."

His hazel eyes meet mine, and he forces a smile to his lips, but he's not fooling me. There a tightness to his jaw, and his hands grip the blankets just enough to betray the fact he's on edge. I nod to him as a farewell, unable to promise that things will be okay when I'm not sure of that myself, and return to the waiting room.

Novik holds up his hand, asking for silence, as I approach. He is pacing the room as he talks on his phone. I sit down and wait for him to finish. I'm getting no clues at all by listening to his side of the conversation.

Finally, he hangs up. "Guess what," he says, the glee plain in his voice. "Some agency just emailed us a whole load of stuff from the inner circle on *The Last Defense*."

I wonder if Rodowski is behind this little info dump. "Awesome. So, Lachlan is off the hook?"

"Well, no, they didn't men—"

"Then why the hell are you wasting my time with that information?" I grumble and push my way past him.

“This is a breakthrough, Jerry. Okay, it doesn’t immediately free your boyfriend, bu—”

I round on him. “What the fuck did you just say?”

Novik stops dead in his tracks. “It was a joke. You know, cos you've been so close to Calhoun, and now you're working so hard to get him off the hook.”

“Funny, some people would call that normal police work.”

Novik rolls his eyes. “It was just a joke.”

“That you wouldn't throw out at any straight guy working so hard on a case.”

“When have I ever had a problem with you being bi, Jer?” Novik snaps. “It was a fucking joke, maybe it was in bad taste bu—”

“You basically called my professionalism into question.”

Novik sighs. “Forget I said anything. Did Newlin help you?”

“He didn't recognize anyone, no, but he hasn't spoken to any cops. Who put the report in?”

“I don't know.”

“If the neighbors called it in, it had to hit dispatch before it went to uniforms or detectives. You need to find out who's name is on that report.”

“And what are you gonna do?”

“I've got some investigating of my own to do,” I say. And that’s all the information I give him.

§

Yeti is a little more accommodating on my return to the body shop, but he still watches my every move. At least I have someone to bounce questions off of.

There are a few group photographs on the wall. I recognize Newlin and Duclos straight away, even in their younger years. Yeti, too, is easy to spot. Calhoun is in a few, and I focus my attention on these. The face I am sure will pop up sooner or later will be in those photographs.

Maybe that's my problem. I *know* who I want to turn up, and I'm dismissing any other likely faces out of hand.

When the wall photos prove fruitless, I look through the albums. Yeti reclines back in Newlin's chair, eliciting a high-pitched squeal from its strained wood. I grit my teeth against the sound and flick through the photos.

After about fifteen minutes of searching, my phone buzzes. It's Novik.

You need to see this. Can you come into the station? his text reads.

I sigh. It feels like I haven't had a moment's peace to get my own work done in days.

"Do you mind if I take some of these?" I ask Yeti and hold up a photograph to indicate what I mean.

He shrugs. "If the boss says it's okay, then it's okay."

I carefully slip the most promising pictures out of the book and stow them in my back pocket. I thank Yeti, who just shrugs, and leave.

I look through the photos while the cab makes its way through the streets. Most of the ones I snagged are from what looked like meetings with other Wolves chapters. The majority were taken at night, and it's a struggle to pick out individual faces, but I'm drawn to them over and over again. There's an answer in them somewhere. Out of desperation I use my phone camera to zoom in. The facial features blur and most of the background people fuzz together, but there's definitely someone in these photos who's pulling my attention.

I glance out of the window to rest my eyes. We're in an industrial-looking area, filled with packing plants and warehouses. "Hey, where are we?" I ask the cab driver.

Silence. He doesn't even spare me a glance. Fearing the worst, I send a quick text to Harris and Novik asking for back up, and give them a basic description of the area I'm in. This isn't going to end well, but hopefully they can use my phone to trace where I am.

Looks like I have two choices. I can jump from a cab going roughly forty miles an hour and hope I hit the ground running, or I can wait it out and see if my back up call nets us some more of these *Last Defense* scum bags. I'd need to run a long way to get help, so I guess that's my mind made up.

The cab driver turns into a narrow alley then maneuvers the car with practiced precision through a loading bay door. I quickly glance at my phone, making sure the GPS is on, then push it as far down inside my pocket as I can get it. It's not going to be hidden from a search there, but at least it's not in plain sight.

The cab driver stops and kills the engine. The inside of the warehouse is dark with only a few slivers of light creeping in around the shutters. I can barely see the cabbie as he opens the door and hauls me out. I give him a hard time then use his momentum to propel us both forward and knock him to the floor under me. He lets out a grunt as he hits the ground hard, but not hard enough to stop him from swinging a fist my way. I block and drive my knuckles into his nose. Blood spurts over his face. His cry echoes off the concrete walls, and blocks out all other sounds. I never hear the footsteps of the person creeping up behind me before they knock me out cold.

§

Whispering voices tickle my ears when I wake up. My head swims unpleasantly as I open my eyes. The stinging light from the one bare bulb in the little room doesn't help either, so I resolve to keep them closed and concentrate on who's talking.

"Well, I'm not doing it."

"Neither am I! This wasn't part of the deal."

"What deal? We agreed we wanted to kill these things."

"Then you do it! I never signed up to hurt humans!"

The voices—both male, New York accents—continue to argue in harsh whispers. They sound young, early twenties maybe. That coupled with the fact they are obviously reluctant to do me harm may stand in my favor.

I sit up, making sure I make enough noise to alert my captors without them being scared into doing something stupid.

"Told you we should have tied him up!"

"I thought we'd have more time."

I rub the back of my head. It's tender, but there's no bump and, more importantly, no blood. The headache has pretty much gone too. The rest of me seems unharmed, undisturbed. My phone and wallet are still in my pockets. Boy, I really am dealing with the amateur division of this group.

"Who's there? Who are you?" I call out. I want to end this; there's no point in dragging it out.

After a whispered, heated debate, one of the men moves forward. He's an awkwardly skinny kid with greasy black hair and a patchy beard covering his chin. He carries a baseball bat and drags the tip along the ground like that is somehow threatening.

"No, who are you?" he growls and points at my face with the bat.

I angrily push it away. The kid panics, and the bat falls to the ground with a *thunk*. We both lunge for it at the same time, but my hand lands on it first. I tap the kid's leg with it—hard enough for a warning and a bruise, then stand up.

"I'll ask again, who are you?"

He glares up at me, his chocolate brown eyes filled with anger. His lip draws up in a snarl as he speaks. "You're a traitor to the human race. You deserve to die!"

"Says who?"

The other kids take this opportunity to run at me. I swing the bat as hard as I can, knowing I'll miss him, but I only want to give him a good scare. This guy has more balls. He swerves out of the way then tries to get inside my guard. I push his arm away and slap him hard across the face. I have no interest in actually hurting these guys if I don't have to, but I'm not above giving them a little bit of humiliation to teach them a lesson. The second kid stumbles to sit next to his friend on the floor and rubs his cheek.

"I don't wanna hurt you guys, and you aren't going to hurt me," I say as I pace in front of them. I smack the baseball bat off the palm of my hand a few times as I talk. "So why don't you just tell me who you are, let me go, and we can forget this whole sorry business ever happened."

They look at each other, and the black-haired one sighs dramatically. "I told you I didn't want mixed up in this shit, Mikey."

Mikey glares at his friend. "Do you wanna save the world or not, Will?"

I laugh. "Save the world? From who? These imaginary things your bosses keep going on about?"

"Who are you gonna believe?" Mikey shouts at his friend. "Us, or this guy?"

Will seems to consider this for a second then gets to his feet. "Gimme the bat?"

I hold it like I am ready to hit a home run. "That's not gonna happen."

He tries to make a grab for me, but I slip out of the way and punch him, back handed, in the thigh. He yelps and grabs his leg.

"Come on, guys," I say wearily. "Do you really wanna do this? Just let me go, and we can forget this whole thing."

Mikey jumps to his feet and runs at me. I feint left then swing right just in time to miss the blade he aims at my chest. Oh, so that's how they want to play? Fuck going on easy on these guys.

Mikey goes for me again, the knife held high as he screams his lungs out. I swing low, catching him across the lower part of his rib cage with the bat, and knock him flat to the ground. Will lands on my back and latches around my neck with both hands. My elbow connects with his ribs a few times, but I can't shake him off. I throw myself backwards, crushing him under me but winding myself in the process. I roll away as quick as I can and grab the bat, ready to swing.

It turns to splinters in my hands.

The shock of the unexpected gunshot from behind me makes all three of us jump. Mikey and his friend stare over my shoulder. Slowly, I look back too.

The person walking towards us is dressed in bike leathers and a helmet. The recently fired gun rests in their hand. "I thought I told you to finish him!" The voice is male, but it's been distorted—artificially deepened and echoed.

"We… we were gonna, Nomad," says Mikey, "but he woke up faster than we thought."

"You gave him time to wake up?!" Nomad shouts. He steps close to me, but all I can see are my own eyes reflected in his visor. "You should've beat him when he was out."

"Yeah, striking from behind and beating a guy when he's out cold is the hero's way," I say dryly.

Nomad laughs. "This fucking guy." He shoves me, and it's almost playful. "You're a funny guy, huh?" His fist slams into my face hard enough that I spin and hit the deck. Blood fills my mouth. I quickly check my teeth with my tongue. Nothing missing. Good.

"That scum," Nomad says, pointing at me, "is the reason we haven't finished off our main target yet. He's always protecting it, always making excuses and hiding it."

"But I thought you said it was—" Mikey begins, but Nomad raises his hand in a command for silence.

"We tried to warn you," Nomad says softly as he squats next to where I'm sprawled. "We gave you so much evidence, so many chances to escape its clutches, and you took none of them." His gloved hand brushes through my hair. I grab his wrist and violently twist his hand until I hear it crack. Nomad howls, pulls away from me, then boots me in the stomach. I curl up tightly on myself and bite my tongue to keep my whine at bay.

"You see!" Nomad shouts at his followers. "This man, this thing that was a man, has chosen a monster over us. We gave him every chance to shake off its shackles, and he chose it! He is no better than it! He doesn't deserve to live."

Nomad nudges my shoulder with his foot, rolling me flat onto my back. He stands over me, gun pointed squarely at my forehead. "Say goodnight, Raven,"

I slam my fist in from the side, catching Nomad's hands just in time. The gun flies from his grip. My second blow hits Nomad squarely in the nuts. He shrieks and falls to the ground at my side.

Blood trickles from my cut lip as I stand. The two kids, having finally grown some sense, keep well out of our way. I kick the gun away from Nomads reach. He lunges, catches me around my waist and forces me to the ground. Stars dance in front of my eyes from the impact. He tries to pin me down, but I throw my weight at his shoulder and roll us over. I straddle his chest. He tries to push me off, but my knees are firmly planted either side of him. I draw them in a little, and squeeze his ribs until he lets out a groan.

"Let's see who you are, buddy," I growl, and reach for his helmet.

"Freeze!"

The building suddenly fills with flashlights and the sound of barking dogs. In the confusion, Nomad throws me off. I grip his helmet, tearing it from him as he slips away. In the beams of the flashlights I can't get a good enough look at him to confirm my suspicions, but I've seen enough to throw my weight behind them.

I kneel on the floor and mesh my hands behind my head. Cops stream by me. Some follow Nomad, and others arrest Mikey and Will, both of whom are now professing their innocence.

A hand lands on my shoulder, and I wait for the cuffs to be slapped on me. Instead I am hauled to my feet and wrapped in a huge bear hug.

"You stupid fuck," Novik whispers into my ear. "You never fucking listen!"

"I wasn't looking for trouble," I say. "I got a text from you saying I had to see something back at the station, and the cab I got into brought me here."

"But I never texted you?" Novik says.

I swipe his hand away when he tries to inspect my face. "I know that, but someone must've used your phone. He busted my lip, that's all." I add when he won't stop staring at my injuries.

"Good."

"He got away," Jameson says as he joins our group. "We sent the dogs after him, but he must've slipped out."

"That's okay. I think I know who he is." I pass the bike helmet onto Jameson. "Plus, we can test this. Bound to be hair and stuff in there."

Jameson looks it over. "Awesome. We'll get it tested as soon as we get back." He pats my shoulder then gives it a friendly squeeze.

"Do you wanna give us a statement at your place or come down to the station? We'll get you check—"

"I'll come with you guys," I say, jumping in before he can finish. "And I'd like to see Lachlan too."

Jameson and Novik exchange a glance, but neither refuses my request.

§

By the time I get to the holding cells I'm exhausted. I've been running on adrenaline all day—from Lachlan's arrest to the fight with Nomad. I'm too jangly to sleep when I have a spare moment in between getting cleaned up and making a statement. I have too many things I want to remember, important details that Jameson and Novik need to know.

I spill my guts to them and tell them every little thing I can remember or have thought about in relation to who Nomad is. I show them the pictures I took from Newlin's albums, circle the face that may hold the answer, and urge them to test the helmet as soon as possible. To my surprise neither dismisses what I have found out or tries to make excuses for it. I wonder if they already had an inkling that Nomad was one of us.

We hatch a plan in secret, just the three of us. Casting the net any wider is just asking for our target to find out. I'm not too happy with the plan—it puts Calhoun right in their hands, albeit under our watchful eyes—but if it means we can get enough evidence to take these guys down once and for all then it's worth it.

And now to face Calhoun without revealing our plan. He can't know anything. He has to be as natural as possible so we don't tip them off.

Novik accompanies me to the cell door and waits as the guard unlocks it. "You can't stay too long," he reminds me. "He is officially under arrest until we can prove otherwise."

I nod then step into the cell.

Calhoun flies into my arms and hugs me tightly. He's shaking. I rub his back in an attempt to soothe him. He looks up as the door bangs shut, and his pale face contorts into a mask of anger. "No! What's going on? I thought—"

"I'm trying," I say. "You'll be out of here soon, I promise." I look quickly around the Spartan cell-it's just a bed and toilet. An uneaten tray of food rests on top of the bare mattress. "You need to eat and keep your strength up,"

"I can't be in here overnight! I need to be there to stop him!"

"Stop who?"

"You know who!" His green eyes are wide, and he continuously clenches his hands. "There could be another attack tonight. I need my phone."

I gently brush his hair back from his face. "You don't have to worry about that. We are slowly closing in on them all."

"No. You don't get it!" He grabs the front of my shirt and shakes me. "It's not the same case. All this shit with these guys has distracted you. Why won't you listen to me?"

"Because the things you're talking about don't exist," I say as calmly as I can. "They can't. It's a gas this gang are using."

Calhoun shoves me away from him. "Open your eyes! You have *seen* things. You've been seeing them your whole life, haven't you?"

"All of this has simple, plausible explanations."

"You're a fool! You don't even know your own nature!" he yells.

"Then speak plainly to me," I say. "Tell me what I don't understand." Calhoun glances towards the cell door. I incline my head in understanding. He doesn't want to be overheard. "Trust me," I whisper. I step closer to him and rub his upper arms. "Just a few hours longer, a day at most."

Calhoun slips his arms around my waist and rests his head on my shoulder. A dry kiss falls against my cheek. "I trust you," he whispers. "But you have to trust me in return."

"I do."

"Then listen to me when I tell you all that stuff isn't hallucinations. You know the truth, you can feel it in you." He lays his hand over my heart. I wonder if he can feel how hard it's beating. "In here, that's where you know. The hallucination might be the more comfortable explanation, but it doesn't sit well with you, and it never will. You know the truth." He pats my chest. "Right here."

Calhoun steps back and looks deep into my eyes before pressing his forehead to mine. "Trust me, please."

His skin is warm, his breath gentle as it drifts over my face. We're so close I could count his eyelashes if I wanted to. My mouth feels dry all of a sudden. My stomach flutters like I'm going down the drop on a roller coaster. Our heads tilt in unison.

The keys rattle in the lock, and we jump apart just in time for the door to swing open.

"Time is up," the guard says. He looks from one of us to the other, maybe making sure Calhoun isn't going to try and make a run for it.

"You'll be out of here before you know it," I whisper. I give his hands a gentle squeeze before leaving the cell.

Novik is waiting for me in the hallway. I nod to him as he falls into step beside me.

"I guess now we just wait it out?" he asks.

"Yup." I say. "After today I doubt they are going to wait too long to try and finish him off."

15

Fly, Raven, Fly

It's the same argument again and again. Myles, as usual, waits until the middle of the night to bring up the case and the fact he thinks he's worked it all out. We talk in the dark for a while, quietly discussing it, but just like every time we've had this chat, Myles eventually switches the light on, grabs his notes and forces me to listen to him reiterate his point of view all over again.

"I get that this is bugging you," I say and try to keep my voice soft, placating. "But we need to get some sleep when we can—this case is eating up all our time."

"But I know what the killer is!" he yells. "I've been studying it closely. Come on, Jay, you *know* I'm making sense."

I flop over onto my back and sigh loudly. "In that case it'll still make sense in the morning. Can we *please* leave it until then?"

Myles lightly slaps my shoulder with his notebook. "This won't wait. There's something big coming. I can feel it." He flips through his notebook and points at a page full of scribbles and doodles. "The end game is coming. We need to kill this thing before then"

"This thing?" I shake my head and laugh. "This thing is just another sicko who's good at covering his tracks."

Myles huffs air through his nose. I can feel his frustration building; it's plain in his white knuckles as he crushes his notebook in his hands. He throws back the blankets, gets out of bed, and starts getting dressed.

"So now you're running out on me?" I say. "Come back to bed, babe. You'll feel better once you've slept."

"Don't fucking 'babe' *me*," he hisses. His freckled cheeks flush red and he shoves his glasses further up his nose. "Your goddamn pig-headedness is gonna get someone else killed, do you hear me?! There'll be blood on your fucking hands."

I keep as calm as I can, and refuse to get into another, blistering, two am argument. "I'm trying my best here! Just like the rest of us." I walk over to him and take his hands. "Babe, this case is driving you nuts. You need to sleep. You've been doing too much."

Myles takes a deep breath. His face smooths out, his anger gone for now. "I *know* what this killer is, and I'm working on finding out how to defeat it. I need your help." He squeezes my hands and gives me his best puppy dog eyes. "Please. Please just do this one thing for me. What's it going to hurt?"

I tilt his head up and gently kiss him. "You need to get some rest. There's no such thing as monsters."

Myles shoves me back from him. "Fuck you!" He storms from the room and I follow him. He grabs his coat and keys. "One day," he growls, "I'm going to be proven right about all this, and you're gonna be eating your fucking words." With his parting shot taken he slams the door behind him on his way out.

This case is going to be the death of our relationship if things carry on this way.

I go back to the bedroom and gather Myles' notebooks and scraps of paper off the bed. I have a little look at them. He could be onto something with all the talk of demons and monsters, but there's nothing. He has a few theories about what we're dealing with, but which one of us doesn't?

The apartment is silent, but despite being awake for close to thirty-six hours, I can't sleep knowing Myles is out there. He'll be down at Eddies or some all-night restaurant, cursing me black and blue over a beer or a slice of pie. I should call him. He's had long enough to calm down.

He doesn't answer any of my calls. After two hours, I've had enough. I get dressed and head out into the night to look for him. It's always better to leave Myles to cool down before trying to talk, but something isn't sitting well with me tonight.

It's quiet out. Pumpkins and decorations litter store fronts, porches, and yards. The air carries the stench of charred gourds, wet leaves, and a hint of snow. Above, the moon is full. I can see clearly all around.

I try Eddie's first but it's locked up for the night. When I call her, she says she hasn't seen him. He's not in any of the bars or diners within walking distance of our apartment either. My worry morphs into anger. I call him again.

I hear a familiar tune on the air, an awful cell phone version of "Run to the Hills" coming from farther down the street. His ring tone for me.

"Myles?" I shout. There's no answer.

With dread slowly coiling around my insides I walk towards the noise. This can't be good. Myles treats his phone like another limb. There's no way he lost it or threw it away.

Myles' cheery greeting invites me to leave a message as his phone goes to voice mail. I quickly hang up then call again. He's right here, around the corner, or his phone is at least. With my heart threatening to beat its way out of my chest I take the final step.

I rush to him. I don't care about the blood. I don't care about the gore. All I care about is the fact my fiancé is lying there, dead. A discarded, broken body on the filthy, back alley concrete.

I scream at him to wake up, but what good will that do? His chest is ripped open and his ribs jut out like jagged teeth. His throat is torn, the spine exposed through shreds of slowly graying flesh. I reach out and the rubbery muscle of his heart indents slightly at my touch. It's cold and still. A few hours ago, it had been hard at work, fueling his anger at me and the flush in his cheeks.

I finally kick myself into action when my own phone starts to ring. It's Novik. Another body has been found—a headless corpse—the final victim. I try to speak or make any sound at all, but my voice comes out in an awful, dry rasp.

Wait, no, this isn't right. Why am I not screaming down the line like I did for real, or in every dream like this since? Where's the creature appearing out of the fog? Myles rising from the dead to finish me off? Why has my nightmare changed?

I hear a croaking behind me. A raven sits in the branches of a tree across the street. It swoops towards me, settles at my feet, and blinks its beady eyes. More join it until I have a small swarm around me. They chatter and squawk amongst themselves, peck at my feet and around Myles' body. I swipe at them. He's not their supper! They fly at me and trap me in a swirling mass of bodies. Slick black feathers cut my skin as they whirl past. I open my mouth to scream but all that comes out is an ugly croak.

You have a second chance to end this.

I search for the source of the voice but can't find any. The soft, male voice sounds almost familiar but I can't lay my finger on why.

You have a second chance to listen, a second chance to end this all forever. Don't repeat the same mistakes.

"Listen to what?" I demand. I swipe the tears from my eyes as if that will let me see through the mass of feathers. "Tell me!"

Not what he seems. Don't be scared.

I look around me, but all I can see are ravens.

Not what he seems, don't be scared. He is the messenger. He has come to sing you his song, but you must listen this time.

Something flashes across my vision. An anonymous street. Fists flying, blood spilling.

Listen to the song. You know every word is true.

Calhoun's thin face, frightened, bloodstained. Hair in a tangled mess of gold and black as he tries to fight off his attackers.

You'll know the truth when you hear it. A beautiful song.

Huge black and gold wings spring from his back and he is suddenly soaring up and away. His thin fingers clutch the handle of the knife buried deep in his stomach.

Angel, Nightingale, Raven. Messengers for gods and emperors. Watch all, see all, listen. Understand.

"Understand what?" I know I've spoken but all I hear is the craw of another raven. My body is morphing, taking another shape. Flames lick along my arms and sooty feathers sprout from my singed skin.

Fly home, Raven. Back to where the clock stopped. To where two kinds of death happened under the full moon. Fly home and seek the truth.

Feathers sprout everywhere—my chest, my legs. A long, sharp beak appears in my line of sight.

Fly, Raven, fly!

My arms, no, my wings move of their own accord. The cloud of ravens around me dissipates and we soar upwards as one. Myles' body, the alley, and eventually the buildings shrink until the whole city is stretched out before me, lit up like a circuit board. The streets are not the wheel and spoke pattern of Boston, though. They are the gridiron streets of New York

The flock surrounds me, and keeps me on the right course as we fly towards the rising sun. It's all so clear now. If only I had realized it before we maybe could have stopped Nomad and his gang ever getting this far. The answer could have been in my closet the whole time, buried with Myles' other things. It's time to dig them up.

The dream ends abruptly and my eyes flutter open. The office is dark save for the glow from Novik's computer screen. The whir of the cooling fan inside it and the ticking of the clock on the wall are the only noises.

I stretch out my arms and back, and rub my stiff neck. Novik's coat slides from me, so I pick it up and drape it over the arm of a chair. I guess I was more tired than I thought.

"Hey, you're awake," Novik says softly.

I nod and try to stifle a yawn. "Any sign of Robertson?"

"Nope, nothing." He nudges a pizza box towards me when I sit beside him, and I take a slice. "It's late, maybe they're going to wait until tomorrow."

"I guess so." I take a bite of pizza. It's cold and a little oily but still good. I pour myself a mug of coffee. The mere smell of it is enough to chase the tendrils of sleep away. The feelings the dream left me with—grief, anger, a little confusion—are taking longer to fade, but going with them is my certainty that I had the answers.

I sit back down and glance at Novik's screen. "What are you doing?"

"Going over those emails we were sent from that hacker," he says without sparing me a glance. "We got a lot here but nothing that ties any of them to these ritualized murders."

I lean in to read over his shoulder. "Are you sure?"

Novik scoots over a little and lets me in at the computer. "Yeah, I'm sure. I've been reading over this stuff whenever I've had a spare moment. A few of us have been."

"They have to be doing them. How else are they sending the letters with all the little changes?"

Novik shrugs. "I'm not saying they're not, but we don't have anything right now pinning them to those kills. All we have is a mention of them in passing. They talk about the Boston case and try to guess when the equivalent murder is going to happen here."

He's right. There's nothing at all in these conversations that sounds like they are planning to murder anyone. "Maybe they were just being careful in case they got caught?"

"I thought you might say that." Novik pulls up another document and gestures to the screen. "Read this."

This conversation lists in detail the plan for Duclos' murder. "Nomad's name is all over this."

"Yup," Novik says. "And they're so open about that and the attack on Newlin. Why not the rest?"

The voice from the dream comes back to me like a whisper. I am listening, and I remember things I saw with my own eyes, but that doesn't make monsters real. I had drugs in my system that could easily account for what I saw. I grab another slice of pizza and eat it to fill the silence while I mull everything over. Novik sits quietly by my side, reading and making notes. He mutters to himself.

"What do you think is going on here?" I ask when being inside my own head is too much. "For real?"

We both glance towards the window into the hallway at the sounds of voices, but neither of the cops we see are the ones we are waiting for. Once they've moved far enough away Novik answers me.

"I don't have any idea," he admits with another shrug of his large shoulders. He taps the computer screen with the end of his pen. "This makes sense though. We're dealing with some sort of terrorist group with enough members in different places that they can do some serious damage. Depending on who their people are, they could do all sorts of shit from murders and covers ups to this gas stuff." He scratches at his chin.

"But?" I say to prompt him.

Novik smiles. "You know, I miss this. Me and you working together."

"Stop being a sap and answer my question," I say but I can't help but grin all the same.

"It's nothing really. I've just be—" He looks sharply towards the window and orders me to get down. I hide under the desk, with my back against the drawers, and wait for Novik's signal.

"Novik?" From the sound of Robertson's voice, he isn't pleased to find someone in the office, least of all Novik. "Working late?"

"Trying to stay one step ahead, as always," Novik replies. He rolls his chair over, shielding me as Robertson takes a seat at his own desk, next to Novik's. I let my breath out slowly, not wanting to make any sound at all to alert him.

"Yeah, I know what you mean." Papers rustle on the desk. A drawer opens. "Well, this is all I came in for," Robertson says. "See you around. Don't work too hard."

Robertson's footsteps grow fainter. The office door opens and closes. Novik remains in front of my hiding space. I hold myself still despite my legs starting to cramp up.

Novik scoots his chair out of the way. "And we're clear."

I crawl out from under the desk. My knee makes a loud popping noise as I stand. "What did Robertson want?"

"Your guess is as good as mine. He took a bag out of his drawer, but I didn't see what was in it," Novik says. He glances towards the door. "Stay here. I'm gonna wander around, make sure they're in the interview room."

"Thanks."

While Novik is away I quickly search Robertson's desk. Most of the drawers are locked, but the ones that are open yield nothing of much use. I didn't expect to find answers here anyway. I hide under Robertson's desk when I hear footsteps. No one comes into the room. I breathe a sigh of relief. Just before I crawl out I spy something stuck into the back corner of the desk. It's a bar code sticker for the furniture, but there's something underneath it—a tell-tale lump betrays it. It's a tiny wad of paper. When I fold it out there's a seven-digit code written on it. I slip it into my wallet for safe keeping and crawl out from under the desk when Novik comes back.

"Hurry," he whispers and beckons me forward with a wave of his hand. "The coast is clear but who knows for how long. Robertson got waylaid by McCray and Harris, and he just got to the interview room."

I fall into step behind him and use his height to shield me from view. There's no one around, just like he said, but the overhead lights are bright, and there's nowhere to hide unless I want to chance my luck diving into a random room or behind a water cooler.

"Do you know what room they've gone to?" I say as I look around.

"Yup." He glances over his shoulder at me. "I waited outside for a bit but only heard normal talking, so I came back to get you."

"Thanks," I reply. "They probably won't try anything right away."

We reach the room without incident. As I open the door Novik gives me a hard shove and swiftly closes it behind him. I angrily grab for the handle then stop. There're voices in the hallway. McCray and Harris. I can't hear what they're talking about, but their voices aren't raised or harsh.

The noise fades as Novik leads them away. Looks like I'm on my own for this one, for now at least. On a shelf under the two-way mirror is a small screen displaying what's going on in the room, and a DVD recorder. I look for the volume button. Good, there's an audio feed too. I make sure there's a disk in the drive, hit record, then wait for Robertson to show his true colors.

Calhoun sits as straight as he can manage with his arms twisted back behind him, no doubt in handcuffs. If he can sense me there, he never once betrays the fact. Robertson and Gordon sit in front of him, their backs to me.

"You will answer my questions," Robertson snaps, and from his exasperated tone, it isn't the first time he has asked.

"I already have," Calhoun says through gritted teeth. His lip looks swollen. A small patch of grazed skin runs parallel to his cheekbone. I clench my fists. They're going to regret laying their hands on him.

Robertson grits his teeth "Not the question I just asked you."

Calhoun glares. "That's because it's stupid. I've never met you."

"Then tell me how you knew." Robertson gets up from the table and walks behind Calhoun. He leans over so he is talking into Calhoun's ear. "How did you know I was an undercover police officer."

"I didn't," Calhoun snaps. "What's the point in all this if you don't want to believe anything I say."

Robertson rests his hand on Calhoun's shoulder and squeezes "If you didn't know then why did you warn the president of the Wolves about me?"

Calhoun's face screws up in confusion as Robertson squeezes his shoulder again. "I never sa—"

The blow is lightning fast. Robertson shakes out his fist as he paces behind Calhoun. "Tell me why you told him!"

Blood drips from Calhoun's nose. He stares almost directly into my eyes even though there's no way he can see me. His rage is plain in his glare and snarl. "I don't have a fucking clue who you are! I didn't give Alex any message."

Robertson's fist slams into the side of Calhoun's face. Gordon doesn't make one single move to try and stop him.

"With that one stupid little warning," Robertson hisses, "you ruined my entire life. This was supposed to be a big break for me! I was gonna be a hero when I brought that gang down."

Son of a bitch! I knew it. Now, come on, Robertson, or should I say, Nomad. Let's hear you brag about your involvement in Rexus' gang.

Calhoun spits blood from his lip onto the floor. "Listen to me, you fucking idiot!" Calhoun growls. "I don't know what you're talking about."

"Are you sure about that?" Robertson says. He grips Calhoun's chin and forces him to look into his eyes. "Are you sure you didn't work your mind magic on people like Chris Duclos? It was him that told you about me. Don't even think about lying because I know it was. He's the only person in that gang I ever met."

Calhoun starts to protest, but Robertson hits him in the stomach. I've seen way more than enough. Leaving the recorder on, I storm from the room and try to open the door. It's locked.

"Robertson!" I roar as I rattle the handle. "Open this fucking door!"

"Jerry!" I hear Calhoun's voice followed by a strangled cry. I pull my gun from its holster and drive my shoulder into the door. It gives way, sending me sprawling into the room. My gun slips from my hand and skids across the floor.

"Well, well, well. Look who's come to the rescue." Robertson laughs.

Gordon hauls me roughly to my feet. "You should have left well enough alone, Jerry," he whispers into my ear as he secures my arms behind my back. "This doesn't concern you."

Calhoun struggles, but Robertson tightens his grip around his neck. I try to slip from Gordon's hold and earn myself a punch to the side of the head. It's a struggle to keep my footing as dizziness sweeps over me.

"Let him go," I demand. "He hasn't done anything."

"Hasn't he?!" Robertson barks. "This shithead ruined my life. He's a manipulative liar. A killer." He presses his forehead to Calhoun's and closes his eyes. "I know how he looks. He's gorgeous, right?" Calhoun squirms as Robertson strokes his hair. "All devils are beautiful. How do you think they lure their victims?"

"The same way you and your sick as fuck friends do, probably," I growl. I wrench my arm out of Gordon's hold and swing my elbow back. I hear a crunch as it connects with Gordon's nose.

Robertson whips a knife from his pocket and presses it to the pulse point in Calhoun's neck. "Take another step, Jerry, and I kill him."

Calhoun is scarily calm. His eyes drift closed as he whispers to himself. My scalp tingles. Robertson shakes him violently and it stops.

"You won't get out of this that way," Robertson says. He buries his nose into Calhoun's hair and sniffs deeply. Calhoun slams his forehead into his face. Robertson howls. I try to pull Calhoun out of Robertson's weakened grasp, but Gordon swings his knee deep into my ribs. I fold over and gasp for breath.

"Make him watch!" Robertson demands.

Gordon grabs a fistful of my hair and wrenches my head back. With his hands cuffed behind his back, Calhoun is powerless to fight Robertson off, but he tries all the same. He drives the heel of his boot into Robertson's shin. Rather than letting go, Robertson tightens his grip around Calhoun's neck.

"Why don't you show us your little trick, then I'll let you go," Robertson says.

"I don't know what you are talking about," Calhoun says. His words are clipped; he can't breathe right.

Robertson cuts him quickly across the cheek. I lunge forward, but Gordon pulls me back. A few strands of my hair tear from my scalp.

"One more move and I kill him. I fucking promise!" Robertson presses the knife point into Calhoun's neck hard enough that a little drop of blood appears on his pale skin. "Come on, now. Don't be an idiot," Robertson whispers to Calhoun. "I saw you do it. The first time you used it to try and escape from us. Do you remember that?" He presses his lips to Calhoun's cheek. "Do you still have that scar?" he says against Calhoun's skin. With his free hand, he traces his blade along the old wound hidden under Calhoun's shirt. "Change!"

"Do it." I don't know what else to say. Maybe if he says he'll change, Robertson will let him go long enough for me to get him away.

Calhoun holds my gaze. His irises flicker between green and gold, and he gives me a sad smile. There're fangs behind his lips. "I'm so sorry, Jerry. I was going to tell you."

His whole body seems to wobble. A blinding flash fills the room and then darkness. The air crackles. A strange scent reaches my nose—reminiscent of lightning storms and hot metal. Gordon's breathing is heavy in my ear. His grip on my hair relaxes. I guess I'm no longer the main threat. A frightened cry fills the room, followed by a screech of metal. Part of what I assume is the table hits my boot. Feathers brush my skin. Gordon gasps. He hits the wall behind me with a heavy thud. The room is silent again.

A gentle breeze ruffles my hair. I stumble away from it and reach out blindly, hoping I'll find Calhoun. He must be in here somewhere, we'll be safer standing together. I back up until I hit the wall.

The lights in the room slowly flicker on. My breath catches in my throat at the sight in front of me. Leaning over Robertson, who is sprawled among the wreckage of the table, is something that just can't exist. Huge black and gold wings sprout from his back, each one crowned with a long, silver claw. Scales in the same colors cover his spine and shoulders. I try to reach the door but all I do is call his attention to me. His eyes are cat-like—with slit pupils and irises a rich gold that fade out to a vivid green. The pupils widen as he looks at me and smiles. Fangs ruin whatever reassurance he intended.

I flatten myself against the wall as he comes closer. His wings rustle as he walks.

"Jerry," he says. He takes my hand in his clawed one. The remains of the handcuffs rattle around his wrist. "It's okay, it's me. Lachlan."

Oh, I know it's him, that was never the issue. But how can he be this, this thing?! I struggle to take a breath as panic coils around my throat. They were right. Rexus and his friends, for all their twisted ideologies, were right!

Calhoun steps closer. He studies my face with his glittering serpentine eyes and frowns. "I know it's a shock, but I can explain."

"A shock!" His understatement surprises a laugh from me. "This… this is some next level bullshit."

Calhoun watches me, calmly, as I put the wreckage of the table between us. "I'm not going to hurt you." He follows my sideways glance to Robertson. "I just knocked him out. I'm not here to hurt anyone unless I have no choice."

"They were right all along," I say, and glance at Robertson again. "You aren't human."

"I'm not a killer either." He holds his hand out in what is supposed to be a comforting gesture, but all I can see are his claws. Are they sharp enough to meticulously carve flesh away from bone?

"What are you?"

Before he can answer Robertson slowly gets up. He rubs his forehead, inspects his hand for blood, then his eyes fall on us. "Now he knows exactly what you are!" he says gleefully.

"Do I?" I say. "Give me one piece of proof that he killed those guys and that this not just some revenge plot."

Robertson's mouth twists up in an ugly snarl. He lunges at us, knife in hand. Calhoun catches him mid-leap, forces him down onto his back, and pins his hands down either side of his head. Calhoun snarls, baring his vicious incisors.

Another flash of light fills the room, and I shield my eyes. Bare seconds after the flash, the door bursts open. Strong hands grab my arms and restrain them behind my back. Calhoun is pulled up too, and to my relief, he's back to normal. Robertson, now faced with a captive audience, puts on the convincing disguise of victim and cowers against the wall.

"What the fuck is going on in here?" Burbank's voice is shrill as he gets right in my face. I bite back on my anger. He glares at Robertson who is still trying to play his role. "What happened?" he demands.

"He attacked me!" Calhoun shouts before Robertson can answer. He struggles against the cops holding him. "Look at my face! He did all of this!"

"He's lying!" Robertson spits through gritted teeth. He jabs his finger at Calhoun. "He attacked me first. Threw me through that damn table."

Calhoun and Robertson shout over each other, throwing accusations this way and that. Burbank's eye twitches and his shoulders tense. He's losing patience.

"It's all on tape," I cut in.

Burbank looks my way. "Excuse me?!"

"I said it's all on tape."

Calhoun glances at me and bites his lip. I don't care if he's worried, we need that tape to prove Robertson and Gordon are part of the gang.

"I'll tell you everything but not in front of him." I jerk my head towards Robertson. "Give me an hour of your time to explain it all, and then you can do with me what you like."

Burbank seems to think this over for a moment. He snaps his fingers and points to the red-haired officer holding Calhoun. "Nolan, take Calhoun and get him patched up. You," he jabs his finger at the other cop—a skinny, heavily freckled, guy with close cropped dark hair— restraining Calhoun, "tell McCray to get his team in here. I don't care if he's hauling their asses out of bed himself, just tell him I want *all* of them. And someone get Gordon to the hospital."

Calhoun and I don't speak as he's led away, but I'm sure he knows me well enough by now. I'm going to do whatever I can to get to the bottom of this, and if Calhoun is responsible, I'll take him down.

"Goldberg, Swanson," Burbank barks at the officers holding me. "Take Higgins somewhere out of my sight and make sure he stays there. As for you," his voice softens as he steps close to Robertson, "you and me are gonna have a little chat."

I let the cops lead me away, satisfied with the look of fear on Robertson's face. Ah, the sweet taste of justice.

16

The Truth

I've always hated waiting. The cops lead me out into another interrogation room and offer me coffee. I guess I can't be in too much trouble. With nothing to distract my attention in the cold gray room, my mind quickly wanders.

The wings. The feathers. The scales. I saw all of that before in those quick flashes in my dream, but he was never a threat to me. Reality may be different. My emotions flip flop through anger, fear and paranoia. Calhoun has the teeth, the claws. He's not human. He's *exactly* what we feared was behind the murders.

But, I've never seen anything that made me think he was dangerous. We've been alone together a lot. I've even fallen asleep around him. If he was going to hurt me he would have already. I'm a good judge of character, goddammit! Claws and sharp teeth do not a killer make.

And yet Rexus and the others tried to warn us all along about a non-human who was murdering these guys. Myles tried to tell me the same thing, and because I ignored him, he was killed. I wearily rub my hands over my face. My dream told me to listen this time around, but the message came too late.

Or did it?

Myles told me he knew what the killer was. He was convinced it wasn't human, and that it could be killed. If Calhoun can sprout wings and claws right in front of my eyes, then who's to say what else is out there? What if Rexus and Robertson are on the right track, but they have the wrong guy?

The pieces are slowly falling into place. There must be more like Calhoun around, and I'm willing to bet that's where all the stories on that website come from—the harmless encounters and the darker tales. Whoever was the spy in the Wolves must have seen something to tip them off about Calhoun. All they needed to do was give Robertson that information, he put two and two together, got five, and blamed Calhoun for blowing his cover. If they already know Calhoun can change from human to what is clearly not, then why not believe he is capable of the type of killings that are happening here? He definitely looks like he could be from the size of his fangs.

So why am I so sure he isn't?

Jameson walks in and sits on the other side of the table.

"You here to interrogate me?" I ask with a little laugh.

"No, just to talk," he says reassuringly. "I've seen the tape. Burbank called all of us in to watch it."

My heart jumps into my mouth. "And?"

He shrugs. "Seems pretty clear cut to me. Robertson attacked him, admitted that he wanted to kill him. Do you think Robertson committed all the murders?"

"I'm not sure. Maybe." I fold my arms on the table top. "Do we know how much Gordon was involved yet?"

"He's still unconscious."

I look down at the scuffed table top and wait for Jameson to ask the inevitable questions about the tape. It takes him a while to say anything.

"I never thought it could be one of us, not from this team," he says. The bitterness and anger is plain in his voice and cold gaze. "I should have, especially with other cops being found through that website."

"Not your fault," I say. "No one thought it was him."

"You did."

"Eventually. And, if I'm honest, I still had a niggle of doubt." I gently rock my half empty coffee cup and watch the liquid swirl. "He can't be the only one. He's barely old enough to be responsible for the ones in Boston, and I don't think he's Nomad either. There was just something different about him, plus Robertson didn't look hurt at all, and I know I hurt Nomad."

Jameson rubs his hand over his close-cropped hair, has a quick scan of the room, then leans closer over the table. "Are you gonna tell Burbank everything?"

"Is there anything I shouldn't be telling him?"

"Well, no. I guess not," he says and tries to look calm by leaning back in the chair, arms folded loosely over his chest. "Everything was done for the good of the case, right?"

"I don't think anyone who helped us get this far has anything to worry about, even if the methods were in a gray area, rule-wise," I add. There, that should cover a whole bunch of things he may be worrying about in relation to the help he gave me.

Jameson acknowledges what I said with a tiny incline of his head. Since he doesn't say whatever else is on his mind, we are silent again for a while. I tap my fingers on the edge of the table, feeling slightly uncomfortable that he hasn't mentioned Calhoun's transformation yet.

When I can wait no longer, I ask, "Was, uh, was there anything else on the tape?"

"Like what?" He looks genuinely puzzled.

"Oh, nothing, I was just wondering."

"They just talk," Jameson explains. "He hits Calhoun a few times, you come in. The tape cuts after that."

I let go of the breath I've been holding. At least we won't have to deal with Calhoun's transformation on top of everything else.

Jameson's expression grows serious and he leans in. "How could he do it though?! How could he stand there, at those crime scenes, see those bodies, the damage he did, and not even flinch? Sick bastard!"

"I have no idea," I admit. "There're some real evil shits out there. We didn't need a demon or a monster for that."

"Would be a hell of a lot easier if it was."

I mull it over. Yeah, it would be. Finding out one of your own is capable of something like that is bound to be a shock to the system.

"I mean he is, was, such a nice guy," Jameson continues. The look he gives me is full of disbelief. "Very quiet but really friendly too, once he got to know us. He was always volunteering for coffee runs and tying to cheer people up if they had a bad day. I just don't get how we could have missed all this. I really don't."

"Like I said, I don't think he's the only one. He's not the top of the pyramid," I say, offering him a rope to cling to. Robertson may be bad, but until we know for sure, he doesn't have to be a sadistic killer.

Before Jameson can react to that, Burbank steps into the room. "Ah, you're still here. Good," he says. "You and me need a little chat, Higgins."

"Good luck," Jameson whispers.

As soon as he leaves Burbank closes the door and sits down heavily in the chair Jameson vacated. He makes me wait as he glances through sheets of messy handwriting—his notes from interviewing Robertson no doubt—and sighs theatrically every so often. I keep my face impassive. Even one little quirk of my lip, one tiny chuckle, could set us off on the wrong foot.

"You've really had some fun here, haven't you?" Burbank says, his eyes still on the notes.

"I wouldn't call it fun, bu—"

Burbank cuts in. "It was a rhetorical question." He massages his graying temples and leans back heavily in his chair. "Okay, let's hear it."

I pick my way carefully through the facts, protecting people who helped me, and keeping the crazier sounding elements out of my story. Burbank's body language reeks of boredom and annoyance. He rests his chin on his upturned hand, rolls his eyes every so often, but he does take notes. Finally, I run out of things to say.

"Interesting," Burbank says even though his tone suggests it's anything but. "I see you still just do what you like and damn the consequences."

"I only did what I thought was right," I say. "And some stuff I got mixed up in without looking for it."

Burbank snorts. "You're always looking for trouble, that's the problem."

I keep my harsh response to myself and look away while Burbank reads. There's nothing else I can do now. I've told him everything, and he can get evidence to back my story up from multiple places. No doubt he'll keep me here for a bit just for his own amusement though.

"Okay, you can go," he says.

My eyebrow quirks up. "That's it?"

He smirks. "What did you expect, a medal?" He steeples his hands in front of his face. "We are done here, for now. I'm sure I don't need to tell you to stay close, in case we need to interview you again."

I frown, confused. "Uh, no. Of course not. I…"

"Something you wanna share?"

"No. I just didn't expect it to be over so soon."

"For you, it is," Burbank says. There's a hard edge to his voice, and I steel myself for the incoming lecture. "We, that's me and my team, will be working on this, piecing everything together. Your job is to be honest in interviews and tell us as much as you can."

"I will, and I have."

"Then keep doing it. You found out who was sending your client those letters, right?"

"I think so," I reply. "But—"

"Then go celebrate a job well done," Burbank says, and a small smile creeps across his mouth. "Let loose for a bit, and if the homicide bug has bitten you again then, for the love of god, apply to join us, like a normal person."

"Are you offering me a job here?" I say. There's no way I can keep the shock out of my voice.

Burbank shrugs nonchalantly. "At least if you're working for me I can keep an eye on whatever shit you get up to." The chair *squeals* as he pushes it back and stands. "I'm not an idiot, Higgins, I know you're a good cop. I may not like the way you do things, and I really pity whoever's cleaning up after you, but you get results. It's something to think about."

"Yeah, uh, thanks." I force a smile to my face. "I'll think about it."

"Good. Now get out of my sight."

"What about Calhoun?" I ask. "I'm not leaving without him."

"Well, isn't it just so damn perfect that Novik is done interviewing him too? At least they should be. You can wait by the doors. There're seats there."

Knowing this is the best I'm going to get I thank him and make my way to the little waiting area by the doors. I've been sitting less than five minutes when Calhoun and Novik approach. The blood has been cleaned from Calhoun's face, the cuts treated, and he's joking around with Novik. All good signs.

"They are letting me go without charge," he says as he walks up to me. "I can't thank you enough, Jerry, I really can't!"

I wave off his attempt to hug me. "Good. I'll take you home."

His jaw clenches, but he agrees all the same.

"I'll call you later," I say to Novik. "I got a few things to sort out first, but I want to run some of them past you before I settle on anything."

"Sure thing, Jer. We'll probably be here a few hours yet."

"Thanks for sticking by me. I know it was a lot to ask with little proof."

"It was as good a lead as any, and it paid off." He claps his hand on my shoulder. "You did good, man."

"Yeah, we did." I smile.

I fall into step beside Calhoun and walk outside.

We head back to the Dakota. It's not my first choice for where this difficult conversation should take place, but Calhoun's insistence that he needs to go home, and his obvious distress about the whole situation, sways me.

We don't speak during the journey—everything I want to say to him can't be said in front of anyone else. Tension crackles between us, and when our eyes do meet, there's fear in his. He's out of the car before it comes to a full stop. I park then follow him upstairs.

The door is wide open—whatever Calhoun needs to do, it looks like it can't wait. I stay in the hallway with my hand on the doorknob so I can make a quick escape if need be. Calhoun clutches a small black backpack to his chest when he steps from the one room in his apartment that's always been locked. He glances at me and sighs.

"I knew this would happen," he mutters half to himself. "I'm not going to hurt you, Jerry. I never would."

"Can you blame me for being a little nervous?" I say as softly as I can. "But I'm here on my own, just the same."

"What are you going to do?" He's never sounded so scared, so vulnerable. I close the apartment door and approach him.

"To be completely honest, that depends on your explanation." My stomach knots up the closer I get to him. If he transforms again, he could easily overpower me, even kill me, and no matter how unlikely that is, I can't keep my nerves at bay. "Can you put the bag down, please?"

Calhoun holds my gaze as he kneels and deposits the backpack on the floor. "Would you like to frisk me for weapons too?"

"Don't get smart," I say sharply. "You've got claws and teeth like a fucking lion. I'm allowed to be a little wary. You owe me an explanation."

He folds his arms over his chest and gives me his best defiant stare. "I owe you nothing."

"Okay, fine." I turn on my heel and march to the door.

"Wait!"

I suppress my smirk and face him. "So, you're going to explain what's going on?"

"Yeah, but I need a drink first."

"You and me both, kid," I sigh.

Calhoun uncorks a bottle of red wine and pours me a glass. I'm not exactly a wine drinker, but it's just as good for numbing the shock as anything else. Calhoun takes his usual place curled up in the armchair and briefly presses his hand to his side while he gets comfy. I sit as far away from him as I can while remaining on the couch and watch him closely. When he doesn't speak, I prompt him.

"Here're the facts, Lachlan. I've spent the past few weeks trying to fight off a supposed monster. I've had you trying to tell me the monster is real. I've had Rexus' gang, who you obviously knew about but didn't bother to mention, tell me the same thing. The problem is they have singled out you." I pause in the hope Calhoun will start to fill in the blanks for me, but he stays deathly silent. "Last night I fought something that could change its shape. It had teeth, claws, and a real lust for violence. I've been shot at, chased, threatened online, and, to top off two weeks of hell, you turn out to be, well, I don't know what. What the fuck is going on?"

Calhoun drums his fingers against his knees. "I work for an organization, agency, whatever you want to call it, a top-secret group of specially trained soldiers, and we've been operating on Earth for years. That thing you saw last night, we call them Veranhiko. It's an ancient name for a type of shape-shifting demon."

When I recover from his sudden burst of information I say, "I've never heard that before. Is it a Scottish legend?"

"Not exactly. I'm not Scottish. I'm not even from this planet."

There's no way I can hold back my laugh, but I quickly quiet when Calhoun doesn't join in. "Shit, you're serious."

Calhoun sighs deeply. "I knew this would be too much. Come here and I'll take away the memory of seeing me as anything but human."

I shake my head. "No! Tell me all of it, please."

"My boss is going to have my head for this," he grumbles. "But they seem to be targeting you too. You should know what you're up against.

"As I said, the agency I work for has been hunting the Veranhiko here on Earth for years, but we've never had any success. We can't track them until it's too late. They just seem to appear out of thin air, do their damage, then disappear. We can't track the humans they are after, because the first kill is always random. The others follow a pattern of birthplaces, physical characteristics, and interests, but the net is too wide, as I'm sure you've seen yourself."

He pauses briefly to sip his wine. "Morrigan and I came here to work a deep cover mission. There are more of us, in different countries and cities all over the world, living our fake lives and staying ever vigilant for signs of the Veranhiko. Living here hasn't helped. They still blind-sided us."

"They must want something from the victims," I say. "The crimes are heavily ritualized."

"We don't know what. We're blind." He scrubs his hands over his face. "And then all the trouble started with those conspiracy theorists. I think there're Veranhiko within their gang who can recognize me for what I am. I can't think of any other way that anyone would have found out. They've been dogging my footsteps, attacking me online."

"Sending the letters?" I add.

"Yes, the letters." Calhoun says flatly. "It's admirable that they want to fight and protect their own, but they have the wrong guy, and they're damaging every attempt we make to help." He wipes his eyes and gathers up the tears that threaten to fall. "I'm so sick of looking over my shoulder all the time and pretending everything is okay. Only a handful of people on this rock know who I really am. I haven't seen my family in years, and on top of all that I have a bunch of humans baying for blood as well as an unstoppable, untraceable monster."

He drops his head into his hands, and his shoulders shudder with his quiet sobs. I cross the room and gently pull him into my arms. He resists but only for a second.

"It's going to be okay," I say into his ear. "That gang is breaking apart as we speak. They won't be a problem for you anymore."

He grips my t-shirt, and his claws scratch my skin. "There're thousands of them, Jerry. They're always going to be a problem."

"Then stop fighting my help like you've done so far." I cup his face in my hands and force him to look at me. "I'm here to help you, Lachlan, and that hasn't changed. If what you need is for me to keep those fuckers off your back so you can destroy these shape-shifting things, then I'll do it. If you want my help in other ways, then tell me." I lean my forehead against his. "I'm not going anywhere."

"You're not going to tell anyone?" He sniffs.

"No. What exactly would it help? And there's nothing on the recording to reveal your true identity either."

Calhoun lets me go and wipes his eyes. "I know. I scrambled the cameras just in case. I knew Robertson was trying to catch me out. If he had evidence that I was—"

"Wait just a minute," I say. "How the hell did you scramble the cameras? You were nowhere near them."

"I think it'll be easier to show you. Can you unplug the TV set?"

Confused, I do as he asks. "Now what?"

"Test it. See if there's any power going into it."

"But I just unplugged it."

Calhoun rolls his eyes. "Will you just do it already?"

I try a couple of times, but of course, the TV doesn't turn on. "Nope, there's definitely no juice in that."

Calhoun steps up to the TV, flexes out his hand, then places it on top of the set. The screen flickers once, twice, and suddenly comes to life. All the little hairs stand up on my arms, like there's a ton of static in the air. It stops when Calhoun takes his hand away.

"What the fuck?" I whisper, more in awe than in fear. "How did you do that?"

"Everyone is born with a certain amount of elemental magic," Calhoun says as if it's the most normal thing in the world. "At least they are where I'm from. Mine is lightning and—" he touches the top of the TV again, and the screen flicks on immediately—"electricity."

A shocked laugh spills from my lips before I can stop it. "This is crazy."

"And you should probably know that there is truth in what Robertson and Rexus said about me. I can, to a certain extent, get into people's heads, change their thoughts around, but I can only lean them toward something they were already thinking. Like tonight, Robertson had a little niggle of doubt about killing me. I tried to make that option seem like the better one, but he realized what I was doing." He pulls his hand from the set and shakes it out.

"If you had some time with him, could you pick out thoughts from his head, like who he's working for?" I ask. It's a long shot, but this could be just the kind of break we're waiting for,

"I guess I could, yeah." He shrugs. "It's worth a shot."

"And with other suspects, would you be able to read from inside their head whether they were human or not?"

"I've never had the chance."

"But if you did?" I ask. "You said you think they could be hiding in the ranks of the Last Defense. That means they're lurking amongst cops, teachers, even the garbage men of this city, because that's the kind of people we've already tracked. It could even be Robertson. He's sending you those letters, right? So, he's either at the crime scenes himself, or he's working very closely with someone who is."

Calhoun chews his lip. "Even if I can single them out that way, that doesn't help us when we can't kill them."

I can't help but smile. "I might know where to get the answer to that, or at least a nudge in the right direction."

Calhoun grins. "Are you serious? How?"

"During the Boston case, my partner told me he had worked out what the killer was and that he knew how to kill it. So, we—"

"That's great. You call him, and we might finally be able to kill those guys."

His interruption catches me off guard. "I can't," I say after a pause.

"Why not?" Calhoun snaps.

"Because he's dead. The murderer ripped his throat out."

Calhoun's shoulders sag. He takes both my hands in his. "I'm so sorry, Jerry. I had no idea"

"It was a long time ago," I say, and give his hands a squeeze. "But I do have a whole heap of his things back home. All we need to do is look through it."

"That's amazing!" His happiness is infectious, and I smile too. "But I really need to get myself sorted before we go anywhere."

"I thought they patched you up?" I say, and point at where he keeps touching his abdomen. "Do you need to see a doctor?"

"No. It's nothing serious. I'll be back in just a second." He wraps his arms around my neck and briefly presses his lips to mine. "Thank you for being so understanding about all this."

"Uh, yeah, no problem," I reply, but he's already on his way out of the living room.

I touch my fingers to my lips. What the hell was that? Just a friendly kiss? We nearly kissed back when he was locked up, at least it seemed that way. I'm not entirely sure I like this change.

To distract myself from thinking about it anymore, I call Novik. "Hey. What's going on?"

"You've been gone for roughly an hour, Jerry," he says. There's a slight grumble to his tone. I try not to take it personally; it's been a long day for us all after all. "Nothing much is going on that wasn't before."

"Is everything cleared up with Calhoun," I ask. "You guys aren't going to arrest him again, are you?"

"No, not from what I can see. Robertson made everything up. There's no evidence from Newlin's place, and he was never interviewed." Novik sighs. "Once we've spoken to Newlin and tested the crime scene for ourselves, we might need to speak to Calhoun again. Why?" His tone is suspicious all of a sudden. "What are you doing?"

"I have a hunch about something, that's all. What's Robertson had to say for himself?"

"Oh, you'll love this," Novik says with a laugh. "He's saying that Calhoun has got you under some sort of spell, and that you've been brainwashed into helping him."

A smile tugs at the side of my mouth. "Got to give him points for creativity."

"He's completely convinced that Calhoun isn't human, but he's equally sure he didn't send any letters. To give him his due, he did look really confused when I asked him about it."

I sit on the windowsill and look out into the street below. "It might not be him. He's guilty of one thing for sure, but we already know this network is huge, and that it probably links back to Boston. Maybe someone else is sending them."

There's a lengthy pause before Novik speaks. "We're still identifying gang members, and we're getting what we can out of the guys that attacked you. Like every other gang-related case, the lackeys fall first."

"Ain't that the truth." There's no sign of Calhoun yet. I hope whatever is wrong with him isn't serious. "So, listen. I have a few things I wanna run past you before I take action on them. I know you're stretched pretty thin right now, so call me when you wake up tomorrow and we'll talk. If that's okay," I add once I realize I'm being pushy.

Novik yawns loudly. "I'll call once I finish here. I won't be able to sleep right away anyway, so might as well do something constructive."

"Okay, that sou—" A whine stops me in my tracks. It came from the bathroom. "Sorry, I got to go. Call me when you're leaving."

I hang up before he can say anything else and rush into the hallway. I knock on the bathroom door and call Calhoun's name, but the only answer I get is a louder cry. A swift kick to the lock forces the door in.

Calhoun jumps back and his wing tips brush the walls at either side of the bathroom. His scales shine in the harsh florescent light, and his chest heaves as he tries to catch his breath. The deep wound on his abdomen stretches and contracts with every movement.

"What the hell are you doing?" I say, shock plain in my voice.

"It's not what it looks like." He holds his hands up as if he can keep me back that way. "I'm trying to fix it." He grits his teeth against a whimper and balls his fists. The wound slowly begins to close.

I drop onto my knees, place my hands on his stomach, and stare at the deep gouge. Right before my eyes the muscle knits back together. Calhoun stretches over me to pick up a small tub from the sink. He smears a green paste into the wound and bites back a whine. The paste melts into his damaged flesh, then it heals fully, leaving behind nothing but slightly pink, tender looking skin.

"What the fuck just happened?" I say, breathless.

"I can't have a wound like that while I'm trying to fight those monsters. He caught my wing too, I had…" He trails off as his legs give way under him.

I catch him before he hits the ground. "Lachlan?!"

"I'm okay," he says, but his weak voice isn't doing anything to convince me. "It takes a lot out of you. I'll be fine in a minute or two."

"Let's get you to bed." I hook his arm over my shoulders and slowly stand. "You need to lie down."

Calhoun leans heavily on me and carefully places one foot in front of the other, like he really has to think about the mechanisms of walking. He sits down on his bed. "Thanks."

I sit next to him. "Did Robertson do that to you?"

He shakes his head. "No. The Veranhiko did last night. I forgot to take any healing cream with me when I moved to the hotel, and I couldn't fix it."

"But you were arrested hours ago." I stare at the little patch on his stomach where the ragged gouge had been before. "You were bleeding. Did they just leave you like that?"

"I'd managed to wrap it." Calhoun says. "Don't worry, it's healed now. No damage done. See?" He places my hand onto his stomach. "It's just as tough as my other skin."

I swallow hard. "Yeah it, it feels just the same."

"And I repaired my wing and a few other little cuts," he says happily.

"I can see that." I gently brush his lip with my thumb. "Good. That looked pretty painful."

Calhoun blushes and takes my hand in his. "You could use it too, if you want."

I slowly breathe out in an attempt to slow my heart down. "I'm fine, really. But thanks."

Calhoun's pupils expand and contract in the dim light. The gold of his irises seems to glitter. I slowly look him over and drink in the sight of his huge wings, scales, and claws. There's something exciting about all of it now that there's no fear attached to it. If I'm completely honest, I think I felt a bit of that before too.

Calhoun loudly clears his throat. "I should go put that stuff back. It's not something you want to get on you by accident." He gets up and heads for the door.

"Lachlan." I get to my feet and try to think of a way to finish my sentence, but all my words wither under his gaze. Instead I close the gap between us, and rest my forehead against his. Calhoun's fingers tangle with mine. I nuzzle my face gently against his. The small cluster of scales on his cheekbones is softer than I expected, more like thicker skin than reptile scales. His hair is silky when I brush my hand through it. The feathers that make up the bottom third of its length are fluffy, like down. With a deep breath, I give in to my desires and press my lips to his.

After a moment's hesitation, Calhoun kisses me back. He slides his hands over my hips and pulls me closer. Feathers gently stroke my shoulders as his wings fold around us.

How did I go so long without this? It's just a kiss, but it's awakening things in me that I haven't felt in years. I want more. I want to feel his skin against mine, hear him moan my name. I want everything he's prepared to give. I trail my hands over his sides and into the dense feathers of his wings. Calhoun kisses my neck. His fangs graze my skin. My pulse races against his lips. He unbuttons my shirt, slides it off my shoulders, and lets it fall to the floor. I wait for a comment about my own secrets—the tribal tattoo that takes up most of my upper arm and the right side of my chest, and the nipple ring that seemed like such a wild thing to do at twenty-one—but there is nothing more than a soft caress over my inked skin. When our lips meet again, Calhoun slides his hand into my underwear.

I grab his wrist. Calhoun frowns, and pulls his hand away. Blood rushes in my ears, my heart threatens to beat out of my chest. It's now or never, Jerry. Do you want him or not? And, if you do, show him!

I pull him close and kiss him like my life depends on it. We fall back onto the bed. Our boots hit the floor with a loud clatter. Clothing follows. Our gazes lock. Calhoun's cheeks are flushed, his lips parted just enough to reveal the points of his teeth. My heart thumps loudly in my chest as I drink in the sight of him. With shaking hands, I trace the small pentagram tattoo on his chest then move lower, taking time to caress the scales on his side as well as his softer skin. I press my lips to his stomach then move lower until I take him in my mouth.

An annoying voice in my head taunts me with the inane idea that I might have forgotten how to pleasure someone, but the sounds Calhoun makes prove those thoughts wrong. He buries his hands in my hair and gently guides the movement of my head.

I pause when he passes me a condom and lube. My hands shake as I uncap the bottle and squeeze a little onto my fingers. I take a few controlled breaths. Is it nerves? Anticipation? A combination of the two? Either way, I don't want to stop.

Calhoun props himself up on his elbows and watches every move I make. For a second I'm lost in the sight of him, a literal angel, wings and all, but he urges me on with a soft whine of my name. I kiss him until he is lying flat again. He slowly strokes me as I slide my fingers inside him

When neither of us can wait any longer, I roll the condom on and push into him.

Calhoun's claws dig into my shoulders, and he throws his head back. He tightens his legs around my waist, encouraging me to go deeper, and I do, slowly savoring every moment. We kiss hard. I seek out his fangs with my tongue and shiver as the sharp point presses into it.

I pull back from him and pick up speed. For a split second, Myles' image splashes across my mind's eye, but I shoo it away with a shake of my head. I've waited so long. I want this! I want

Calhoun more than I ever thought possible.

Calhoun whimpers my name like a mantra. Claws rake down my back. Heat pools in my stomach. I don't want this to end, but I can't fight it off any longer. I bury myself deep inside him as I fall. Our voices harmonize as Calhoun gives in too.

Slowly, we untangle from each other. I roll onto my back and sigh happily. My mind and body feel completely relaxed for the first time in weeks, maybe even months. Calhoun takes my hand and slides his fingers in between mine.

The buzzing, warm high fades away only to be replaced with a prickly anxiousness. I can't put my finger on what's wrong, it's just a general uneasiness—like the ground is unsteady beneath my feet.

I reach over onto the nightstand for the wrapper. Calhoun watches me quietly as I dispose of the condom then sit on the edge of the bed. I can't look at him, not directly in the eye anyway.

Was this a mistake? I barely know Calhoun, and yet I destroyed a decade of self-imposed celibacy in one move without a second thought. But it's not a big deal. I've had sex plenty of times before, and I was the one pushing for more. It's about time I moved on, isn't it?

Calhoun touches my arm unexpectedly. I flinch.

"Are you okay?" he asks quietly.

"Yup. Fine. You?"

He's not fooled by the false cheeriness in my voice, but he doesn't ask any more questions. I squeeze his hand. "I'm fine, really. I'm just feeling a little… shock isn't the right word, but after all that's happened these last few weeks—"

Calhoun presses his finger to my lips. "I get it. You don't have to explain. I wasn't expecting this either."

I take a few deep breaths then finally look him in the eye. He smooths my hair back behind my ear.

"Are you sure you're okay?" he whispers.

"Just… just been a while, that's all," I say, and force a smile. It's as much of the truth as he's going to get tonight. Why kill the mood further?

I lie back down and motion for Calhoun to join me. He gives me a confused frown but rests his head on my shoulder just the same.

"Are you worrying about another murder?" Calhoun asks after a short pause.

"No," I say. "Well, a little I suppose. Or some sort of retaliation after arresting Robertson."

Calhoun picks his jeans up from the floor, and takes his phone from his pocket. He opens up what, at first, looks like a standard GPS app. A tap on the screen brings up an incomprehensible menu, then he selects an option that throws a familiar symbol onto different locations on the map. "This is the only warning we get of the Veranhiko being nearby, and we only get the alert when a portal opens. Red ones are dead portals—ones that's have been used and are no longer active. If they show up in amber, it means they're active."

"That's the symbol we found at the crime scenes. I thought you'd seen it on the news when you drew it on the wall."

"You're not wrong," he admits with a shrug. "But it's not the only place I've seen it."

"And one of these has opened before every kill?"

"Closed too." Calhoun places his phone on the nightstand and snuggles into me with his head back on my shoulder. "We can rest easy."

"What about the ones that might be hiding out with The Last Defense?"

He gently strokes my side as he talks. "They've never killed anyone so far. Like I said, the portal always opens first. We will have those few seconds of warning, and any other problems will be human made and easy to handle."

We fall into silence. I run my fingers through Calhoun's hair—the motion comforts me. There's a niggling thought in the back of my head, and it tells me to run, get as far away from Calhoun and all this change as possible. I stay put. If I run away from this now, I'll probably never move on. Do I really want to live the rest of my life alone?

"Do you want to come to Boston with me?" I say. Might as well jump into this change stuff with both feet.

"I'd like to, yeah." His cautious tone suggests he doesn't think my request is genuine.

"Novik is going to call me when he's finished at work. We're going to meet up and talk over how to proceed from there. After that, we'll go to Boston" I kiss the top of his head. "We won't be gone long, and we'll keep an eye on your alert thing just in case we need to come back sooner."

Calhoun sits up, stretches, and changes back to his human form. Spots dance in front of my eyes from the flash. "That's all we can do. Wait." He gently brushes his lips against mine.

I rest my hand against his cheek and gaze up into his green eyes. With each passing moment, the strange, untethered feeling that hit me straight after we had sex slowly fades. Now is not the time to over think. There's too much going on to even contemplate dating or even talking about how we feel, so why not just enjoy this for what it is?

Calhoun smiles when I kiss him. I press my lips to his face, then his neck. His soft hair brushes my face, and I breathe in the sweet scent of his shampoo. My phone starts to ring as soon as our lips meet again.

I curse under my breath. "I have to get that," I say by way of an apology. Calhoun nods, smiles, and gets up from the bed.

"Hey, Novik," I say. "Do you still want to meet up now?"

"Yeah," he grumbles. It sounds like he's outside; I can hear traffic. "We'll be back at the hotel in about a half hour. We're gonna stop off somewhere and get some coffee and something to eat. We'll bring you back something."

"Could you get something for Lachlan too?" I ask "I'll pay you back when I see you."

There's a brief pause. "Okay. We'll seen you then," Novik says and hangs up.

17

Hidden Talents

Novik and Harris arrive at the hotel not long after we do. They look beat—their shoulders sag, their skin looks paler than normal.

"I don't know what the hell was up with McCray," Harris says, his words clipped by anger, "but he seemed to have more and more shit for us to do. I know we had a breakthrough tonight, but why keep just *us* there."

I frown, confused. "He sent all his usual guys home?"

"Yup," Novik confirms. "I'm gonna talk to him about it as soon as I'm not in danger of ripping his or anyone else's head off." He hands me a tray of coffee cups, then fishes his key from his pocket. "So, what do you want to talk about?"

"It can wait, honestly. You both look like you could use some sleep."

"And we will after we talk," Novik says firmly. He strides into the building and pulls us along in his wake.

"Any news?" I ask in an attempt to break through his foul mood.

"Nothing," he grunts. "McCray was interviewing Robertson, and the other guys we picked up seem to have taken a vow of silence. They didn't say one damn word. We'll get shit out of them eventually."

"We've got them under surveillance," Harris adds. "We think there's a chance they might try to kill themselves rather than spill what they know."

I look at Calhoun. "It's a possibility," I say. He nods in agreement.

The elevator climbs lethargically and my stomach sinks. At first, I think nothing of it, but the feeling intensifies and wraps itself around my insides like barbed wire. I glance at Calhoun and then at my friends. We fall silent one after another and watch the numbers creep upward. The elevator *ding* when it reaches our floor is like a death knell. The doors open and we all release our held breaths. Novik moves forward.

Calhoun steps in front of him. "This isn't safe. You need to go back down."

"Don't be dumb," Novik growls. "You guys go if you like, but I'm going to my room either way." He pushes past Calhoun and into the hallway. We all follow.

On the outside, nothing appears to be wrong, but the air feels thick and heavy, like before a storm. It puts pressure on my sinuses, and every cut, bruise, and broken bone I've picked up over the past few weeks throbs.

Calhoun takes my hand. "We should go. It isn't safe."

"It's just stress. We've been on edge too long and we're seeing threats everywhere." Harris says but he lacks conviction.

All four of us hang back, and stare down the undisturbed hallway with its locked doors. With cautious steps, we approach our rooms. Novik's is closest to the elevator. After a moment's hesitation, he unlocks the door and pushes it open.

Nothing happens.

Novik switches the light on. The place has been ransacked. Novik's belongings are strewn carelessly around the room, the bedding slashed.

"Those fucks," he hisses under his breath. "Is this their revenge for us taking down Robertson and Gordon?"

"It's much worse than that," Calhoun says. There's a slight tremor to his voice. Is he scared?

"Who else would trash it?" Novik asks with an angry shrug. "They're just trying to scare us. Go check your rooms," he says and points at Harris and me. "I bet they've turned them over too."

We reluctantly move towards our own rooms. Mine is farthest down the hallway. The pain in my sinuses grows, and pushes towards migraine intensity. Calhoun positions himself in the middle of the hallway, and watches all three of us warily. In unison, Harris and I unlock our doors.

"You were right," Harris says with an angry sigh. "Good job all the files are at the station. They won't find anything helpful here."

I turn on the light in my own room, ready to see the same, but what greets me makes my blood run cold. I take a cautious step inside, not quite believing what's plainly in front of me.

Crimson streaks cover the cream wall behind the bed. The headboard and bedding are spattered with blood too. Underneath the blankets, with their remaining arms around one another, are the two missing halves of the subway bodies.

"Don't touch anything!" Harris yells. All three of them crowd the doorway.

"I'm not an idiot," I say. My voice sounds tiny, distant, and not like my own at all.

"Then get out the room," he hisses. "Before you—"

A seam of red appears along Harris' forehead, just above his eyebrows. He slumps forward, and the top of his head slides off the rest of his skull. It hits the floor with a wet squelch.

"Run!" Calhoun screams.

I try to, but Novik and Calhoun are shoved into the room with me. The door slams with a deafening bang. Glass rains down on us from the shattered ceiling light, and we are plunged into darkness. The small seam of streetlamp glow that leaks through the drapes isn't enough— I can't see my hand in front of my face. I draw my gun and hear Novik do the same. His back rests against mine. I reach out blindly for Calhoun with my other hand, and pull him into a tight huddle with us. No one can sneak up behind us now.

Laughter echoes in the dark. It's impossible to pinpoint exactly where it's coming from. We huddle closer together—shoulder to shoulder, back to back, in a tight triangle. I control my breathing in an attempt to stay calm, and wait for the bastard to make a mistake.

Novik and I shoot when a squeaky floorboard gives the killers position away. The muzzle flashes illuminate the room for a split second and leave spots in front of our eyes.

The silence seems louder somehow.

My wrist is grabbed and I'm hauled forward. I fire again. A screech echoes around the room. A stench like rotting meat fills my nose. Clanging metal and cries of fury and pain fill the air as we fight blindly. Razor sharp claws rip at my skin, hair is yanked from my scalp, and fists raise lumps all over my body. I fight back, but my true goal is the bed. There's a reading lamp on the nightstand. If I can reach that then I can see what we're fighting and get a clear shot.

My fist sinks into the soft, spongy flesh of the killer's face. Sharp teeth graze my knuckles as he yelps. A heavy blow to my side lifts me off my feet and sends me spinning through the air. I land heavily on my stomach. Stars dance in front of my eyes. Fighting through the pain, I rush for the light switch, punch it with my elbow, and fire as soon as I can see clearly.

Time seems to slow down. Novik falls to the floor. Calhoun lunges, his dagger whistles through the air before it slices with the killer's neck. He's a little shorter than I expected, but my shot finds its mark anyway. The murderer's head snaps back, and his dark hair fans out behind him. The scream is the same ear-splitting one I heard in the alley.

Burning fury floods me. This guy has attacked me twice, no, three times! I caught him red handed torturing Mads, the sixth victim, and he killed my friend! I lunge at him, wrap my hands around his throat, and squeeze.

Thick, gray goo seeps through my hands. I jab my thumbs into the wound Calhoun made and prise it open. Why won't this bastard die already? I blew a hole in his forehead, and he's still breathing, still struggling. Just die!

Our eyes lock. The killer's irises flicker from their original hazel to blue, then green, then through a heap of fantastical colors. Smoke curls around my fingers and fills my lungs with an acrid stench. The murderer's struggles grow desperate—he claws at my arms and thrashes around like a fish out of water. Flames burst out of the gash in his throat and quickly spread. In shock, I let him go. In a surprisingly short time all that is left is ash and a greasy stain on the carpet.

I wipe my hands off on my pants, then turn my attention to Novik. His face is bloody and lumpy. He's missing a front tooth and one eye is swollen shut. Blood stains his torn clothing, and when he stands he struggles to put weight on his right foot. Calhoun too, is covered in bruises and scratches. He falls to his knees and gingerly touches the remains.

"He… he's gone," he says shakily. He looks at me with wide, unblinking eyes.

"Good," I say through gritted teeth.

Harris, or what's left of him, is slumped near the door. The remains of his brain are more on the floor than in his skull. I step back from the blood seeping into the carpet.

"I never heard a thing, I swear," Calhoun says from behind us.

"I thought your little app thingy told you when they were around?" I ask without turning to face him. The sight of Harris' open skull demands every bit of my attention.

"Not this time." The defeat is plain in his flat, almost emotionless tone.

Novik pushes away from me and sits down heavily on the floor. "People don't just…" he says but then trails off into his own thoughts. He looks around the room—at the bodies in the bed, the stain lying in the middle of my trashed belongings, and finally back to Harris. "At least it was quick. Harris never knew a thing, did he?"

I nod. "Course he didn't. He was gone as soon as he was hit."

Novik scrambles around in his pockets for his phone, calls someone at the station, and relays the story in an increasingly shaky voice. Calhoun slips his arm around me. I lean against him a little, thankful for the comfort.

"This just got real personal, didn't it?" I ask even though I know the answer. "He knew where to find us, all three of us. This is a message, some sort of payback." I look over at the pile of gray dust. "And now he's dead and gone. There'll be more though, won't there?"

"It's a possibility, yeah," Calhoun admits.

"We have to stop them," I say in a harsh whisper—I don't want Novik to overhear us. "We know they can die now. Look at the mess of him." I point towards the stain on the floor. "There's nothing left."

"I've seen them repair themselves before," Calhoun says. "Regrow limbs, even heads. There's no guarantee that it's dead."

I swallow my reply when four uniformed officers burst into the room, guns aimed, and force us to kneel with hands locked behind our heads. Novik shows his badge and explains what happened. I guess there was no witness silencing fog this time since someone farther down the hall called nine-one-one on us. When I try to stand my head swims. The floor goes out from under me, and I howl in pain as Calhoun grazes my side in his attempt to catch me.

There's blood on his hands, my blood, and a lot of it, too.

"I need to get to the hospital," I tell the uniformed officers.

One of them, a female officer with her dark hair in a tight bun, looks me over. "Stay still, I'll radio for an ambulance."

"It's fine," Calhoun says. "He's hurt but there's no need for an ambulance. Trust me." When the cop insists, Calhoun steps forward and gently takes her hand. "I am trained as a doctor. Trust me, he's fine. I'm going to take him to the hospital myself." The little hairs on my body respond to the electricity in the air. The other cops watch the two of them, but no one tries to stop him. "When the detectives get here," Calhoun continues, his tone hypnotic, "tell them that we had to go to hospital, all three of us. You will tell them that you called an ambulance. You will also tell them that the killer escaped. You chased him, but he got away. You can do that, right?"

The cop nods, and her fellow officers mimic her but with less conviction. The magic he's using must be rubbing up against my brain too. I can almost believe that the stain on the floor was not once some murderous monster.

Once the officer has repeated what Calhoun told her, he lets her go and drags Novik and me from the room. The strange static feeling on my skin doesn't fade until we are on the street. Calhoun grabs my car keys from my pocket and ushers me and Novik into the back of the car.

"What the hell happened back there?" Novik shouts at him. "Where are we going?"

Calhoun starts the car. "We're going somewhere where you two can heal, and fast." He glances at us both through the rear-view mirror. "You're going to need to be in top condition for what's coming. Jerry, keep your hand pressed to your side."

I do as he asks. My shirt is soaked in blood. Underneath, the flesh feels swollen, misshapen. I press my hand in harder as Calhoun speeds towards wherever he is headed.

Before long we pull up in front of an apartment block on fifth avenue. My legs shake as I try to stand. My pulse pounds in my ears. Shit, I'm losing a lot of blood. Novik slings my arm over his shoulder and drags me with him into the building even though he is limping himself. My vision blurs on and off as dizziness floods my brain. Novik wraps his arm tighter around my waist and follows Calhoun.

I don't catch much of what's going on, just voices, the tell-tale static tingle of Calhoun's power at work, and the whir of an elevator. The floor beneath my feet changes from marble tiles to rich burgundy carpet then to shining wood. We are in someone's apartment. There're voices all around me. The light is too bright. All I want to do is lie down and sleep.

It seems I'm getting my wish. The bed is the most comfortable thing I've ever lain on, and it supports me in all the right places. I wipe my face on one of the pillows in an attempt to cool down and smear sweat onto the clean, white linen. Someone sits near my head and places their hands on my shoulders. All I can see is a blur of black around peachy skin tones, but the size of the hands means it must be Novik holding me.

I wince as my shirt is pulled away from the wound in my side. “This will hurt,” Calhoun says. His voice is so clear it’s like he's talking directly into my head. “But, in no time at all, you'll be good as new.”

There's a sting somewhere between my ribs and my hip, then a strange cold tingle spreads out over my body. My flesh begins to itch. It starts deep inside my body, as if my organs need to be scratched. I squirm as I try to relieve the discomfort, but all I get for my troubles is nauseating dizziness.

Then the pain really starts.

Calhoun sits on my legs. Novik's grip tightens on my shoulders. I howl and arch off the bed. It's like being shot—the pain is pinpoint sharp before radiating out from the tear in my flesh. It won't stop. It pulses over and over again, moving over my stomach like a wave of fire. Needles jab into my nerves. I try to fight out of their hold but they hold me down.

“Help him!” Novik shouts.

“He'll be okay,” Calhoun says. He touches my forehead. The tiny brush of his hand is like a razor moving over my skin. “This is the worst of it, Jerry. You'll be okay.”

The pain is so bad I can barely breath. Tears stream down my cheeks. I whine and sob and beg for release from the torture. Just when I think I can take no more, it stops. The relief is immediate, exhausting, blissful. For a second, I float on the wave of euphoria, but sleep rushes up in its place. I gladly let it take me.

When I wake up, shafts of sunlight are spilling over the bedspread. The room is painfully bright. The walls are cream, and everything from dresser to the linens on the bed is white. My clothes, lying folded up on an ornately carved chair in the corner, are the only things with any color in the whole room. I feel like I'm messing the place up just by being here.

I pat my hands over my body. There's a large dressing on my side, but there's only a tiny twinge when I press my fingers to it. My skin is free of bruises and cuts, even the small scar I had on the back of my leg from falling off my roller blades as a kid is gone. I feel better than I have in years, healthier, stronger.

It takes me a few seconds to realize I'm not alone. Novik lies on his side beside me. His back is to me, so I lean over him. His eye is no longer swollen and I'm willing to bet a tooth has miraculously grown where the other was knocked out. He's still asleep, but it appears natural. It's probably best not to wake him. He was in bad need of sleep before last night.

Raised voices farther into the apartment pull my attention away from our miraculous recovery. My bare feet sink into the cream carpet. It muffles my footsteps as I pad towards the door, open it, and peak out into the hallway beyond.

I recognize Calhoun's voice immediately. Even though he isn't speaking English, his musical accent is pretty much the same. The other voice is softer, feminine, and vaguely familiar. I step back into the room, and pull on my pants and shirt. All my clothes have been cleaned and repaired. Even my shirt, which was soaked in blood. I don't bother with my boots or socks—I want to move as quietly as possible. I creep back out of the room and across the hall.

I find a good vantage point where I can see into the living room yet remain mostly hidden by a large display case full of crystal animals in the hallway. Calhoun paces the pale purple living room, talking and gesticulating. I can't see who he's talking to, but now that I'm closer to them and can hear better, I realize it's Pendragon. This must be her place.

My name being dropped intrigues me. Is Calhoun telling her what happened? If that's the case then maybe the ball is already rolling on a plan to rid the world of these bastards once and for all.

"Jerry," Pendragon calls from the living room. "We know you're there. Come in and sit with us.

My cheeks flush with the embarrassment of being found so easily. When I enter the living room Calhoun rushes to me and we hug tightly.

"How are you feeling?" He steps back and cups my face in his hands. "No residual dizziness? Any pain?"

"I feel great actually, better than I have in a long time."

His grin widens at that. "And Novik?"

"He's still sleeping."

Pendragon clears her throat. We both face her. "Lachlan was just informing me what happened tonight."

"Someone left a little surprise in my bed, then attacked us," I say in brief summation.

"So I heard." Her smile doesn't have any warmth to it. "And you managed to kill one of the Veranhiko?"

I take Calhoun's hand in mine. After witnessing my friends murder, I really need his silent support. "Lachlan slashed his neck. I shot him in the head then throttled him. He started to burn up after that."

Pendragon and Calhoun share a glance. "We've been talking about what happened since we treated you and your friend," Pendragon says then takes a moment to straighten out her long flowing skirts. "And we think we may have a plan."

"Let's hear it, I'm all ears." I sit down on the couch when she motions for me to. Calhoun sits close to me.

"We can't wait for them to come to us," Pendragon begins. "If we do then we are risking the death of someone else, maybe even ourselves. What we need is a lure, and I think we have the perfect one. The man you saved, the one currently in a coma, is the one that got away."

"What we need is a sure-fire way to kill them." I look at Calhoun, and he encourages me to go on. "We can't lure them without first knowing we can take them out, that would be suicide. I think I may be able to find out how to do that, but I need to go home first."

"And if this turns out to be a dead end?"

I shrug. "Then we're right back here, and we try your plan without that knowledge. We'll have no choice."

Pendragon takes her time reaching for her glass. "Lachlan told me about this lead." She pauses to sip her drink. "It was something your partner found out, am I right?"

"Yeah," I bristle at her tone. It's the same one she used when I interviewed her—patronizing and snide. "He told me he knew what the murderer was and how to kill it."

"But you realize you managed to kill one tonight, right?" Pendragon says.

Her question shocks me into silence. I try to order my thoughts to get my answer out. "That might be the case, but we need something concrete. We can't just rely on blind luck. What if there's more of them? It took three of us to take down one."

Pendragon shakes her head slowly. "Lachlan, if you're going to tell someone what we're doing here, then I really do wish that you tell them the whole truth."

Calhoun suddenly takes a lot of interest in his boots. "I was following orders. I had no proof until…"

The strange, uneven footing feeling is back. I let go of his hand. "No proof of what?"

Pendragon's deep blue eyes sparkle. Is she getting enjoyment out if my discomfort? "That you're a carrier of powerful magic."

A laugh bursts from my throat, more from surprise than amusement. "Good one. I needed to hear something funny."

"It's true," Calhoun whispers. "I saw it in you tonight. The Veranhiko didn't burst into flame on its own. *You* burned him."

"That's impossible!" I shout. "I'm human. I have a completely human family who I'm blood related to. There's nothing about me that isn't normal."

Pendragon settles back in her armchair completely at ease. "Are you sure about that? There's nothing that's happened during your life that makes you think there might be something different about you?"

I roll my eyes. "Apart from this case and the one in Boston, no. And none of the weird shit was caused by me."

Calhoun pats my hand. He probably means for it to be comforting, but it comes off as patronizing. "No one on Earth knows they have these powers, that's the whole point. They're supposed to be hidden. They can be in any person, anywhere in the world. We don't know who they are, but more importantly, the Veranhiko don't know where they are."

"I thought you didn't know what they're after?" I say. My heart pounds in my chest. What else did he forget to tell me before?

He bites his lip and looks away. At least he has the good grace to feel guilty about lying. "I told you what you needed to know. The last thing I wanted was you trying to track down the next victim and getting yourself killed, but things have changed." He meets my gaze without flinching. "You are one of the people they're after. You need to know how to protect yourself from them."

"And others," Pendragon adds. "You can kill these monsters, Jerry. You saw with your own eyes what you can do to them. Are you prepared to do it again?"

"This is fucking stupid," I snap. "Myles never mentioned anything about this shit. He has the answer. All I have to do is—"

"He was talking about you," Pendragon insists. "He maybe didn't know he was, but that doesn't change the facts. It's the finest irony. The only people that can destroy the Veranhiko don't even know they have the power."

"But it's just fire." The pitch of my voice rises in my confused state. "Grab a match and—"

"Hey, what's going on?" Novik says. His voice thick with sleep.

"Good to see you're awake," Pendragon says. She crosses the room and takes his hand in a motherly gesture. "We need to have a little chat. Come along." She leads him from the room. Novik throws me a confused look on his way out.

"What's she doing?" I whisper so Novik can't hear.

"She's going to rewrite his memories so he won't remember seeing a monster or anything about the healing," Calhoun says just as quietly. "It's what he, a normal human, wants to believe anyway." I make for the door but Calhoun moves at lightning speed and closes it. "Let her do it, please. It's better this way."

"Better for who, Lachlan?" I can't keep the anger out of my tone any longer. "They're after him too. He needs to know what they are."

Calhoun doesn't flinch. He tries to guide me back to the couch, but I won't move. "He's not going to be involved in this fight."

"Everyone is involved, don't you get that? We don't know who our enemy is or where they'll spring from next." I make a grab for the door, but he slaps my hand away. "You're leaving me with no support here."

"Morrigan and I will support you," Calhoun says.

"Three of us against god knows how many of them?"

Calhoun falls silent but keeps his gaze on me. "Trust me, Jerry," he finally says. "We're trying to do the right thing with the minimum amount of impact."

With a frustrated growl, I sit back down. "This is fucking bullshit."

Calhoun takes a seat next to me. "I'm sorry,"

"No, you're not." The words come out harsher than I intended, but in light of all he's kept from me I'm not going to take them back.

"I am!" he insists. "That's the other reason I healed you both, as an apology for dragging you into this."

My knuckles pop when I clench my fists. "An apology? Do you think healing my body makes up for dicking around with my friend's brains, probably mine too?"

"I saved your life!"

"You put me in danger in the first place!"

"You put yourself in danger," Calhoun jabs his finger at me. "I told you to go home. I ordered you all to stay out of those hotel rooms. Now look where we are."

"Boys," Pendragon says, having suddenly appeared at the door. "Do we really have time for petty squabbles right now?"

"You're fucking around in my friend's head," I say through gritted teeth. "Just who the hell do you two think you are?"

Pendragon doesn't flinch. "Your friend is sitting on my balcony right now, and he is free from the burden of knowing that monsters are real."

"What did you tell him?" I demand

"I told him a truth he could accept," she says firmly. "That members of The Last Defense retaliated for the arrest and sent one of their number to attack the three of you. He killed your friend, and hurt you both badly. You went to hospital and came here afterward, somewhere you knew was safe."

I scrub my hands over my face. "You've given a cop who just had his partner killed right in front of him a chance at revenge. Do you know how dangerous that is?"

Pendragon glares. "He appears to be the type of man that can show restraint."

"Unlike me you mean?"

"With all due respect, *Detective,*" Pendragon says sharply, "I barely know you."

"You two are morally fucking bankrupt," My voice shakes with anger. "Who in their right mind thinks pulling this kinda shit is okay?"

"The kind of people who can see the bigger picture." Pendragon points into the hallway. "Your friend is dealing with this all alone, distraught. Is arguing with me really that important?"

I force my anger down and brush past her. The kitchen is dominated by large glass doors that open onto a balcony heavily laden with plants and potted trees. The room itself is in the same pale color as everywhere else, down to the blond pine floors. Even the counter tops are soft peach marble, polished to a mirror shine. She's probably never cooked in here. It doesn't look used. I head out onto the balcony and stand at the railing next to Novik.

"How you doing?" I ask, and raise my voice over the drone of traffic.

"I don't know," he says. He never looks away from the road below.

I rub his back in the hope that that physical comfort will help when I can't find the words to do the job.

Novik scrubs one large hand over his face. "We gotta tell Kelly. And the kids. Fuck!" Novik bangs his fist against the wrought iron railing. "Those poor girls just lost their dad."

"They're not going to send us back to do that," I say as softly as I can. "Someone will have called back home and—"

"*I* should be the one telling her," Novik says. There's a sharp edge to his words. "He was my partner."

"I know, man, I know," I soothe. "But we don't want her finding out through some stupid Facebook post or in the papers. What if someone calls her to offer condolences before she's even found out?"

He pauses for a minute. "I don't want her finding out like that, but that doesn't change how I feel about it.

We fall into silence again. There's no point in arguing about something neither of us can change.

"We're going to get this bastard," I say half to myself. "No matter what it takes, no matter who it turns out to be, we're going to destroy them."

Novik laughs and chokes on cigarette smoke. "Yeah, things are looking just great for us." He stares down onto the busy Fifth Avenue traffic. "Harris was standing right beside me. Our arms were touching, we were that close together." His breath hitches, and he wipes his eyes. "And I could do nothing."

I attempt to pull him tighter to my side, but he's hard to move if he doesn't want to, so I get closer instead. He leans his head against mine when I press my cheek to his shoulder.

The sun continues its lazy arc across the sky while we stand there, silently mourning our friend. It's unbearably cruel what Pendragon has left Novik with—the crystal-clear memory of Harris' death, most of the details of the fight, and the belief that, somewhere out there, is the murderer. He's already gone, Harris already avenged, but Novik will never know that. Hopefully putting an end to this for good will give him some comfort.

Eventually we return inside. Novik, at my insistence, heads off to try and grab some sleep in the same room we used earlier. I consider going with him, keeping silent company just like he did with me after Myles passed, but I have something too important to ignore that I must deal with first.

Calhoun steps towards me as I enter the living room. I raise my hands to stop him from hugging me, then sit down on one of Pendragon's couches.

"Here's what's going to happen," I say, and force my voice to remain level. "You are going to tell me exactly what's going on here, from the moment you two arrived in New York up to this conversation. I want no secrets, no hiding behind whatever agency you work for. I want the truth, and if I don't get it I'm going to be really pissed."

"Don't threaten me," Pendragon says haughtily.

"Why, what're you going to do to me? Fry my brain?" I shake my head dismissively. "If you were going to do that you would have already. You want me to remember this stuff. He—" I jab my finger at Calhoun— "wants me to remember or he would've taken care of my little memory of seeing him change and sent me back to my hotel." A light bulb goes on in my head and I face Calhoun. "Did you know they were going to attack us?"

Calhoun shakes his head vigorously. "No, I swear. I wouldn't have let any of you go near if I thought so."

"But you insisted we go back to your apartment. You transformed again. You probably used those little mind powers of yours to—"

"Don't you dare," he snarls. "You wanted me just as much as I wanted you. I didn't do anything to force your decision."

I smirk. "Prove it."

"I have never made anyone do something against their will."

"Like I said, prove it."

He crosses the room with lightning fast speed and slaps me hard enough to knock me off the couch. "You fucking asshole," he snarls. "Do you think I'm so desperate for sex that I tricked some middle aged, pot-bellied, moper into bed?"

Despite declaring to myself that I don't care what he thinks of me I glance at my stomach. "I'm not fat!"

"And I'm not a sexual predator!" He sits back down, arms folded over his chest.

Pendragon glares at him, and they mutter back and forth in a singsong language I can't make head nor tail of. I rub my stinging cheek and take my seat again.

"Enough!" I shout as their muttering turns to yelling. "Lachlan, I'm sorry. I'm pissed off and, right now, I don't know what to think about either of you or this magic you seem to have." I look him straight in the eye in the hopes that will show him how serious I am. "I don't think you tricked me into bed, but the possibility my memories have been tampered with at other times is pretty real right now. Please tell me what I need to know."

Pendragon smooths out her faintly pink skirts. "Fine, since you've been so insistent. We came here five years ago with the orders to build a life in this city. We both created back stories, and slowly gained friends, employees, and a special place in the gossip webs of this city. Do you know how free people are with stories when someone is inking their skin or serving them drinks? We probably heard more than most therapists."

She pauses and flicks away a little bit of fluff that she picked from her clothes. "When we came here we had very little information to go on about who we should be looking out for. It was hoped that we would have a better idea having lived here for a bit, but there's never been any clues to what magic the Veranhiko will come after."

"I already know most of this," I say with a roll of my eyes. "You came here to protect potential targets, people like me apparently, but due to no clues, no magical pings or whatever, you've never managed to save one. But I have," I can't help throwing in.

Pendragon huffs air through her nose. "If you already know, then what do you want us to help with?"

"I need to know how all of this fits together," I say. "Why was Calhoun being trailed while working with Newlin? Why were you mixed up with them in the first place? And why did I find part of Calhoun's painter's smock at one of the scenes?"

Calhoun rubs the back of his neck. "When I get a ping on the app I showed you, I have to drop everything and go. I was wearing my smock when I fought one of them. I know it got ripped, but I only noticed after I got back to my apartment. It was too late to do anything about it then."

Pendragon's face flushes a dark pink and her eyes narrow. "I've been running around after you," she spits at Calhoun. "Cleaning up your messes. Pulling evidence that could get you killed from under the nose of the police, and you just keep messing up."

"I don't exactly get a chance to clean up after myself when I've been fighting them," Calhoun replies. His voice rises an octave with rage.

Pendragon shakes her head. "You've got to be amongst the most useless undercover agents I've ever worked with."

"Your friendship is another lie then?" I say with a derisive laugh.

"We're agents," Pendragon says firmly. "Yes, we are friends too, we couldn't work so long together without being close, but we are colleagues first and foremost."

It seems like she is the only one to feel that way because Calhoun stares at her like she slapped him. Tears fill his eyes. I almost feel sorry for him.

"How about you finish explaining all this to me," I say. "You guys can argue later."

Calhoun bows his head. Pendragon stares at him for a moment then glances at me.

"Early on in our time here, we heard rumors that led us both to believe Alex Newlin was a viable candidate for having elemental powers. We planned to have Lachlan show up looking to join his biker gang, but Newlin found his own way to us. Another reason we thought he was a possible target. Lachlan worked within the gang until we were sure Newlin was nothing more than an ordinary human."

I nod to show I'm following. "And how exactly did you find that out?"

"By closely monitoring him for just over a year. We have tests, crude at best, but they assess traits closely linked with the magic we're looking for. In Newlin's case it's the same as Lachlan's and my own, lightning. The humans that carry the lightning magic have three major traits. They are drawn towards careers such as psychologists, coders, artists—careers that require a great deal of lateral thinking and creativity. They are usually born in the fall months. And, our biggest clue, they almost always report hearing voices."

"Voices?" I say, confused. "You mean inside their head, right?"

"It depends how powerful the magic is in them," she says. "This is not the first set of murders concerning carriers of lightning, and we've seen from medical records and anecdotes that the manifestation of their powers ranges from what they assume to be extremely good people skills to misdiagnosed schizophrenia."

"But none of the victims this time around had any history of that?"

"I said it varies." Pendragon says sharply. "Some embrace it and consider it a psychic ability. For others, it's too strong, too troubling. A small number work out what it really is, that they can hear other people's thoughts, and the reactions to that knowledge vary widely. It's not going to show up in their medical records if they believe they have a gift."

I wave her explanation away. "What happened after that? Did you orchestrate your way out of the gang, or was that all a coincidence too?"

Calhoun looks sick as he starts to speak. "I set up a way to get out of the gang. Duclos and I were friends back then. He didn't know about my relationship with Newlin, but I arranged for him to find us, hoping Newlin would get enough of a scare to push me out. He didn't. He stitched Duclos up instead, and Duclos turned on me."

"Are you sure he was your friend and not just using you to give information to that site?"

"I'm sure." Calhoun says. "He told me too much of his own secrets for that."

I roll my eyes. "That's how people pull you in."

"I'm aware of that," Calhoun says firmly. "Duclos and I were friends for a long time. I tested his loyalty from time to time by giving him false information. Nothing I told him made its way onto that site. I never had a reason not to trust him."

I bite my lip against my snide reply. He's right, they knew each other for years. No matter what I think I know, I have to take Calhoun's word on Duclos.

Calhoun looks down at his feet and appears to gather his thoughts for a moment. "Before I was attacked I had been using little twists on Newlin's thoughts to gradually force us apart. I guess it worked because he dropped me pretty quick as soon as I ended up in hospital." He folds his arms over his chest defensively. "Don't feel too sorry for him. I can't make people think things they aren't considering to some degree already." He pushes his hair back behind his ears. "After Duclos saved my life, we made peace with each other and aired out our differences. He told me that he knew who had attacked me. They were a small group within his own gang, but he had nothing to do with it. I believed him. I had no reason not to. That was when we hatched a plan. He read those in his gang the riot act for trying to kill me then let them think he'd been persuaded to their cause. He got access to *Thelastdefense.com* and was included in top secret conversations. All that information he passed onto me. A few weeks before his death his membership to the secret sections of the site was rescinded. It happened to a few others. I did try to tell him to take more precautions, but he didn't listen."

"Did you kill him?" I say almost immediately.

Calhoun stares at me in shock. "Of course not! He was my friend, my ally. And all he wanted in return was a chance to travel to my home with me. I never hurt a hair on his head."

My eyebrow quirks up. "Even though he told me he wasn't your friend and denied knowing about the attack?"

"I told him to," Calhoun says sharply. He looks directly into my eyes, defiant. "I knew you would see through him. You're not stupid. It was a way of directing your investigation where I wanted it to go, but you went your own way."

I steadfastly refuse to look away from him. "I'm a private investigator. It's my job to investigate things, funnily enough."

Pendragon clears her throat. "Do you want an explanation or not?"

"Did Duclos send the letters to you?" I ask without sparing Pendragon a glance.

Calhoun and Pendragon look at one another for a long time. Calhoun bites his lip, and all the anger in his expression melts into worry and regret. Oh, this can't be good.

"We've been sending them," Calhoun admits in a barely audible voice. "We've been using our knowledge of the other murders and anything new I've seen while fighting these monsters." He scrubs his hands over his face. "I didn't send the crude ones, I'm not sure who did, but they gave me the idea."

I clasp my hands to stop them from shaking. The ten seconds I take before answering is not enough to cool my temper. "So, the whole reason I'm here is a lie?"

"No, not a lie." Pendragon says. "We needed to bring you here because we knew someone on the Boston case had figured out how to kill these monsters. We just didn't know that the answer would be hidden inside another Boston detective."

"Why didn't you just ask me about it?" I say sharply. "Pretend to be a cop working on the case? Someone writing a book about it? Why make up such a stupid lie and not know if you were going to get any answers at all?"

Calhoun looks helplessly at Pendragon. "Because this seemed like the best way," Pendragon says apologetically. "It had to fit in with back stories we had already created."

"You hauled me from my life." I punch the couch. "You made me and my friends targets. Not only of these killers, but a group of radicalized conspiracy theorists too. You might as well have killed Harris your damn self!"

"I never meant to hurt you," Calhoun pleads. "I was just trying to do my job. I had no idea you were carrying these powers yourself."

I rub my forehead in exasperation. "So, you two have been running around behind my back, taking evidence, fucking around in people's heads, and lying through your back teeth at every turn?" I point in their faces. "You realize you're responsible for every damn death in this case, right?" When they protest I motion for them both to be quiet. "We're done! Hand over your phone. I'll track these bastards myself."

Calhoun holds his hands up as if asking for calm. "We can work this out. This is bigger than all of us."

"What part of done don't you understand?" I snap. I push my face close to his. "You lied to me about everything. You have fucked up my entire life. Stay out of my way if you know what's good for you."

I storm through to wake Novik. Calhoun follows me.

"I'm sorry, Jerry."

"I don't give a shit," I say. I hate the tremble in my voice but I can't get rid of it "I trusted you. I cared about you. I put my life on the line to keep you safe from a threat that didn't even exist. If I never see you again, it'll be too fucking soon."

"I know it looks bad, but what happened between me and you has got noth—"

"There is no me and you."

He forces himself between me and the door to the room. "Please listen to me!"

"Give me one reason why I should."

"I didn't get involved with you because it was part of this mission. What happened with Newlin wasn't part of some plan either."

"It's kinda convenient, though, that the two people that you were supposed to seek out ended up in bed with you, huh?" I take a deep breath and try to calm myself a little bit. "If I didn't need to speak to Novik we could be in Boston by now. So, when would you have told me the truth? Once those things were killed? Maybe once we'd fucked a few more times, or I'd fallen for you? Or maybe you'd just run off after all this was done. Mission over, see ya later, Jer."

"No, I…"

I cross my arms over my chest and wait from him to answer. "Well?" I prompt. When his silence continues I shove him out of my way and step into the room.

"Time to go, Marty," I say, and shake Novik awake. He grumbles and sleepily swipes out at me, but eventually sits up.

"What the hurry?" he asks and rubs his eyes. "Do we need to go to the station?"

"No one's called yet," I say. "We better go is all."

"Go where, Jerry? Our hotel rooms are crime scenes."

"Then we'll stay somewhere else." I pull my boots on. "Let's go."

Novik frowns but gets ready to go all the same. Calhoun hands over my keys without any further fight. I don't spare him a glance as we leave.

"Maybe we should just go to the station rather than them chasing us?" Novik quietly suggests. "They're probably trying to give us time to grieve. I don't know about you, but I'd rather be doing something constructive."

"It's not like we've got anywhere else to go," I say with a shrug.

He looks me up and down then shakes his head slowly. "I think I must've had a weird dream about you. Well, not just you, but that whole thing last night."

I fight hard to keep my expression neutral. "What did you see?"

"I don't know, it's kind of fuzzy now. I kind of remember seeing something burning, and you had orange eyes. I know it was just a dream, but something feels off."

It's only the fear that telling him the truth will screw his mind up further that stops me setting him straight. "It was a pretty hectic night. Everything happened so fast and mostly in the dark. I'm not surprised you dreamed weird shit after that."

"Yeah, that's probably it." Novik steps from the elevator, limping slightly on his twisted ankle. Why leave that unhealed but fix his face? Is this some way of giving our bullshit story credence? At least it doesn't seem as bad as it was.

At the station, everyone talks to us in hushed voices, like they're scared a louder tone is going to hurt us. Novik warmly accepts their hugs, but I hang back, scared their well-meaning gestures will break the fragile hold I have on my emotions.

The statements are hard to write, and not just because we have to painstakingly recount Harris' death. I should have found out exactly what Novik's memory had been changed to, down to the letter. One tiny detail that doesn't match is going to cause us a problem.

After I'm done with that, I put the whole incident out of my mind and deflect any questions my friends have. I focus instead on finding some good in a bad situation. I can discard so much of the investigation that confused me before. The letters aren't a link, but there is still information passing between Rexus' gang and the Veranhiko, how else would one of the shape-shifters have known where to find us? If I hadn't seen the gray sludge spilling from the guy that killed Harris, I would have put this all down the Rexus' gang, and that's how I must play it to the others. All the suspects we bring in can still be tested to see whether they're human or not, it's as simple as taking a blood sample or pricking their finger. The change is just on the surface.

Jameson sits down next to me, disturbing my thoughts. "Novik is gonna stay with me. You're welcome to too."

I force a smile. "Thanks, man. I really appreciate it."

He squeezes my shoulder. "We're leaving now. Are you coming? You look like you could use a break too."

I look down at the pile of notes on the desk. "Sure. You don't mind if I work at your place, do you?"

"Be my guest." Jameson pats my back then stands. I get up too.

"Where're you guys going?" McCray asks.

"Higgins and Novik are going to stay with me," Jameson explains. "We're heading out but I'll be back in a few hours. I need to get some rest."

"Can you stay behind, Higgins," McCray asks. "I need to speak to you about something."

I bite my tongue so I can't tell him to go fuck himself. I'm just cranky, nothing to do with McCray. "Sure."

Jameson nods then squeezes my shoulder. "See you in a bit."

Novik hugs me before he follows Jameson out. We don't speak. We have nothing we wish to discuss in front of everyone else. I so badly want to go with them that it hurts to stay still.

I pull another chair over to McCray's desk. "How are you holding up?" I ask.

McCray shrugs. "I didn't know him as well as you did."

"I guess not." I smooth my hair back behind my ears. "So, what did you want to talk to me about?"

McCray leans back in his chair. "What's your thoughts on what happened last night?"

I frown. "Didn't I write this all down in my statement?"

"Yeah, but I was thinking there might be insights you didn't want to put on paper."

"Uh, no. Like I said in my statement we got back to the hotel, found our rooms trashed and the bodies in my bed. Some guy attacked us. We tried to stop him but he got away."

McCray nods and glances at his computer screen. "Did you get a good look at the guy?"

I huff air angrily through my nose. "It was pitch black. Do you want to tell me what this is really about?"

"I'm just double checking your story while I have you here. This guy killed one of our own. I'm not leaving any stone unturned." He studies his computer screen again. "Anyway, that's everything. You can go now. I'll walk you out."

"That really isn't necessary," I say and make a valiant effort to keep the annoyance from my voice.

McCray shrugs. "I'm going out anyway. We might as well go together."

My jaw hurts from how tightly I have it clamped shut. McCray stands, bangs his desk with his gut, and knocks over a take-out coffee cup. The scalding liquid splashes onto my arm. I yelp and jump back out of the way. McCray wipes at his soaked shirt, hisses, then shakes his hand.

"Well that was fucking dumb," he says with a laugh. He takes the paper towels I've grabbed from the side of the coffee machine, cleans his desk up, and pats at his shirt.

Little red marks appear on my skin. McCray got hit with a lot more of it than me. How is he so calm? "Are you okay?" I ask.

"Yeah. It'll wash out. Come on, let's get out of here." He takes a step, and his face screws up with pain. "Shit, I guess I pulled a muscle jumping up like that."

I look him up and down as he takes another step. He's definitely dragging his leg, but it seems to ease the more he walks on it. I fall into step beside him.

"You try to get some rest, okay Jer?" he says as we step outside. "We're gonna need to be sharp to see this through to the end."

"Yeah, I'll get right on that. Gimme a call if you need anything." I say and get into my car.

McCray nods and gets into his own car. My hands shake badly when I try to put my keys in the ignition. I fumble with them one too many times and drop them. It's such a stupid thing, seeing my keys on the floor of the car, but it's the last straw. I punch the steering wheel as hard as I can, and the horn blares. My roar of frustration is louder. I slump forward, lay my head against the steering wheel, and let my emotions take over.

The shrill ring of my phone is a welcome interruption. I wipe tears from my eyes, see Novik's name on the screen, and answer.

"Ah, Detective Higgins. I did wonder when we would have a chance to talk."

I frown. The voice on the other end of the phone is deep and echoey. There's no discernible accent. "Who's this?"

"That's not important. Do you want to know what is? I have your friends, and if you don't do exactly what I say, then I'm going to kill them. And I'm really going to enjoy taking my time about it too."

There's no one around that I can catch the attention of so I stay calm and ask, “What do you want?”

“You, my friend. No matter how hard I try I can't seem to keep you down. It was more of an irritant before, but you just had to go and kill one of my best soldiers, didn't you?” There’s a hint of amusement to the caller’s tone.

“Self-defense,” I say flatly.

“Well then, consider this self-preservation for me and my soldiers,” he says. “Here's what you're going to do. You will meet me in two hours next to the turtle pond in Central Park. Not two hours and one minute, or one hour fifty-nine. Two hours. If you come with me quietly, then your friends will go free. If you cause any trouble, bring any cops along for the ride, or tell them where you're going, then I'll kill them and make you watch every deliciously gory minute of it.”

My hands are shaking again, but it's not sadness this time. “Two hours, Central Park turtle pond. Got it.”

“Oh, and one more thing, Jerry. Be a dear and bring that nice man you took to the hospital with you. He's supposed to come with us, you see, and we're not leaving without him.”

He hangs up before I can answer, but not before letting me hear Novik and Jameson shouting in the background. They don't sound harmed in any way, but if this bastard is even half as sadistic as our murderer, then I doubt that’ll last for long.

First thing I do is call in an anonymous tip and inform dispatch that our guitarist, Mads, could be in danger. Next, I swallow my pride and head back to Pendragon's. After a brief discussion with the doorman, I am ushered up to her apartment.

“Back so soon?” she smirks.

“Don't even start,” I snap. “Is Calhoun still here? I need to speak to you both. Now.”

Pendragon stalks towards another of the bedrooms in her apartment. Calhoun is lying on the bed, curled up on his side and sobbing softly. Despite all the anger I feel towards him, my heart clenches at the sight of his tears.

He sits up quickly and wipes his eyes when he sees me. "Jerry, you came back!"

"Don't get your hopes up. This is nothing more than business." I say in as neutral a tone as I can manage. "These monsters have two of my friends, and they are blackmailing me into handing over the victim I saved. You want to prove to me you're not some manipulative asshole who used me for his own gains, then help me beat them."

"Anything! Just tell me what you want me to do."

"You're sure I can kill these things, right?" I look at them both and search for any doubt in their faces. "It was definitely something I did that killed him?"

Calhoun nods vigorously. "It was your magic. I'm sure of it."

"Okay, in that case, why doesn't your magic work?"

His face falls. "I…. I have no idea. I didn't know anything could kill them until you did."

"It's true," Pendragon says. "This has always been a kind of suicide mission."

"My heart bleeds for you," I reply, and my voice drips with sarcasm. "If my powers are the key to this then how do I get them to work?"

Calhoun chews his painted nail as he thinks. "You have fire, so anger would probably be the easiest thing, given the circumstances. I imagine they work similar to ours. You just direct it with your thoughts or gestures. Will the magic out."

"That's it?" I say skeptically. "All this apparent god-like magic, and it boils down to abracadabra?"

Pendragon snorts a laugh. "A cynic to the last."

I wave her comment away. "Okay, I have less than two hours to hatch a plan and get to Central Park, and I have to try and hit the time exactly. The guy that called knows I can kill their kind, or he has been told that I've killed one of their agents. Either way, we need to prepare for the worst-case scenario that we'll be facing the Veranhiko again." I hold out my hand to him. "Will you help me?"

Calhoun immediately shakes my hand. "I'll do everything in my power."

Pendragon and Calhoun listen to my rough idea the help me refine it. Once I'm satisfied we're as organized as we're going to be I leave the apartment with a half hour to spare to source another possible ally.

The guy specifically said no cops. He didn't say anything about not bringing a biker gang as back up.

18

Showdown

Central Park is eerily quiet. Although I've seen a lot of it from above since Calhoun's apartment looks into it, I've never actually walked around. It's huge. I keep an eye on my phone screen as the seconds tick by. The turtle pond is silent. There's not a single person around, no animals, no birds. It's not natural. At exactly one a.m.—two hours to the second since he called me—I receive a text from Novik's phone.

Approach the castle. I will meet you halfway. Any funny business and I'll flay them both and feed you their skin.

I look around. I can't sense anyone nearby, but I know that Newlin and his guys have this place surrounded. They don't think or move like cops. They know how to keep hidden, and they'll fight dirty if needs be too. I wish I had some way of contacting them, but any kind of earpiece or hand signal would just give the whole thing away. They're watching and they are ready to move in. That's what's important.

Calhoun doesn't react at all as I hoist him back up over my shoulder. Who knew he could play a person in a coma so well? His freshly dyed hair still carries its chemical scent, and it clashes harshly with the earthy smell of the park itself. The sword strapped to his chest digs into me, so I shift him over a little. The path is well lit. The shadows outside of the pools of light are inky black. If I have to move off the walkway I'm going to be pretty much blind for a few seconds.

Someone walks towards me. They are dressed all in black, and their face is obscured by a baseball cap. Their long coat billows out around their feet as they walk. I stop when they do, about two feet from them, and watch carefully for their next move. I can't see their face at all—I can't read them.

"Lay him down here," he commands. It's the same voice from the phone call—deep, echoey, and devoid of accent.

"Where are my friends?" I ask in a forceful but calm voice.

"First, fulfill your end of the bargain." He points at the ground between us. "Leave him there. Let me check that he is the man I'm looking for, then you'll see your friends again."

I pause before I answer. "They could be dead for all I know. Prove to me they're alive."

The guy sighs heavily and makes a beckoning motion towards the castle. Shit. There's more than one of them. I should have known! The second man is taller and heavier built, but that's all I can make out through his dark clothing. He holds Novik tightly by the arm and hurries him along.

"There," the shorter one says. "He's right here and still breathing. How long that stays true is up to you."

"Where's the other cop you took?"

"Hand over the guy, and I'll bring him out."

Calhoun subtly nods, just enough for me to feel the movement. He's right, I have to give these bastards something to keep them playing. Novik looks completely unhurt, and I can only hope the same is true for Jameson. I walk forward then carefully lay Calhoun on the ground. He's wrapped up tight with the sword hidden from view. His face is completely serene. If I didn't know any better, I'd think he was really out of it.

"Good, now step away."

"Let my friend go first."

Shorty looks back at his taller companion, then jerks his head towards me. "Release him."

Beanpole releases his grip on Novik, who moves to stand by my side. I flex my hands, and watch the men in black carefully.

"I've fulfilled my end of the bargain, now step back." Shorty waves his hand as if shooing me away.

I back off; Novik walks with me. Calhoun lies deathly still even as Shorty leans in to get a better look at him. The light is a hell of a lot brighter than I bargained for. I hope Calhoun's disguise is good enough. My heart hammers in my chest, but I keep my breathing controlled and my eyes on them.

Shorty looks Calhoun over then straightens up. "Well, you did get the right guy after all."

"I'm a man of my word," I say firmly. "Release my other friend, now."

Shorty laughs. "Bring the other one out."

Beanpole appears a few moments later with Jameson. Oh, thank god! They're both unharmed. Jameson snatches his arm back from Beanpole and throws him a glare before walking over to me. He looks from Calhoun to me, his eyebrows knitted in confusion. I try to convey to him with just a simple look that I have it all under control, but I'm scared even the simplest lift of my eyebrow will give the plan away.

We didn't think we'd get this far without them finding out it's all a trick.

Shorty extends his arm, as if inviting me to take his hand. "You remember our deal, don't you?"

"I remember," I say as calmly as I can.

Jameson grabs my arm. "You can't go," he says in a harsh whisper. "He'll kill you."

"I promised," I say. "Don't worry."

Jameson narrows his eyes as if he is trying to read me, and lets me go. I wish I could see the face of either one of our enemies. Are they smirking? Do they look nervous? Is there any clue at all to what they are thinking in their expressions? Their body language gives little away. Shorty is maybe a little too confident His arm is still outstretched, and nothing about him looks tensed up. Beanpole is pretty much the same with his relaxed posture and both arms loose at his sides. I measure my reach carefully in my head, planning what could be my only shot, and wait for Calhoun's signal.

As soon as Shorty has his hand on my arm, Calhoun yells, "now!"

I grab the dagger from my pocket, sweep around in a wide arc, and slash it across Shorty's throat. The blade jams into something hard, but just for a second before the momentum of my blow dislodges it. A small, gray box on a Velcro collar hits the walkway. I pick it up and take a closer look. It's a voice modulator.

Shorty gurgles and gasps. Blood spurts an impressive distance from his throat. He falls to his knees, and claws at his torn neck. Come on, change! Show me the monster you really are. Where's the gray goo, the red eyes? Too late, I realize what I've done. Now I can see Shorty's face. His blue eyes are frozen in shock, and his blood-spattered lips open and close with each failed attempt at breathing.

He's just a kid!

Beanpole stares at the fountain of red spurting from his friend's neck for a second longer before he turns on his heel and runs. Calhoun gives chase, but I tackle him to the ground.

"They're fucking kids!" I roar in his face. "You swore to me they were monsters."

"We *have* been fighting monsters. You saw one of them yourself." Calhoun tries to force me up and away from him, but I pin his wrists to the pathway. "They must be using members of the Last Defense, just like I said!" Calhoun insists.

"How do I know it's not a memory plant, just like what you did to Novik?" I get up, and drag Calhoun with me. "Look at him!" I grab his hair and force his face close to Shorty's. "Does he look like a monster to you?"

I flinch as a large hand closes around my arm. "He's trouble," Novik says softly. "He forced you into making this mistake. Set it right. Call it in, and blame him."

"I can't do that. It was my fault. I have to tell—"

"Why die for a monster, a liar, a killer," Novik whispers almost directly into my ear. "He's been leading you along all this time, twisting your thoughts, getting what he wants, including you."

"He did. I've nearly busted him twice, and he's always weaseled his way out."

"Then call it in, anonymously if you have—"

He stops mid-sentence, his mouth frozen in an 'O' of surprise. My hand sinks deeper into his abdomen, following the dagger I drove into him.

"Next time you wanna fool someone." I twist the blade this way and that, "make sure you know what information the person you are pretending to be has."

Gray sludge pours from the gaping wound and over my arm. Novik's face starts to lose shape like a deflating balloon. There're no bones, no organs, no blood. Just clay-like… stuff.

"Tell me where my friends are," I demand. The monster's eyes flicker green to red and back again. It smiles at me with sickly gray lips but doesn't speak. I twist the dagger again. "Tell me or you die!"

"We can't die, idiot!" Jameson snarls as he walks towards us. "We were here when the universe began. We will survive its end. You are a mere inconvenience. You got lucky last time, but that won't happen again."

I try to pull my arm free, ready to defend myself, but I'm stuck fast. Calhoun moves in, but the demon in Jameson's shape grabs me around the throat. Needle like claws press into my skin.

"One move from you," he warns Calhoun, "and I kill him. The same goes for your friends in the woods." He lifts my free hand, cuts my palm with his claw, then licks the blood off. "I'd know that taste anywhere, son of fire." He sighs then pats fake Novik's shoulder. "Bring them to the circle."

Fake Novik restrains Calhoun and me against his putty-like skin. It molds over us, and binds us to his chest. Struggling only earns us a few slaps and a fat lip. We aren't led far, just around the path until we are on the shore of the turtle pond. The walkway has been swept clean.

"I've been waiting a long time for this moment," fake Jameson says as he surveys the area. "To stand in front of a carrier of elemental power and explain just how much they've been used by the people supposedly trying to save them." He steps close to me, red eyes blazing. "Do you know what you are, Jerry."

"The guy that's going to kick your ass," I say, and force as much aggression into it as I can. I spit in his face and struggle to free myself.

Jameson laughs. "You have his fighting spirit. Good."

"Who's?"

Fake Jameson gently pets my hair and winds a lock around his fingers. "He really told you nothing, didn't he?" he says and jerks his head towards Calhoun. "You have a power in you, a magic, and it was gifted to you by a god. Not just to you, of course, or even your ancestors, but the human race as a whole. Through thousands of years of evolution, births, deaths, wars, migrations, that magic has found its way into you. We want it."

"Then take it," I say. "I never asked for it."

Fake Jameson laughs. "If it was that easy, we would have all six already. Every kill we make sends the magic into someone else. It doesn't reside in any part of the human body that we can remove. We've done our experiments to find that out, as I'm sure you've already seen from the bodies we've left behind. It seems the only way to get the magic back home is to take you alive."

Suddenly Calhoun is spat out from Novik's chest and sprawls on the ground. Jameson grabs him by the hair and hauls him across the path. Calhoun twists and tries to tear himself free, but Jameson's fingers elongate, snake down through Calhoun's hair, and wrap him up tight. He stands Calhoun in the middle of the swept path, and with his free hand, he cuts a line across Calhoun's cheek. He flicks the blood onto the ground. It sizzles and sparks like gunpowder and etches a small curve on the path.

I try to haul my arms and legs free, but the substance that makes up my captor's body tightens. It crushes around my chest until I'm struggling to draw breath. Jameson cuts Calhoun's cheek again, and spatters the ground with more of his blood. The pattern grows. He raises the knife again and pulls Calhoun's head back. The artery in Calhoun's neck throbs. I can't get enough breath to scream.

Suddenly, Jameson's face explodes outwards, and spatters the ground and us with gobs of smoking, putrid goo. The larger pieces still retain parts of Jameson's features. His disembodied eye blinks at me from the shore of the lake. He drops Calhoun and claws at his face. Calhoun rolls as he hits the ground and leaps for Novik. He drives his sword so close to the back of my shoulder that the point slices my shirt. Novik howls and spits me onto the ground.

"Now, Jerry!" Calhoun screams. "Use it!"

I point both hands at Novik and concentrate as hard as I can. My hands heat up, sweat breaks out on my brow.

Nothing happens.

Wolf-like howls break out in the woods around us, and Newlin's gang spills onto the path. One of the Wolves crashes to the ground, a knife buried deep in his back. His attacker pulls the weapon out and swings it at another. A gunshot rings out, and the rogue biker's head explodes in a shower of gray goo.

They're everywhere!

Calhoun and I jump into the fray. The numbers of changelings in Newlin's gang are small, but they don't go down easy, and the ones that do don't stay down. The one with the exploded head joins the fight again with only half of his face regrown. Hacking off limbs doesn't slow them down. Cutting them open stops them for a few minutes, but their strength is just the same when they repair their bodies. I quickly run out of bullets and resort to what I can scavenge. Luckily, I find a machete lodged between the shoulder blades of another biker. I haul it out and drive it through the skull of a guy rushing at me, knife held high. Blood spurts from the wound, and he falls to the ground before his eyes have dimmed.

Shit! We can't fight them if we don't know who's our enemy and who's not!

I scream as a blinding pain blooms from deep in my right shoulder. I run my hand over my skin, and look for the handle of a knife or some other weapon, but my fingers sink into a ragged hole instead. Fuck, the bullet must be lodged in my arm somewhere. There's no exit wound.

A snarling heavy-built guy with scraggly blond hair rushes at me. I block his clumsy knife blow with my own weapon, but his next attack comes from the other side and forces me to use my damaged arm. The impact sends shock-waves up the bones and deep into my shoulder. My brain fuzzes with the pain.

With a loud roar Newlin runs in and drives his fist into the guy's face. He goes down hard, and instantly loses consciousness.

"Bleeding," Newlin mutters, and points at the small river trickling from the guy's temple. "Those other things don't bleed." He grabs my wrist. "Stay with me so we know we got another human with us."

I let him pull me along. He has a gash on the shaved side of his head, right through his wolf's head tattoo, and half of his face is crimson. If he is in any pain he shows no signs of it. I take his fresh, bleeding wound as a sign he isn't one of the Veranhiko.

Newlin moves through the chaos and uses well aimed punches to determine who he can trust and who he can't. Soon, we have a group of about ten confirmed humans. We hold our ground, back to back, and add to our circle when we find others. My shirt sticks to my back. My right arm is pretty much useless from the gunshot to my shoulder. Blood—my own and others'—drips from my hair and into my eyes. I swing my machete as a half-formed humanoid blob shuffles towards me. A spray of gray joins the stripes of red on the walkway.

A loud scream rattles the air. One of the monsters holds a struggling biker off the ground and chants loudly through its misshapen maw. It slits the biker's neck. Blood pours from him and onto the walkway. The ground shudders as the circular pattern etches into the path, throwing up sparks and flame. Calhoun rushes forward, roars in fury, and transforms on the move. Wings spread, he jumps into the air. His sword comes down in a sweeping arc right through the center of the monster. The top half of its putty-like body slides off and hits the walkway with a squelch.

It's too late, though. The portal is already opening.

Calhoun stumbles back. I move towards the glowing portal, ready to help him fight off whatever is growling on the other side. Without warning, he screams and rises from the ground. Blood sprays my face as a blade bursts through his back. It severs his bones, muscle, and skin as he is cleaved in half. His killer pulls itself free of the portal, wipes its gore-covered blade through its clay hand, then lifts one foot in the air. Our eyes meet as its foot hardens then slams down onto Calhoun's skull.

Time seems to slow down. More creatures spill from the portal, but all I can see is the fucker in front of me. It attempts a smile with its misshapen features, rubs its foot into Calhoun's skull, and crushes what's left of his face.

A wave of nausea hits me and rises fast into my throat. An inhuman, echoing roar bursts forth in place of the vomit I expected. My skin tingles all over. I thrust my hands at him. The heat on my palms is intense. The monster bursts into flame. It writhes, screams and frantically pats at its smoldering flesh. My body moves of its own accord. I stride forward and kick the creature back through the portal.

I move swiftly through the Veranhiko and rip heads from clay bodies before immolating the remains. Flames lick at the trees and grass of the park. The stench of burning skin and leather fills my nostrils, but nothing deters me from getting my revenge.

The monsters flee from me and back into their portal. I wave my hand, sending fire after them, and laugh as their bodies bubble and burst with the heat. Flames lick along my fingers, but I feel nothing, just warmth and a sick satisfaction. As the last one runs for the gateway I make a leap for it. We hit the ground together.

And fall right through it.

I tumble forward onto hard-packed, cracked earth, choke on my first breath of ice filled air, and sweep my hair out of my eyes. Where the fuck am I?

The sky is full of steel gray, swirling clouds. Jagged mountains thrust upwards from the cracked, dry earth. There's nothing here. No grass, no life, nothing but twisted gray things in their barren gray world. Then I hear it. The roar of thousands of feet all pounding towards me. An army of Veranhiko march on the portal, running as if their lives depend on catching me. I quickly look around. There's nowhere to go. The portal symbol is ashes under my feet. Well, if this is how I'm supposed to die then at least let me go out with a bang. I raise my hands towards the army and force every last piece of energy I have towards them. The leading line explodes in a fury of flame and smoke, closely followed by the second. But there are more, and they're still coming.

Something clamps around my ankle. I look down. A hand and forearm protrude from the gateway and, as I watch, it yanks my ankle, hard.

I fall back through the cracked earth just as the front line reaches the perimeter of the portal. The noisy ruin of Central Park thunders into existence. Smoke fills my lungs before I fall into the turtle pond, and cool water takes its place. I surface, coughing and spluttering.

"It's okay," Newlin shouts over the roar of burning trees. "Stay low to the water, out of the smoke."

I have no choice but to do as he says. Sirens burst through the other noises, but there's no way the emergency services can get to us. We're surrounded by a wall of crackling trees and burning earth. I return Newlin's hug, and we both settle in for the wait.

It gets harder to breathe. Newlin wheezes and coughs at my side, even with his soaked shirt pulled up over his nose and mouth. I can't see a thing through the dense air, and my eyelids are heavy. My head lolls forward.

Newlin shakes me. “Don't fall asleep, okay? Just a little longer.”

I nod but slump against him. I can no longer hear him speaking, but the timbre of his voice is comforting. After what seems like an age there's a change in his tone, and he tries to move me. Many hands are on me, they lift me up, and then I'm being laid down on a solid surface. The air that hits my lungs is fresh and cool.

It's safe now. There's no more danger, no more waiting for rescue, just let go, sleep.

Jerry, open your eyes.

“Fuck you,” I mumble. “We're safe, let me sleep.”

It's important. Open them!

I try my best to ignore it, but the voice is persistent. I slowly open my eyes. The sky above me is a soft pink, and the clouds are dusted with gold. A gentle breeze carries the scent of freshly mown grass. I bask in it for a moment, then it hits me. Where's the burning woods of Central Park, the acrid stench of singed hair and melting skin? I force myself to my feet and whip around. I'm in my backyard. No, my parents' backyard. My childhood home sits where it always has, on top of the gentle slope of the lawn, but its colors are muted, the whole picture hazy. Beyond the fence should be other yards, other homes, but there's nothing except a moving wall of cloud.

“I thought you'd feel safest here,” says a deep male voice.

He steps towards me from behind the oak tree that always dominated the lawn, and I back away. He looks, well, he looks like me—long black hair, thin built. I'm not sure my jaw is so angular though.

“I'm not you, Jerry,” he says. He even has my accent. “But we are, for lack of a better word, related.”

"Who the fuck are you?" I demand, and look around for a way out.

"I guess you could say I'm your father."

I laugh so hard I double over. "I know who my dad is, you wierdo. I've known him my whole life. I was named after him."

My almost-twin stops in front of me. Now that he's up close I can see more differences—the faint age lines around his eyes and mouth, the strange tiger striping of tattoos that I took for shadows at first glance. He studies me in the same way, then smiles.

"I didn't say I fathered you. I had absolutely nothing to do with you coming into this world. Your parents, the ones you have known and loved for forty years, they *are* yours. However, I did have a hand in making you, well, you." He rests his hand on my shoulder. His warmth seeps through my clothes. "Come sit with me, and I'll explain."

My curiosity overrides everything else, and I let myself be led into the shade of the oak tree. Everything feels so real—the bark of the tree, the grass underfoot, even the breeze.

"Am I dead?" I ask.

"No, not dead, but you are close to it. That's how I could pull you out. Your body won't miss you right now, not while it's fighting to repair itself." He makes himself comfy against the tree and stretches his legs out in front of him. "I'm sorry you had to go through all that. We have no choice where our magic goes."

"Magic?" I look down at my hands. The flames are long gone, not a trace of them remains. "Oh, I guess you must be. . ." I leave the question unfinished. Even here, in this strange frozen moment, it seems ridiculous to say.

"Yes, I am the god they mentioned. My name is Lasair, and I'm—"

The ground under us shakes violently, but it passes in seconds. Lasair looks around then takes both my hands in his.

"We don't have much time, so listen well," he says. "The magic in you is awake now. You're aware of it, but don't think you can control it yet. It's sentient in a way. It will try to protect itself, and you, like you saw tonight. Rage, a threat to your life, these are triggers for it, but other emotions cause smaller reactions. You can learn to control it through experimentation. It's important that you do." He pauses as another, stronger quake rumbles under us. "Changes have already begun in you. You'll see the first one when you wake up. Don't be alarmed. It's easy to hide."

"What if other people see it? They're going to know."

"Don't worry. You'll be surprised the lengths people go to so they can normalize situations for themselves." He lays his hand against my cheek before brushing his fingers through my hair. His skin is warm and dry, his touch strangely comforting. "I know you're scared, and you have every right to be, so I want to give you a gift. Those monsters are greatly weakened thanks to you. You have destroyed so many of them on their home world that portals can no longer be opened. With that link broken, the Veranhiko left behind on Earth will slowly lose their powers, but they could still come for you. They're still dangerous. With that in mind, I give you the gift of true sight so you can identify them. Just like me, you'll be able to see the heat in the blood of all living things. You'll be able to sense that warmth, that pulse of life, that none of the Veranhiko have." Another tremor silences him for a moment. "My son," he whispers, and presses his forehead to mine. "Take this gift, and know."

The ground shakes, splits underneath us, and throws me down into its depths. I hurtle through the air with the wind whistling past my ears and stealing my voice. There's light at the bottom of the chasm. It grows brighter until…

Shapes fill my blurry vision. Slowly, they become clearer, and bring noises with them—the bleeps of machinery, and fast paced chatter. I try to speak, but my tongue refuses to cooperate. The fuzzy figures move, merge, and fill the air with a soft glow, almost like each of them is carrying a small candle. Someone calls my name. A face appears in front of mine. Deep brown eyes are the first thing I see clearly.

"Jerry, can you hear me?" she asks.

It takes an inhuman amount of effort for me to nod, but I manage it.

"Can you tell me your full name?"

To my ears I sound drunk, but the doctor only nods as I tell her my name. She turns to her colleagues and speaks quickly, using a whole bunch of medical jargon I can't begin to understand, then looks at me again.

"You've been shot in your right shoulder. We've got the bullet out, and pinned the bones back together but it's going to be sore for a while. We're going to move you to a room now. Rest. You're going to be okay."

The parts of the doctor's face I can see over her mask glow with a soft, golden light. No matter what the skin color of the people I see—dark like the doctor, or pale like the nurse closest to me—they all carry the same sunset colors. I raise my hand as much as I can, and the doctor takes it in her own. Maybe she thought I was reaching for her? Gold shimmers along her arm and down to the tips of her fingers, following the branching of her veins and arteries. My own hand glows the same way.

"You're real," I mumble. I grip her hand with all my might, which isn't much right now. "You shine." I want to say more, explain what I mean to the confused doctor, but it's taking every bit of effort I have to keep my eyes open.

"Don't fight it," she whispers, and gently pats my hand. "You need your rest. I'll be right here while we move you to your room."

True to her word she holds my hand the whole way to the unit, and chats softly with the staff pushing my bed. The soft buzz of conversation is enough to make me lose my battle with exhaustion, and I slip back into the comforting embrace of sleep.

The shining people I saw when I woke up in the recovery room are quickly explained over the next few days. My left eye is injured and my vision blurry, perhaps permanently. I see the glow on and off, but it's just another symptom of the damage I received. Despite knowing something’s wrong, the doctors and even an eye specialist can't figure out what exactly it is. Discoloration of my iris—it’s now gold instead of blue—is the only physical change they can find. At a loss of what else to do to help they give me an eye patch to wear over my good eye in the hopes the muscles in the other will strengthen and improve my vision. For me, it's more important to hide my gold iris, so the eye patch eventually ends up permanently over my left eye.

My shoulder is my only other acute injury. My splintered bones were pinned back together, and my shoulder joint realigned before I woke up in recovery. It takes a few days for the pain to become manageable without strong pain relief, but at least I will regain full movement in my arm eventually.

Rodowski visits every day. Through her I begin to get a picture of how the events in Central Park are being reported. There's no mention of monsters or portals, not that I expected there to be, but the fire, the involvement of the Last Defense, the Wolves, and members of the NYPD, has been twisted up into some kind of gang war. I give my version of events to everyone that will listen, not just Rodowski but the detectives from other departments who are part of the investigation. The Wolves are not going to get the blame for this, they were there to help.

On the seventh day of my hospital stay a package is left for me. Inside is a flash drive, a small, shining black box, and a letter from Pendragon.

Jerry,

Let me begin by saying that anyone injured in the Central Park fire will have their medical bills paid for, it's the least we could do. Secondly, during our own investigation of the park we found enough material from our enemy to fashion an identification device. Obviously, we have don't have the means to test it on living Veranhiko, but it does accurately identify their genetic signature from samples that we have. Please take this as our gift to you. Hopefully you will never hear it go off.

By the time you get this letter Lachlan, all our fellow agents, and I will be long gone. We have erased the memories of everyone who had the slightest inkling what really happened in the park. Your human police will eventually gather enough evidence to identify members of the Last Defense as the arsonists. We have planted the false memory that the Last Defense kidnapped your friends and tried to kill you in the belief you were an inhuman. They set fire to the park when the Wolves tried to free you all. Please stick to the story.

With regards to Lachlan, he will be listed among the dead from Central Park. There will be no funeral for him on Earth, and no memorial. Everyone who needs to know what happened to him will believe he was repatriated to Scotland. He will be buried according to the customs of our people.

Because your powers are no longer dormant we have not altered what you remember. I understand this knowledge could be a burden to you, but it's more important that you understand this magic you carry. Experiment with it, study it, but most importantly, learn to control it.

Lachlan left you a message, you will find it on the pen drive in this package. Watch it, discard it, it's up to you.

Sincerely

Morrigan Pendragon.

I read her letter a couple of times. It doesn't surprise me that she left this way. She had no connection to me, and she probably feels like she owed me nothing, but it still stings.

As soon as I'm discharged I visit Jameson and Novik. Both of them, the real ones, were found drugged and tied to a tree not far from where we had fought the fake versions. Novik's hands are heavily bandaged, but he's in good spirits. Just like Pendragon promised he doesn't remember a thing about the shape-shifters. It's probably for the best. Jameson is asleep. His face is burned, and he too has bandages on his hands. Bile rises in my throat at the sight of them. I'm the sole reason Central Park burned. They were hurt because of me.

I have one last hope that I won't be on my own with the truth. Newlin was heavily guarded last time he was in the hospital, and chances are the same happened again. As long as the bikers on his door had not thought about ditching their duties then Morrigan wouldn't have had a chance in persuading them to move.

After visiting hours are over I try to get in touch with Newlin. When the number he gave me continually rings, I go to the body shop instead. A new face, one belonging to a short, older man with gray hair, greets me at the desk.

"Is Alex here?" I say before he can speak.

The old guy shrugs apologetically. "Sorry. Newlin's gone away for a few weeks."

I hold his gaze and he doesn't flinch. He doesn't appear to be lying. "Do you know where?"

"Somewhere on the west coast, I think." He gives a lazy shrug. "I can get a message to him if you like."

I sigh. "It doesn't matter. I'll call him myself. Thanks for your help."

Newlin's phone goes to voice mail when I try to call him on the way to my car. I guess I just have to face facts, he doesn't want to talk to me. Who can blame him? He probably doesn't remember a thing about Calhoun or the Veranhiko, just like everyone else, and wants to get as far away as possible from the one who dragged him into a war zone.

Is there any worse feeling than suddenly realizing that you're completely on your own?

Just as I start the car my phone rings. It's Newlin.

"Hey," he says. There's a bit of a weary sigh to his voice. "Sorry I missed your calls. I've been busy."

"That's okay," I reassure him. "I was going to ask if we can talk but I don't want to have this conversation over the phone. It can wait until you come back."

"I haven't gone yet. Flight's tonight." There's a pause. In the background, I can hear Newlin's fingers tapping on a desk or table. "I'll give you my address. I was hoping to talk to you anyway. As long as you're here before four, we can talk."

I scribble down the address on an old receipt. Newlin's place is not far from where I am, but it's enough of a drive to give me time to think of exactly what I'm going to say.

19

The Last of the Last Defense

I pull up in front of a town house with large trees in the yard. This was not what I was expecting at all. Newlin opens the door before I get a chance to knock.

"You found it okay then?" he says with a smile. He still looks pretty beat up. A large dressing covers the shaved side of his head, and his left hand is heavily bandaged. He has a lot of cuts and bruises too.

"Yeah, it's an easy enough neighborhood to find," I reply.

He steps back and leads me into the house. The living room is organized chaos. A mishmash of furniture crowds the room. Shelves covered with dusty photos and curios hide most of the faded floral wallpaper.

"It's my grandmother's place," Newlin says almost apologetically. "I was staying here to care for her up until a few months ago, and I haven't got around to clearing it."

"It's a cool place," I say.

Newlin rolls his eyes then leads me into the kitchen. It's spotlessly clean and more modern than the living room. A large window above the sink faces into the yard. Trees form a natural fence around the lawn, and some sprout from the grass itself. One has an aging swing attached to a low hanging limb. “This is kinda like my parents’ place actually,” I say half to myself.

Newlin carefully measures ground coffee into the machine. “Oh yeah? Is your mom a hoarder too?”

“Well, kinda actually,” I say with a smile. “But I meant more the look of the house and the yard.”

He joins me by the window. “Yeah, it's homely. Anyways, I wanted to meet you here so we could talk alone.” Newlin turns and leans back against the counter-top. “I want you to know I'm not going to tell anyone. You're a good guy, and you're obviously on our side.”

My eyebrow twitches up. “Tell anyone what?”

Newlin frowns, confused. “You know? About the flames and the freaking lions roar. To be honest, I think it's kinda cool that you're… whatever you are.”

“I'm human,” I say with a little bit of bite to my voice. “Just like you.”

“I can do a lot of pretty cool shit, Jerry, but throwing fire out my hands ain’t one of them.” He laughs but quickly stops when I don't join in. “So, yeah. You're on our side. You have fucking awesome powers. It's like having our own personal superhero.”

I roll my eyes. “Not by a long shot.”

“But you could be, right?” He pours the coffee into two mugs and hands me one. “Like with a bit of training and support. You could control it?”

“Uh, maybe. I don't know. I've not tried to do anything with it since then.” I point at his bandaged arm. “Maybe it’s better if I don't.”

"Don't worry about that," Newlin says. "I only got this cos I pulled you out of that portal."

"You remember it all, don't you?" I say. I can't keep the shock out of my voice. I'm not on my own after all!

Newlin sighs. "I wish I didn't but…"

"So do I," I say softly. "No, scratch that. I wish there was nothing to remember. It shouldn't have happened at all."

"And that's why I think we should do something about it." He stares into the depths of his coffee cup. "Me and you, together."

I frown. "You're really confusing me here, Alex. Do you wanna just spit out whatever it is you have to say?"

Newlin scratches at the side of his mouth. "Now this is going to sound a little out there, but hear me out, okay."

A smirk pulls at my lips. "I'm listening."

"I'm setting up an army, and I want you to run it with me."

I wait for him to laugh. Instead, the silence stretches on and on. "Are you serious?" I finally ask.

"Deadly." Newlin raises his burned arm. "This is small potatoes compared to what those fuckers did to other people. We need to be prepared for when they come back."

"They're not going to come back," I say without much conviction. I look out into the yard again.

"How do you know that?" he snaps. "Some of my own brothers turned into monsters that night. People that I'd known and trusted for years. I'm not taking any chances."

"So, you fear them but you don't fear me?" As much as I'm dreading the answer, the question has to be asked if he expects me to work with him.

Newlin rolls his eyes. "Why, because you can shoot fireballs?"

"Well, that would put off most people, yeah."

"I'm not afraid of you," Newlin says defiantly. "I have no reason to be. You're on our side. You've always been on my side, which is why I'm asking for your help now. You can kill them with your magic or whatever the hell it is. I've got the means to get weapons, build what we need, maybe even learn to track them." He claps his hand down on my shoulder. "My cousin is flying in from New Zealand. He's got all sorts of know how that could help us. You're the last piece of this puzzle, so what do you say?"

I can't answer at first. It's a tempting offer—being on the front line just in case they come back, but I have a whole life to go back to in Boston. "Can I think about it?"

It's obviously not the answer Newlin was expecting. His eyes narrow in anger. "What's there to think about? You either wanna solve this problem, or you're sitting back and letting it happen."

"If there's any sign of them again, I'll be right here fighting beside you, I promise. Until then I need time to think." I dig the little package out of my pocket, open it, pull the scanner out and give it to Newlin. "You need this more than I do. It was a gift from Lachlan and the people he worked with. This will tell you if any of those monsters are near you. Don't wait for my answer. You don't need me. Build your army and your weapons and I'll let you know my choice as soon as I make it, I promise."

Newlin looks down at the device. "We really need you with us."

"You have my number and I have yours. Boston is only six hours away, less if I fly."

Newlin leans back against the counter. His shoulders sag as he sighs. "Well, okay. The only thing worse than you not helping would be you staying here under duress."

"I'm not cutting ties with you. Call me, talk to me if you need to, come see me if you want. I'll probably do the same because we're the only two people in the world that know for sure that those monsters were real. That this," I lift the eye patch and show him my gold eye, "isn't just damage to my iris."

Newlin barely notices it. "All the more reason you should stay."

Fuck, I really am a dumbass. This isn't about army building, not really. He wants my support. We need each other even if it is just to reassure each other that we're not crazy. His posture stiffens a little when I hug him, but then he relaxes and hugs me too. His large hand pats my back. The force rattles through my shattered shoulder.

"I mean it, you can call me," I whisper. "You don't have to suffer alone."

"Neither do you," he says, and hugs me a little tighter.

I let him go before the lump in my throat gets any bigger. "I need to get back home. Like I said I'll give you an answer either way."

"In the meantime, I guess we just hope this little thing doesn't go off?" he says with a laugh.

I nod in agreement. "The chances of that happening are pretty slim."

"Any chance is too much," he says.

"Yeah, you're right, but—" I pick up my coffee cup and the handle breaks. It falls from my hand and smashes on the tiles. "Shit. I'm sorry,"

I bend down with Newlin to pick up the fragments. Suddenly a light—bulb goes off in my head. I quickly help Newlin clean up as my mind races over all the evidence at my disposal—the convenient limp, no reaction to hot coffee being spilled on his stomach, the weird questions he asked that were probably a stalling tactic. Shit! How have I been so blind.

I make my apologies to Newlin, promise that I'll call him with my answer, then rush from the house. I call Rodowski as I run to my car.

"Are you at the station?"

"Yeah, I am," she says, confused. "You're just out of the hospital. Shouldn't you be resting?"

"Something important has come up." I get into my car and put my keys in the ignition. "Do you have Robertson's call records?"

"Not on me, but, yeah, I have them."

"Can I take a look? I'll explain when I get there."

"Okay," she says in a questioning tone. "I'll meet you out front."

"And don't tell anyone what I'm coming in to check." I say firmly. "I'll explain what's going on face to face. You can refuse to help me then if it doesn't sit right with you."

Rodowski pauses for so long I wonder if the line has gone dead. "We'll deal with that when we get to it," she finally says.

I'm at the station as fast as I can manage in Manhattan traffic. Rodowski is outside. "Is this something we need to work out in secret?"

I head into the building and she falls into step beside me. "I found a code. It could be a password or something for a keypad, but I think it might be part of a phone number."

We go into the empty office, and Rodowski pulls the call logs from her desk drawer. "The highlighted ones are pre-paid phones. That's probably your best place to start."

"Definitely. Thanks."

I take the scrap out of my wallet and lay it flat on the table. Slowly, I work through the list. The code I found is three digits short of a standard phone number, but why would he keep a full code? This was probably just enough to remind him of who to call. Just as my uncovered eye is growing blurry from looking at so many digits, I find it.

Fuck. I really hoped I was on the wrong track with this one. I fix my face into a weary smile and turn to Rodowski, who's been diligently checking with me.

"Sorry to waste your time. The number doesn't match anything here."

Rodowski leans back heavily in her chair. "Another dead lead. Great."

"It was just a little thing," I say. "This scrap could be anything, but I thought I'd check, just in case." Rodowski gathers up the papers. I commit the number I saw to memory as quickly as I can before it's gone from view. "Thanks for your help."

"Any time," Rodowski says. Her smile looks forced. "Now go home and get some rest."

As soon as I'm back in my car I program the number into my phone. I consider calling it right away to confirm my suspicions, but all that will do is let them know I'm on their trail. If I'm going to be confronting the person I think I am, then I can't afford to make any wrong moves.

§

If there's one thing I was always praised for as a cop it was the ability to stay calm under pressure, and boy do I need that skill now. Waiting for my suspect to show himself is hard. I don't want to sit around, I want action, I want this to end! Finally, I see him. He's on foot, so I abandon my car and follow him. I position my hat down low enough to shield my eyes and pull my scarf up over my nose. Thankfully, the wind is bitter, and I'm not the only person wrapped up against the cold. He stops by a convenience store and buys a pack of cigarettes and a newspaper, then catches the subway into Brooklyn. I watch him from across the busy carriage. He does nothing but read and occasionally glance out of the window.

I step off the train when he does. The crowd swarms around us as we head back up onto street level. Twice I lose sight of him, only for him to reappear in my line of sight just when I'm about to give up.

The longer I tail him the less I'm sure of my suspicions. He seems like just a normal guy doing his normal routine, but Newlin though that about members of his gang too. I have to follow this through. If he is one of the Veranhiko, like I suspect, then he's too dangerous to be left alive.

Finally, he heads into an old brownstone. I creep up the stairs, and keep a floor behind him so he can't see me if he looks back. My blood pounds in my ears. This is too easy. It's a set up, he *has* to know I'm following him.

He never acknowledges me.

The reason why becomes clear when he takes his earphones out and lays the chord around his neck. I could have stomped my way upstairs and he wouldn't have heard a thing. When he slips his key into the lock I call the number from Robertson's logs. My heart sinks when my suspect reaches into his pocket and pulls out a ringing phone.

"Hi, McCray," I say flatly. I hold up my phone to show I called him.

McCray looks from me to his phone and back again. "Did you really need to do both? Why not just say hi like a normal person?"

"Because I ain't normal," I step up into the hallway beside him. "But you already knew that, right?"

McCray laughs. "I dunno what the fuck your talking about, but I think you must've hit your head pretty bad as well as busting your shoulder."

"I'm going to give you one chance to tell me the truth. Why are you here and what do you want?"

"I'm here cos this is my home," McCray says gruffly. "And what I want is to go inside, maybe eat, then go to bed."

He turns his back on me. I kick him savagely in the spine. McCray stumbles through door and lands hard on his knees before rolling onto his back. I kick the door shut with my heel then kneel by McCray's side.

"The number I called you on was found taped under Robertson's desk," I say softly. "It's not your phone number, cos I have that, so why do you have a second one?"

"You must have got the number wrong." McCray insists. "I have no idea why Robertson would have my other number. Only one other person does! I… I'm having an affair."

I laugh. "You aren't married. I've never heard you mention dating either." I take his wrist and turn his hand palm side up. "This will barely hurt. If you bleed I'll bandage you up and take you into the station. If not…" I leave the threat hanging as I draw a knife from my pocket. Our eyes meet and his frightened face stalls me a second too long.

Something snakes around my waist and then pulls me up. I'm thrown back against the door, but land on my feet. McCray rushes at me. His body loses most of its shape as he lashes out with whip like tentacles. I slash at his limbs, and block as best as I can with my right arm pretty much a dead weight. He gets a few stinging blows in, but I gain the upper hand and force him back. The living room is soon spattered gray and smelling like the inside of a sewage pipe.

"Why are you here?" I say sharply. I hack off McCray's fist when he tries to punch me.

"Fuck you!" He spits through gritted teeth. He bites off his tongue and spits it at me. Gray slime hits me in the face with a sickening squelch. McCray takes advantage of the distraction to go for my injured shoulder. His hardened fist slams into the pinned bones. I scream—the extra padding I put around it is not enough to dull the pain.

McCray pulls back. His fist molds into a stone block. If he hits me with that it's going to break a bone for sure. I slip nimbly inside his guard before he can bring it down, and drive my knife into his throat.

"What do you and your fucking friends want? Is it really all about these powers?" I demand. McCray sputters and gasps. I pull the knife out. "Don't play that game. I know you can regrow every bit I cut off. If I have to, I'll take you apart bit by bit."

McCray howls when I stab him in the stomach. I pull my hand back before he can close his flesh around it.

"You can't win," he croaks. A smile forms on his misshapen face. "I was right under your nose for almost twelve years, and you knew nothing. You have no idea how many others are hiding and you never will."

"Won't I?" I pull my eye patch off. Immediately, the edges of my vision blur as my right eye compensates for my damaged left, but the color of my iris has the desired effect. McCray's distorted mouth opens wide with shock. His gaze darts all over my face. "Aw, did no one tell you?" I say with a smirk. "You're not the only one that's been hiding in plain sight."

He backs away from me. Just in time, I realize he's making for the window. I rush after him, grab his shirt front, and haul him close. I'm pretty much defenseless. I don't have the strength in my right arm to block or use my knife, but all the power I need should be literally in the palm of my hands. I concentrate hard, and let all my rage slowly flow into my veins.

"I've never done anything to you." McCray's words come out in a rapid high-pitched squeal. "Okay, I'm not human, but neither are you! You can't hurt me for being different."

"Do you really think this is all about differences?" I say through gritted teeth. "Every one of your kind I've met has tried to kill me, or been in the process of trying to kill someone else. The sole reason you're here is to track people like me down. Isn't it?" I shake him roughly when he doesn't answer. All the fight has drained out of him. His limbs, they're too malformed and too numerous to be arms any longer, hang uselessly by his sides. His face is the picture of fear—wide eyes, gaping mouth, even his breathing is rapid.

"You're right," he sputters. "You're absolutely right. But we're not all the same, and I left Boston during those murders, remember? I may be the same species but I don't work for them, not anymore."

"Then why did you stop me leaving with Jameson and Novik? You stalled me so others in your little group could kidnap them and lure me in."

McCray shakes his head violently. "No! I needed to clear up parts of your statement, that's all. I'm just trying to live a normal life despite what I am."

I look him up and down. My anger quickly cools. He's not a threat to me, he's pretty much cowering at my feet. "But you're Nomad, aren't you? You must be. Robertson had your number taped under his desk. Nomad knew I was working with the cops, and you had a limp just like Nomad should have after our…" I relax my grip on his shirt. Fuck. Have I got him all wrong?

"It's all just coincidence, Jerry," he whispers. The hairs along my arms lift with the static in the air. "You made a mistake, but it's okay. No harm done."

A flicker of movement to my left catches my eye. I spin away just before McCray's fist, now fashioned into a sharp blade, can hit me. This time I give him no time to worm his way back inside my head. I grab him around the throat with both hands, and force all my anger into him.

As the flames spring up from his flesh, it's not McCray's face that looks up at me, but Myles'.

"They'll come for you," he says. He even has Myles' voice. "You'll just be getting used to the idea of bein' safe, and they'll be back."

I keep my hands on him. It doesn't matter what he looks like, it's all a trick. I know what he is, and he's too dangerous to live!

"Let them," I say sharply. "I can kill you easy enough now. Imagine what I'll be able to do by the time they come back for me."

Flames lick at his blond curls and turn them quickly to ash. He smiles at me, the same smile the real Myles used to have. "You can kill my kind, but you have no fuckin' clue what kind of surprise they have waiting for you."

His laughter quickly turns to screams as the last of his body is consumed. I don't let go of him, not until all that's left under my fingers is ashes.

I sit down heavily on the floor. My body shakes. My head swims unpleasantly, but the effects of using so much energy pass pretty quick. I look at the pile of grease and dust. I had no choice, yet I can't help feeling a pang of remorse. He was one of the Veranhiko, and a dangerous monster, but he was also someone I counted as a friend, or at least an ally, for years. If I thought locking him up would be the end of the trouble he could cause then I would have taken that route.

I stay in the apartment long enough to dispose of the ashes down the toilet, and do a quick sweep of the place for recording equipment and any useful evidence. Once I'm sure there's nothing, I slip on a pair of woolen gloves and slide his phone into my pocket. With my scarf wrapped tight over the bottom half of my face and my hat pulled down low over my eyes I make my way back into Manhattan, and stop just once to throw McCray's phone into the East River.

§

My apartment is a little cold, but it hasn't been lived in for a few weeks. I turn the thermostat up and go straight to the kitchen to make some coffee. My shoulder is aching after the long drive, so I pop some painkillers and wait for the coffee to brew.

It's so quiet here. I plug in the radio on the windowsill and smile when the familiar riff of "Creeping Death" by Metallica floods the room. It's still tuned to the rock station I used to listen to. I sing along under my breath, pour myself a cup of joe, then start making a list of the groceries I need. Suddenly it hits me. This is the first time I've played music in my home since Myles died.

Ten years to the day tomorrow. I check my phone just to make sure and it's there in black and white. October thirtieth. My finger hovers over the off switch on the radio but I haul it away. I'm not going back to living like that. I can't. I need to get my life back.

I turn the radio up and force myself to relax, drink my coffee, and think what to do next. Unpacking should be my first priority, but before I move on fully, maybe I should put the events of the last few weeks to bed first.

I take the little package out of my bag and fish the flash drive out of it. My laptop was in my hotel room so it's still with forensics while they close the investigation, but I have an older one. Hopefully it will play the video.

It works, and I'm confronted with Calhoun's tear-stained face. He wipes his eyes, then starts to speak. "Jerry, I know that you probably never want to speak to me again, but I have to explain myself. I need you to know that you weren't part of my plan. Well, you were, but only insofar as I was supposed to find you and try to get information about the old case from you." He pauses and wipes his eyes. "I know it was stupid to get involved with you, but you already knew I was undercover, and you made the first move. I didn't think you cared about my secrets."

"You were still keeping things from me though," I mutter.

"I want you to know that I consider you a friend. It's a relationship built on necessary lies, but we could have got past that, right? Maybe we'll have time, I don't know. You've made it pretty clear you don't want to talk to me anymore."

He drops his head almost out of camera view, but I can hear his sobbing. A lump rises in my throat. I didn't mean to hurt him so badly, but after all the lies, how could I just forgive him?

Calhoun makes a valiant effort to control himself before continuing. "I'm lonely, Jerry. It's not the only reason I slept with you, or the sole reason I got together with Newlin, but it is part of it. Like I told you, I've lived here for five years. No one knows who I really am apart from Pendragon. I have no one else I can really talk to, and I needed… something. I don't know. You showed me so much compassion, you really cared for me and my safety. I needed that much more than I needed anything physical with you."

He scrubs his hand through his hair. "So, yes, I suppose you could say I used you in that respect. I needed to feel wanted, cared for, maybe even loved on some level. It was selfish of me, and I'm sorry. I have no idea how to make it up to you, but allow me to start with this. The truth about me." He takes a deep breath. "My real name is Siffik Madriana. I'm twenty-eight years old. My birthdate would correspond to the thirty-first of October on Earth, if my conversion is right. I live with my father. My mother and my older brother died in the crash I told you about. There's no way I'd ever lie about something like that. I am a fully licensed and trained tattoo artist here and back home. I've been in the agency I work for since I was sixteen years old, and this mission is my second one. I'm due to go home once the threat has passed."

I shake my head sadly and wipe at my eyes. "You didn't deserve to die like that," I whisper. "You weren't a bad person."

"Well, that's all," he says with a little shrug. "I know it isn't much, and I don't expect it to make up for anything, but I wanted you to know something about me after all the false information you were given. I hope we get a chance to speak again, and I can explain myself in person."

The video cuts off abruptly. I sniff loudly and rub my eyes, but the tears keep falling. I cover my face with my hands and sob. This is so fucking unfair. His only crime was lying to me, and as much as it hurt, I get why he had to do it.

"Jerry!"

I flinch and almost knock my computer off my lap. Calhoun's face fills my screen. His hair is shining black, obviously covered with dye.

"You've just left my apartment. I don't have long to speak, but this is important. This plan you have, it should work, but if it doesn't I want you to get this message." He holds up a piece of paper. "This is a printout of the email I have sent to my superiors. It states that, should they refuse my request to stay on Earth for longer, or in the event of my death, then the apartment in the Dakota is yours. This is not some strange apology on my part. This is practical. I know that you'll refuse the option to have your memories altered, and since you have magic, it won't be forced on you either. You'll remember everything, and you'll want some way to fight back." He wipes a drip of dye off of his forehead. "In my apartment is a locked room. Inside you'll find a whole heap of things to help you. I've asked in the email that the computer systems get updated into English, so you can read them. If you decide to take the apartment, a manual will be sent to you explaining what everything is. If I can remain on Earth, I'll explain it all myself. I just needed a contingency plan in place."

He holds the piece of paper up to the camera. "Write this down. If you want to take me up on my offer then email this address telling them you accept, and give them a secure postal address. They will send everything to you, and then the apartment and everything in it is yours. All my personal things will have been cleared out. There are no rent payments on the place; we bought it outright. You can do what you like with it, just, please, make sure the stuff in that room doesn't fall into anyone else's hands."

A sad smile spreads across his face. "You're a good man, Jerry. A brave one too. It's been an honor to work with you."

The screen goes black again. I wait in case there is another little video. There's nothing but silence. A horrible thought hits me. Did he know he wasn't going to get out alive? Pendragon did say this mission was pretty much suicide. Did he come here knowing he would never go home?

I push my laptop off onto the other side of the couch. Once I start crying, I can't stop. All the pain and grief that I've stored up over the last few weeks, maybe even longer, comes tumbling out of me in shaking sobs. I'll never see Harris again. I'll never know if Calhoun and I could have been more than a hook up. The last month has just been one long parade of loss and shattered futures.

When there are no more tears left to cry, my eyes sting like crazy, my throat is raw, and my nose is stuffy. However, the horrible heavy feeling in my chest seems to have lifted. My mind feels clearer too.

I go into the bathroom and splash cold water onto my face. My reflection is almost unrecognizable. I guess I wasn't eating or sleeping right while running around after those monsters—my face seems thinner. The gold eye is a gleaming reminder that even if I did sink back into my old life, I'm not the same person. I blow my nose, scrub my face, and take a deep breath.

No, I'm not settling back into my old habits, not after everything that's happened. It's time to make some real, long-lasting changes.

§

Two weeks later I walk along a driveway carpeted in red and gold. An early November frost makes the fallen leaves crunch underfoot. There're a few other people wandering in the cemetery, some carrying flowers, others simply paying their respects with words. I have an entirely different tribute in mind, one tailor made for the person I'm visiting.

I've avoided this place for years, but my feet know the way, and before long I'm standing in front of a headstone bearing the name *Myles Sebastian Delaney.* The grave site is tidy, and there's a fresh bouquet resting on it. I grimace at that. Flowers weren't exactly Myles' thing, but whoever left them had their heart in the right place. I wonder who else visits here nowadays apart from his mom and brother?

I set the coffee cup down carefully on the base of the stone and place an Oreo cupcake beside it.

"Hey," I say, and feel ridiculous as soon as I open my mouth. I push past it though. "I got you your favorite, and coffee too. Don't worry, it's none of that milky, syrup-filled stuff you used to make fun of me for drinking. It's just how you like it. Black, two sugars."

I hug myself against the cold. "Harris had a good send off. Even some of Newlin's gang showed up to pay their respects. No one's really sure what happened to him. There're loads of rumors, but all the evidence gathering is causing plenty of fingers to point at this gang McCray and Robertson were involved with. I don't think it's right that Robertson might go down for murders he didn't commit, but he was willing to kill Lachlan. He isn't exactly innocent. At least McCray got what was coming to him."

I pause even though I know I won't get a response. "You were right. It wasn't something human," I continue in a quieter voice. "I thought maybe you'd have some definitive answer on how to kill them, but I've checked every notebook of yours since I got back, and I can't find anything. Just a load of disjointed ramblings. What did you find out? If it was about this power that I have, you would've told me, right?"

A sip of coffee chases the cold away from my lips for a moment. "For what it's worth, I'm sorry. I should have listened to you, or at least not let you leave. I was a dick. I'm so sorry. I've regretted that night ever since. So, I…" I pause and clear my throat. Why am I so nervous speaking to him about this? My mind is made up already. "So, I hope you understand that I've learned my lesson, and that means I can't afford not to listen any more. That's why I'm moving to New York.

"I've not sold our place. I rented it out to this really cool couple. It'll be their first home together, just like it was for us. I found so much shit when I was cleaning out, and I gave your mom a lot of your stuff. I kept some too, including your notebooks. I hope that's okay?"

A crisp wind sighs through the trees. In the strangely comforting silence I wonder if Myles could be nearby listening to me. If demons and winged humanoids can be real, then why not ghosts?

"If you meet Lachlan or Harris up there," I say, my voice thick with tears, "please tell them I'm sorry." I lay my hand on his headstone. "I love you, Myles. I always will."

I pick up my offering because to anyone else it'll look like garbage, and throw it in a trash can on my way out. I check that the back of the U Haul is locked tight, and that the letter Calhoun's superiors sent me is safely in my glove compartment. I won't be living in his apartment— that's too weird—but I need to know what's in that room. At the very least it could give me some real answers about what the hell I am, and hopefully some clue as to how to control my power.

I turn on the radio, twist the dial until I find a classic rock station, then leave Boston behind.

Detective Jerry Higgins

will return in 2018 in

The Raven and the Wolves

The Corvid Chronicles

Book Two

Cover Design by:

TatteredWolf Studios is the joint venture of husband and wife team Brad and Megan Baker (otherwise known as Loni and Tatiyana Wolf). The goal of TWS is to bring their unique design aesthetic to the world through traditional, digital, and video game art.

They can be found at www.TatteredWolfStudios.com.

80211688R00207

Made in the USA
Columbia, SC
14 November 2017